Sandra Howard was one of the leading fashion models of the 1960s. She is married to the former British Conservative Party leader Michael Howard. Her first novel, *Glass Houses*, was published in 2006 to wide acclaim.

Also by Sandra Howard

Glass Houses

To Eleanor

Ursula's Story

SANDRA HOWARD

with warmest wishes

**POCKET
BOOKS**

LONDON · SYDNEY · NEW YORK · TORONTO

First published in Great Britain by Simon & Schuster UK Ltd, 2007
This edition published by Pocket Books, 2008
An imprint of Simon & Schuster UK Ltd
A CBS COMPANY

5 7 9 10 8 6 4

Simon & Schuster UK Ltd
Africa House
64–78 Kingsway
London WC2B 6AH

www.simonsays.co.uk

Simon & Schuster Australia
Sydney

A CIP catalogue record for this book
is available from the British Library

ISBN: 978-1-4165-2199-0

Typeset in Garamond by M Rules
Printed and bound in Great Britain by
CPI Cox & Wyman Ltd, Reading, Berkshire

In memory of my mother.

Acknowledgements

I would like to thank a number of people for their help with this story. First and foremost, my wonderful editor, Suzanne Baboneau, whose constant guidance and infinite patience is such a sure, steadying hand at all times. Enormous thanks too, to Sue, Rochelle, Grainne, Libby and all at Simon & Schuster. My agent, Michael Sissons, is a tower of strength, and warmest thanks too, to Carol and Fiona at PFD.

I'm immensely grateful to the experts for their wise advice. Any errors and misunderstandings are, of course, entirely my own. Ray Bull, Professor of Forensic Psychology, University of Leicester, who spared precious time to answer a host of questions with unfailing good humour; Louise Bowers, consultant forensic psychologist, for her spirited involvement and specialist knowledge that gave such invaluable insights into the mind of my disturbed character. Chris Smart for so generously sharing his detective's intelligence with spontaneous warmth and attention to detail; my doctor, Jonathan Munday, for his informed, good-natured help; and the Terrence Higgins Trust, whose provision of Aids tests and selfless work with patients should be supported and held in awe.

Armando Iannucci deserves special thanks for bidding in a charity auction to lend his name to a character in this book. The two charities concerned, Students Partnership Worldwide and Learning Through Leisure, benefited greatly from his generosity. I chose the character . . . Page 66 is the place to look.

I am greatly indebted too, to John Sprague at Sotheran's in Piccadilly and Marrins in Folkestone for their kind and enlightening instruction in the ways of the antiquarian book trade, Rodney Fletcher, who has a wine business and whose expertise was so helpful and who is, happily for us, quite unlike my character with a similar business, and to Natasha Foulkes, who, at thirteen, knew exactly the habits, likes and foibles of Ursula's daughters.

My fervent thanks also to my poetry-writing friends who have so graciously allowed Ursula to borrow from their lines: Ben Moorhead, a taste of whose inspired work can be found on page 293, my sister Carma Roamer, for the lines on page 289, and Hilary Johnson, for her engaging front-piece verses and all other extracts included.

And finally, and from the heart, a big thank you hug and kiss to Michael for his wondrous forbearance, and to the rest of the family and all our understanding friends.

Ring the changes,
Toll the bell;
Marriage peals
Or parting knell.

Change of heart
Means change of wife.
Change your partners,
Change of life.

Ring the changes,
The bell rope swings,
Life's a circus:
Change the rings.

HILARY JOHNSON

Ursula's Story

CHAPTER 1

Bill is marrying her today. I glance at the clock, clear and bright in my blacked-out bedroom, the red digits glowing like fireflies. It's on Bill's side. I still stretch across every morning to switch off the alarm. Only half-past five, I'll never get back to sleep.

Perhaps a new smaller bed might be good – like the one I saw in Brearfield with a card on it saying, 'The Occasional Two'. Or would it be better to move, to downsize, which would certainly help Bill. Still, round here, though, the girls have had enough upheaval.

A buyer shouldn't be too much problem with the wonderful garden and London little more than an hour away. I do love the house. The wisteria is always so glorious before the dry papery petals come fluttering down like confetti. I love the circle of gravel, the glossy-white front door.

I love the symmetry of the tall Victorian sash windows. They have folding casement shutters that usually help with sleep. I draw the curtains too, at night, but now the blackness feels constraining. Scrambling out of bed to open them I climb back in and lie hugging my knees watching the curtains lifting in the light breeze; both sashes are pushed up a little, as far as the window-locks will allow. The daylight is gathering, creeping in cautiously, gingerly, like a child who knows its parents won't enjoy being woken. Bill's lucky, it looks a perfect spring day.

His proprietor, Oscar Bluemont, who never does things by halves, is giving the reception, opening up his lavish Kensington home whose garden might be a greenhouse at Kew. It's not something every newspaper editor could expect, but then not many marry a government minister and ask the Prime Minister and half the Cabinet along.

The press will be back here again, after down-at-the-mouth pictures and quotes. They won't get them. 'His ex-wife Ursula, forty-three, was unavailable for comment.'

It will be on the evening news. '. . . And now the wedding we've all been waiting for! Health Minister Victoria James and William Osborne, editor of *The Post* – better known, of course, from his current-affairs programme on television, *The Firing Line*.'

Bill is a tough operator, I think with frustration. Clever and charismatic in the way he presents that programme, lulling interviewees then homing in for the kill. He was a household name even before his great affair with Victoria James. Will she take his name and become Victoria Osborne at work?

Her teenage daughter will be pointed out: the girls and Tom too, probably. '. . . William's three children by his first marriage.' My children, I think angrily, imagining my mother glued to the set.

The day's tensions are already forming, tightening into a ball in my stomach. There'll be all the tacky headlines in tomorrow's papers, too. 'Editor and Minister spliced!' 'Victoria weds her slick Willie.' Endless photographs. It's so pissing-off.

The telephone rings and I reach across, fantasizing for one childish moment that it's Bill changing his mind. I don't even want him to. It's sure to be Julian; he will know I'm awake and all wound-up already and he'll be feeling resentful; it does really get to him. I suppose, though, it's hard for a man even to begin to understand the pain of losing out to another woman, the obsessive consuming quality of the jealousy. Julian thinks I'm indulging in an orgy of hurt pride and should rise above it. I have to accept he's right, but it's not that easy and very irritating of him, expecting it of me.

'Is that Mrs Osborne?' The sickly saccharine voice on the end of the line sounds ominous. 'I just wondered how you're possibly feeling about today's wedding . . .'

It's the press. They've got a cheek, calling this early. Controlling myself with difficulty I answer through tight teeth, 'Sorry, no comment,' and slam down the phone. Lying across the bed I pull the phone out at the socket then I reach for my mobile and fall back breathing heavily, clutching it to my chest. My heart's thumping. I need Julian's call.

When it comes minutes later I'm still raging and tense. 'Hi,' I mutter, quite bad-temperedly.

'That's not very friendly – were you thinking it might be William having regrets?'

'God, Julian. I've just had the press on actually – at this hour! I don't see why I should be given such aggro when she's treated like Mother Teresa. So she almost lost her life in a riot, terrible obviously, but does that make her so wonderful and whiter than virginal white?' Why do I have to keep on endlessly repeating it all and souring up Julian? I'm like some automated message machine that everyone's heard till they want to scream.

'They forget the long deceitful affair, all the hurt,' I add, laying it on while I'm at it. 'Some ministerial example . . .'

'And were you so very pure, clinging on in a fake empty marriage?'

'It wasn't fake, we just grew apart.' I almost tag on 'because of you', which would have weakened my case, but instead go on piously, 'And it wasn't clinging, putting Emma and Jessie first. I wish they didn't have to go to this wretched wedding. *And* stay the night. Tom's coming for them. Victoria is driven round in that ministerial car so she lets him use her Mini Cooper the whole time, now. She's ingratiating herself, it's sick-making; I can't stand it.'

'Why? Why can't you just be grateful? Tom's an impoverished art student, it gets him home to you more at weekends.'

'He shouldn't be living in that basement flat of theirs anyway; he was fine in halls at college. She shouldn't be influencing my children so much, letting Tom drive that fast car.'

'She'll want to avoid being seen in it these days, I expect, it's not environmentally friendly. Tom's fine, he's got his head screwed on and he's a good safe driver.'

'Probably about as safe as eggs in a paper bag – and you're just trying to be soothing, you haven't got a clue either way.'

'Yes, I have. I used to let him drive quite often when I gave him lifts to London.'

'I don't believe it, your precious old Porsche? You're in love with that car!'

'No, only with you. I'll come round later, about seven this evening. If that's what you want.'

I've made him angry, I think, lying back with my silent mobile, he was sounding cold. I'm always spiky and showing my worst side then longing to undo it. It's so hard to relax at the moment. The edginess is no effort, as instinctive as survival – if having the opposite effect.

Julian won't put up with much more. I need him; I need the sex. His body is lean and hard from some past other life; the slightest brush of his arm and my spine turns to jelly. He can plump up my shrivelled morale like a raisin in rum and make me feel sky high.

We first met at his father's funeral in Brearfield seven years ago. Julian had been away for years, living in Greece, Africa, wherever, and writing travel books, but came rushing back when his father was dying of cancer. A year or two before then he'd had the terrible tragedy of his mother and sister killed in a car crash: his father's death must have been extra heartbreaking.

After the funeral there were pub drinks and sandwiches and we'd talked. His face had held such anguish, like a wounded defenceless animal. His topaz eyes had been latched on to mine; his hair was unkempt. I had longed to take him into my arms.

Julian's hair is well cut and tamed now and it's fairer than its natural mouse since he goes abroad a lot, on trips to Africa. He's always tanned. Good-looking in a quiet unassuming sort of way: just short of six foot, a lean well-structured face, straight nose, those steady golden-brown eyes – a touch of the Hollywood fighter pilot, perhaps. He hates conforming and leading a conventional life, but that's part of the problem, it's so ingrained in me.

His father, Sir Peter Bridgewater, had been a respected permanent secretary in the civil service who'd retired to Brearfield and opened an antiquarian bookshop. Julian kept it going, surprisingly, even moving in and creating an upstairs flat. It's a rickety Tudor building in the market square; the upper half hangs over the shop like a beer belly.

People were pleased. The shop was popular, particularly with Brearfield's retired old colonels – there are quite a few – whom Julian impresses no end with his knowledge of military history. Even so, and in spite of the travel books he's written, there were murmurings about his past. And his marriage to a local girl lasting less than a year didn't help.

I never went near the bookshop during the time he was married. It was completely irrational on my part. Our contact had been minimal. I was married too, with two small daughters, Tom was still at school.

Julian's books are good. I loved his wry account of an Englishman farming on a Greek island. He says his new book on Uganda, about a time when people's lives were cheaper than a bunch of bananas, is very harrowing and I shouldn't bother reading it. I was going to anyway but my copy seems to have got packed up with Bill's things.

Four years of guarded bottled-up attraction – until that extraordinary spur of the moment, split second of time at Val and Chris's party when I almost left Bill. Circumstances conspired, though, and it didn't happen. Bill started his affair soon after, which came as a shock and cut deep, but it was, as Julian well knows, more to do with hurt pride at that stage.

Then came the break-up. I could never have picked up with him in all the crippling glare of Bill's exposure, the ceaseless battery of humiliating press. Julian was sensitive to that and never once pushed it.

The media caravan rolled on. I had licked my wounds interminably like a cat, succumbed to more melodramatic outbursts than a hormonal top model, aged my mother by years and still felt blood raw. Julian took me out, we did things together, but he knew I needed time.

When we finally made love it had a rare significance, a grace even, after all the waiting; we had known it would happen for so long. It was of the moment and had needed no looks, no raised questioning eyebrows. I'd chanced on him in the market square one late afternoon when the girls were at a friend's for tea. We had gone into the bookshop, straight upstairs to his low-ceilinged bedroom with the small four-poster, undressed and climbed into the cool luxury of Egyptian cotton sheets. There had been no sense of awkward newness, every nook and curve of our bodies had felt completely familiar after five long years of abstinence.

And now I'm obsessed with the physical side, I think of nothing else and feel frightened that it's locking me in.

It wouldn't work. I'm in a total tangle. There's so much about Julian I don't understand. He's never talked marriage. I think he loves me, but how long would it last? I'm six months older, he'd get bored, push off to wherever, whoever . . .

It's all about being starved of sex. Bill might have lied and let me down, but he never sexually dissembled. He maintained a distance in bed like parallel ships at sea.

'Mum, you asleep?'

'Hi, Ems. No, I've been awake ages, lying here like an idle slob.'

'Jessie's the slob, I went in her room and couldn't wake her – and she's got her legs flopped right back like giving birth. It's disgusting. And her mouth's open. If she was old she'd be snoring.' Emma's in Tom's old maroon-striped pyjamas and, giving the trousers a hefty hitch, she climbs on the bed on her father's side. 'Dad's so mean, getting married this Thursday instead of next, when term's started, we could have had a day off.'

'I'm sure he thought of that.'

'Jess wants to wear her stretch pants suit. I said she can't keep changing her mind and in any case Gran would see it on telly and die a death, but she thinks Gran will be far too busy ogling all the VIPs.' Ems is sitting cross-legged, carefully inspecting her toenails, her pearlized aqua varnish. 'Jess is not to cling all day, Mum. She crowds me, she's a pain.'

'Be nice to her, love. And try and talk her into the red skirt, trousers would be wrong.'

'You're as bad as Gran! Even loads of brides wear them these days. Will Victoria wear white, do you think, as there's the church blessing?'

'Not a white pants suit, I'm sure.'

'Can I ask something?'

'Depends what.'

'Are you and Julian going to get married soon, too?'

'Certainly not! He's just a friend.'

'Oh, come on, Mum! He's much more than that. Tom says he's been in love with you for years. He says Julian reads you like one of those old books of his. Tom thinks—'

'Well, Tom can just jolly well keep his thoughts to himself!' It's infuriating of him, talking like that to his 12-year-old sister. I swing my legs out of bed and smile back at her. 'Time we got going, Ems – and wear the new tights, no ladders for Dad's big day.'

At the door she looks back with an evil grin. 'And Tom said—'

'Go and get dressed!' God knows what she'll come out with at the reception. Bill's drunken untrustworthy journalist mates might pick up quite a few little nuggets for their wretched columns.

Cleaning my teeth I think about Julian staying the night. He never has, even on Bill's weekends with the girls, but tonight they'll be in London and if ever there was a time . . . Best just see if it happens.

I feel a cold wet nose pressing against my thigh. Emma must have gone downstairs and let out Misty. 'No walkies today,' I murmur, fondling his head. 'Shitty pressmen.'

Misty was a present from Bill, just before he starting commuting. One evening he had appeared with a tiny ball of golden fluff, the retriever puppy I had longed for, and said cheerily, kissing me, 'To guard and keep you company! It's only going to be a couple of mid-week nights. I shall hate being away, though.' At the time it had seemed sensible and his investment in a one-bedroom central London flat, shrewd and sound.

I let Misty out into the garden and pick up the papers from the front step: *The Times* and *The Post*. Why keep on with *The Post* and being constantly reminded? Why is it so hard to let go?

Victoria's face shines out. 'Health Minister marries *The Post*'s editor today.'

Her accident set the seal. She had been Housing Minister then and on a private trip to see the proposed site for a controversial huge new housing development, quite close to Brearfield. Her visit sparked a riot of local protestors and more were bussed in. There were too few police, it got out of hand, and a random stone striking her head had caused life-threatening pressure of blood on the brain. They had operated just in time.

Bill threw caution and me to the winds and made a wild dash to the hospital where he stayed for hours. It was media open season after that. The press invaded and ransacked our lives; they feasted like medieval kings. 'Family values editor at minister's bedside.' 'William Osborne's vigil.' 'Editor and minister's secret tryst.' No sacking her over a deceitful affair; she was praised for her courage and made Minister of Health instead of Housing.

It was life-and-death drama and romance; people had felt fascinated sympathy. That my privacy was stripped away like the bark of a tree, that I was raw, unprotected and bleeding, meant nothing. And William Osborne was a well-known television personality, permitted to fail his wife.

I yell routinely to the girls to come for breakfast, still half reading the papers. Victoria is sharing the front page with a heart-gripping account of a young girl abducted from her garden. My skin crawls at the thought of it happening to one of mine; it's too awful to contemplate. A shiver runs through me, a shaft of icy stomach-clenching fear. I'm overwrought and being overemotional; I've got to smile through the next few hours.

My mother's on the phone when Tom speeds up and brakes sharply on the gravel. The kitchen has windows to the front and side of the house and lets me see people arriving. It's huge and light, two opened-up rooms, with a long pine refectory table at the garden end. There's a door leading off to a laundry area and a small study beyond that used to be Bill's. It's mine now.

The black Mini Cooper is giving off vibrations; good ones, obviously, to Tom, the music is at full pitch. I lose the thread of what my mother is saying: some rant at Bill coupled with absorbed fascination about the wedding. She has a split personality where Bill is concerned. Concern on my behalf, but she's always responded to his drive and television fame, her daughter married to a success story. I love her and we're close, but she drives me mad; even talking on the phone I can end up screaming my head off at her.

Letting in Tom, the phone still pressed to my ear, the sight of my tall dark angular twenty-year-old in his ancient jeans swells my heart. There's an eight-year gap between him and Emma. Having married and had him so young I'd felt tied, in spite of adoring him, deprived of downtime with girlfriends and sudden jaunts with Bill. My job on an interiors magazine had had to become part-time – with all Tom's fizzing energy he had needed a greyhound track, not a South London maisonette. Bill had been working long hours on the paper, it seemed folly to think of having another child.

Bill became Home Affairs Editor, then Deputy Editor of *The Post*. We moved to Brearfield, close to the downs. Bill was being loving, planning the garden; I had a beautiful new home and soon two baby girls in quick succession. Those early Brearfield years were really our happiest time.

Tom mouths 'Hi!' then goes to the banister to drape over the suit and tie he's holding before coming to give me a kiss.

I need to get my mother off the line and thrusting the phone at him, whisper, 'It's Gran – say a quick hello, darling.'

He takes it a touch wearily. 'Hi Gran, how you doing?' He listens with his face screwed up in a pained quizzy grin. 'OK, OK, keep your hair on. Promise I'll be in a tie. But I have got this wicked silver ring through my right eyebrow now . . .' I shake my head, frowning. 'Only kidding, Gran . . . We're seeing you, Sunday? That's cool.'

Tom clicks off and hands back the phone. 'You do know the press are out there, Mum?' I shrug, as if to say, who cares? He carries on rather undiplomatically, 'We, um, should really be going quite soon. There's lunch first, you see, with Victoria's brother and family, her parents and Nattie—' He dries up then, more uncomfortably aware of my sensitivities.

I hate picturing the scene. And that daughter of hers, Nattie, is seventeen, she'll be giving mine ideas; they're only eleven and twelve. 'Ease up a bit, Mum,' Tom says, with a very endearing smile.

It's a madhouse getting them off. Emma raids my shoe-cupboard and stands clutching a pair of summer espadrilles. 'Please! I can tighten them to fit . . .' In the high wedges and a fifties frock with blue corn-flower heads, blue as her eyes, she looks at least fifteen.

Tom's shirt is missing a button. 'It won't show, don't fuss,' he insists. I sew one on.

Emma's holding her hair in a tail and letting it loose again. It's very fair like mine. Tom and Jessie have their father's dark hair. 'You won't mope or anything, Mum?' she urges. 'Victoria's so, so nice! If you could only just get to know her . . .' I smile, a little tightly. Tom's glaring, but Ems isn't letting go. 'She's not stuck-up or a meanie, you really would get on . . .'

Jessie is nodding, agreeing vigorously. It shouldn't hurt, but it does. She's Bill's secret favourite; she looks up at him with those big solemn violety-chocolate eyes and he smoothes her tumbling hair or tugs at her ponytail with an achingly melting expression.

The break-up hit her hardest. She put up walls, closed doors, there was no way in; she was always bottled-up and buried in a book. Bill was sick with guilt, but I saw it most closely. If Jessie is accepting Victoria now, he can relax, and that feels like a defeat. Jess has been an ally to me, a compatriot in adversity. She can't start liking her stepmother.

Books are her great love, one she shares with Julian. He is so good with her; they get on really well. He's made her see and feel the romance of old books and talks to her very adultly about pseudo-nyms, blocking and bindings. She absorbs it all with keen attention, which I can tell he enjoys.

She was often with me the times I used to call at the bookshop on some painfully transparent pretext. Julian would give her beautifully illustrated old classics to look at while we stood gazing at poetry book spines, our bodies close, but not touching.

I write poems. It's my release: light years from the telephone research I do for an executive recruitment firm, school runs, the duty calls from Bill – all the small print of life.

The children are gone. Reporters on the doorstep repelled, I'm feeling hermetically sealed inside the house and fighting an urge to call Julian. Resisting the need for contact has become a habit and it's a hard one to break. An Irish friend once talked of the ecstasy of abstinence. I'm no Catholic priest, though, and those years of unspoken longings were painful. I'm free now, but still holding back. It's a fear of rebound, of making impulsive mistakes, of becoming engulfed, subsumed like an insect in a sticky tropical plant and then spewed out and discarded.

Thoughts of Bill swim in. Meeting him when I'd just started at Leeds University. He'd been on the *Barnsley Echo* and had come to cover a student demo. I'd gone to it out of mild curiosity and stayed at the back of the hall. Bill came close beside me and whispered I was beautiful. He pursued me keenly, if briefly, after that, chasing up and down the motorway in a ropey old banger before leaving to take up a new job in London.

A sensitive philosophy student had dried my tears. Three years later, though, and a year into my own job on the interiors magazine, I'd been buying a paper in a South London corner shop when Bill had walked in.

He'd looked confident, in charge: wonderful. His reuniting stare across the frozen foods chest had been compelling. 'Have you got a flat near here?' he asked easily. 'Come back to mine – come for breakfast. Can we get married? Whose flat?'

'Mine's full of sleeping flatmates.'

'Then there's nothing more to decide.'

My chest feels ready to burst. Racing upstairs and flinging on the bed, a few heaving orgasmic sobs do the trick. I get my hair washed then and make purposefully for the study to tackle some outstanding work for my executive recruitment firm. I do the very early stages and I'm presently whittling down a list of candidates to captain a cruise-ship based out of Miami. I'm on the outgoing line, calling up Scandinavians with impossible names, talking round the job, mentioning relocation, when my mobile goes and my heart leaps. It's not Julian, though, but Val.

As a solicitor Val is capable and friendly, a big-boned woman who fixes clients with a very level-headed gaze. As a close friend she's all. Warm, loyal, always ready with a healthy blast of common sense. We're a group of three; there's also Susie, who is blonde, trim, athletic and into aromatic oils and pyramid selling. She has other-women problems and I hate seeing those sad eyes of hers. Val and I play bridge, her husband Chris doesn't, and she and Susie play golf.

'Anything I can get for you?' Val asks briskly. 'I'm sure the press are hanging around and you'll want to stay put.'

I tell her Julian's coming this evening and what a favour it would be if she'd pick up a couple of steaks. She sounds pleased. She and Susie are showing clear signs of weariness at all my indecision.

Settling back to work I consider breaking into the case of excellent claret Bill left me. He was good like that, never mean. Wouldn't it seem a bit over-the-top, though?

And I'm cross with Julian, too; it feels like he's getting at me for being such a misery Minnie; the least he could do is be more gentle and ready with the tea and sympathy.

My mobile goes again, giving me another start. It's Bill, though, which I was hardly expecting. He knows I won't be answering the landline; my press problems should be tattooed on his conscience for life.

'Just thought you might like knowing they're here, safe and sound, and all's well.'

It was thoughtful of him, considerate. 'Thanks,' I say, feeling much warmer than minutes ago and saved from having to call Tom and sound overfussy.

'And from me, too,' Bill says. 'It means a lot, um, having them with me today.'

'Yes, well . . .'

'Victoria's parents will look after them and I've warned them, Ems especially, about what not to say and who to watch out for!'

I resist a sharp remark. 'Well, hope it all goes wonderfully well – and good luck, I guess, in your second life.'

CHAPTER 2

I'm in the bedroom thinking about second lives when Julian drives up. The press have probably gone by now, the wedding is a done thing, after all. I wouldn't have minded them seeing my lover turning up in a sexy sports car – anything to avoid being endlessly slotted into a sour rejected ex-wife box. I suppose it suits their copy lines better or something.

Julian hasn't called all day and I've just watched the evening news on two channels and seen the wedding twice over. The girls and Tom were easy to spot, standing behind the happy pair with smiles all over their faces. They weren't mentioned by name, it could have been worse. What really gets to me, the real deep-down root of it all, is Bill being so blissfully sorted. He's flying into the future while I'm still so bogged down in the now.

It's been such a balmy shower-free April day. Julian's car-top is down and standing at the bedroom window I watch him running his hands through his hair before picking up a brown-paper-wrapped parcel and jumping out. I have a quick go at my own hair, which is very fair – Susie, whose own is high-lighted and helped along, is fond of saying mine makes hers look in need of a wash. People comment a lot on my natural fairness. Bill liked my hair hanging in a sweep and used to complain when I took it back with combs. He said I had a refined look, the lure of unavailability. I don't want that, I'm much keener on being approached.

Julian is unsmiling as he hands over the parcel. 'It's instead of champagne,' he says pointedly. 'You were making clear you didn't think it was a day for celebrating.'

'Thanks, but there was no need for either.' I smile, ignoring the unveiled sarcasm. Standing with my arms down, the package resting against grey silk trousers that feel cool to my thighs, I admire the mellow sky behind him. There are crimson highlights in a wash of coppery gold.

'That stunning sky was reflected in your eyes,' Julian says, coming in. He closes the door and turns. 'And now they're as deep a violet as your sweater. You look wonderful.'

'No I don't, but your car does, it's gleaming.' I'm bad at accepting compliments and he's still being cool, in a prickly mood. 'You must clean it as often as your teeth—'

'That's making assumptions about my oral hygiene.'

'True.' I meet his eyes uncertainly. 'But reasonable ones.'

Julian takes the present out of my hands and throws it at the hall refectory table where it scuttles along polished oak. I feel the force of his kiss in the empty house. I want to be transported upstairs, to have him lifting off the violet sweater, to feel more of his strength.

He separates and stands staring. 'You're not opening your present.'

I nod at the table. 'You threw it over there.' We're very close and my lips are parted, but he doesn't give in. It makes me angry and I walk off, picking up the present and saying irritably over my shoulder, playing it his way, 'Come in the kitchen and let me get you a drink.'

There's a bottle of Sauvignon Blanc in the fridge. Julian pulls the cork for me and his eyes alight on Bill's claret that I've opened and left standing. 'That's a very classy bottle.'

'Yes, Bill bequeathed me a case. It's conscience wine – you don't mind drinking it?'

'It's a great honour.'

'You could try and be a little bit nicer.'

He comes and presses his cheek to mine. 'Sorry. Shall we go and have this next door?'

I feel better when we're close together, settled on the sitting-room sofa. Julian pours the wine and I unwrap his present, which is a slim leather-bound volume entitled, *A Romance. By Jane Greenmantle.* I smile with my eyes and lean to give him a kiss.

'It's eighteen-thirties,' he says, his arm along the sofa-back. 'That won't have been her real name, of course. It must have been quite fun choosing the pseudonyms.'

'It looks far too valuable – I don't approve! Does it have a happy ending?'

'That's for you to find out. A woman came in with it only this afternoon, along with a few military histories. Probably her late husband's and she needed the money. I felt sorry for her and gave her a good price. She looked so forlorn in her cameo brooch, a sort of left-behind anachronism in today's world.' It makes me think of stories in the papers, the girl just abducted, terrorism, gay marriages. 'The military stuff will do well on the Net,' Julian remarks rather absently, his eyes wandering round at the paintings in the room.

Bill took some delicate watercolours painted by a close friend of his who'd recently died of lung cancer, but the pictures he really loves, the bold vibrant oils, paintings he threw reckless money at, still remain.

As do the antique Spanish threshing-table converted into a coffee table, the huge textured-white sofas. There's little in here of me.

'You should let William have one or two of those paintings.'

'I don't see why. Possibly, if and when I decide to move – stop trying to get me mad!'

Julian smiles and turns my face for a kiss and I feel the tension evaporating, vanishing like dew. Leaning into him companionably I ask an awkward question that's hard to word. 'What I've often wondered . . . is why you ever married Marion in the first place.'

His arm is round my shoulders, his hand fondling my hair. 'It was a safety valve, an outlet. I'd had to do something or explode. I knew I was in for a long wait, that you weren't going to leave William in a hurry. I felt sure of your feelings, but then suddenly I just couldn't stand it. And such intense frustration felt dangerous, I had to needle you and get some sort of reaction, some sign.'

It's very flattering and unnerving; I stare at him, unsure what to think. 'It couldn't have been all about me. You married her; you must have felt things. And you never so much as hinted at it, but you could probably have edged me into an affair.'

'I wanted all of you, not a few cheap pickings. I felt such loathing for William in those days, I was blinded by it and obsessed. I could have murdered him.'

It's a stark shocking phrase that isn't a joke and quite frightens me. Julian doesn't use words loosely. He wants to shake me up, I think; it's deliberate. 'There's a quote from La Bruyère,' he goes on, his face more gentle. '"As long as love endures, it lives on itself, and even at times on what might destroy it: on caprices, harshnesses, absence, jealousy."'

The lines are sobering. I love him quoting poetry and prose; it's always moving and unexpected. 'Of course now,' he smiles and kisses my lips, 'I rather respect William; he showed emotional honesty by leaving.'

'But why her?' I persist, seeing Marion in my mind's eye, manageress of a fitness club and also a masseuse. 'And what did you find to talk about?' I add bitchily.

'Not a lot. She had other talents . . . like choral singing . . .' He grins and I glare, hating to think of the sex. 'I wasn't quite up to celibacy, waiting around for you all that time.

'I asked her at the Brearfield fete. William was on the water-pistol stall soaked to the skin and a group of teenage girls were lapping it up, giggling as his shirt became transparent. Marion said all that chest-hair did nothing for her, but you were looking on with such a fond indulgent smile. I wanted your eyes. And when you wouldn't even look at me I felt so bitter and violently frustrated I turned and asked if she'd like to get married.'

'What about your own chest-hair, that didn't worry her at all?' I ask facetiously.

'It didn't seem to be an obstacle. It wasn't a marriage I really expected or wanted to last.'

'But that's shocking! No one gets married with that attitude. And what about her? You couldn't have been that cynical and heartless. I don't believe it. What if you'd had children?'

'She couldn't. Her ovaries didn't work. She'd told me all about it – something called Turner's Syndrome. I'm ashamed at having to admit it, but that did play a part.'

'And you had no qualms or conscience at all?' I'm feeling more and more horrified, half wishing I'd never asked about Marion, but flattered too, in an awful way.

'It's certainly something I'm not proud of, as I said, but I was so obsessively in love with you. I had told Marion it was all a bit of a gamble, a sort of on-the-rebound situation . . . She's fine now – living with a councillor in Brighton. Sends me postcards. She had none of your delicate compelling beauty, but she knew how to make a man feel wanted . . .' That cuts deep; I look down, hurt and bitter.

'What really got to me today,' he says, drawing me closer, his hand unerringly finding the G spot through my trousers, 'what got me quite so uptight was thinking you only wanted the sex, that it was all about morale-boosting and evening the score. I do really understand you, I know your feelings almost better than you, but just sometimes I lose faith and wonder.'

'I should get some food going,' I mumble, pulling free and standing up abruptly.

Val had appeared at the end of her lunch hour with no time to stay – although she does overtime as comforter in my hour of need and it might have been part deliberate. She had typically brought a little present of some asparagus as well as the steaks I'd asked for.

I've made a lemon tart and the wine, Gruaud-Larose '89, is perfection. Julian enjoys the meal and we both start to be more relaxed. 'Will you stay the night?' I ask him, smiling across the table.

The phone on the far side of the kitchen starts ringing. We both get up. Julian hands it to me and I lean against his chest, loving the feel of him fondling my hair as I answer.

'Hi, Mum! Thought you'd like us to call. We've been having such a cool, cool time!'

'Hi, darling.' Emma's sounding on such a high and it gets to me, I can't face a blow-by-blow account of the wedding.

'There were so many famous people,' she goes on with hardly a breath. 'I talked to Jeremy thingy on television and the Secretary of State who's Victoria's boss. He's got a big domed head, and you'll never guess! He asked if I went clubbing!!! And then the Prime Minister arrived, Mum, and it was really funny. Tom said it was in the news today that the Foreign Secretary's supposed to be plotting against him and there they were, sort of accidentally standing back to back. It would have looked awful in the papers, Tom said, but Victoria somehow put herself between them and manoeuvred the Prime Minister away! She wasn't in white, Mum, it was a kind of apricoty satin suit – the colour of sunrise, some journalist woman said – yuk, yuk! And Dad was so funny in his speech, he—'

'Can I say hi to Jess, now,' I break in resentfully, wishing Julian wasn't holding me in his arms and able to hear every word.

'In just a mo, Mum. And Tom's girlfriend Maudie was there. She's got these fantastic bright green eyes. Tom got so mad and kept hissing for us to get lost! And there was this terrific woman with huuuge boobs who's a brilliant artist, Tom says, and Victoria's best friend. She had on a snakeskin suit with a snake's head zip that curled right up between the boobs and she gave Dad the most enormous great kiss and everyone cheered.'

'Give it me, you beast, I want to tell Mum things.' Jessie's grabbing the phone, sounding just as overexcited. They should be in bed; it's nearly ten. 'Hi, Mum! Victoria's parents have got their dog with them, he's a liver and white spaniel called Christie, so gorgeous and friendly! Can Nattie come and stay soon? Please say yes! She's a proper stepsister now. I was telling her all about Julian's shop and how he—'

'He's here actually. You can say hello.'

I'm still leaning against his chest, using him as a prop, and hand him up the phone. It was impossible not to react and stiffen, hearing all that guff, which he's sure to feel. The mood had been so good and now I'm winding us up again. All the wedding chat was bad enough, let alone the thought of Victoria's daughter coming to stay. Does she really have to? Surely she'd be bored stiff with girls of eleven and twelve?

'Hello lovely Jess.' Julian has such a smile in his voice and Jessie's reply, that I can hear quite clearly, is so elated; it's making me feel irritably jealous.

'Nattie's given me a really old Katy book,' Jessie goes on, 'and it's got brilliant illustrations, Julian, they wore full-length skirts and boater hats to school!' There's a pause. 'Have you asked Mum yet? Is she OK about it?'

'Not yet. And she might think you're a bit young, don't get too excited.'

'But you will ask?'

I frown at Julian. It's maddening, not knowing what's going on. Separating and taking the phone to lecture about bed and say goodnight, I return it to its stand with compressed lips before muttering tightly, 'What was all that about, what's going on?'

'Jess wants to come and help me in the shop on Saturday mornings; she's all worked up about it. What do you think?'

'Wouldn't she just be under your feet? And you're not always there, I wouldn't feel comfortable with Roy in charge.' Julian's assistant is a bit weird, always excavating in his enormous nose, and he has a curious sideways walk like a crab.

'God, nor would I! No, obviously only when I was around and it wasn't one of William's weekends. I'd love having her, that's no

problem. She'd be a real asset and it would be a positive help, actually. Roy's been nagging for more time off, he's got so stuck into
entomology, even enrolled on a course at the Science Museum. It's
his big new thing in life.'

We go back to the table. I'm thinking more about the wedding
and the new Mrs Osborne than Jessie and the bookshop, but Julian
is still pursuing it. 'She's so keen! I showed her the client base when
you left her the other day. It has all their interests, that sort of stuff,
and Jess thought of an 1802 book on Nelson's Battle of the Nile for
a guy in Denver. I emailed and think he might bite – it's worth a
couple of grand! Fascinating account by a clergyman, Cooper
Willyams: such a decisive period . . .'

I stare, hardly absorbing a word. 'Good idea. Sure you won't mind
her around?' His smile makes clear that's not an issue and I retreat
inwards again.

It's Marion, getting to me, I think, and Julian talking of losing
faith. I do care and I really need him just now. Why fight it, then?
It's all Bill's fault, his doing, his media bun-fight, he's got me into this
mucked-up emotional tangle.

Julian helps clear up the supper things. We're both silent. I glance
at him, biting my lower lip, and he stares back thoughtfully. 'I should
go and put up the car-top,' he says, looking on quite tenderly. 'Then
I think, perhaps, it might really be best if I went home.'

I don't want him going. Does he expect me to start begging him
to stay? I turn abruptly away, holding on to the sink, and keep my
back to him. 'Do what you like,' I mutter. Misty senses the tension
and gets out of his basket to come to lick my hand.

'I'm staying with the Pearsons this weekend,' Julian says mildly.
'I'll call. It was a wonderful meal.'

I turn and see him leaving the room. Misty starts to follow, but stops when I make no move, looking back reproachfully at hearing the click of the front door.

I feel like screaming. Why do I have to plead, why must it be pushed on to me? There's no sound of the car. He's not rushing off.

The security light flashes on as I step outside. At least the press have gone, I think distractedly, Misty's not barking. Julian has seen to the top and he's in the car, but hasn't turned on the engine. The driver's window is down, his blue-shirted elbow sticking out. The Porsche, like a powerful stallion, has a reek of male energy – and Julian has, too.

'You could have said goodnight,' I call rather petulantly.

'So could you.' He gets out of the car, but stays leaning against it. 'I know it's been a hard-to-take day, I do understand, but there was no great love lost, no broken hearts. William's generous; your children have adjusted. I suppose I had a vain hope you might see it as the moment to draw a line and even,' he pauses, 'give a little thought to us.'

It's dark, hard to see his expression. 'You think I haven't?' I call. 'Impossible not to, considering the way you've been acting tonight. On the one hand I don't make you feel wanted enough, on the other you're convinced all I want is . . .'

'A fuck,' Julian finishes. 'And a poodle administering it.'

I'm being made to feel small and don't like it. The outside light has gone off too; I can't see his face. Stepping out makes the light come on again. 'And, anyway,' I grouse, getting up close, 'what if that was all I wanted? You've used people when it suited your purpose, by all recent accounts . . .'

'Ah well, if you just want a tame stud . . . That's no hardship, you're no bad fuck as it happens.'

I don't trust the look in his eye. Anger, fury, he looks like a schoolmaster holding a cane, but there's something irritatingly akin to amusement. He sweeps me off my feet then, catching me unawares, and with such a tight hold I'm powerless to resist. I can hardly breathe let alone struggle and as much as I kick out, I can't free my arms to pummel him. I've lost weight, but I'm still no sylph and quite tall and he's carrying me with ease. How can he be so fit and strong?

'Put me down, Julian, you, you – stop hauling me round like a log!'

'I have done some lumbering in my time . . .' He kicks back at the door and it slams shut. 'Want it upstairs or down?'

'Oh, I get to choose, do I? You've just shut Misty out.'

'Misty's fine.'

Halfway up the stairs he presses me against the wall, panting. His face is close, his body giving off the hot damp sexual smell of exertion. 'Hard pounding,' he grins, 'I should have slung you over the hall table. I was being too kind.'

'Kind – did you say kind?'

We're at the top of the stairs. I'm carried into my bedroom and dropped heavily on to the bed. Julian's hanging over me, pinning my spreadeagled arms, trapping me with his weight. Then he's pulling off my trousers, pushing me back when I try to struggle up. He's straddling me again, leaning back down on my arms. He's in a commanding position and his eyes have concentrated holding power. I feel tethered.

His eyes stay trained. Lifting up he unbuckles a thick leather belt and pulls it free of his jeans. I feel a spurt of pure undiluted adrenaline, concentrated fear; my heart's thumping like a fist.

'You're planning to beat me with that thing?' I say, keeping my cool.

'That what you want? It's not what you asked for.' He chucks the belt at a chair. 'I'm only giving you what you asked for. My terms, though: a no-frills fuck. Wham bam.'

'Sounds more like rape to me. That's what a court would believe.'

He's unbuttoning his jeans. 'I wouldn't be too sure. "She was asking for it, m' Lud, I was only giving her what she asked for."'

He's driving into me, hard and fast. No kissing and tenderness, no lifting off of the violet sweater, no fondling of breasts. I feel hammered and nailed to the bed. It's rough, painful and raw. It's a new experience, being a receptacle, an available hole, and I'm fighting tears.

And then I'm in his arms, his wet face pressed to me, and I'm hugging him. We're rolling together, clutching and clinging, his kisses are pouring out. I feel loved, overwhelmingly so, and there's no way of holding back tears.

'The judge might side with you,' Julian says, his fingers trailing my arm.

'No, you'd be all right. They don't like interfering in domestic scenes.'

'Is that what we are?' It's a provocative question that prompts nervous thoughts, but the need to answer is overtaken by some prolonged, very plaintive barking.

'Oh, Christ,' Julian groans. 'Sorry Misty!' I start to sit up but he swings off the bed and hitches and zips his jeans. 'I'll go, I've got more on – but I expect you'd probably rather I went altogether now, anyway.'

'No, don't. Can't you stay the night? I want you to.'

He kisses me and rests his forehead to my face, his eyelashes brushing. 'As long as you'll sleep in my arms. I'll lock up and see to Misty then we can have a bath together. And if I can share your toothbrush I'd be living up to those reasonable assumptions you made.'

CHAPTER 3

'Mrs Osborne? It's Merrill Winslow. I know *The Courier* has been in touch about doing an interview for us, but I was hoping personally to persuade you. You could put your side of the story fairly and in context and it would be of such interest and help to women in similar positions. It's been far harder for you, of course, with everything so centre stage . . .'

'Sorry, I don't give interviews.'

'We don't usually, but I'd be happy to let you see the piece in advance?'

I stand my ground. I'm not baring my soul in print and certainly not for *The Courier*, Bill's bitter rival. Deserted wives often do open up, though. Perhaps it helps to feel a soothing wash of readers' sympathy. Might I want to if I didn't have Julian?

He wants me to go to stay with his friends, Henry and Lauren Pearson, at their weekend place in Cambridgeshire. I've more or less agreed to, next time Bill has the girls.

Henry was at school with Julian and they were at Cambridge together, too. He's a barrister and his wife, who's American, is a food writer and wine buff and often on television. According to Julian she's wonderfully easy company, a brilliant cook, obviously, and very down to earth. He does go on about her.

It's late. I should be getting up, not lying here stark naked, being idle as sin. Before leaving, Julian brought me tea then slid back into bed and into me again. Easily, comfortably, with my leg slung over his pelvis.

It felt too good. He'd been obsessed with me all those years, more than I had thought. But now he's got me and won't he soon have had me? My eyes are more open, post-Bill.

And suppose I had been the one to leave? I'd have got a whole lot more flak than Bill did, but none of the hideously demoralizing humiliation. I came so close to it that night of Val and Chris's party, so very nearly changed the course of my whole life.

The party had been just a summer get-together. Bill had stayed home, bored rigid at the very thought; it was the full suburbia as far as he was concerned. He could have made more of an effort. But even then, pre-Victoria, we were as guests in a hotel, sharing a roof and little else.

Val is such a close friend, but of mine, not Bill's. She's not in his sphere. I'd gone to the party feeling less put out, thinking of that, and keenly anticipating seeing Julian. Her husband, Chris, is an architect and the house worships at the altar of space. Pale wood floors, a state-of-the-art kitchen, it's so uncluttered and unlike mine.

It was a hot July night, everyone outdoors. Julian was nowhere to be seen, which had made me feel at a frustrated loose end, a keen sense of anticlimax.

I had wandered into the kitchen where Chris was pulling corks and talked about Tom. He'd been so set on going to art college and turning down a top university place. Chris had taken my son's side and argued passionately. 'Art is so enriching and expanding, he'll see things in a whole new light. Tom's got the talent – don't be so hidebound, Ursula! Wish I'd done it. I'm jealous if truth be told.'

All very well, that, from a highly qualified architect. 'He's got to earn a living,' I shot back, idly picking up a towel and an upturned glass. 'Art can still be his great interest.'

Chris relieved me of my towel and took over the drying. 'Don't relegate it to a hobby, for Christ's sake, not when he's got such genuine ability. Give him his head, let him—' He had stopped, his attention held, and I turned to see where he was looking.

Julian was standing in the doorway. Something about his expressionless face had spoken to me. Its very blankness had caught Chris's attention too, but I could feel the intensity behind the façade and it was drawing me like a spell. 'I'd promised Julian a dance,' I lied, looking back at Chris with a smile, needing any excuse, any reason, any means, for abruptly walking out of the kitchen and getting away.

We had never danced together. We'd had lunch a few times at the Thai place opposite the bookshop, mostly with a solemn-faced little Jessie along. Julian had involved her in our poetry chat, almost comically given her age, but she had listened attentively, gazing up like an adoring fan. She had been my cover and helped keep the gossip at bay.

Dancing with Julian our bodies had slotted together like the two sides of a zip. His cheek had felt warm and male, pressed to mine. He had lifted up his head at one moment and looked at me carefully, then rested his cheek again, entwining our fingers more tightly. I had felt completely at ease with the intimacy and had no thought for Bill or anything else.

A space in the sitting room had been cleared, Val and Chris's 15-year-old son Jack was in charge of the disco, but the barbecue was in full swing, we were the only couple dancing. When Jack upped the pace and one or two of his teenage friends came in, it seemed the moment to go.

There was a crowd round the barbecue. We had wandered into the garden with no one paying attention. I can remember the heady scent of the shrub roses, a resplendent show of tall hollyhocks that had acted as a screen. I was in a filmy green dress with shoestring straps, Julian in shirtsleeves. Right at the bottom of the garden we had leaned our elbows on a high wooden fence and stared out to the playing fields beyond.

That soft caressing night had wrought its magic; we leapfrogged over the niceties and concertinaed years; our longings no longer hidden and silent, we had spoken our feelings that night, known the certainties and where we wanted to go.

Julian had asked me to come away with him. 'Just for a night. We need to make plans. William's at home with Emma and Jess. Call, tell him you're staying with a friend and will be back tomorrow – in good time for him to leave for the paper.' Julian had been so confident and sure, on to the detail, the next stage. The battle raging in me was one he'd already fought. But I had known that the night, the hour, the moment had been unique.

I'd heard the footsteps and sensed the intrusion with a feeling of drowning; my throat had closed up as though constricted by a coiling snake. Claud Jeremy, the vicar, had been bearing down on us, his wavy brown hair bouncing with each stride. 'Hasn't it been another perfect evening,' he called out. 'They are always so lucky with the weather!'

'Divine intervention,' Julian muttered.

'Whenever you're ready Ursula, just say the word.' Claud beamed, his pointy nose giving its customary twitch.

I was often out on my own in Brearfield and he had made it his vicarly duty always to see me to my car. I hadn't suspected his interest at the time, but after the break-up he had made quite persistent, if coy, advances.

'I'll take Ursula to her car, you needn't worry, she'll be quite safe,' Julian had said with glacial sarcasm, raising the conversational drawbridge. Giving an equally icy smile he had rudely turned back to the fence.

Claud had had no option but to wander away, but his brief unwanted presence had brought home all the ripples of my actions. The dust of conformity settled back on my skin in suffocating layers. The consequences were inescapable. A chance, a butterfly vision had fluttered into view, but fluttered just as quickly away.

When we left and were beside my car, I had leaned against it, facing Julian. 'It's too hard, I haven't the strength, not right now. Can you understand?'

He kissed me lightly and held me. His arms round my bare back, his tracing fingers, the nearness: I had arched my back and felt him take hold of my sticking-out shoulder blades, grasping them like the bony bases of a bird's wings.

'You'll need all your strength,' he said, his fingers still gripping. 'It will be harder now, but it's going to happen.' He kissed me again. 'And then you can have all of mine.'

Twelve o'clock, why aren't they back yet? It's the time agreed. The phone rings and leaping to it anxiously, I assume it's Tom, but Julian answers. 'Just in case you're worried, they've stopped off here. It was Jessie's doing, I think. She wants to know if it's all right about coming here tomorrow to help me.'

'But aren't you away this weekend?'

'Not going till after lunch. I should do a morning and give Roy his time off, especially as I'm off to Uganda again quite soon, if you remember? I shall hate not seeing you.'

I'm pleased about Jess, less so about the trip. It makes me feel irrationally hard-done-by and I start whinging about the orgy of wedding pictures in the papers. Julian makes no comment. He lets me rant on, but all I'd wanted was a soothing sympathetic response.

When he gently reminds me that Jess is waiting to know about tomorrow, I snappily respond. 'It's fine,' adding then for good measure, 'Emma might kick up a bit.'

'I've worried about that. Think I've sorted it, though – more or less.'

The family arrive back in a tired, niggly morning-after grump. Emma doesn't stop needling her sister about the bookshop; maybe it's not so sorted after all. I tell them to lay the table and they snatch forks, arguing and being very babyish.

'Jess is so sucking up to Julian, Mum, she's such a skanky little flirt.'

'Stoppit you minger, I'm not even getting any money.'

'Don't stick your tongue out, Jess. What's this about money?'

'Julian says I'm an apprentice,' she carefully separates out the syllables, 'that's sort of training and he says you don't really get paid. But he's giving us all a book, Mum, Tom too: first editions and they do grow in value, you know. It's a sort of advance bonus – and manky Emma's not even earning hers so she can shut her stupid face.'

*

On Sunday, with their grandmother due, Emma is looking quite tidy. Jessie's a mess. Tangled hair and she's sulking, hunching her shoulders, sticking out her lower lip. She's a sexy child, I think, watching her pick up a book and flop down on a rug on the floor. She sits with elbows on wide-apart knees, the book open on the floor between them. Emma's more bashfully aware of her body; her breasts are developing, one very slightly bigger than the other. She's obsessed about it, but I've told her it's quite usual and not to worry.

I watch from the kitchen as my mother, Barbara, parks her safe little Vauxhall Astra as far away from the house as possible; you'd think I was lunching an army of VIPs. And she's hardly crunching the gravel, it's a sort of tiptoeing of wheels.

Letting her in, getting a mild lecture about the state of the front grass, I worry about her lonely eyed look, the fair hair fading to white. She has more lines at seventy than she deserves. It's lack of a man, I think, and never treating herself. Her prettiness was there in early photographs, but always an aura of reticence, as though she felt it wrong, almost sinful, to be looking good. She works part-time as a doctor's receptionist. My father died young, at only fifty, and diplomats' wives were discouraged from having careers.

My father's death from a stroke just before the start of my first term at university affected me deeply. I'd written spare dark desolate poems at the time. They had moved Bill, I think, and played into his need to get involved.

> Outside,
> Rain ran down the road
> In streams;

And down my face,
The tears of grief.

My brother, Harry, is a diplomat, too; he's out in Colombia, hoping to make ambassador next posting. He married late, a feisty Colombian artist. My mother thinks it might affect his promotion and she's probably right.

At lunch I bring up the possibility of moving. From my mother's face I might have just suggested emigration to Iraq. 'But you love this house! And it's the children's home, you can't disrupt them even more.' It wasn't me who did the disrupting, I think sarcastically.

'It's not like that, Gran,' Tom says. 'Mum needs her own space, a whole new life.'

'She doesn't need a new house.'

'I am here you know.'

Jessie's very quiet and it strikes me suddenly that she hasn't once mentioned the bookshop job to her grandmother. She was pink with excitement yesterday, when Julian dropped her back, telling us how they'd been so busy doing the catalogue on the computer they'd almost missed a customer coming in.

'Jessie's a working girl, now.' I smile and fill in my mother about the job.

She looks horrified all over again. 'Darling, she's far too young! You left her there the whole morning? I really don't think this is a good idea.' She turns to Jessie with an anxious frown. 'You didn't go out in that busy market square, I hope?'

'No I didn't.' Her lips are tight-pressed; she looks defiant, vulnerable and upset.

'Books are Jessie's thing,' Tom says. 'It's great for her, she'll learn a lot. Julian gives her so much of his time.' He stands up, duty done by the family. 'Well, guess I should really be getting back. He grins at his kid sister. 'Might just pay my respects to Elton, though . . . Coming?' Jessie's guinea pig is her passion and point of refuge. She noisily scrapes back her chair and gratefully makes her escape.

The bookshop subject is dropped, but later when we're alone in the kitchen and clearing up, my mother returns to it. 'Jess is only eleven. I do hope that assistant of Julian's was around to help keep an eye.'

'For God's sake! Julian's hugely responsible – you just don't understand him, you don't even try.'

'No,' she answers simply, 'I don't. He's led such a funny life and there was that business of the failed quickie marriage as well. His father was such a nice man, I secretly wonder if his son mightn't have been just the tiniest bit of a disappointment to him.'

The disappointing son calls me at midnight. I'm in bed, deep in a book, written just post-war, about a French girl breaking up a solid middle-class marriage.

I'm relieved and glad to hear Julian; I've missed him. The girls have squabbled all evening and dragged their heels about homework. I feel due a little cosseting.

Turning pleasurably on my side I feel my nipples beginning to tingle and prick. It's too physical, this relationship, too binding in. I tell him about Jessie. 'She's thrilled to bits, so full of the job – it was odd, though, she didn't breathe a word of it to my mother at lunch today.'

'When I was telling her how brilliantly she'd done I did say people would be wrong to think her too young. Perhaps it was that. She is an exceptionally quick and intelligent child, you know.' I do know, but it still seems unusually astute of Jess to have guessed so exactly her grandmother's reaction.

The apprentice idea was inspired, I tell Julian, and saying a lingering goodnight, put the tiny sand-grain of uncertainty out of my mind. He is so good with the girls.

I'm nervous about meeting his friends, Henry and Lauren Pearson. They belong to a side of Julian I never see. Then he's off on this trip to Uganda, some project or other to do with a village school. And I'll be here on my own.

CHAPTER 4

'Misty, come here!' I yell furiously. We're out on the downs and he's deep into every rabbit hole. I battle on over grassy hummocks and stones with the wind billowing my shirt back like a sail. It's a good feeling, being up here. I love seeing Brearfield far below, glinting in the May sunlight. Hemple Benton too, in the distance, its church spire looks silver-dipped. Did someone climb up centuries ago, and conceive that tall tapering spire pointing so gracefully skywards? I feel in the mood for writing a poem, thoughts forming.

> A memory so sharp that surely
> Another lies beneath.
> Somewhere much deeper . . .

This is no good; I've got to get going. Val is expecting me for lunch and Susie is coming, too.

We settle down at the glass-topped table with lunch all spread out. A delicious-looking salad studded with black olives, Feta cheese, crusty French bread: raspberries, brownies – Val's idea of a quick snack. She's in office gear, grey skirt and jacket; Susie's looking very trendy and nautical in tight white canvasy jeans and a navy top.

They're such opposites, my friends. Val is a rock, the most common-sense person in the world. Susie is more vulnerable and I suppose, in a lesser way, I'm a sort of rock to her; she thinks I partic-ularly understand about being married to a womanizer. I do, although as far as I know Bill stuck to one woman. And even married her.

'Myrtle's gone north to see her mother,' I say, peeved with my babysitter, for all her special qualities. Myrtle has cropped dark hair and a cross-looking face that is quaintly at odds with her immensely caring nature. 'Just when Julian's got tickets tomorrow, for the Edwardian revival at the Haymarket. There's a parents' evening at school too, though, so the writing was on the wall.'

'Julian can always take me,' Susie says wistfully. Her husband, Phil, is such a shit.

I grimace. 'No chance. He's taking his best friend's wife. She's American.'

Val looks wry. 'Anything wrong in that? You don't sound terribly keen . . .'

'I haven't met her, but she's one of those achieving women who make you feel weary at the thought. I'm going for a weekend with them soon and I'll feel so inadequate.'

'Don't be mad,' Susie snorts, 'with your looks? Be a nice change, good for you. I saw Jessie in the bookshop on Saturday,' she goes on, 'being quite the proper little assistant. She was working on the com-puter with Julian alongside. They were doing catalogue entries. He says it's all Internet and catalogue now; no one has antiquarian shops any more.' I stare, finding that unsettling, was he hinting it's time to move on? 'I got Julian to buy tickets for the Women in Health dance,' Susie says proudly.

'Not sure how!' I laugh, falsely cheerful, thinking charity dances are hardly his thing, even one Susie is chairing. It's a charity Bill always supported in *The Post* and being reminded of that brings back memories. I can't help having a small attack of wistful fondness.

'You still thinking of moving?' Val asks. 'Blossom Cottage is coming on the market, I'm told. It's worth having a look at. Take Julian if you do, old George Farley is one of his greatest fans.'

She's imagining the cottage as a cosy little outcome, just the love-nest job. I'm not shacking up with Julian to please my friends, I think angrily, he's never even suggested it. Why move at all? Why be worried about Bill's outgoings? I've got enough problems of my own.

Driving home Susie's husband, Phil, is on my mind. He was one of those men who came out of the woodwork like greedy worms the moment Bill was gone. They would call round, stand oppressively close; suggest fixing my window, fitting a new washer. Services offered with arms casually draped, hands dipping into my resistant body. It's an ongoing problem; Phil still tries it on.

Did Bill have a string of affairs before Victoria? I'll never know. And Julian? He isn't a Phil, I'm sure of that, but we don't live together. There could be other women.

On Saturday Julian comes for supper. Just macaroni cheese with the girls, but he never minds and fits in with familiar ease. Jessie is holding forth, being very full of her second bookshop morning and blatantly showing off. 'Books have less value with foxing,' she says airily. 'That's those little brown spots they get with age. You know! Like old ladies do.'

'And old men,' I say defensively, glaring at Julian who's giving me a cruelly teasing grin. But his topaz eyes, with their lights and depths, are soft and my heart gives a leap. His face has a sort of high-boned thoroughbred look. I love its contours. He's smiling fondly at Jess and I wonder if he misses having children of his own.

He touches my hand. 'She's being the most fantastic help, picking it up so fast.'

'I sold two books today, Mum, and one for fifty pounds! The men buy them, the ladies just look and then put them back in all the wrong places.' I can imagine Jessie's solemn sales pitch winning over susceptible males.

We're at the garden end of the kitchen. The sun is very low and the quality of light is richly golden as though down to its purest essence. Long dark-edged shadows from the trees are in sombrely beautiful contrast. There's one magnificent presiding oak that sires so many acorn offspring, I'm constantly having to weed out tiny fledgling trees.

I finally get the girls off upstairs. Then after a decent interval Julian gets me to bed too, and we make noiseless, slightly inhibited love behind my closed bedroom door.

When he's gone, in the still, lonely silence after his departed throaty car, I find myself dwelling on his trip to the theatre with Lauren. Henry had been away overnight apparently, in Germany. 'What's a British barrister doing out there?' I'd demanded suspiciously.

'An army court martial.' Julian said. 'He's quite often away on cases.'

Lauren is keeping me awake; she feels a threat, his best friend's wife. She'd been available that night of the theatre – had Julian stayed in London or come home?

*

On Tuesday nights Val and I have a regular bridge evening with a retired admiral and his wife. We go there, as he's wheelchair-bound, but Myrtle, my babysitter, is back home and it's no problem.

We're fond of the couple, but the fire always smokes, they have snuffling pug dogs and the admiral constantly yells at his wife across the green baize – quite as explosively as he must have at his ratings. She maintains an impervious calm.

I play badly, gazing at silver photograph frames on the grand piano, even trumping one of Val's tricks. She raises a generous dark querying eyebrow, but it's simply my impatience to get to Julian's flat. I'm feeling in need of him and can't keep Myrtle up too long.

There's an alley behind the market square, a backdoor into the shop. We're hungry for each other, Julian wanting me, too. His kisses are devouring and rapacious and we make slow progress up the rickety little staircase to his flat; he's unbuttoning my shirt, dragging down its sleeves. And then in the bedroom, he's burying deep in my breasts, parting my willing thighs.

It can't last, I think, lying in the crook of his arm, luxuriating in the cool crispness of fresh white cotton sheets; and after all the wonderful passion, what then?

'It's late, I should go . . .' I don't want to, Julian's arm is round me so protectively. My eyes wander round lazily and I marvel at what he's achieved with two small rooms above the shop. A kitchen fitted along one wall of the main room is prettily tiled and unobtrusive, shielded by Japanese screens; there's a mini-bathroom where previously existed only a loo. No room for a washing machine, no drying socks, his laundry bills must be huge.

The rooms are beamed and whitewashed and the wide old floorboards creak with a language of their own. He has a charming little desk with mother-of-pearl diamonds over the keyholes and there's a delicate early pen drawing of an Italian village on the wall above that I particularly love.

'Don't you miss having a garden, any outdoors?' I turn to him, smiling.

'I do miss growing things, but I'm away so often – it's not so bad.'

'Did you have to sell your father's house?' I'd been to it once with Bill when Julian's father was still alive and loved it: a Georgian house on the outskirts of Hemple Benton and an ideal size. The furniture, too, had been a stylish mix of contemporary and old.

'I couldn't have stayed there with all the memories,' Julian says simply.

I lift up and kiss his cheek feeling moved, thinking of his mother and younger sister killed in that terrible car crash just months before Bill and I moved to Brearfield. I'd heard people talking, criticizing Julian for going abroad again so soon afterwards and leaving his father.

I'd asked him about it once. Julian said he'd had to go back to Uganda for a time and his father had wanted it, but he had felt really wretched, being out of the country when a terminal cancer had been diagnosed. I'd wanted to find out why he needed to go, what it was all about, but asking questions had seemed insensitive in all the circumstances, intrusive.

I feel for him, having lost his whole family. It must be unbearable sometimes and I'm sure he thinks of his friend Henry Pearson almost as a brother. They've known each other since childhood.

'I sold the house at a good time,' Julian says, bringing me back, 'which was very useful. I'd wanted to put some money into an Aids hospital in Uganda. There was inheritance tax, of course, but Dad had some shares.'

'Did you sell the furniture too?'

'No, that's in store.' There's an awkward pause, unvoiced thoughts floating around.

'Really must go, poor Myrtle!' It's hard untangling myself, but I have to and begin rounding up my clothes. 'Oh, by the way, Susie's ecstatic you've bought tickets for that dance . . .'

'Not sure if I can make it, it's about when I'm going to Uganda. Depends on the flights.'

'Let me know soon as you can,' I say, feeling irritated, stepping into my shoes. 'Susie would be quite hurt if I don't go, I'll need to make amends.'

Julian hunches on his shirt and pulls me close. 'The tickets are for you. Take someone else if I'm away.'

'Who like – my mother?' I lean my head to him. Julian picks up my face and I can't help saying rather wetly, gazing into his eyes, 'But you might be able to come?'

'Depends. I need to be back for the summer Olympia Book Fair: it's fitting everything in.' He gives me a kiss and a squeeze of the hand, then reaches for his keys heaving a small sigh – one I'm probably not supposed to hear. 'Come on,' he says then with a big cheerful grin, 'in the absence of Claud I'll see you to your car.'

CHAPTER 5

Wednesday is market day in Brearfield and I'm lucky to find a place in the car park. After days of rain, a bright dewy morning is giving the town a freshly spring-cleaned look and lifting spirits. People are calling from opposite pavements, cheerily waving, and when I go to the market the stallholders are on wisecracking good form.

It's a very gentrified little market. Local honey, home-made chutneys, dried herbs in Provençal pouches, fat shiny olives and salamis; no back-of-a-lorry cheap gadgets or clothes.

There is an excellent fish stall with glistening cod, skate, tiger prawns, hunks of meaty tuna, all tidily laid out. Joe is the fishmonger, whose shortage of teeth is quite striking. Buying monkfish I wonder how he manages to chew. But he's in good voice and informs me that Victoria's government needs to get its effing collective finger out.

I bypass the rare plants stall, run by a woman in a melon green dress who looks as palely refined as her stock, and make for Bert's with the summer bedding. He has trailing geraniums, a lovely burgundy colour, and some healthy-looking white petunia plants.

Buying a tray of each I say beaming, as he hands over the petunias,

'I'll just get this to the car. Be back for the geraniums.' I like old Bert, he's solid and decent.

'Make it soon, if you can, Mrs O,' he urges, 'I'm packing up early today.'

At the car I rest the tray on the roof and dig around for my car keys. Out of the corner of my eye I see, to my dismay, Erica Barkston weaving through the cars. It's too late, she's gesticulating and coming over. Shit. She's about the only person to be able to drag me down on such a glorious blue-sky day — someone I'd cross more than a car park to avoid. Erica is the worst sort of net-curtain-tweaking troublemaking gossip, which is being generous, and she's making a very determined beeline. There's no escape, I'm in a sea of cars, pinned in between my old navy Mercedes estate and a much newer, cleaner Volvo.

'Glad I caught you, Ursula!' She's panting a bit, so keen is she to catch me. 'I do need a very private word.' Her bulbous grey eyes do a quick privacy-seeking circuit of the car park, but she'll be longing to be overheard. I wouldn't trust Erica to post a letter for me without steaming it open first; it might contain some hot gossip.

She has bobbed brown hair and my eyes keep being drawn to the thick white parting, straight as a Roman road. And she's clutching the most hideous floral straw bag. 'How can I help?' My smile is stiff as rigor mortis. 'I am in a bit of a hurry . . .'

'I'm sure you are, Ursula, but this is extremely serious,' she says importantly, in a breathy whisper. 'It's a particularly delicate matter, in fact I hardly know how to begin.'

'Goodness. Well, hadn't you just better tell me straight?'

'It is very difficult . . .'

She's looking sly and I begin to feel genuinely alarmed. And she's crowding me in her too-tight trousers, making me have to take a step back.

The sly look becomes more artfully complacent and giving a quick backward glance she leans even closer. 'I must say it, I'd never forgive myself if, well, God forbid, anything happened. It's about Julian and your daughter, you see . . .' She pauses to let that sink in and my stomach begins to churn.

'Ursula, don't you think you're really being too terribly trusting? I mean leaving Jessie alone with him at the bookshop all morning; I wouldn't with my child. I do happen to know, actually, that his assistant, Roy, has time off when she's there and, when you remember Julian's flat is just upstairs . . . Can't you see the risk, the temptation you're putting his way?'

There's a pounding in my head, a scream in my throat. 'That's the most appalling unfounded slur, Erica, how can you even think such a thing, let alone say it? I can hardly believe what I'm hearing.'

'He is of good background, of course,' she carries on with a snobbish sneer. 'His father was well respected, but who knows why Julian spent all those years abroad. There was sure to be some very good reason. And he may be a *close* friend of yours, but it's in just those sort of circumstances, where a child feels relaxed and comfortable, that these terrible things can happen.'

'What things?' I demand. 'Just think what you're actually insinuating, Erica.' I've raised my voice and look round in alarm; there are people dotted about, a woman returning to a nearby van. With a supreme effort of will I contain the fury, the blind urge to strike her and pull out tufts of hair; it's almost blurring my vision.

I swallow, desperate not to talk loudly and draw attention. 'You

make that ludicrous disgusting allegation, you've no basis, no shred
of evidence . . .'

'Yes I have.' Her eyes have a gleam of victory and my legs go weak.
She looks theatrically over her shoulder and carries on. 'I went in the
shop last Saturday, quite by chance, and the door wasn't quite closed;
that old brass bell didn't ring. Jessie was playing on the computer and
Julian was pressed right up close. His arm was round her, Ursula, he
only took it away when I coughed and made myself known.'

'Wasn't it just along the back of her chair?' I demand in a furious
whisper, determined not to let her see me shaken. 'Two people working on a computer would have to sit close. And the door was ajar,
you said. It was a Saturday, for God's sake! Customers coming in.'

Erica's mouth sets a little more tightly, but she's still looking sick-
eningly smug. 'Just don't go spreading that around,' I hiss, aware of
someone looking over. 'Have you got it in for Julian or something?
Excuse me now, but I really have to go.' I flash the key at the car,
fling myself in, then, lowering the window, add bitterly, 'Think of
the harm, Erica, it's the most dreadful thing to have inferred.'

'Your tray of plants is still on the roof,' she says with infuriating
complacency, 'shall I hand it in? Forewarned is forearmed, I say –
you'll be grateful to me when you've calmed down.'

I get out of the car, grab the tray, get in again and slam the door.
My knuckles are white as I grip the steering wheel, throw the car into
reverse and back away.

She'll tell the whole of Brearfield, I can just hear her, 'I mean,
would you really let your daughter . . .?'

I've got to ignore it, forget it. I can't, it's too awful – she can do
such needless harm.

I'm minutes from home when a powerfully potent image suddenly fills my mind. It makes me brake sharply and slow down. I can smell him, feel him, Julian pressed up close on the sofa that night, nuzzling my neck, fondling my hair. My stomach goes concave and my heart is thumping like a drumming fist. But that was me he was caressing – me, the woman he loves. I'm overwrought, not seeing straight. God what has that woman done?

I pull over in the quiet lane and stop the car. Val will be with a client. I can't possibly bother her. Yes I can, I think, feverishly digging out my mobile.

A secretary answers, but Val takes over the phone. Her next appointment, she tells me, can wait. She listens in silence, but in the very telling I can imagine how melodramatic I must sound. Val will dismiss it out of hand.

'It's all about trust,' she says thoughtfully. 'You shouldn't give a toss what Erica says or tries to insinuate. She's seeing what she wants to see, looking for trouble, itching for a real-life drama. Your own views are what count. She doesn't know Julian. You do and you had no qualms. Has Erica really said anything to make you change your mind?'

'No . . . and I do trust him, of course I do, but – well can't you see how evil she is, Val,' I cry, 'the mischief she can do?'

'Hardly. She's an interfering small-minded small-town bitch and known to be. Evil's too big a word. Go with your instincts, Ursula. You were happy to leave Jessie with Julian and nothing Erica has said adds up to a single row of beans. She's tried and failed to make trouble, that's all.'

I go home feeling calmer, reassured and grateful. But Erica will still talk and some of it will stick. And how will I rise above any infinitesimal seeds of suspicion sown? It will be hard not to start looking for signs.

As I'm opening the garage door a rusty old white van drives up. I keep my back turned, hurriedly wiping my eyes and cursing the intrusion, longing to be left alone.

It's Bert, from the market. 'I was just passing,' he says diffidently. 'I've got your geraniums in the van. Sorry I had to pack up early. It's me little granddaughter's birthday today and I'm helping at the party.' He's opening the back, getting out the tray. Handing it over his face is solemnly concerned. 'You OK, Mrs Osborne? You're looking a little pale. Nothing wrong is there?'

'No, no, nothing at all. It's so good of you bringing this, really kind. Sorry to give you the bother, I got a bit held up. Can you hang on a mo, Bert?' I smile. 'Just while I nip in and find a little something for your granddaughter. I'd like to do that.'

CHAPTER 6

I plant the petunias in boxy containers either side of the front door. They look fresh and unfussy. The geraniums are for the weathered stone urns on the back terrace. I've carried them round, but still have to put them in. The terrace is my favourite place, a suntrap. There are doors out from the sitting room and kitchen, the Gloire de Dijon roses Bill planted years ago have scaled the heights, and sun-loving plants seed themselves between paving stones with glorious promiscuous abandon.

I'm feeling just as abandoned, seductively lured by the late-May sun when I should be working – researching a new finance director for a weed-killer giant. The sun is hypnotizing and all embracing, though, and it's bringing a sense of elation absent in weed-killer companies. I'm not even planting the geraniums. Just lying back on the wrought-iron bench, a cushion under my head, legs dangling, trying to soak up some sun for the Pearson weekend. And for Bill: he's coming for the girls tomorrow and it's a matter of pride that he sees me, and the house, looking our best.

Half-past eleven, he said. Jessie wants to do an hour in the book-shop first. I would have vetoed that, but she's so keen and Julian seems content about it. And part of me is hoping Erica will see her there again. I don't want that woman thinking she's won.

Taking Jess into Brearfield in the morning I avoid the car park and manage to find a twenty-minute bay in the market square. Jessie jumps out looking cute as can be in a denim jacket and cut-offs: too pert and sexy, I think anxiously, as people smile her way.

She stops for a word with a middle-aged man on a bench in the square, whom she seems to know. His dog, a Jack Russell, is rather adorable and Jessie squats to give it a friendly pat. I leave her there a second and go across the market square to post a letter.

'I feel sad for that man,' she says waving back at him as we go over to the bookshop. 'He came in and looked through the old paper-backs box last week and told me his mother's just died. Julian was a bit mean, saying he'd never buy anything and wasn't to be trusted. And Julian asked if he had a job, which I thought was quite rude really. He's a security guard, working nights, and very nice, Mum.'

'Julian has to watch out for shoplifters, I expect. He knows best, darling. You must do as he says.' Erica wouldn't approve – telling Jessie that. God, she's a dreadful person.

The brass bell sounds as we go in. My daughter leads through into the main body of the shop where she takes off her jacket, draping it over a wooden chair like an executive arriving at the office. She looks round appraisingly with sweet proprietary pride.

There are framed old prints laid out on a side-table; drawers underneath for the unframed ones, glass containers for the more pre-cious books. The floor-to-ceiling shelves are well stocked, boxes of second-hand bargains – it's a browsing book-lover's paradise.

Julian comes down from his flat with a mug of coffee, which he sets down. I fix to be back for Jess at eleven then smile awkwardly, feeling stupidly nervous about our weekend. 'You'll pick me up a bit later? Bill will have gone by twelve.'

He touches my cheek. 'Sure. We can have lunch on the way, stop at a pub, perhaps.'

I meet his eyes, tense with anticipation, then glance over his shoulder and see Jessie darting upstairs. It makes me instantly freeze. 'Where are you going?' I call out shrilly.

'Must have a pee. See you, Mum!'

Erica can't do this, I tell myself, all the way home; I can't let her, mustn't.

As I pack a few things for the weekend Emma keeps me company – sitting hugging her knees on the bed and being quite quizzy. 'Julian says it's really casual,' I say self-consciously, 'but I still need something for tonight.'

'Your paisley midi that kicks out. It's cool.' She jumps off the bed, flicks through my hangers and holds an apricot silk shirt aloft. 'And wear it with this – and that belt from Spain, the one with the big old studs.'

'Quite the little style guru, aren't we! You all packed for Dad?' She rolls her eyes, hands on hips, and then stomps off out with an exaggerated sigh.

I take too long applying minimal make-up, I'd hate Bill thinking I've made an effort. Yesterday's sun is helping, though, after Erica had caused such skin-draining gloom.

Greeting Bill, I find myself in the arc of another pair of compelling brown eyes. It's a curious mix of strangeness and familiarity, seeing him now, when any real connection or emotion is historic. I feel the sway of his considerable charisma, but without being physically drawn.

Bill's eyes on me are warm, conciliatory. He's probably just wondering how close I am to being sorted and off his conscience, I think irritably and, staring back, say with sniffy sarcasm, 'How's married life?'

'It's good,' he smiles, diluting any sharpness of mine. Then his smile broadens and widens as the girls come running and he squats for Emma to fling her arms round his neck. Jess stays back, but he reaches out and draws her in, too. 'A hug-a-rug's what I need,' he says, enveloping her along with Emma and pressing their heads to his chest.

He has come in Victoria's car. 'Will Nattie be home?' I hear Jessie asking eagerly as they pile in. Why can't I loosen up and just be glad they all get on?

I go round the house checking on window-locks, impatient to hear Julian's car. I can't wait to see him, although Erica's mischief has made unwanted images of physical closeness to Jessie keep creeping in. They won't go away, like violent scenes in films.

I've got to stop this. I'm a free woman, about to go off in a sports car for a night away with a man I trust and can't wait to be in bed with. I might even like his friends.

Julian is looking serious getting out of his car. I'm outside, hanging back by the front door, and he comes close with his eyes on me so intently my head and heart pound. 'You've got a golden glow,' he says, kissing my nose and pressing his body hard to mine. 'The woman I love.'

I want more than a kiss on the nose, but he separates and picks up my bag, stowing it on the floor by the passenger seat. With Misty coming there's no space behind. 'You're spared having the top down,' Julian says, tipping the seat forward for Misty. 'They say it might rain. Jessie was worrying about Elton — she did remember to feed him?'

'An entire lettuce, my prime baby carrots, he's a guinea pig gourmet! Are you sure the Pearsons really don't mind about Misty, you have asked?'

'Of course. They're delighted.'

Driving through Brearfield Julian turns with such a look of contact that I wonder, though it's wistfully fanciful, if he's thinking like I am of future drives and weekends. 'Lauren called just as I was leaving and wants us there for lunch,' he says, looking ahead again. 'Can you hang on?'

I tell him food's the least of it, but can't explain about my ball of nerves. I'm feeling so out of practice with movers and shakers. Bill used to ask them down, journalist colleagues, politicians, artists, tycoons; he never stinted on drink and, like the wine, good rowdy conversation flowed. Lauren is one of those doers and success stories, exactly what I'm not. And she's a mother with twin sons of sixteen, although they won't be there this weekend.

Erica and the bookshop won't leave my head. The thought of it lingering, hanging over the weekend like a spectre, makes me suddenly decide to clear the air. 'I had a bad scene with a school mum this week,' I say, surprising myself. 'Erica Barkston.'

'Who else! Was it about me? She's been in and out of the shop, snooping, making very clear her view of my new young apprentice — quite convinced, it seems, that I'm a raving depraved paedophile. She'll be looking me up on the sex register next!'

My face must be showing the incredible weight he's just lifted. 'Actually,' Julian says, glancing over absorbing my relief, I'm sure, 'Erica's helped me in a rather extraordinary way.'

'Can't think how. She's not renowned for her helping skills.'

'I've been wanting to do a biography, possibly of someone who's committed a dark crime – a bit like *In Cold Blood*, a sort of poor man's Truman Capote. It would be fascinating to write a psychological thriller, a real-life account, and delve inside the mind for the triggers that tip people over. There was a child abductor case, years ago, that I thought about doing at the time and Erica has made me decide to get on with it.'

It reminds me of the case in the news right now, the girl taken from her garden. It's still all over the papers. I tell Julian how much it haunts and distresses me.

'This other situation was heartbreaking, too,' he says. 'A 10-year-old girl held captive for weeks, but just as the police were finally closing in and attempting to get a dialogue going, her captor suddenly strangled her. There had been no sexual interference, nothing like that, and I can't believe there wasn't some way of getting through to that man and saving her life.'

'Think of the parents knowing she'd been alive all that time. The awfulness of it is beyond belief. It would be so hard to read a book like that, so horrifying. But I suppose that would be the point.'

'I've just done a little preliminary research. I can't interview the abductor, he took his own life in prison, but there are the psychiatrist's notes. I might somehow manage to get hold of them. So you see,' he reaches for my hand, 'Erica's done me a good turn!'

Julian pulls into a lay-by and kisses me, which is what I badly need. The story he wants to write, the girl in the garden, Erica – so much is sitting heavily. He makes me feel comforted.

We're on the road again and I drop my head down on his lap. Julian takes one hand off the wheel and smoothes my hair. 'All I ask is that you trust me, I'll never tell you lies. But you have to work out your own feelings. You know mine, the rest depends on you.'

I sit up and kiss his cheek, saying nothing, staring ahead feeling emotional, watching the car eat up the road. It's not my own feelings I worry about; it's his. The thought they won't last, the fear of future hurt. Where's the long-term security?

'I'm sure you'll like Lauren and Henry,' Julian remarks. 'The house is quite remote, a pair of knocked-through cottages; modernized and spare, but big on creature comforts, American style. It's stark country-side roundabout. No hedgerows, just vast fields with endless expanses of single crops – it's not unlike America's Midwest, fields and fields and nothing else. I remember crossing a state line there once and seeing a sign that said "Welcome to South Dakota, land of infinite variety!"'

I turn to smile and Julian gives a rather shy grin. 'I love the bleak-ness, though: it's a sort of invigorating beauty that gets to me.'

'It must be all the more so in winter, and cold.'

'Arctic! The wind belts across.'

'You made very good time.' Lauren has a wide smile as we climb out, stretching our stiff limbs. Julian kisses her and she squeezes his hand, saying softly, 'Hi!' She encompasses me then, seeming very warm. 'Welcome! It's so good to meet you at last.' Her smiling green eyes flit to the car. 'You're lucky, he let you off! You weren't being blown stir-crazy with the top down.' The Americanism emphasizes her accent, which is still strong after years of living here. 'Julian overdoes the fresh air,' she adds, a remark that somehow seems more suited to bedrooms than cars.

Misty's relief at escaping from his midget cramped quarters is so amusingly obvious that he gets all our attention and canine introductions are duly made.

'It's wonderful of you to have him,' I say, 'and me!'

'We're absolutely delighted.' Henry has come to stand beside his beaming auburn-haired wife. He's immensely tall and angular, slightly stooped, inevitably, and appealingly intellectual-looking. His arm encircles Lauren's waist, whose proportions bear no witness to her cooking skills, and he remonstrates at length about the wine Julian has brought before insisting on carrying bags.

Soon we are having lunch at a sizeable old scrubbed-pine table. Simple food: a cold ham that Henry is haphazardly carving, hot minty new potatoes and salad. There's an Aga, attractive Mexican tiles; plenty of space and light. The kitchen is large, the living room too, with contemporary furniture aside from two inviting-looking squashy blue sofas either side of a huge inglenook fireplace.

Lauren adeptly puts me at ease. 'It isn't very American-touristy countryside,' she says charmingly, 'but we're quite soppy about this part. I was over doing a year at a Cambridge college, Henry came back for a reunion dinner . . . and, well, that was that!'

I smile, deciding she's younger than I am. It's hard not to feel responsive warmth, though. 'Julian was saying how much he loves it round here.' I glance at him needing some reassuring eye-contact. 'He thinks it's invigorating!' Lauren is not really a beauty, too freckly, but with her lit-up green eyes, immense charm and tumbling shoulder-length burnished hair it's a striking package.

Talking of her cookery-discussion programme on television I ask, 'Does it get easier? Do you stop thinking of the million or so viewers out there, people like me?'

'To a degree: it's toughest when I'm out of routine, being interviewed or something – that's when I need the worry beads!' She gives me an awkward look. 'I'm going on *The Firing Line* this Friday . . . but I won't ask for any tips!' She says it so engagingly that I feel almost a kind of bond. Bill is so confrontational in his television programme, almost more so than as editor of *The Post*. And he's ruthless and tough enough at that.

'Told you William would follow up,' Julian exclaims. How is he involved in it? I feel confused and left out, instantly suspicious. My hackles spring into place like security spikes in the road and I flash Julian a fiercely inquisitive demanding glance, determined to extract an explanation and know what's it's all about. He meets my razor-eyed glare with an easy smile, quite unfazed. 'I was in London for one of those Sunday Russell Square book fairs last weekend and ended up bumming a meal off Lauren and Henry, as usual.'

'Not bumming,' Lauren chips in, 'nor as usual. I insisted! We had a few coming for dinner, the Osbornes included. Ministers are only ever free on Sundays. William mentioned me doing *The Firing Line* then, but I'd thought he was just being polite.'

'That's hardly his style, not what he's best known for at *The Post*!' I say, trying to laugh it off, but feeling bitterly put out. Turning to Julian, making a great effort to sound no more than casually curious, I add, 'So you actually met Victoria. You kept that very dark!'

'On past form,' he grins, 'I didn't think my impressions would cut much ice . . .'

I handle that as well as can be expected – although my smile is rather set as Henry, in an attempt to iron out the little wrinkle, chats on about other guests. 'Armando Iannucci had us all under the table with laughter. He produces such terrific stuff, I think he's the best satirist around and we should see more of him – don't you, darling?' Henry turns to his wife for backup and she nods. 'Armando's such a natural and it's not often people are equally accomplished on radio and television.'

'Lauren's pretty nifty at both, herself,' Julian says, chatting up his smiling host.

We move on and talk about some neighbours coming for a drink later on. Henry gets to his feet after that, saying we must all have a walk. Misty thumps his tail loudly.

Julian and I have an hour upstairs before dinner. The bedroom has stripped and varnished boards, fresh blue and white fabrics, soft rugs. I stand looking out of the window. A single field stretches away as far as the eye can see, slightly mounded at its centre, sloping distantly out in all directions. It's starkly dramatic, rather daunting.

Turning back to face Julian I say heatedly, 'You could have mentioned about that dinner and meeting Victoria. It made me seem such a twit, not knowing.'

I've been feeling sensitively resentful ever since. All the time we were out walking, and it was my sort of afternoon too, Julian hanging on to my hand, a bracing wind. I'd felt intensely happy on one level, but also deeply mistrustful. The beautiful desolate countryside had passed me by; it was like having the radio on without absorbing a word. What had really got me down was thinking about a whole side of Julian's life unknown to me. I feel vulnerable and shut out. It's as though he's deliberately keeping something hidden.

I'm still standing by the window and he comes close. 'Sorry! But you wouldn't have wanted to hear that I liked her – which I did. It seemed pointless telling you when there wasn't any upside.'

'But you keep so much of your life private,' I complain, fishing, wishing he didn't.

'That dinner was very last-minute and so unimportant. I'd called Lauren about something and she needed a spare man.'

'Who was the spare woman?' I'm full of suspicion, more interested in why he was calling Lauren. A stray spare woman seems much less of a threat.

'Only Lauren's agent,' he answers, 'whose predilections are quite another way . . .'

He's kissing me then, melting me, closing off the outside world with its spare women and auburn-haired hosts, taking me into his arms and inside his cocoon. It feels such a safe welcoming place. No one can get in here with us, I feel protected and loved.

We're showered and changed, ready to go down, dreading the neighbours coming for drinks. 'They're going on to a function,' Julian grins. 'It could be worse.'

We're first downstairs. There's a crackling fire, champagne and glasses put ready. Julian pours us both a glass and when Lauren comes in, pours one for her too. He hands it over in such a familiar way that I feel myself winding up again fast. Julian treats this house as home, I think, he's acting almost like a second husband.

The neighbours arrive. A farming couple and a local solicitor whose wife seems unable to stop staring at me. I'm William Osborne's left-behind wife, notorious by proxy: it's hateful. The men are in dinner jackets, the women in décolleté dresses exposing winter-white shoulders and arms. Julian is as remote from these conventional people as I am from Victoria, but he changes gear with impeccable manners and charm. 'How's your wonderful daughter,' he asks the farmer's wife. 'Bet you gave in over that pony!'

The solicitor's wife is still staring. Henry notices. 'My Frühlingsgold rose is in full flower, Nancy,' he says, taking her elbow and steering her doorwards. 'You must come and see it in all its glory.' He is a nice man.

At dinner we talk books and Catholicism. The candles are low. We've been drinking Julian's excellent wine and moved on to camomile tea. Lauren's meal was light and good, fresh tomato soup, baked fish; nothing too showy and produced with effortless ease.

'I've been reading an Anthony Powell essay on Graham Greene,' Henry tells us. 'Vulgarized Conrad, tedious Roman Catholic propaganda, he doesn't hold back! It's strong stuff.'

'Brave of Powell, though, slating someone so universally acclaimed,' I say, enjoying Julian's eyes on me. If I'm looking good, he's the cause of it.

'Powell had a point,' Julian says, entering the discussion, continuing to stare at me as though we're quite alone. 'Catholic writers can be quite idle, the way they use religion – at times, I think. They make it a short cut to rounding out characters. I read somewhere Waugh and Greene were particularly lavish in their praise of any writer who'd converted.'

We cover more literary ground. Brearfield feels distant. I find I can contribute and hold my own; it's like the shock of an absorbed political truth, this weird new feeling of being very much at home.

Later, though, upstairs and alone, I shed a few skins. Julian's obvious closeness to Lauren is obsessing me and bringing a sense of defeat. I feel up against fast runners in a race. And my resentful pique about 'the Osbornes', and Julian meeting Victoria without telling me, has ballooned up again.

I can't help harping on about it when we're in bed. 'Did you really like her all that much?' I query, lying pointedly apart.

'You're back on Victoria?' I shrug, trying to ignore his tracing fingers. 'Yes, I did. They seemed exceptionally well suited, really right for each other – perfectly attuned. She won't take any flak. It'll be a feisty give-and-take relationship.' All take on her part, I think sarcastically, being dreadfully distracted by Julian's lightly trailing nails.

I give in and roll closer. He knows my body so well, knows exactly how to bring it to an intense pitch of desire, swirling senses, total and intoxicating.

And how to keep me poised. 'I can feel you coming,' he whispers, 'we're perfectly attuned. And I love you, what's more.'

In the night I'm suddenly wide awake, still half in a disturbing dream. A strange man has been sweet-talking me while another person, unseen, like a confessional priest, was urging me to beware. The image is vague and elusive. It makes me feel threatened.

We leave after lunch. I'm silent in the car, tightly withdrawn. Julian will put it down to thoughts of Emma and Jessie being full of sparkle after a weekend with their father, but it's nothing like that. It's Lauren. Seeing them alone together this morning, overhearing things, the sense of shifting ground. I'd been feeling wonderful, securely in Julian's groove, but now the needle's splaying, scratching across the turntable. It's a harsh jangling sound and bringing me crashing down.

We had a lazy Sunday breakfast, boiled eggs, croissants; newspapers spread around. I finally stirred myself to take Misty out for a quick turn. Getting back the front door had been ajar, Mozart playing. Henry was out pottering in the garage. He'd shown me the ancient Ford they kept to use locally, joking it was a lot greener and more practical than Julian's Porsche. I'd wandered indoors after that, relaxed, happy, leaving Misty outside exploring smells.

From the hall I had a clear view through to the kitchen. Julian and Lauren were standing together by the table. Her hand resting on his arm had made me hold back, feeling icy shivers. I edged forward, any sound I made masked by the music, getting as close as possible and trying to listen in.

They had no idea I was there. Lauren's hand had been gently rubbing his arm and she seemed concerned. 'Wouldn't it be best just to tell her?'

'It's very hard,' Julian had answered, looking down. 'It doesn't feel the right time.'

'But women sense these things, she'll know there's a corner of you where the shades are down.'

'I'm still not sure she could take it. It's too soon.'

'When will it ever not be?'

He had looked up at that, with a wry, yet wistful expression. 'We're so close and still so far apart . . .'

Misty had come racing in then, panting noisily, and made straight for the kitchen and his water bowl. I'd followed and Julian and Lauren had turned to greet me with warm easy smiles.

We're nearly home. The only sense I can make of it all is that Julian and Lauren are involved. He can't face telling me or bring himself to end it. She thinks he should. Maybe he doesn't really want to. I do believe he genuinely cares and men can, after all, love two women. It's no basis for a future together. It's exactly the hell I've lived through all the last year.

Arriving back at Brearfield makes me think of Erica Barkston; she'll be spreading her gossip far and wide, leaving no stone or school mother unturned. At least the weekend with Julian, for all its vicissitudes, served to put that awful scene out of my mind. It's right back in again now, thoughts of the repercussions, how rumours get around.

Julian's normal natural reaction, joking about Erica, talking about his biography, had been reassuring. My faith in him took a knock this morning, but I do trust him over Jessie. It's insane. I feel hot rage that Erica could even think, let alone say, such things.

I'm kneading my hands in my lap and Julian covers them with one of his. It feels warmly encompassing. 'You're brooding,' he says, giving a glance. 'If it's about Lauren you mustn't start imagining things, she's a very close friend, but just that. I can talk to her in a way I can't even to Henry.'

'More than you can talk to me?' I feel torn, wanting to, but uncertain how much really to trust him.

'Yes. Other things get in the way with you – like how I'm feeling right now. I'm going to miss you tonight.' His eyes are back on the road, but he hasn't taken away his hand. 'Oh, by the way. I've booked a flight to Entebbe for the day after the dance. You still on for that? Or are you fixed up to go with another?'

'No,' I say tiredly, feeling wretched as the car turns in the gate, 'I've done nothing about it. Susie will be very pleased.'

CHAPTER 7

Susie is drawing up in her Volvo. I go outside and Emma comes running. Jessie is still at school having a flute lesson. This is the last week of school runs. There's a brand new bus service starting on Monday that's going to make quite a difference to our lives.

Emma's in her pleated navy skirt, canvas bag hanging half off her shoulder; she's looking extremely pink-faced. It is baking hot. 'Hi, Mum. We had to stay in at break today. Just because Brad and Kevin were twanging bra-straps, it wasn't fair!' She's not sounding too unhappy about it, I think, giving her a quick hug. She's impatient to get indoors and hurries off calling back, 'Need a drink, I'm hot as a radiator.'

I look over to the car. Susie's getting out, although her teenage son, Luke, is in the back and she would normally drive straight off. It puts me slightly on edge; I've told her the full horrors about Erica.

She's in pink striped drainpipes and mauve Ralph Lauren sports shirt and I say, putting on a grin, 'You're looking very together – showing me up in my old jeans!' Lowering my voice and with an eye to the car I go on, 'Any talk? Any gossip?'

Susie shifts hips and pushes at the sunglasses in her short blonde hair. 'Well, a bit . . . People are saying it's not even legal, that you've got to register with the council and be fourteen.'

'That's only if you're paid and Jessie isn't,' I exclaim angrily, my insides knotting up. 'This is all so silly. You did try and tell people it's not like that, Susie? Julian is a family friend, Jess just learning about books. You did say what ridiculous claptrap all this is?'

I'm sounding a little critical and she looks hurt. 'Of course I did! I told everyone how sweet he is with Jess, and fond of her, always encouraging her interest in books.'

People will read what they like into that, I think morosely, it wasn't Susie at her best.

I should be thanking her, not picking holes. Telling her she's a wonderful friend I suddenly can't stop myself continuing, 'I'm really depressed about Julian, actually. It's not connected with Erica, that's just crazy, but I think he's involved with someone, you see. He'll soon pack up and go.'

'Oh, I'm sure not,' she says, without having a clue. 'Julian loves you and it shows, believe me. Why not go to London and buy a new dress for the dance? Treat yourself. It's what I do when Phil's got me down, have a slug of botox or something. Not that he ever notices or that it does much good.'

Watching her drive off I wonder how much longer she'll put up with Phil. It's so sad, she loves life in Brearfield in all other respects. It's where she grew up. She's the youngest of five and her parents, whom she adores, still live nearby and are getting on in age.

I've come to loathe it. I chose Brearfield; it isn't the sort of real country that lifts me, but it seemed right at the time with Tom growing so fast and commuting to London possible. And in those early days when we moved here Bill was being loving and pouring energy into my veins before his own world took him over.

Then I met Julian, with all the intense undercurrents. And now Brearfield feels so confining, more claustrophobic than a stuck lift. It's a maze, high-hedged paths leading to nowhere. It's a castellated fortress of a town. I'll never find a way out.

In London I head for the M & S car park in the King's Road. Will Lauren just happen to be buying food, or new underwear like me? She and Henry are sure to live somewhere like Chelsea. Even trailing round the shops and boutiques for a dress, I'm half-expecting to see her. Swinging along the pavement, auburn-haired, arm in arm with Julian.

In fighting spirit I buy a pricey, flashy, slashed-fronted dress. 'It's got your name on it,' the assistant urges.

At home after hustling the girls to bed, I'm just in time to watch *The Firing Line* and see Lauren being interviewed by Bill. The debate is on how far the NHS should pick up the tab for obesity. Bill's attacking style is first to disarm people with a winsome grin then to tear into his poor unsuspecting victims and rip them to strips like a shredder.

The debate is passing me by. I feel so jealous. Lauren's even getting round Bill, he's putty in her hands. She's the one doing the disarming, I think, wishing she were easier to hate. It's that starry green-eyed smile, it's giving off such a bright light.

Bill sharpens up. 'You foodies do a good job, school dinners, upping standards, but you don't go near bingeing and compulsion eating. Why not?'

'Television cooking is in a different box; it's all about enjoyment of food. But perhaps it is time we got off our butts and tackled eating disorders . . .' She grins.

The phone goes. It's Julian, which catches me by surprise. 'I'm watching your "very close friend", actually,' I say with barbed emphasis, scowling with no one to see.

'You still on about Lauren? Of course, it's *The Firing Line* tonight. I forgot – better tune in. It's been a bit manic this week. I told you about the Olympia Book Fair straight after Uganda. That's serious bucks, worth being around for. All the big buyers are over.'

He'll have set the programme to record, I think distrustfully. It wouldn't be inconsistent or telling a lie.

'I'll come about eight tomorrow,' he says. 'Or will Susie want you to be prompt?'

'Probably, but that's too bad. I hate the whole idea of this dance – almost as much as you do.' I can't stop being crabby and difficult. Julian has called often since the weekend and on Tuesday when we met after bridge he was very tender, talking of dreading three weeks apart. At least Lauren is unlikely to be going to Uganda.

I phone my mother in the morning and describe my new dress. 'It's sort of milky-navy, backless and practically frontless – Emma thinks it's wildly sexy! Actually, Mum, I'm on the scrounge. Can you stay on after lunch tomorrow? I want to take Julian to the airport.'

The phone wires sag under the weight of her dubiousness about him. She's happy to help, she promises, but then says with excruciating transparency, 'Perhaps you might make some nice new interesting friends at this dance.'

'Christ, Mum, it's a load of bed-hopping middle-aged couples, not a bloody dating shop. It's for charity; people don't go to enjoy themselves.'

'You're sounding very tense and jaundiced, dear. Are you all right?'

'I'm fine, Mum, just fine.'

Julian arrives ahead of Myrtle, who is in for a long babysit. Seeing him in a dinner jacket is a rare sight. His eyes on me are serious and constant. It's a carrier-pigeon look, a transmitter of inner thoughts that seem deep; had I been feeling less thrown off-course I would have believed they were straight from the heart. I wish he wasn't going away.

The girls are glued to a television pop contest, watching in the sitting room, and with my new dress slashed practically to the waist his hand effortlessly finds its way to an uplifted tit – hoisted up with clever invisible engineering. 'Don't flaunt it,' he whispers, kissing me, massaging the nipple, 'leave that to those who need to.'

'God, why not just say you hate the bloody dress!' I pull away in childish pique, but he keeps hold of my arm, his fingers digging in to the point of bruising.

'Fuck that. Fuck the dress.' He's angry, kissing me roughly. But I'm angry, too.

We ignore the ringing doorbell. 'Door!' Emma yells as if no one else has heard it, clearly, though, not about to go herself. 'Mum – you there?' Julian releases me and I let in Myrtle.

'*Very* glam!' Her warm voice belies that permanent frown of hers. She looks over my shoulder. 'Isn't it a beautiful dress, Mr Bridgewater!'

'Beautiful. How are you, Myrtle? I'll try not to get her back too late.'

I yell for Emma and Jessie and seeing them Julian's face opens up into a broad spontaneous smile. 'Hey, you guys! Was that the actual finals? Did the one with the pink hair win? He had much the best voice.'

It seems he did. 'Hadn't we better be off?' I say impatiently, with ill grace.

'Mum, can you come . . .?' Emma nods towards the kitchen, indicating a need for privacy. 'Julian's kissed off all your lipstick,' she whispers, when I follow her there, still feeling irritated. 'It, um, sort of shows.'

I hurry upstairs, grateful. Coming down again, repaired if little better tempered, I sense Jessie's mood is even worse than mine. She's oozing resentment, moping, drooping like an unwatered plant. Is it just tiredness? She was with Julian all morning.

I smile at him for appearances' sake, hiding a scowl. 'Ready, now! We should go.'

He gathers up Jessie and kisses the top of her head. 'Night, my young apprentice, sorry I'll be away. You've got a weekend with Dad, only two missed Saturdays.'

He blows Emma a more adult kiss goodbye, charms Myrtle with a handsome grin, opens the front door and, as I step down on to the gravel, unsmilingly takes my hand.

The commodity broker John Bragg, who's providing the marquee for the dance, has a large mock-Tudor house and acres of garden, but parking is in a nearby field. I stubbornly refuse to be dropped off and teeter beside Julian with my heels sticking in the turf. He drove the short distance fast and we didn't speak. The onus is on me, it seems, to lift the veil of impasse.

'I can take you to the airport,' I say, weakening, feeling I had been quite adolescent. 'I've asked Mum to stay on after lunch – unless, of course, you've got other plans.'

'No other plans and I'd like that.' He entwines our fingers as we stumble across the dark field and squeezing them tight adds, 'Thanks.'

We're late. People are peering at the seating plan, a huge sheet on an easel, and filtering through to their tables. We are on Susie's, which since she's chairing the dance, is in prime position, far away from the serving passage and flapping exits.

The tent is lined in cream silk, the supporting poles garlanded with flowers – although the fresh blooms are showing up the tired-looking ivy frameworks used for the Braggs' daughter's wedding last week. The ivy is looking like dried old hops.

Val and Chris are on our table, the Braggs too, John and Molly, who are basking in excesses of gratitude for the use of the wedding marquee. They look remarkably revived after the big event. Both have chunky waistlines and plump soft hands; Molly is the shape of the Gherkin building – or an upended seal.

There's a couple I don't know just arriving, who are on our table. Susie introduces them. 'This is Jane and Perry Maynard. They've come all the way from Hampshire!'

'I sell wine.' Perry grins. 'And it's not so far – and Susie and Phil are very good customers . . .'

He has grey-blue eyes, a crinkly smile, and the assured air of someone supremely confident of his background. Slipping an arm round Susie's waist in her big-occasion blue taffeta he gives her a cuddly squeeze. 'I'd have come twice as far, any day!'

His wife Jane would clearly have rather they'd stayed home. My smile at her falls on stony ground. Julian exchanges a few pleasantries. 'I knew Perry at school,' he says, but in a flat tone that suggests her husband is no long lost friend. Julian has unfailing good manners, but I can tell when his toes are scrunching in his shoes, when it's a façade.

The marquee is fuggy — and full of verbal hot air as the drink kicks in and people bray and shriek across the tables. I'm pleased for Susie, who's looking proud of her dragooned troops, all loyally and determinedly having a good time. Erica is there, but on a table that I'm pleased to see is right in the path of a rabbit run to the Portaloos.

We pull out chairs and sit down. Perry is on my right, Chris, the other side. Julian is opposite, between Val and Molly Bragg. He's refusing to look over at me for some reason that I don't understand. I had hoped we were over our little spat.

'I've done a plan for this school extension Julian's planning in Uganda,' Chris says, breaking into my thoughts. 'Just as a guide, impossible, really, without seeing the site.'

'I'm sure it'll be a cut above any local architect's,' I smile, peeved that he seems so in the know when I'm feeling excluded. Julian is always incredibly unforthcoming about his Uganda trips.

The main course arrives, an unappetizing hunk of lamb. Perry eats speedily then turns fully sideways. 'I especially wanted to meet you,' he mutters confidentially, crinkling his eyes. 'It actually tipped the balance into coming — Jane thought it was mad!' He gives another warmly connecting smile. 'I was longing to tell you what exceptional courage and dignity you showed.' He's keeping his voice low. 'God knows, what an ordeal! Never a day without those acres of newsprint about your husband and Victoria James . . .'

'Ex-husband, he has married her!'

'It showed such inner strength,' Perry carries on unperturbed. 'No whinging quotes in the press. I almost dropped you a note!' The grey-blue eyes are full of sympathy and admiration. I'm aware of being chatted-up, of Jane looking glacial across the table — very aware of Julian's transmitted resentment while sounding bland, talking to Molly Bragg.

It's still hard not to feel flattered and be warm in response. Perry gets my best self-deprecating smile and I say coyly, 'That's all in the past. Over and done!'

He is dark, dark as Bill, though with curly, expensively groomed hair. His chin has a pronounced cleft and his upper lip, too, is rather oddly indented: a scar or a natural defect, perhaps. But the flaws are part of the attraction. Something he clearly well knows.

'Tell me about selling wine.' I give a flirty grin.

'It started off as a hobby, then I went in with a friend and set it up properly. I love all the trips to France, the new discoveries. Good wine is more than just a mellow drink from a well-bred grape, it's a total experience.'

'How lucky, having such a passion and being in business with a friend.'

'Oh, the friend got bored and moved on. But the business was well set up; it worked out fine. Do you have any special passions?' he asks, his crinkly eyes keeping hold.

He's much more focussed on the chat-up, I think, couldn't give a fig about any interest of mine. I answer quite seriously, though. 'Well, yes I do, writing poems – but only published people should dare to admit that!' I'm embarrassed to think of Julian hearing and avoid his eyes across the table.

Perry doesn't pursue the poetry line; his glazed-over look implies it's just what he would have expected: one more bored middle-aged divorcee doing writing classes and turning out trite poems. Remembering Bill's enthusiasm for my poems helps. He did think they had merit. I've never shown them to Julian, he's too expert, immersed in every serious poet going, although I would value his criticism. One day, perhaps . . .

I'd hoped Julian would, but Perry soon asks me to dance. Looking over from the floor I can see Val and Julian talking. He is being so spiky, deliberately not catching my eye.

Perry is firming his grip, his hand on my bare back drawing me close, putting his cheek to mine. He's a big, broad-shouldered man who's certainly enjoying this dance.

'Perhaps we had better get back,' I smile, easing away. We've been on the floor for an age. I've been stuck fast, feeling his thighs, even thinking up satirical verse as we dance.

> He's confident, with *savoir faire*,
> Dressed with style, that certain flair
> Which speaks of cash in good supply –
> Look at the cloth on that muscled thigh!

Perry gives a last press of his body and leads me off the floor.

Weaving back through the tables, people I know are keen to chat and I have to keep introducing him. Two of Brearfield's colonels are lavishly complimentary about my dress.

Back at our table he asks Susie to dance and Chris takes Val. They are a close, well-matched couple, hardworking, but never dull company. I can't help thinking of Julian talking of Bill and Victoria, describing them as perfectly attuned. He said we were too, and it makes me sigh.

Phil is about to ask for his turn, but one thigh-pressing married male is quite enough in an evening and to avoid any awkwardness, I call over to Julian, 'We haven't had a dance!' He'd have had to be quite a heel to refuse, but he still gets up with an embarrassing lack of enthusiasm.

Our bodies slot in familiarly on the floor, although I can feel the rage lifting off him like a child's fever. 'I want to go now,' he mutters bitterly. 'Let's get the hell out of here.'

It gets me worked up and quite as angry; it was only a mild flirt. Julian is being impossible. I might have been a bit too long on the floor, but at least I was thinking up a sarky poem. 'It's only eleven,' I say plaintively. 'Can't we at least have a dance or two? You are going away.'

'I'm well aware of that.'

'Don't be like this, I hate it.'

'You think I'm enjoying it?'

'Please, Julian. Whatever's wrong with you? If we are going, can it be to the flat?'

'No, I'm taking you home.'

We stumble across the field in silence and have another fast, non-speaking drive. He's like an exposed wire, touching him is clearly not a good idea. I would have felt jealous if he'd been making a play, but I was on the receiving end, not instigating it, hardly being much more than polite. And after his closeness to Lauren last weekend it seems doubly unfair.

I'm going to miss him. Uganda is a long way. I'm in urgent need of loving physical contact, not of being worked up into a defensive resentful retaliatory rage.

Julian brakes sharply on the gravel then comes round to help me out of the car, so exaggeratedly observing formalities that I feel like pummelling him with both fists.

'Julian, can't we just be close? I hate you going away.' He gives me a look that burns through to my backbone and says nothing. I fumble for the door key in a fury.

Myrtle is surprised to see us. 'I'll just pack up my knitting! They were very good – well, Jessie was just in the tiniest bit of a grump. Probably a scrap overtired, poor love.'

'She had a long morning in the bookshop,' I mumble, mainly to myself since Myrtle has gone for her things and Julian is communing with the floor. I regret the dig, getting at him through Jessie; I feel ashamed of myself and biting my lip I try to find the right money for Myrtle.

After seeing her out we stand in the hall listening for the last of her car.

'I'll go too,' Julian says, turning to me. 'I haven't finished packing.'

'You can't, not without telling me what this is all about.' I almost say darling, it's so much the sort of row only two very intimate people are capable of, but I have never called him that and don't feel about to start. We're both avoiding it; Julian has never said it either.

He shed his bow tie in the car and looks compellingly attractive in his open-neck shirt. 'Must we really keep up this farce,' I plead, touching his arm.

'Oh, is that what it is?'

'For God's sake!' I turn on my heel at that and look down at the hall table, not quite able, though, to tell him to go home and pack all bloody night, if that's what he wants. I need him too much.

Julian swings me to face him and grasps my wrist. His fingers and thumb join round, gripping, keeping me manacled. I let myself be marched into the sitting room, where he pushes the door shut with a backwards foot. At least he's being mindful of Emma and Jess and the need for closed doors.

He takes hold of my other wrist too, and we stand staring. 'I've got to go to Uganda,' he says, driving into me with gimlet eyes. 'It's important, there's a real need. You can do what you like while I'm away, obviously: fuck around as you please. You might just try a bit harder not to tarnish what we've had.'

I'm shaking, feel wretched, hating the way he said 'had'. Is he using this hurtful row as an out? All the same I answer with plenty of fight, staring back with just as piercing eyes. 'What's that supposed to mean? I've no plans to "fuck around" actually — or are you trying to tell me something?'

'"No plans,"' Julian says icily, 'is a political phrase meaning having every intention. And I am trying to tell you something.' His voice is less cold. 'Look, Perry Maynard is a shit, a lousy womanizing shit. I know him. He'll shag you a few times and move on. He'll use you — you'll be a married man's temporary little plaything. Is that what you want?' He lets go my wrists and steps back quivering, his eyes still accusing. 'Is it?'

'For Christ's sake, Julian, what kind of an overreaction is that?' My ribcage feels tight. 'I was put next to that man at dinner, I didn't choose to be. He asked me to dance — should I have refused? It wouldn't have been very polite. And the logic of what you've just said is that it's fine for me to have any man as long as he's not a married so-called shit. And why on earth should Perry ever get in touch? And who are you to talk? You've got London friends, another life . . .'

'Friends yes. Only one woman I love.'

'But the friends are there for the shagging?'

'Don't make me sick.'

'And don't you speak to me like that.' I can't help the tears then, they come spilling out. Julian takes me in his arms and I bury my face, taking refuge.

He picks up my chin. 'I'm sorry – let me try to explain. Maynard knew you'd be there, Susie would have told him. He came to that dance as a predator, couldn't resist an attractive divorced woman and he's conceited enough to think he can have anyone he likes. He's another Phil, same endgame.' I feel surprised and slightly shaken that Julian should be clued into Phil.

'Maynard will call by with a case of wine, you wait and see. He won't tell you his wife doesn't understand him, he'll have a good plausible line and complete confidence in winning you over.' Julian takes his arms away and steps back with a sort of acid-faced look, as though soured by his own words. He goes on, 'Just don't expect me to stick around waiting for the scales to fall from your eyes.'

I wipe at my tears. 'Why are you goading me like this and pushing so hard?'

'I'll go now. I'm sure you want me to.'

'No don't, not like this. Please don't. Can't you kiss me?' He puts his lips to mine, but he's too uptight, past any breakthrough point. There's no softening, only a dry dutiful kiss that has to carry all the baggage of unfinished business.

He's going away without making love to me. What right has he to indulge in such an excess of jealousy? I feel desolate, following him into the hall and to the door.

He turns back, staring levelly. 'You needn't feel you still have to take me to the airport.'

'That means you don't want me to? This tawdry petty row is all your making.'

'And you had no part in it?'

I'm shivering with rage and misery. And filled with guilt about flirting the night before he's going away. It had something to do with Lauren. 'I'll be round at three, I'll take you to Heathrow,' I say, holding off the tears, 'we'll stick to the plan.'

'Thanks. But if you change your mind, let me know in time to get a taxi.'

He's hating this as much as me; too proud to climb down. We could so easily fall into each other's arms, but it's not going to happen. He's not even looking back, going out of the door with his eyes cast down.

The car's gone. I lock up, kick off my shoes, hitch up my skirt and bolt upstairs. Was that a door closing? Was it Jessie? Did she wake up and hear us rowing? No point worrying. I fall across the bed and, burying my face, think of all the practice I've had lately at floods of self-pitying sobs. Not for the first time I think that somehow I've got to get tougher, sort myself out and get on with life.

CHAPTER 8

We're halfway to the airport. The traffic's bad and Julian seems really desperate not to miss the plane. Why is it so vital? He's looking drained, staring intently ahead, rubbing his knuckles and studying his watch. It's making me feel even more down.

'Sorry about last night,' he says, without sounding terribly contrite about it.

'So am I.' Glancing while driving I smile beseechingly, wanting him to know that I really mean it. We've spoken little and said nothing about the row. Trying to clear the air, I bring it up in a joking way. 'You do seem to hate Perry Maynard quite a lot!'

'I despise him. It goes back to our schooldays. Then a good friend of mine went into the wine business with him – he put in his last penny and taught Maynard all he knows. But do you think that shit could care? He casually cut out my friend the moment he'd served his purpose and took pleasure in it. Maynard would carve up innocent little garden worms.'

'But you can't really know all the ins and outs,' I say, thinking of Perry talking about his wine partner at dinner in a light easy way. Julian could have it wrong.

'Shall we drop this particular subject?'

I should never have brought it up. We crawl on, stopping and starting, with Perry a great elephant in the car. I keep thinking of Julian saying he wouldn't stick around waiting for the scales to fall from my eyes. It's like the overheard conversation with Lauren, something that's out, that's slipped its collar and can't be rounded up again.   .

At the airport check-in I stay queuing with Julian, shuffling along in the cordoned-off lanes. Businessmen, holidaymakers, Africans, Asians, we're a crawl of resigned bag-carrying humanity. An African woman in a colourful orange headwrap has a baby strapped to her bosom, a small whining child at her skirts. Julian might not get much sleep on the flight.

When he's gone I walk slowly back to the car park.

I have a feeling of foreboding, of catastrophe even, that's quite inexplicable. It's not terror of bombs, his plane crashing, nothing like that. I'm not an alarmist. But Julian was so uptight last night, deliberately leading me to the deep-end of the swimming pool. Is it that? The fact I have to face that our relationship is coming to a head? It's very powerful.

I feel in a vacuum too, which brings back memories of my father's stroke years ago that had been such a bolt from hell. I'd felt the same numbness then, a sort of shell-shocked paralysis. It was a whole day before the grief had torn into me and released all the wrenching pain.

The atmosphere at home keeps pace with my mood. The girls are slumped over their homework; it's clearly been a dismal drizzly afternoon.

My mother looks done in. Her faded fair hair is flat to her head, her skin as grey and lifeless as last night's ashes in the grate. Going out with her to the car, her face, in the remaining twilight, is a road map of lines. 'What's wrong, Mum? Something is. Has Jess been in one of her moods?'

'Not exactly. I'm worried about her, though. I know she can be a little madam, but she's so in on herself and I'm sure it's to do with Julian. It's not healthy.'

I feel my stomach tightening. 'What do you mean?'

'I think Jessie's convinced herself he's not coming back from this trip and feels very insecure. It's so soon after all the upset of William leaving, the strain of the press, school friends' reactions, the whole business. She'd get over it in time,' Barbara adds hurriedly, 'but not knowing isn't helping.'

She hadn't been thinking along Erica lines, which is a relief, but her gentle reproach is like a drill on a raw nerve. 'Of course he's coming back! It's only a three-week trip – Jessie's just missing her Saturday mornings at the bookshop. And that's such amazing experience for her, Mum,' I go on. 'You do see that? You must. She's really learning about the antiquarian book trade, it's going to be a great future interest. Julian wants to take her to that famous shop in Piccadilly, Sotheran's. We could all have a day in London, I thought. Emma and I could go shopping.'

'You're feeling more serious about him, are you dear? To be honest I can't see him settling down.'

'Give us a break!' I smile wanly. 'Julian lets me have space. It was a bruising business, being dumped so publicly – on practically every page of every national paper – and having to stomach Victoria being let off so lightly.'

'William's married her now,' my mother says, unmoved. 'It's a fact and you'd better get used to it. I know very well what you went

through, but that's the past. And she is a government minister. Tom
and the girls will be meeting such interesting people . . .'

'God, I don't believe this! That woman is so bloody damn perfect
she's opening doors for my children, now.' I angrily yank open the
one on my mother's car. 'And actually, as it happens, I am quite keen
on Julian – so there!'

'But it would be nice if you had other friends, too. Julian might
decide to stay away. He has done before . . .' She smiles at me gently,
with fond maternal eyes, and gets in the car. 'I can always come at
weekends to help and babysit,' she says, lowering the window.
Raising it then, she concentrates on the gears and drives off.

Hysteria starts bubbling up as her car disappears, spurting like an
artesian well. Julian has a return ticket; I know the flight number.
Roy can't keep on manning the shop indefinitely.

Suddenly a rush of hot shame burns through me. How selfish can
I be that it takes my mother to see and understand Jessie's fears? I go
indoors feeling full of self-loathing, miserable at the thought of my
poor daughter so unsettled and insecure.

The homework has been abandoned. Jessie's reading, Emma is
tuned into a satirical half-hour on television. She's more intrigued by
politics since Victoria. 'Time for bed,' I say, mainly to the wall since
both girls are choosing to ignore me.

Jessie goes up first. She's still deep in her book when I go in to say
goodnight, lying turned to the wall. Edging myself on to the bed I
talk to her back, feeling helpless.

'What's the book, Jess?'

'*Mansfield Park.*' She keeps facing away, dark hair tumbling over
the pillow. 'Julian lent it me. He said it was too old for me, but it's
not. I like it.'

She's determined to read it and prove him wrong, I think, sitting more on the bed and fondling her spread hair. 'Well, when he's back you can tell him that!'

She swings round then and two large tears dribble out of her velvety eyes. 'He's not coming back, not really properly – he's going to sell the shop. He told me so.'

'He was just thinking about it, I expect.' I kiss her head, wondering if he had been preparing the ground. There was the time he told Susie no one had antiquarian bookshops any more . . . I try to smile. 'I'm sure he was just talking long-term.'

'No, Mum, he is going to,' Jessie insists. 'People buy online and from catalogues. He'll sell the shop and go away from here.'

'He won't in a hurry,' I say soothingly, more aware I can't string her along. 'Maybe, at some future time if things between us should change. Julian and I are special friends, but it's not . . . well, quite like a marriage – and we all know what can happen to those! He's not away long, angel, and you'll be seeing Dad next weekend.'

'You don't understand,' she says impatiently, sitting bolt upright in bed. 'Dad's Dad, that's separate. Julian's my friend. He can't go away and leave me, he's my friend.'

The tears spill out more freely and I draw her close with an aching heart – grateful when she doesn't pull away. 'Tell you what,' I say smiling, 'Julian's plane gets back quite late on a Friday, well after school; we could all go and meet him if you like.' She shrugs in my arms, then extricates herself and settles for sleep, keeping her place in the Jane Austen with a bookmark and depositing it on the floor. Her bamboo bedside table is littered with all her special things: books, lucky keepsakes, a miniature house not yet added to her collection, bangles, her I-pod and mobile.

The borrowed book on the floor is in excellent condition, its spine and top edge elaborately blocked in gilt. 'You will take good care of that,' I say automatically. 'It looks valuable.'

Jessie glances over her shoulder at me, glaring. 'Julian trusts me with his books even if you don't.'

With that she hunches round the duvet, prickly and defiant to the last, her unhappiness bouncing back off the wall she's facing. Nothing is sorted, nothing resolved.

On Wednesday I get a letter from Perry Maynard. The post comes late, it's nearly lunchtime and I fix myself some bread and cheese, taking it out to the terrace with a newspaper and Perry's letter as well to reread.

The sun, when there's a decent break in the fast-moving clouds, is burning hot; Misty is stretched out panting. Garden scents are reaching me, heavenly smells. Is it the philadelphus, the jasmine? No plant seems to be hiding its head, there's a feeling of show-time, full dress rehearsal, and the roses will be performing for weeks. It's such a work-intensive time in the garden. I need more help than the few hours old Cyril gives me on a Friday. Shall I ask Bill?

Julian rang at midnight last night. He'd called on arrival, three days ago, and said with feeling that he was missing me, but a car had been waiting or something and he'd been brief.

Last night was different. They are ahead in time and it would have been in the small hours, so what was he doing up so late? He talked of heavy tropical rainstorms when the dry season should be starting, managing to sound very loving while talking of such things, and he took an expensively long time ending the call.

I didn't ask about selling the shop, but I've thought of nothing else. I can't believe he told Jessie before me. It's playing into the feathers of fear that keep brushing my skin. But he would never do anything to her, I'd stake my life on that.

She is so bound up in him, though, twitchy and insecure. It brings back that strange sense of foreboding I was feeling at the airport. Perhaps Jess is leading Julian on? Calling an adult her friend, children just don't do that. She has a way of getting round her father that's close to flirting. Very different from Emma, who's so sweetly uncomplicated.

Time to get back to work. I swig the last of my water bottle and pick up Perry's note. It's on company paper, not from home.

. . . I got your address from Susie; hope you don't mind. I'd really like to bring you a mixed case of wine (I am a salesman, remember!) but thought you mightn't appreciate an unannounced call. I'm nearby this Friday if that would suit? Do phone my office or mobile if not, otherwise I'll come about eleven and much look forward to it.

I did so much enjoy the other night.

Perry. PS. The wines are for everyday drinking, nothing at all special!

It's an open, jolly little note – even if it does prove Julian undeniably right. Quite neat of Perry, putting the ball in my court; it would seem churlish telling him not to come, easier, really, to do nothing about it.

Friday morning is close and muggy. I dress in a new pair of plum-coloured cut-offs and a classic cream silk shirt. It's one Julian gave me. I hesitate for a second about wearing it, but then think how ridiculous that is.

Perry turns up in a silver Series Seven BMW at exactly eleven. From the kitchen window I watch him open the boot and lift out a case of wine.

He has it pressed to the wall as I open the door, freeing up a hand for the bell.

'Hi! Where would you like this?' He's grinning broadly and looking more raffish in a yellow-striped shirt and rust-coloured trousers than in a sober dinner jacket. 'They're absolutely just for trying, no question of the bill in the post!'

'Perhaps in here on the table if you can.' I lead on into the kitchen. 'Have you time for some coffee?'

'I was hoping you might say that! I'm driving straight on to the Channel Tunnel.'

'On a wine mission?' I smile over my shoulder, filling the kettle at the sink.

'Yes, I'm always hopping across. Can't I put this away properly for you somewhere?'

'Thanks, I guess it would be a help.' Flicking the kettle switch, I walk over to the door to the walk-in larder that has a few wine racks above a broad marble shelf and hold it open. 'I know I should use the cellar,' I laugh, conscious of bodily closeness as he manoeuvres past.

'This seems cool enough, they're really nothing special.'

He's well built, too tall to be stocky. I get a faint whiff of some very refined cologne and it seems an unexpected little vanity, somehow rather out of place.

With the coffee and a plate of freshly made flapjacks on a tray, I suggest having it out on the terrace.

Perry takes the tray from my hands. 'You lead on. These flapjacks look amazing!'

'They're for Cyril the gardener, you came on the right day.' I grin back at him.

The geraniums are tumbling out of their urns, the paving awash with cushioning daisies and thymes; even the sun is trying to come out. I find myself trying a bit too, and say chattily, handing over a cup of coffee, 'It's great having new wines to try, but I never really drink on my own – don't expect a large instant order!'

He's crinkling his eyes at me over his cup, and replies, as though checking on the relationship, 'I'm sure Julian will help out . . .' Tip them down the drain more likely, I think, with that bitter row still fresh in my mind.

'Julian is away right now, on a trip to Uganda. Do you know him quite well?' I prompt, curious as to how Perry might respond.

He rubs his sexy cleft chin in a relaxed considering way. 'Not really, it's more that we've got friends in common, the old school thing. I was the year above. I really admire him, though. His exceptional taste in women, of course,' more creasing of the grey-blue eyes, 'and then all those good works out in Africa. Right at the height of the Aids explosion, too. When you think of the ghastly statistics, almost 30 per cent, you have to admire Julian for taking such huge brave risks.'

'What do you mean?' I stare at him uncertainly, wondering. There's no love lost on Julian's side, but it usually cuts both ways. I don't trust Perry's praise an inch.

'Well, he was living and working with the locals, manual work, sugar factories and things, so my old wine partner told me. That took guts. I'd have been worried about cuts and scratches, a brush of infected blood getting into a nick or cut of my own. Sugar cane is vicious to handle. Don't get me wrong, not look so alarmed – I didn't mean sleeping around!'

That thought had immediately flashed in. I remember Julian once mentioning a doctor girlfriend, years ago, someone out doing humanitarian work too, I suppose. How will he be spending his time on this trip? Does he have a circle of old friends? Will he sleep with one of them? I've never asked enough questions about his life out there.

'I haven't read his book on Uganda, I'm afraid,' Perry says, smiling.

I'm too ashamed to admit that I haven't either. 'More coffee?' I offer, keeping my eyes lowered, reaching for his cup. 'Uganda was the first African country to be brave and bold about getting people to use condoms,' I remark, trying to sound well versed. 'Julian says they've really turned things round. He's given financial help to an Aids hospital.' I'm painfully conscious of having little clue about his doings, of talking with false authority.

Perry leans for a flapjack. 'However did we get on to this gloomy subject!'

He admires the garden, tells about his three teenage sons acquiring expensive tastes in wine – continues to be good company, eyeing me appreciatively, but not overtly so. It's flattering and I have to admit to rather revelling in it. Good-looking, sexy, sophisticated men don't grow on trees in Brearfield.

Cyril is trying to catch my eye, he wants to cut the grass. I smile apologetically at Perry, hoping he'll make a move.

He takes his cue. 'Time I was off, outstaying my welcome. I'll, um, be driving past again on Sunday morning, why don't we sample one of those bottles? Just a quick drink –I'd get stick if I wasn't back for a late lunch!'

My thoughts dart about like silverfish. Emma and Jess will be with Bill, Tom's probably coming home for a change. 'Be nice!' I smile. 'My mother and my 20-year-old son might be around, but it's one of William's weekends with the girls, so quite peaceful.'

'It's a date!'

I see him to the door and receive a warm parting kiss on the cheek.

Bill arrives in a brand new hybrid car. Maybe I can ask for more gardening help after all. 'It was time I went green,' he says ruefully, talking over the girls' heads while hugging them. 'I'm having to toe the line a bit. Tom thinks it's very funny.'

I'm less than amused. It's all very well, his dancing to Victoria's tune; he never did to mine. 'Henpecked already?' I grin, trying to avoid it becoming a grimace.

'More a bit of give and take,' he says with a smile. Which seems one up to him.

Emma is in awe of the new car's gismos. Jessie takes no particular interest.

As soon as goodbyes are said, return times agreed and the car has disappeared out of the drive, I make a beeline for the study.

It's been consuming me, keeping me awake, the thought that took root the moment Perry left; it's clinging insidiously like bindweed. It made me guardedly reserved when Julian called. I could hardly have asked all the burning questions, long-distance, though, that won't leave my mind. 'Have you ever thought about being HIV positive? Have you had a test, omitted to tell me, seen no need? You would have, wouldn't you, if . . .?'

Of course he would, he's responsible, honest. This is crazy. But suppose, having a doctor girlfriend at the time, he simply hadn't given cuts and scratches a single thought?

I stare at my computer screen. Was Perry just mixing it and doing the dirty? I trust Julian, it's such an extremely remote possibility. Suppose I had a test myself? Isn't that the only way to clear up any lingering doubt?

I bring up all the information I can find on HIV Aids, sexually transmitted diseases, and sift through the links. Genito-urinary medicine: GUM clinics, there are sixty within the M25. God, how can I even begin to decide where to go, let alone face having a test?

There's a number for NHS Direct. Getting through I stumble out the words and, being told to wait, keep my fists clenched as though about to have a set of dentist's injections.

A sympathetic and professional-sounding male nurse finally comes on the line. 'Most clinics are attached to hospitals,' he says. 'They are all completely confidential, your doctor needn't be informed. You can go anonymously and give a false name.'

He reels off a raft of detail then suggests that a Terrence Higgins Trust centre in London might suit me best.

'I'd go to one of their rapid-test drop-in clinics. You'll get the result right away.'

The extreme tension begins to ease. It's strange, though; not once in all the times Julian had spoken of how wretched things were in Uganda, of the courageous condom drive embarked on by President Museveni. Nor when he'd talked of all the frustration at its recent subversion by the President's wife – her demands for an abstinence-only policy that was undoing so much good. Not once had the thought of HIV entered my mind.

I trust Julian; I'm not seeing straight. Or have I just been wrapped in cotton-wool false security? I could have asked if he'd ever had a test. I've no reason to feel let down.

He might have been tempted by casual sex in that seductive sultry climate . . . For heaven's sake! He'd have taken precautions.

It's certainly overreacting to be thinking of having a test. I could wait and ask him. That would be hard to do and embarrassing, though, and, however reassuring he was, wouldn't there still be the tiniest of question marks?

Getting to bed, lonely, the children with Bill, Julian thousands of miles away, I'm resigned to hours of wakefulness. It's like the night before travelling, checking off a list in my mind and feeling in a spin of agitation, far too strung-out for sleep.

There are other questions crowding in and they're all about Julian. I'll never believe he could harm Jess, that's just absurd, but she is so worryingly wrapped up in him. And Erica's heavy hints about a shady past play to my own feelings of ignorance – I felt it even more so, overhearing Lauren talking of a part of him where the shades are down.

Perry was implying Julian could have Aids. It's a far-fetched thought and Perry's motives are suspect, but he could have some inside knowledge. There's my mother, who thinks Julian won't settle. She doesn't want me hurt, it's with the best of intentions, but it's too late. I'm hurting already. Still believing in him, deep down. Missing him.

CHAPTER 9

'Your daughter, Mrs Sinclair, turned every head at the dance. My wife said I was bound to be on her doorstep selling wine . . . and here I am! What's your verdict on this one – quite reasonable, don't you think?' Perry grins easily and my mother almost purrs, certainly flutters her eyes at him.

'It is very nice and light. No, no more, really not. I do have to drive back to Hove!' She's opening up like a sun-loving flower. Her powdery cheeks are aglow as though lit from inside.

'I love that bit of coast,' he goes on. 'Hove is so delightfully staid after jazzy Brighton: those quiet sleepy streets, the wonderful Victorian terraces with their steep front gardens.'

Perry's coaxing away her every inhibition, which is a rare feat. He describes a great little pub she might know in a village near Hove and then says, looking over to me, that I really must come there for a bite, sometime.

'And now I must definitely be on my way.' He's beside my mother on the sofa and leans to kiss her flushed cheek before rising to his full bulky height and saying his goodbyes.

I go out into the hall with him, and to the door. He takes hold of my shoulders, staring hard. 'I do want to see you again, I think you need a bit of looking after. Can we have lunch?' I smile at him, feeling unsure. 'Next week.' His eyes are fixed on me. 'I'll call.'

Giving him my numbers, watching as he jots them in a small black diary, I feel embarrassed and uncomfortably disloyal. It's a relief hearing Tom's car. 'That's my son arriving, throwing up gravel!'

I reach for the door, but Perry restrains my hand. 'We do have a date?'

'Sure,' I say neutrally, turning the door-catch and feeling his lips brush my cheek.

Tom is just slotting in his key and seems slightly surprised to see us, although he's been primed to expect Perry. 'Mr Maynard's just leaving, Tom. We've been trying one of his delicious wines. Not much left for you, I'm afraid – Gran's been knocking it back!'

'She has been known to . . .'

'You must try one of the others,' Perry says. 'The Chateau de L'Hurbe, perhaps, and give your mother a view. You might think it a little routine, but it has some depth.' He continues talking wine, attributing a stash of knowledge to Tom in a socially exaggerating way, as though my art-student son in his unironed shirt were a bibulous hedge-fund manager. He eyes the Mini Cooper. 'You pleased with that, find it quite nippy?'

'Pretty terrific,' Tom says politely, if a bit shortly. He doesn't elaborate on its borrowed status so I'm spared any talk of Victoria. I do resent his closeness to her; it's to do with living in that basement flat of theirs, which means she sees him a whole lot more than I do. The house is Georgian, on a main road in South London, Tom says, but set well back with good big rooms and a garden. Still unsuitably far from college.

Perry kisses my cheek again, saying cheerily, 'I'll call.' Then slinging his well-toned bulk into his top-of-the-range machine, he's off and away.

I hug my son tight, feeling uplifted at seeing him, a mixture of love and joy and pride. How would he handle being told I was HIV? I must stop this and be more rational, it's so remote – no matter how long Julian was in Uganda or how bad things were.

Tom and I go indoors. 'What do you reckon on Perry Maynard?' I query curiously.

Tom wrinkles his nose dismissively. 'Too full of himself, bit of a poser, I'd say.' He looks beyond me with an impish grin. 'Hi Gran! I hear you've been hitting the bottle, succumbing to that smoothie Mr Maynard's charms.'

Tom is sweet with her at lunch – and with me. He jokes and tells stories, sitting with one of his long lean legs hitched on the rim of his chair, his arms clasped round his knee. His fingers are interlocked in a way that so reminds me of Bill; they're his fingers too, tapered, elegant. Tom has Bill's looks, mannerisms, charisma, but none of his ruthless drive. Will a gentler nature make it harder to get on in life? I hope not.

He can't stop bringing the talk round to his girlfriend, Maudie, as if obsessed, thinking of nothing else. It jars a bit. She's such a friend of Victoria's daughter, Nattie, they're at the same school, both in the middle of A-level exams. I can't help but mind Tom being so joined at the hip with that whole family.

'Maudie's got a provisional place at Edinburgh, Mum. It's a disaster!'

'Why, Tom?' his grandmother asks disingenuously. It must be the wine.

'It's bloody miles away, Gran, cost a fortune, getting up there. And,' he turns to me with despairing raised eyebrows, 'she's dead keen to go to Africa in her gap year. She wants some advice. Do you think I can ask Julian to help?'

'Of course, I'm sure he would. He knows Uganda best, though, and that's possibly not her first choice . . .'

Tom leaves before tea, which makes me sad – saying he's behind with work. As I go outside to see him off, he hesitates and shifts his feet. 'What's eating you, Tom?'

'Well, Victoria will be with Dad when he bring the girls back later. They're in one car, coming straight from her constituency and the new cottage. Things worked out fine over that, Mum, after all the trouble. Will you at least say hello? Just do that one thing for me?'

Why for him? And I don't want to hear any more about this new constituency cottage. Tom's told me quite enough, that it's next to a twelfth-century church in the same village as her old one – which her ex-husband, Barney, had wanted to keep on. Hearing about the problems they'd had trying to dissuade him I'd said sarkily that I could see two husbands in the constituency might be an embarrassment, and only one was likely to vote for her.

Tom has always insisted that Barney's a dreadful man and defended Victoria to the last. He's doing it now and it hurts.

'Why must I say hello to her, Tom? I'm not sure there's much need, is there?' It comes out dully, if defiantly, the shine rubbed off my last precious minutes with him.

'It's the right thing, Mum. Emma and Jess want it, too. Time you relaxed about it all. You do read her very wrong, you know. You're actually quite unfair.'

How can he say that when she took Bill? He's still making me feel

like a child roundly scolded for its messy room and I argue obsti-
nately. 'I'm not – she's closing the A&E unit at that hospital near
Crawley, it's such an uncaring thing to do. Is that reading her very
wrong? Hardly much saving for the Treasury.' It's an unreasonable
attack, unconnected, a stupidly petty thing to have said.

'You don't know the facts and nor do I,' Tom says, grinding it in.
'It's nothing to do with her as a person. She's very straightforward,
and prepared to take the rap, at least, unlike some ministers.' He's
looking hurt and angry.

I kiss him goodbye, feeling chastened, and promise not to disgrace
him. I'm soon seeing off his grandmother too, and left waiting with
butterflies – after changing back into the new wraparound summery
dress I'd worn for the drink with Perry and carefully redoing my
minimal make-up – to meet the new Mrs Osborne.

The car arrives, Bill at the wheel. Emma leaps out like a dog from the
trap and comes racing over. I'm outside to greet them, but holding
back, staying by the front steps. Emma whispers urgently, 'You will
say hello, Mum, and be nice? We were just at a fete,' she goes on
more loudly, 'I won some bath-salts for you and a coconut!'

Bill is opening the door for his new wife – is that partly for my
benefit? I stay where I am with Emma keeping guard, watching Jessie
tug at the strap of her bag, which seems to have got stuck in the car
door. Her father turns to help and Victoria comes over alone.

Her face has an unexpectedly anxious look. She's self-consciously
brushing back the brown hair falling into her eyes.

They're wide, gently smiling eyes, not the eyes of a closer of A&E
units. Their holding power comes through in photographs, but now,
trained on me, I feel more compellingly in their sway. There's no hint

of 'I've won, he's mine', none of the peanut-brittle hardness I'd expected, no slick varnished veneer.

'I know this must be hard for you,' she says, 'but I'm so glad of a chance to meet. And I must tell you your children are wonderful! William never has to be strict.'

'He overdoes being lenient, you mean! It's good to meet you, too.' I'm glad she calls him William, it's a tiny distinction that allows me to keep separate the past, those early years he and I once had. 'Are you in a rush?' I hear myself asking. 'Have you time for a drink?' Bill's joined us and I look from one to the other, dreading the reply. It would be too painful.

He glances at her, deferring, which he never did with me, and Victoria answers. 'Thanks, that's really kind, but I've got a most horrible amount of work still to do. And Emma and Jessie must be tired after a hectic day.'

'We're not, you must come in! Be really nice.' Emma's tugging at her arm. It wouldn't, though, and nobody pushes it. One tiny fragile step at a time.

First thing next day I phone a Terrence Higgins Trust centre.

There's a sexual health clinic every Tuesday morning, I'm told. 'You don't need an appointment. Just turn up any time.'

I think obsessively all day about whether to have a test, sleep little that night, but it feels a sort of solution, a means of reassurance: something that must be done.

I get the girls off to school and decide to go by train. My nerves really set in when there are people I know in the carriage, a local estate agent opposite and a school mother across the aisle. She leans towards me, eyeing my deliberately played-down jeans, and asks if

I'm going up to shop. I smile and nod, heart thudding, legs tight-crossed, then glue my eyes unseeingly to the paper. It's *The Post*, my daily reminder of Bill.

Nearing Waterloo I stare out at London's great grey sprawl: drab offices, pockets of wasteland, grimy terraced houses. Trains come in by a city's backdoor, I think, there's no window-box colour or welcome-mat, no cheery light in the porch.

The centre is quite far down Gray's Inn Road. I keep walking and finally find it. There's a bright reception area with chairs in primary colours and indigo-painted walls. And young helpers around, watching out for patients like me whose nerves must give them away.

A pale girl with ginger hair comes over. 'You for the clinic? It's just through here.' She shows me into a windowless waiting room, pointing to forms to complete. 'And the tea and coffee's right there,' she says indicating, and leaves me.

My hand is shaking, spooning Café Direct coffee granules into a mug. I hold it under a spout and squirt hot water, determined to stay calm. It's fine, just a simple sensible precaution. Sitting down, resting the mug on the floor, I tackle the forms, writing in my maiden name, Sinclair, and giving a mobile number, but no address.

There are five others waiting: three men, a pretty teenage black girl with hair scraped back in a ponytail and another young girl who's white and wretchedly haggard-looking, with sunken cheeks like an old pensioner. She's rattling and seems badly in need of a fix.

People are summoned into a consulting room and leave with hard-to-read faces. God knows what must be going on inside. Then it's my turn. The woman who receives me is in jeans. 'I am a nurse,' she says, correctly reading my concern. 'We wear regular clothes, some clients can find the stiff starched look a little inhibiting.'

She asks what brought me here, questions my sexual history and explains that three months need to have elapsed since any sex or exposure to risk for an accurate result. I'm dry-mouthed. Suppose, just suppose . . . It's pointless panicking, so unlikely. I lean on Julian and trust him. If only things were less of a mess and I felt freer to love. But then there's always Lauren.

The nurse is watching, waiting for a gap in my thoughts. 'It's a rapid test with an instant result,' she says, pulling on rubber gloves, 'but quite safe and sure.' She has a glass capillary tube ready to draw up the blood and takes my hand. 'Just a pin prick.' I study her fair head intently as she bends over the task.

'This is the magic ingredient,' she smiles, placing the tube on a testing strip. 'One red line it's negative, two it's positive. Don't worry now . . .'

There it is, one red line, clear as the number on a footballer's strip. Panic over.

On the train going home it feels as if my captive's hood has been lifted and I'm seeing daylight again, life back on track. It was only temporarily derailed, but I've been staring into a deep dark abyss and feel as shaky now, when there's no need, as having survived some extreme and more immediate life-threatening situation. I stare down at my trembling hands: funny thing about delayed reactions.

Why don't I feel more bitter and angry? Perry was trying, and not so subtly, to put me off Julian, it was disgustingly underhand. He wouldn't, I suspect, be pleased to know how conclusively his under-mining tactics have failed. I'm glad now, though, to have had the test and be feeling more reassured – almost grateful to him. Perhaps that's it.

There's certainly no love lost. Julian's attitude, picking that fight and losing his cool, was extreme, but Perry does need supping with a long spoon.

Do I have lunch with him? He's very keen, only half dislikeable . . . The whole Perry thing, I think, trying to analyse it, is tied up with that terrible female trait of feeling rejected and vulnerable, responding too eagerly to an attractive man's advances.

The train's almost empty leaving London in the middle of the day. Only a couple more stations to go now; there are fields out of the window, sunlight. I had stuffed *The Post* into my oversized squashy handbag and dig it out. Although I'm hardly much more in the mood for reading a newspaper than I was on the way in.

There's no breakthrough in the case of the girl taken from her garden. Bill is blasting off in lurid news-speak at the police. The child was taken in full daylight, seen by no one. What, he storms, is going on?

The grieving mother and her partner are pictured holding hands on a sofa. It's heartrending. The girl's father lives in Scotland and is thought not to be involved. As the train draws into Brearfield I sigh deeply and leave the depressing paper on the seat.

At home there's an answermachine message from Perry, one on my mobile, too. I'll have to decide about lunch finally and call him back. Why am I fiddling about with a married man at all when Julian never once leaves my mind and I was bitter enough about Victoria? It seems dreadfully disloyal, especially after the Aids thing. Somehow or other, though, I've got to break out and try to be independent and build up a protective self-support system.

It's only lunch. I'm more wised-up and in control now, too, and could keep Perry contained, I'm sure. I must stand back from Julian. Could I have fallen for him as a defence? Had I seen what was coming with Bill so much in London and needed to feel Julian was there? It's like sitting an impossible exam, this feeling of denseness.

Julian is going to sell the shop, that's obvious. He's made up his mind and even told Jessie before me, which hurts and saps my confidence levels. He builds them up easily enough, but they're dry of juice, the tank is empty now that I feel so sure he's leaving Brearfield. I've got to get going, move house, find a proper job and rev up my life a bit.

I pick up the phone to Perry and think up good reasons not to have lunch till next week. It leaves time to cancel. I do feel guilty about it at heart and so unsettled.

Work can wait, I think, having an urge to call Val – not that I could off-load about the Terrence Higgins Trust and the test. I couldn't, not even to my closest friend. But Jessie's relationship with Julian and her sense of insecurity is such a worry; I do need to talk it through.

'Jess is very aware,' Val says, 'and with her sharp mind she can tell things aren't right between you and Julian.' Is it that obvious to Val as well?

'He told her he's going to sell the shop: he hasn't told me,' I say testily.

'Preparing the ground for poor Jess, I expect. You can hardly blame him. You've been so priggish and prickly, making clear you don't choose to know your own mind.'

'I'm scared to show my feelings, Val. Scared of being alone, of getting burned. There's a side of Julian . . . well, where the shades are down,' I say, quoting Lauren, 'that makes me hold back.' I pause a moment then carry on, 'And Perry Maynard, that wine man from the dance, is sniffing around. I've agreed to have lunch.' It's clear Val doesn't go a bundle on that and I snap, irritated, 'Now who's being priggy? It is only lunch. So what if he has got a wife?'

'You've had quite a bit to say about such things in the past, if I remember. Just don't tell Susie, she'll be jealous.'

I compress my lips, feeling put-upon. And Val hasn't made my anxiety about Jess any less. Much of it is Erica's doing, but I feel despairing and need to try to explain. 'It's hard, Val, I do worry so about Julian and Jess. She called him her friend, but he's an adult and that seems sort of a bit unnatural . . .'

'She likes him and all the attention he gives her. It's her chance to shine. And I suppose,' Val ponders, 'however much Jess accepts the new wife, she might still feel resentful at her father going.'

Val has a client waiting and we end the call. Thinking about Erica is a bad idea and I try to push her out of my mind. Perhaps, after all, Julian selling the shop might really be for the best. But that thought in itself puts me in even blacker despair.

It's hard to concentrate. Bill knows nothing about the Erica business. There's little point telling him if Julian is shutting up shop anyway, but should I perhaps just mention it in passing, being joking and dismissive about it?

He'd had no worries in the first place when I told him about Jessie's little job. And Bill edits a national newspaper, he knows what goes on; grim stories, ones like that poor girl abducted from her garden, must cross his desk every day.

CHAPTER 10

It's another golden June evening and almost the longest day. I'm still gardening at nearly ten, deadheading roses on the terrace. It's time to go in now, though, late for the girls to be getting to bed.

All the doors are open and I can hear them bitching; it sounds nasty and I put down my secateurs and basket and race indoors.

'God, not the waterworks again!' Emma is saying, in her worst goading tone. 'Daddy-waddy's little darling is missing her darling Julian, then? You're such a sucking-up little show-off, Jess. Have you run out of friends? Did that creepy larry, Luke, finally dump you? I'm not surprised.'

'Fuck off you, I hate you. Just fuck off, you're only jealous.'

I burst in on them shouting, 'Jess! I never want to hear language like that again, do you hear?' They both spin round looking shaken. Jess is red-eyed. She has her legs curled under her on the window-seat and hurriedly swings them down. Emma's in front of the television and gets to her feet, too. 'And you've got nothing to smile about,' I shriek at her. 'Talking to your sister like that, you should be ashamed. You had both better apologize and fast!'

'Sorry.' Emma says with a nostril-flaring sneer.

'Sorry, little Mummy-wummy's girl.' Jessie glares, sticking out her tongue at her sister and rushing out of the room. I hear her feet go pounding upstairs and wait for the slam of her bedroom door.

I'm going to have to calm them down. Do I punish them? At least Jessie is in her room already, I think, turning to have another go at Emma who is back in front of the television, keeping a low profile. 'Upstairs this minute,' I say, 'and you'll both be going to bed a lot earlier tomorrow night, that's for sure.'

Upstairs I try to appeal to them to be sweeter, more helpful, perfect little paragons. They seem quite guilty and cowed. A sense of proportion is needed, I tell myself, longing for advice, wishing Julian was around – wishing it hadn't been all about him.

He calls in the night. It's a couple of days since the last time. I've been in bed for hours, failing to get to sleep, and feel wonderfully relieved. 'You're ringing very late,' I complain warmly.

'I had a feeling you'd be awake.'

I tell him Emma and Jessie have been rowing, that Jess is upset, that she's told me he's selling the shop. 'I'd actually rather not have had to hear about something like that, third hand,' I add, sliding into bitterness.

'Who was the second hand?'

'Susie – well obliquely.' I'm close to crying now, far too wound up.

'I'll explain about it all when I'm back. It's to do with writing the book I told you about. I had to level with Jessie, since her Saturday apprenticeship is to be so short-lived. I do hope she's not too upset.'

'She certainly is,' I sniff, lifted, for all my tense misery and misgivings, by his gentle tone. Just hearing his voice does for me every time; it causes physical feelings. 'I could come and meet your plane next Friday if you like? I'd bring the girls. Or are you already being met . . .?'

'No, that'd be great. Can we have some time alone together after-wards, though?'

'Sure.' What does he think? It was bad enough that he went off in such a miserably off-key way. I'd like a more passionate return.

'Has Maynard appeared on your doorstep yet with his wine?'

I can't easily lie. 'Yes, he did turn up with a case. You were right about that!'

'And you've seen him since?' Julian asks tonelessly, managing to transmit with ease that it's something he knows very well, exactly as expected.

It makes me feel both cringing and angry. 'Perry offered to help sample some of the wine he brought, so I suggested a Sunday lunchtime drink with my mother. That's all. Hardly a hanging offence.' It's a cool, defensive reply, and we're awkward with each other winding up the call, a bad note to end on.

It's raining when Perry arrives, a steady relentless downpour. He's armed with engaging smiles and a big black umbrella, but then taking me to his car, he holds the brolly at such an inefficient angle that I'll have wet bedraggled hair. Perhaps the rain will mean less people about, I think hopefully, fewer of Brearfield's gossipmongers around to take careful note of who's inside passing glamorous cars.

'It's nothing much, this place we're going to,' Perry says confi-dently. 'Quite quaintly appealing, though, one of those pubs where the regulars look like they've forgotten to go home.' He glances to see if I found that entertaining then reaches out and fingers my hair. 'It's so soft and stunning, nothing out of a bottle about your hair! You're far too beautiful. God, this weather, I can hardly see the road.'

I feel slightly unclean. He's not going to lunge like Phil, but however much more stylish his pitch, it comes to the same thing. Perry wants steamy sex in tucked-away country pubs and hotels, a risqué affair. Is that what I want out of this? It's hardly a stable long-term relationship with a man I love and admire . . .

We're off the motorway now, criss-crossing the countryside, driving in dark-green oppressively overhung lanes. Swollen raindrops are clattering down, spattering on Perry's smooth-running car that I'm beginning to find claustrophobic. It's a relief to see a sign saying we're entering the village of Slatter, our destination.

The pub is at the thin end of a triangular green and also in heavy shade, towered over by a huge dripping horse-chestnut tree. A brass bell rings in a clanking way as we go in, and a few old codgers in the public bar swing round and briefly stare.

'I love the old oak booths here,' Perry says, going through into an eating area and making for a reserved table. 'They're so nice and private.'

Our drink order is taken. I stick to a spritzer, although pressed to join Perry in a glass of red wine. We decide on steak pie and salad, it seems a good idea on a gloomy day.

Will Julian at this very moment, with his telepathic waves, be imagining me having lunch with Perry in some tucked-away rained-on pub?

He was so determined to paint him a cold callous shit and a scoundrel, but is the man crinkling his eyes across the table, gazing so openly and appreciatively, really that bad?

I try to remember that between this and the last time Perry and I met, just over a week ago, I've been through hell and back over Aids because of him. It won't do to have any illusions.

'Julian says they've been having gigantic rainstorms in the dry season out there,' I observe, keen to talk naturally and positively about Uganda and make clear Perry hasn't succeeded in making trouble. 'It's not only raining with us!'

'What exactly is he up to out there?'

'A school extension project.'

'He does seem wedded to the place. Julian was well known for his great passions and amours, you know,' Perry says, 'his love of faraway places, but then always being off to pastures new. He's not the most stable person. Uganda's doing well!'

'You seem awfully determined to do him down, and not that subtly,' I retort.

'What do you expect? I've thought of nothing and no one else since the moment I set eyes on you.' Perry's hand stretches out over the table and covers mine.

We can't be seen, it's a carefully chosen pub and he's talking in low tones. There are people in other booths, though, and while his hand is pleasurably warm, his sudden look of intensity feels dangerous. He's no longer smiling. 'It's been the most ghastly terrible strain. Accused of being distant at home, not wanting to scare you off . . .'

Perry has to pause then as, with poor timing, a hot-looking waitress brings two steaming oval earthenware pie-dishes to the table. He waits patiently while she fusses over the salads, alternately beaming at her and decanting the contents of his pie dish on to a large oval plate.

He has a few mouthfuls before carrying on as though without interruption, 'And, less selfishly, I'd been feeling in such sympathy with you from afar. Reading all those columns of stuff on William and Victoria – I think I fell in love with you in print!' Perry has another bite or two then looks up with an ardent potent gaze. 'Julian's a loner, not the man for you. He's flawed.'

I'll decide who is or isn't for me, I think, feeling enraged. Perry can't start laying down the law. 'Most people have flaws. Are you so perfect that you haven't a single one?' I flash him a furious glare. It's extremely irritating, too, the way he's tucking into the food.

He gets the message and sets down his knife and fork, grinning. 'You're wonderful in a rage! And very loyally protective, I like that.' His face becomes grave. 'My biggest flaw,' he says, with his expression more solemnly aligned, 'is not loving my wife. In fact, I actually rather hate her.' I stare at him, startled. For all the cold unpleasant sentiment he's suddenly sounding alarmingly more genuine. 'And another flaw is, I suppose,' he looks rueful, 'that I'm very good at hiding it. It keeps me going, a sort of sick private game I play. The serious problem now, though, is that it's beginning to pall. Married nineteen years and suddenly you come along. It's a new and overwhelming feeling and my mask is slipping, I fear.'

His look is concentrated and I stare down at my little-touched piecrust in embarrassment. I'm not taken in, even though he's banking on me being gullible, still hurt and confused. But Bill and I had also been married nineteen years when he fell for Victoria and the coincidence is slightly unnerving.

Perry freely declaring hatred for his wife is shocking, but his very ability to come out with such a thing has a sort of arrogant honesty that gives me slight pause. He can't seriously be falling for me? It must be a ruse, a way of getting through, of taking care of any possible infidelity sensitivities of mine, and having his way.

She's the mother of his children, I think, disgusted, remembering him talking so naturally about his sons of fourteen, sixteen and eighteen, laughing at their fast acquired taste for fine wine.

'It's the children who get hurt,' I say with feeling, my thoughts inevitably leaping to Jessie, 'and the scars seem to last.' I'm anxious to sound remote, personally distant, in the role of a sympathetic friend. Could Perry's marriage really be cracking up? Even if it is, I can't possibly be the cause.

The waitress is back. Perry orders apple crumble and talks engagingly about his love of France. He does have charm. I sneak a look at my watch, feeling like a guest at a modestly good party who's decided, on balance, that staying home was the better idea.

He doesn't ask after my children and how they've coped with the break-up, in spite of my earlier remarks. I'm glad about that, although it would have been a natural and solicitous thing to do.

'Of course, Jane has always minded about my brother,' Perry says, returning to the strains of his marriage. 'I even find it a bit hard myself at times. It's a beautiful estate, wonderful fishing. Rough justice!' He is letting on in an amusingly blatant way that there's a title in the family. I don't ask questions and give him openings, to his evident chagrin. He still takes my hand more than once, rubbing his thumb over it rhythmically and saying I've upturned his world.

When we leave his arm is round my shoulders and then in one of the dark overhung lanes he stops the car and takes my hand. 'Can I call you from time to time? I'm married, I more than understand your feelings, but,' he touches my cheek, 'I'd be grateful for any crumbs.'

He kisses me then. It doesn't overwhelm me, it's a curiously conventional kiss, reasonably sexy and turning-on, but not a perfect fit. I'm able to extricate myself with ease.

Which I do, with a warm smile. 'Really must get home now . . . Sorry!'

As I'm getting out of the car I find myself submitting to another ardent kiss. Perry is leaving me in no doubt of his keenness to win through. 'You'll let me call once or twice?' He fingers my hand. 'I do need to. And I'm here for you any time you need me. You will remember that?'

CHAPTER 11

We're at the airport, in arrivals, waiting in the area where the passengers come through.

Emma's fidgeting and bored. 'Mum, can I just nip and look in Smiths quickly?'

I let her go. Jess is fidgeting too, and has a stubborn little pout on her face. People are giving her glances; she has a way of making her presence felt, like a child film star used to being feted. The frayed-edge denim skirt and black ballet pumps she's wearing are her choice. And the pink T-shirt stretched tight over two small beginnings of breasts; Jessie's quite fashion conscious in her own way.

I go over to where I can thumb at Emma, but, as so often happens, at exactly that moment Julian comes through. Turning back I see he's with Jessie and giving her a hug. His eyes alight on me then and stay fixed. It does for me, his look; it's real, radiating feelings of love and need. I've been battling with secret dark thoughts that have prowled like wolves in his absence and now they're slinking away. He's very tanned; it can't have rained all the time out there.

'Hi – welcome home!' I say, smiling quite shyly, returning his gaze.

'It's so good to be back, seeing you . . .' He leaves Jessie and the luggage trolley and comes close, giving me a kiss on the mouth, squeezing my hand very tightly. It's swift and electric and very brief, we separate in seconds. Emma's rushing up.

She gets a hug too, then Julian says, 'I got you guys a few bits and pieces out there. Not a lot to buy, I'm afraid, they're very big on carved animals and stuff.'

'It's cool!' She loves any sort of present and grins with delight. I wish Jessie would. 'Can I buy *Bliss* on the way out, Mum?' Emma tugs at my arm. 'It'll only take a sec.'

Julian's mobile rings when we're in the car. He's smiling into the phone. It's Lauren, I'm sure, listening intently, but only able to hear one side.

'Yes, great . . . Yes, all sorted on that front. Just a case of waiting and desperately hoping now, on the other . . .' Lauren seems so in the know; it's maddening, I feel miserably left out. Julian turns, his smile directed at me. 'Yes, we're in the car – yes, I'll tell her. You both really are serious about the plan? That's amazing and generous. And it is the best way.' He clicks off, looking thoughtful, and pockets the phone.

It's well past the girls' bedtime when we get back to Brearfield. As I draw up in the alley behind the bookshop, Julian looks relieved to see his car still parked there.

'Shall I come round in a bit?' he asks as he gets out.

'Sure.' I get out too, and stand idly by while he lifts out his bags, fishes for the girls' presents and hands them over. 'In about an hour?' he says, turning back to me. 'We do need to talk.'

That sounds so impersonal, like two colleagues in an office. Then Jessie is out of the car, annoyingly, staring up at him with a serious face. 'Can I come tomorrow? It is Saturday.'

The bookshop was far from my thoughts and I can't help a tiny reactive flicker crossing my eyes. I blink it away and smile at Julian. 'Won't you be far too busy after being away?'

His look is questioning, he took in that fractional uncertainty and stiffening on my part. 'She'd be a wonderful help – but, of course, it's up to you.'

I'm angry with myself, hating to think he saw my reaction. 'Back in the car now, Jess,' I say awkwardly, giving tense tacit permission, 'or you'll be far too tired.'

Driving home my pulse is racing. I need Julian; my body needs him, and very badly, but there are negatively charged pulls too, fighting the need. They feel like incompatible electrons in an inhospitable field.

Emma's enjoying her present. 'The necklace says "real gems" and Julian's brought me some horn bangles too, Mum. They're really fun.'

'And is yours the same, Jess?'

'No, it's a different sort of bangle. "Vine bracelets made from recycled paper,"' she reads, '"by people displaced by Northern Uganda's twenty-year war . . ." He cares that they haven't got homes, you see,' she adds in an accusing tone.

When we're back in ours and I'm upstairs hugging her goodnight, it becomes clear that Jessie overheard Julian's aside, his mention of needing to talk. 'He'll say about selling the shop, Mum. I wish he wasn't going away.'

She's speaking into my chest and I stroke her hair. 'Even if he does, darling, he'll still be your friend. Those things don't change.' But they do, I think, as I'm kissing the top of her head, when adult emotions muck everything up and get in the way. Leaving her room, going to mine to get ready for Julian, I'm feeling very adult emotions and anticipation.

Julian is facing me in the hall. His hands are on my breasts and I know, we both know, that if he kisses me we'll be in it deep. I flick my eyes to the upstairs landing; it's possible the girls aren't yet asleep. He stares a moment, then pulls me into the kitchen, on past the larder with the wine racks and Perry's wine, and into my study. There he turns the stiff rusty old key in the door that's never been used. It makes a squeaky complaining clunk and we fall on each other with smothered giggles, kissing with violent passion – and in ecstasy.

The room is in near darkness, as if hidden from the world. The blank computer screen is the only watching eye, the only invader of our private hungry heaven. I can't feel the hardness of the cold stripped floorboards, the nailheads, the splintery cracks, and if I could it would be the least of my cares.

We stay lying together on the floor, very still. My head is resting on Julian's shoulder and I have a sense of him as a house with solid walls, safe and secure.

'Did you miss me?' he asks, kissing each of my fingers in turn.

I've ached for him, but had terrible moments of black fear. How can I explain all that? 'You've just made up handsomely for being away! But did you miss me, though?'

'I love you, it's self-evident I'd miss you.' He turns my face to him. 'It's a given – but will you promise to remember that? It's funda-mental, essential to what I'm about to say.'

'You needn't sound so formal and patronizing. If you're moving on, selling the shop, if this is goodbye, why can't you just say it out-right?' I jerk away and my head slips off Julian and on to the floor.

It makes a dull knock, a thud. I don't try to lift myself up. The lights have gone out, the electric glow, the thrill, the glorious brightness has drained away. Why does he bother wrapping it up so laboriously, why can't he just come out with it?

I feel his hand sliding under my head, supporting it, and he's leaning over me, staring into my eyes. 'You only half trust me. It's not enough. You have to know that nothing, nothing matters except the love I feel for you and it's what you want – that there's no room for shits coming round with cases of wine.'

I look away and mutter, 'I'm getting cold.' Neither of us makes a move, then I struggle up to a sitting position and pull on my trousers without pants, my shirt without a bra. Turning back with a half glance I demand, 'So what exactly are you saying?'

'I'm going away from Brearfield, we can't go on as we are. I'll research and write the book and give you time.' He's getting dressed as he speaks, purposefully, in preparation to leave. 'I can have the use of Henry and Lauren's Cambridgeshire house. It's empty all week and helpfully near the Radcinowitz Institute for Criminal Research. I'll go to book fairs at weekends, do short trips away or use their London house when they're in Cambridgeshire so they have some time to themselves.'

'And the shop?' I'm hugging myself with crossed arms for warmth.

'It'll be on the market. I'll take the most valuable books and Roy will look after the rest. He can show people round.'

'Well, that's it then.' I can't accuse him of walking out on Jess, on us both, having made clear enough ever since Bill left that I didn't want to feel beholden or tied. 'Jess will be very upset,' I say, by way of a statement.

'But not you?'

'God, Julian! Don't start pushing it on to me. Of course I don't want you to go. I actually thought what we've just done was pretty special and wonderful . . . But if you've had enough and are on to new pastures, then that's your affair. You want a little doormat, someone swearing undying love? Well, I've been one of those. It's not how I want to live now.'

'You were no doormat. You and William just weren't a natural fit. It happens – all too often.'

'And three children? That doesn't feature in your calculations?'

'Not much. Your children need a loving home, not one with all the colour and energy gone. They don't need parents whose relationship was getting weaker by the day like losing blood.'

I'm feeling bloodless right now, standing with my hand turning the key in the door, both wanting to bar his exit and feeling I should tell him to go.

'There's no one else,' he says, coming and touching my lips, 'it's all for you. And I know you have genuine feelings, too. Let me know if you ever get round to discovering them. My mobile will always be on.'

His arm is round me going to the front door. I can't shrug it off. I need it there badly; I'm feeling too weak for challenging gestures, too numb and disbelieving. This isn't happening, it can't be; it isn't the end.

It is, though, and as he clicks up the latch the panic erupts and I have to suppress an urge to physically restrain him. 'I was going to ask you to come and see round Blossom Cottage,' I say lightly, without pride. 'It's on the market and Val thinks George Farley is such a fan of yours, you'd be the one to clinch the deal.'

'Val's wrong about Blossom Cottage – she's not about much. This house isn't the problem; it's Brearfield. Your future,' he says, meeting my eyes, 'isn't in this town.' Then with a quick press of his cheek, his body, he's out of the house and gone.

Turning from the door I look up and catch a glimpse of Jessie on the landing in her pyjamas; she sees me looking and darts back into her room.

A long week has gone by, I think, driving to Brearfield at lunchtime on Friday to pick up Val. She's coming with me to see Blossom Cottage.

I've convinced myself it's Julian who's wrong, not Val. Moving, releasing capital, would give me a little independence. I could get help and commute to London, do a proper job – possibly try to re-establish links with the magazine I worked on fifteen years ago. I could have done that before, without capital . . . but I wanted to be in Brearfield, close to Julian. Now I must stand on my own two feet.

Shouldn't I look at London properties, too? The money would go nowhere. And the girls would hate leaving their happy life here for a suburban semi or alien city flat.

Val's waiting and we set off the other way out of Brearfield. The cottage is next to riding stables. I'd like the sound of horses clopping past. It looks out over fields that contain a row of pylons. I'd get used to them, they don't really spoil the view . . .

I push on the slatted wooden gate and we walk up a short paved path. The garden looks too tidy. That's easy to change.

Mrs Farley, with dimpled arms and fluffy white hair, is effusive in her welcome. George Farley, also white-haired, standing with his backside to a rangy inglenook fireplace, springs forward with hospitable offers of medium sherry. We have a job declining them. 'And here's Victor to say hello,' Mrs Farley says fondly, as an aged terrier staggers stiffly out of a smelly round basket.

Victor approaches us snarling, baring exceptionally yellow fangs, his growling reaching a climax that might result in a teeth-sinking snap. 'Grumpy old stick,' his mistress says, patting his head lovingly and leading him back to his basket. 'Shall we start upstairs?'

I stare vaguely at an expanse of dusky pink carpet in the master bedroom. The low ceilings and beams make me think of Julian's flat.

I'd felt desperate, taking Jessie in for a last Saturday morning with him, but I couldn't refuse. She wanted to say goodbye. Julian dropped her back, having apparently promised to send books, but since telling me that Jess has barely opened her mouth.

She's been so in on herself. Tom tried to bring her out when he was down for Sunday lunch next day. They went into the garden to see Elton, but Tom gave me the thumbs down, coming in again. He's called her too, but I could hear her being monosyllabic into the phone. Emma's been no help – she's secretly pleased the bookshop job is no more, I think. It wouldn't have been her thing, but it inevitably caused a bit of jealousy.

Mrs Farley is opening cupboard after fitted cupboard and Val is stalwartly holding the fort. I can't bring myself to show the proper amount of interest and communicate.

By Wednesday, in Brearfield, the bookshop already had a 'For Sale' board up. People had come up and questioned me inquisitively, deeply shocked at its closing. The town was justly proud of its anti-quarian bookshop.

Erica Barkston had caught my eye from across the street. She had a look on her face as if to say, 'I was right, he was running scared.'

She's the only one who will derive any satisfaction from the bookshop's demise, I think, as Mrs Farley shows us smaller unused bedrooms with nestling cuddly toys piled on top shelves.

The rooms would be suitable for Emma and Jess, but I fail to say so. My mind won't stay put.

Going downstairs again Val gives me a hefty nudge. 'Try a bit harder, can't you? It shows! Let's go for a quick sandwich from here.'

George Farley has poured the sherry. We can't refuse. 'We're moving to Bristol to be near our children,' he says. 'Still upset at Julian Bridgewater closing down though. I suppose it didn't pay?' He looks at me.

'Antiquarian books are mostly sold on the Internet, now.'

'Pity, it was such a draw. Is he leaving Brearfield altogether?'

Mrs Farley is frowning, seeing my discomfort. She presses home-made cheese straws. She's not as fluffy as she looks.

Val asks after the septic tank, which slows us up, as George Farley seems immensely proud of it. When we finally make our escape, Victor's parting growls rumble on in our wake like distant rolls of thunder.

The teashop in the market square has one customer, a man in a three-piece suit, although it's a hot June day. He's doing a 'quick' crossword; with luck he'll soon be gone. I tell Val all about Lauren in full technicolor detail, perhaps over-richly, like butter on a crois-sant, but I need to get across how extra hard it is that Julian is going to be right there, living in her house. How can he expect me to sort myself out and decide whether I trust him totally in those circum-stances? It's like asking a scared horse not to bolt. I think for the first time Val sees the force of my dilemma.

She gives up trying to press the delights of Blossom Cottage.

'I'm sure Julian does care,' I say as an afterthought, staring down at four small triangles of white-bread ham sandwich. 'He just wants things on his terms.'

'Which are?'

'That he'd like to dip in and out of me, I suppose, that I'd always be there.'

'You didn't ask about his plans, what happens after the book – where he'll be living?' I keep silent. What would have been the point? 'You might, in fact, have it all wrong,' Val goes on. 'Lauren might be on your side.' I raise an eyebrow at her, sky-high. 'But the key must be, surely, feeling in love enough to get hurt, and,' she looks at me quite fiercely, 'not caring a fig what anyone thinks – not even your own mother.'

I've told Val my mother's overcautious view of Julian, but answer defensively, 'Mum's had little chance to get to know him. He could easily have won her round.'

'That's not the point. She's no fool, your mother. She wants you safely, acceptably married and you shouldn't let that influence you, Ursula. It's your life, not hers.'

'You're safely, acceptably married, so what's wrong in that?'

'Nothing. But we're us, not you and Julian. You've got a very defiant streak, it's where Jessie gets it from, and deep down you fight the conventional – you'd give Julian a run for his money if you'd only get going!'

We order the teashop's filter coffee. I tell Val that Jessie is taking things badly, missing Julian, I think. Probably escaping into her own little world and creating an imagined one, as a younger child might do, where she's lost and lonely in a wooded wilderness, battling against dark dangerous forces.

A solid parental front would help, which is the whole irony. I can't even appeal to Bill without a huge loss of pride and, anyway, he's part of the problem.

We pay the bill and leave. I feel as desolate as in the months after the night of Val and Chris's party when I had so nearly run away with Julian. Where would he and I be now, if Claud the vicar, like an interfering industrious spider, hadn't woven his sticky web and held me back from flight?

Lauren is the spell-breaker this time. That Cambridgeshire weekend had been wonderful until, with the overheard conversation, she had shattered the mirror, the glass, the window I'd just looked through onto a world with Julian and me.

Val asks why I've never confronted him about what I'd heard. She's reading my thoughts. 'I wasn't up to it,' I say honestly. 'I couldn't bear to accelerate things and force a decision. I didn't want to lose him . . .'

'Don't say "and now I have",' Val chips in. 'Julian would have told you if it was over. Think about that. And use the time he's given you. Decide if he's worth all the pain and then give him the answer.'

Val walks with me to my car and, as I'm getting in, touches my arm. Her eyes are soft and she has a humorous smile. 'Not sure if this will make you laugh or cry, but Erica's putting it about that Julian's doing a runner, that he's had child trouble in the past and thinks it's time to move on. She's convinced that's why he's selling the shop. I'd like to think Brearfield has more sanity than to believe her. Erica's take on life is almost medieval, pity she's living so out of time.'

CHAPTER 12

The school's new bus arrangements are panning out well. No more hanging around at the school gates. With so many women at work the waiting mums' scene will soon be just a photograph in a book of contemporary history. I must get a full-time job.

Jessie has an after-school flute lesson today, though, and for a change I'm waiting outside to collect her, lounging on a playground bench, enjoying the warm sun.

It clouds over when Erica Barkston walks out of the building – dressed as for a Governors' meeting in dull beige trouser-suit and with another of her frightful handbags on her arm, a twin-handled mock-croc affair.

'Hello, Ursula. We don't often see you at school.' Leaving me no time to reply, she goes on, 'After Julian's extremely odd, very sudden departure, I think, perhaps, you might concede I was right!' She's trying not to look too triumphant, but failing handsomely. 'I'm sure you had some private concerns and must be secretly a little relieved,' she suggests solicitously, still with her nauseating smile. 'I had discussed it with the Head, you know, and felt it my duty to raise it with the Council. It's so important to stay within the law.'

God, she's insufferable. I bite my tongue. 'There was nothing odd or particularly sudden about his going,' I say, managing a cold smile. 'Julian's been thinking for some time about closing the shop and being free to work on a book. He needed some country quiet. I've been to the house where he's staying, it's very remote and peaceful.'

'Ah, but you don't *know* that's where he is, do you?' Her eyes gleam challengingly. 'You've split up with him, you're not going to go there and check. There's something in his past and your daughter was at risk, I'm sure of that. I know he's got things to hide.'

How do you, you cow? I think furiously. Staring at her with hard eyes I say tightly, 'There is such a thing as trust in a friend, Erica. Here's Jess. We must be off.'

Erica beams at her. 'A little more time at weekends now, Jessie?'

'I've got books to read. Mr Bridgewater sends me them.'

It was a neat answer. I feel pride and an enormous outflow of love, hurrying my daughter away before Erica, like the rats, can get at her. And me: how dare she impugn Julian in that way. I think of Lauren's call in the car and of him thanking her for the loan of the house – then remember, with a tiny jolt, that he had thanked her for something else, but hadn't spelled out what that was.

I shiver internally. This is madness: that ghastly woman is warping my mind.

As we reach the car I say brightly, 'Another Jiffy bag came for you today, Jess!' She shrugs, as though nothing in life, not even books from Julian, has any special significance. Which weighs heavily on my already sagging spirits.

Jess rushes off to change, picking up her package from the hall table on the way. I've been staring jealously at that envelope ever since it arrived, but without noticing whether it had a

Cambridgeshire postmark. As I start wondering about that now, I fume at myself for letting Erica get to me.

The telephone goes. It's Perry again, who's been calling regularly. He asks after my job-hunting and I tell him the interiors magazine I used to work for has nothing, only an occasional book review.

'It felt like being offered a day as a film-extra in a crowd scene!'

'Couldn't you work full time for your executive search firm?'

'They've got their top people in place. Frankly I've had enough. And so had someone I called up today, a Norfolk lawyer whom I was sussing out for an in-house job with a pharmaceutical company. He was leaving his wife, he said – and then proposed to me blind! Begged me to come away with him and grow oranges in Portugal. Just on seeing my picture in the press, it was hard to believe!'

'A man after my own heart,' Perry sighs theatrically. 'I've got a proposal to make, too . . .' I'm silent, annoyed at myself for giving him the opening. 'It's time you were taken out for a really decent dinner. You can't go on having a row of telly suppers, you'll be coming to the door in curlers and slippers next!'

He has a point. It would be dinner with strings, though, and I feel so starved of Julian, the way he talks about life, books – all the extraordinary travel tales. I'm distracted, as Perry is talking, remembering one of Julian's whimsical stories about African tribesmen who gave male visitors, as a sign of approval, a cone-shaped basket hat for their dicks.

I try to concentrate more as Perry carries on. 'I've discovered a terrific Michelin-starred place just up the coast from the Channel Tunnel. It's a tiny hotel in the French style – hardly any rooms, just fabulous food.' He leaves a meaningful pause. 'I do need to see you.

I'm finding it so hard. Why not get a sitter next Friday and come down? It won't be heavy pressure, promise! I've got friends nearby who might join us. You can drive back afterwards if you must, but I'll book you a room in case. It might be wiser to stay over.'

'I'll think about it,' I say, knowing the friends wouldn't be free and it would be the full candle-lit flowing-wine seduction scene. If only I felt able to run to Julian. No one understands, not even my mother, the fear of getting emotionally dependent again so soon. If Julian wanted to marry me he would have said so, I'm sure of that.

He likes the travel, the freedom – if I hitched my star to his wagon I'd live in misery, desperate about what he was doing all the time. I can't ask what Val had thought the obvious question, what his plans are for after the book, I'm too scared of the answer.

Seeing a bit of Perry might help me build up some confidence. I do feel more on top with him, caring as little as I do. Then if I get a London job, meet people; get around a bit . . . Better than feeling all these emotional pulls and pangs when I'm still too bruised to think straight.

'Mum, I'm thinking of having a night away. Perry Maynard wants me to join him for dinner with friends down on the coast. He's going to be there on his way to France and would book me a hotel room. I can't quite decide. I doubt his wife will be around . . .'

'You'd like me to come and stay the night? I don't finish at the surgery till six.'

'It's next Friday. The girls have an after-school swimming lesson. I can drop them off at the Leisure Centre and I'm sure Susie would take over for me and have them till you come. Perhaps you could collect them from her house? But in any case I haven't quite decided. It's probably a bad idea. There is his wife – although I must say she doesn't seem to feature much on his radar.'

'He might have some interesting friends. You do need to start meeting a few new people, darling, and he did seem an extremely pleasant, considerate man. I think you're really quite attracted!'

My mother's being incorrigible, egging me on. I can hardly believe it. She speaks four languages and is no fool and yet is completely taken in. Perry did a brilliant con job.

Or am I just being horribly cynical and influenced by Julian's detestation? Suppose Perry's marriage is genuinely on the rocks? He could even have fallen for me – as he does keep saying. It happens. Not in his case. Who am I trying to kid?

There isn't much to lose. It's an hour and a half's drive, so no absolute need to stay over. I don't have to jump into bed with him and be ticked off his list. I can string him along, do just as the mood takes me . . .

My mother ends the call by saying a nice little break is exactly what I need, do me a power of good.

I call Susie about it. 'No probs,' she assures in a flat voice. 'I can be there by the end of swimming, but not any earlier, not to stay and watch. They'll be OK if it's a class, won't they, if I'm there by six? I've got some aromatherapy oils to deliver.'

'Sure. Thanks – that's great, Susie.' She's sounding down and it's easy to tell she's been crying. Her voice has a catch, a sort of jerky frailty and smallness that I've all too often heard in my own. 'Want to come round?' I suggest, feeling a surge, a great Mexican wave of sympathy for Susie – for a whole army of crying women. We're all in the same sinking boat.

'Just for a quick chat,' she says gratefully, 'before school comes out.'

There's only an hour left so I wouldn't have got much done. I make a pot of coffee and have a few minutes with the papers.

The Post has thick black headlines about the girl in the garden case. A body has been found in a canal, obviously hers. Clothes found, too. The mother's partner is now said to be helping the police with their inquiries.

It surely can't be him? Images from television pour into my head: the couple grieving, holding hands, his kind supportive way. He's a systems operator, educated; he couldn't sound more normal. Erica's dark hints and accusations about Julian are playing around in the corners of my mind. I want to scream and drive them out.

Who do I believe? Erica – or Julian? The fog seems to clear then, I know the answer, I'd entrust Julian with everything I hold dear.

I turn to *The Times* and read an article about the case saying the Internet has a lot to answer for. The piece is on the same page as the paper's diary column, whose lead item, I see curiously, is about Bill.

'William Osborne, budding TV star who moonlights as editor of *The Post*, is spitting venom about the NHS and A&E closures. He's not sparing his pen. "It's no good being taken to a state-of-the-art facility," he rants, "if you're dead by the time you get there. The Health Minister has to think again." And who should that knife-wielding closer of these units be? Why, none other than Victoria Osborne, his fragrant new bride.'

I turn back to *The Post* to find the story and it certainly is a rant. It must be hateful to read stuff like that. I never thought I'd have feelings of sympathy for Victoria, but the press don't win any prizes for moderation and Bill is worse than most. Did he and Victoria fight it out over the breakfast table? Did he dare to take home the first edition last night? Whatever can have made her go into politics? I must ask Tom.

Susie is here, getting out of her car looking trim and fresh in crisply laundered Bermudas. She's incapable of looking a mess. 'Hi! Sorry to do this to you,' she says as I take her through to the kitchen, 'I hate breaking into your day.'

'Don't be mad!' I exclaim, taking in her red-rimmed eyes as she pulls out a chair. 'Coffee? Here, have one of these brownies. Is it Phil?'

'It's the woman in the flower shop, the new owner.' Susie smiles wanly. 'I was so pleased when Phil came home with flowers the other night, but then we went on to the Jones's drinks party and I saw him curling his foot round hers. I wanted to rush home for the freesias and hurl them back in his face.'

Susie has a habit of pulling at her fingers and now it seems sadly symbolic, like trying to take off rings. 'You've got to live with it somehow, or leave,' I say. 'He's playing around, it doesn't mean much. He loves you – he's just being a stupid fool.' Phil's the womanizing equivalent of a small-time crook, I think, weak and self-ish as they come.

'I'd try making him jealous,' I smile. 'Leave your mobile at home sometime and send it a passionate text or two, even a voice message if he doesn't answer. He might think you're trying to reach him and have a look. And you could try putting down the phone in a hurry, just as he comes into the room.'

She's looking dubious. 'It's not that easy, Ursula.' Which is cer-tainly true. Sipping her coffee she looks up then with a game attempt at a smile. 'So who's your hot date next Friday?'

Susie loves Perry's flirting and flattery; she would, as Val said, be quite jealous. 'Only a friend of my mother's,' I say, trying to make the lie a white one. 'It's a dinner right down on the coast, that's why I'd have to get off early.'

It feels like cheating on Susie, I think, as I see her out – almost as bad as Phil. Oh, hell, I'm going to go, I may as well try to enjoy it. Perry is an attractive man.

The girls get home, Emma chatty, Jessie subdued. It can't last, can it, this lowness of Jessie's? Surely it's not just the bookshop job – is she minding about Julian on some other level?

They change out of school clothes and potter. Emma's in the kitchen with me, Jessie has disappeared outdoors.

I get a shock when she's suddenly at the open backdoor, panting, wide-eyed, looking terrified, really desperate. 'Mummy, Mum, come quick, please hurry and come, it's something awful. Elton's not right – he's just lying there.' She turns and runs.

Pulling my hands out of the sink where I was washing a lettuce, I grab a dishcloth and follow, running after her down the garden. Emma comes too, catching up behind.

Poor Elton, he's obviously dead. 'I'm sorry, Jess, darling,' I say, feeling agonized, my arm going round her shaking shoulders. 'He was very old for a guinea pig and he'd had such a good happy life.'

Jessie is distraught, sobbing and catching her breath in great big gulps. Elton was much loved by us all. I can feel my own tears pricking. I gather her up and we rock together, both crying. It's a very sad day.

We bury him in the vegetable patch and mark his grave with a little basket lined with lettuce leaves. Jessie puts in baby carrots and some roses on top. We say a few prayers and I give a tiny eulogy.

'Here lies Elton who will be very much missed. But he had a wonderful full long life and wouldn't want us to be grieving and shedding tears, only to remember the sunny joyful times.'

It's not going to work, suggesting getting another, even in the weeks ahead. Elton was irreplaceable.

I call and tell Bill the news. 'Elton's died.'

'Oh no! Oh dear. Can I talk to her?'

Jessie comes to the phone, silent, sullenly miserable. I watch her nodding a few times, saying nothing, then finally muttering, 'Yes, Dad,' and 'Bye.'

I take back the phone and, since Jess has gone out of the room, tell Bill I was going out on Friday, possibly away overnight, but that I'm worried about leaving Jessie in this wretchedly upset state. I do hate the thought of not being there for her when she's low.

Bill says she is eleven, after all, and that everyone's pets have to die. I sense his curiosity about my movements. Has he heard via Lauren that Julian has gone away?

CHAPTER 13

I wake early on Friday. It's mainly the heat. The day promises to be incredibly muggy and airless with thunderstorms forecast, which is predictable in the first week of Wimbledon, but Perry and heavy rain do seem to go hand in hand.

It's the usual headache getting the girls off to school. Jessie's dragging her heels, sulking and looking grumpy, and Emma won't stop whinging.

'Must we go to Susie's? Why can't we just be at home with Myrtle?'

They've no business acting up, I think, it's not as if I'm out every night. 'You know she works at the hospice, Emma – now where's Jessie gone, for heaven's sake! The bus will be here.' Going into the hall I stand yelling, 'Buck up, Jess!' then race upstairs in frustration. She's sitting on her bed holding a photo of Elton, and looking forlorn.

I go to her side, guilty. 'Would you like me to stay home, love? You've only to say.'

She ignores me for a moment then mutters, 'No, it's OK, Mum, you go. You want to.'

We hear Emma shrieking up from the hall, 'It's the bus! It's hooting like mad!'

Jess hesitates ominously then grabs her school bag and runs. I do too, chasing out after them to see them safely off.

Coming back in I remind myself that Jess was arguing with Emma at breakfast about who they'd rather meet, Justin Timberlake or Beyoncé. She'll be fine at school with her friends. But she is very down and in on herself and I do worry. It's nearly three weeks since Julian left Brearfield and she hasn't mentioned him once.

I've tried saying people have to cocoon themselves away when researching and writing books, but it gets me nowhere. It's hard talking about him, anyway, feeling so sensitive and sore myself.

I do miss him. Term's ending soon. It was this time last year, the start of the summer holidays, when Bill walked out. Will these holidays be any better?

Time seems curiously suspended as I go about the day. I get some work done, but with a feeling of hiatus like waiting for exam results or medical tests. And thoughts fill my head: Lauren leaving London for Cambridgeshire early on a Friday, hours before Henry. Julian meeting her at the station, driving her home in his fast car, rushing her upstairs . . .

I pack a small holdall: nightdress, clean pants, T-shirt and trousers, with almost a sense of dread. Staying the night feels a huge mistake. But I'm free, being taken out to dinner, branching out. It's all experience. He's not free, though. Don't I care about that?

By the time the girls get back I've walked Misty in readiness for leaving and dressed in a sheer, tea-dance style dress, blues and browns over a cream slip. Repainted my toenails too, and slung on a pair of strappy sandals. It's been bare-leg weather for weeks. The shoes are high, not ideal for driving in, but I'm in a mood for breaking out.

We have a quick turnaround tea with Jessie still being sullen and difficult. 'I don't want to swim, Mum. I'll just watch.'

'Don't be silly, you love swimming and it's so hot! Go and get your things, now. We must go.'

'She hated it at school, Mum,' Emma whispers when we're alone. 'People are going round saying Julian's, well, done something bad in the past . . . not to Jess's face. But then Zoë was bugging her about it today and they had a fight.'

Zoë's not in her immediate group of friends, I think, as my indignation boils. I'm about to ask Emma a whole load of questions, only Jessie's back with her things, towel hanging out of a canvas bag. Collecting my own little holdall, I hurry them out.

Emma's changed into a yellow and white halter-neck sundress; Jessie's in pink shorts and a T-shirt with a big blue heart on it that has 'Love' in shocking pink scrawled diagonally across it. Even with her sulky frowning face and stuck-out lower lip that's trembling slightly she's managing to look appealing. I scrunch them both up in an emotional hug.

The swimming pool, now called a leisure centre, is situated in the rougher end of town. But it is opposite a big expanse of playing fields and is a popular well-run amenity. I kiss the girls a last time, begging them to be good for Susie and sweet to their grandmother, then watch them run off into the changing rooms.

Driving away there's Wimbledon on the radio, good listening that gets me involved, until a sudden downpour inevitably stops play. It's still fine over Sussex and Kent, though, and in spite of half wishing I wasn't going, just being free of responsibilities and on a jaunt to the coast brings a light-hearted sense of release.

I think about Perry's wife with little guilt. Jane Maynard had seemed so coldly resigned, as though all his doings were beneath her and he could just get on with it – what did she care? I have an image of her flapping her hand at his cheating, more as with swatting midges away on a balmy night than slapping both sides of his face. I'd hate to feel that detached.

Guilt suddenly gets more of a hold and I feel shocked at myself. There's no excuse for what I'm doing, none at all. Victoria probably had much stronger and deeper feelings of guilt, I think, as she inevitably comes to mind. She was ditching one husband and taking mine, but at least there was real emotion. Should I be using lack of emotion as an excuse? Isn't that acting just like Phil or Perry?

I've been trying to force my thoughts off Julian, but it's no good. He can probably sense whom I'm on my way to see. It feels as if he's tracking my car, training a long lens, shining a light inside my head. It would kill any feelings of love for me stone dead. Is it defiance? Am I trying to spite him in some way? Self-destructiveness, like a moth to the candle flame, a fly to sticky paper? Or just plain despair?

He wants me to come running and say I love him, but there are so many loose ends. Lauren, who never leaves my mind, frissons about Julian's past – that's all Erica's mischief, but now the rumours are even percolating down to the children at school.

Perry calls to check my progress. I've reached Folkestone and found the coast road. As I drive along there are Regency houses, shops, modern blocks of flats all looking straight out over the Channel to France. I see Perry then, watching out for me. He's standing on the sea wall and flags me down, indicating I should park right across the road from the small hotel. It has a flat façade, centrally placed door and shuttered windows and looks like a child's drawing of a house.

The evocative smells, seaweed, the damp salty air, the sea's swell and vastness make me feel uplifted and exhilarated as Perry helps me out. 'I think it must be wonderful, overlooking the sea and hearing that sound all day,' I say, trying to avoid kisses and overpersonal greetings, 'like living on a very stable ship!'

It's a lost cause. Perry's arms come firmly round, clutching me close, his cheek against mine, his breath hotly fanning my hair. 'I can't believe you're here,' he murmurs. 'Couldn't wait to see you. You're the most wonderful thing to come into my life.'

Only since the last girl you snared, I think sardonically, amused – now that I'm attuned to it – by the typical patter and stock phraseology, the lack of sincerity. But he's still pressing my body close, nuzzling my neck and there's a physicality, a tangible sexuality that's hard to ignore. My body is feeling it. With the sound of the waves hard against their retaining wall, the tang, the sea's silvery sultriness and hidden dark deeps, it's an intoxicating package.

'Even on a calm humid night like this you can still feel the sea's threatening power,' I say elatedly, breaking away. 'Conrad called it the accomplice of human restlessness and that's just how I feel! Can we walk along the sea wall a bit? It's so hypnotic, that sound.'

Perry takes my shoulders and rubs noses. 'I'd rather be sharing a nice bottle of cold white wine! And I'm sure you'll want a little clean-up and they're sticklers for being on time, the food is the thing.'

I feel cheated, a lot keener on nearness to the sea than this big broad-shouldered man who wants my body. Then he's reaching into the car for my bag that I'd intended leaving there – at least for a while. I smile obligingly though, and dutifully give in, letting him take my hand and lead me firmly across the road and up the hotel steps.

The hotel's owners – an English couple just returned from

working in one of France's finest restaurants – make a big fawning fuss of him. He's obviously a regular customer.

'They're good at the buttering up,' he whispers on the stairs, having suggested I use the room to freshen up since it's booked and paid for, rather than the lady's loo. 'You'll like the charming decor, it's spriggy and light, very country-house.'

Seeing me into the room he hovers, ominously. He needn't think he's staying while I pee and wash. I ask pertly, knowing the answer, 'Is anyone joining us? Those friends you mentioned?'

'I had no intention of sharing you! I've lived for tonight, thought of nothing else.' He pulls me tight to his chest and touches my hair. 'I still can't believe all this silky wonderful blondeness.' Lifting it away he murmurs sexily into my ear, 'I long to be exploring and discovering more of you. Blonde pubes do it for me, there's nothing more turning on.'

Something goes click in my head. Those are not the words of a man in the grip of a great love, who's found the woman to rock his marriage. They're jarring and cheap, but they've just unlocked a door, the only trigger needed. A truth, a simple understanding, can lie hidden for ever; the greatest minds can stumble unseeing along emotional paths, missing neon-lit signs. I was only seeing shallowness, but now – perhaps with the help of the powerful sea outside – I've grasped a reality, a single deep truth.

'You go on downstairs, Perry, I'll be right there.' I smile warmly, pushing him out, feeling perfectly able to hide the gut loathing that's suddenly crawling all over my skin. Then closing the door firmly, hugging myself with crossed arms, I can't help a great smile from spreading all over my face, can't help the shooting shivers, my fast-beating heart.

It's easy. I love Julian. I'll suffer sharing him with Lauren if I have to, I'll cope with his comings and goings, any wrongdoing in his past. I've loved him since the day of his father's funeral. I felt numbness for Bill after that. Having seen the way once, I lost it and have been blindly digging my own holes and falling deeper in them ever since.

Funny it should take a lying ruthless bastard, devoid of decency and normal feelings, a king of the sewer to light the way. I will go downstairs, have a drink, smile and walk out. It will be dinner for one. Perry alone. And when I'm out of range of his radar, I'll stop the car and call Julian. Will he have turned to Lauren in despair or will he give me a second chance?

'You use this place quite often?' I inquire when we're sitting down, omitting to add 'for this sort of thing', but with a look and tone that imply it. I sip my Chablis glancing round, taking in the safe, cherry-coloured loose covers, repro side-tables, seascapes, copies of *Country Life* and *The Field*. Bringing my eyes back I give him another teasing smile.

Perry is opposite, on a small sofa, his legs stretched out, and answers a bit edgily, 'Sure. It's great food, handy for trips to France.' Snapping himself more upright, he pats the spare space. 'Come over here. You can't keep giving me looks like that. It's making me quite desperate!'

My mobile starts ringing in my bag. It's only just after seven; is it one of the girls, playing up and being difficult? My mother can't have got there yet and wouldn't Susie just cope? A fluttering of nerves starts up. I get to the phone in time and see with a pang of more active fear that it's Val calling. Why? She knows what I'm doing – doesn't entirely approve, but would never think of intruding without good cause.

'Ursula, you must come back immediately. It's desperately serious. Jessie's gone missing from the baths. We've searched everywhere, covered everything. The police have just arrived.'

My chest starts heaving and pounding, it feels strapped round with pain. My stomach goes concave, gripped by an icy hand. 'She can't have. From the baths? Oh God. Tell me this isn't happening. She must be somewhere – could she have run home?' There has to be an explanation, I think wildly, struggling up out of the small low armchair. Images of horror are forming so fast I can't black them out.

Grabbing my handbag I keep talking, 'Val, Val, I'm on my way – keep hanging on, keep on the phone can you, till I'm in the car.' Making for the door my legs feel weak. Cold sweat is breaking out and an uncontrollable attack of shivers.

Perry grips my arm, restraining me before I can get to the hall. 'Calm down, now. Don't get hysterical. Is it one of your daughters playing up? It'll sort itself, I'm sure. Leave it to the people on the spot. There's nothing you can do. Much the best, just relax.'

As he tries to pull me close I wrench free, 'She's missing, you idiot, let me go, you bastard. Fuck off – get out of my sight.'

I'm both seeing and blind to the one or two people drawn towards the commotion and go racing out of the main entrance and down the steps, still half hearing the sea. Crossing the road I cause a van to swerve and I fumble desperately for my key to the continuous sound of a furious horn. Finding it, flashing it at the car, I jump in still clutching my mobile, pull out and roar away.

'Val, are you still there? I'm in the car; I can talk. Is my mother there yet? Have you called Jessie's mobile? I could do it now.'

'Her mobile's here with her swimming things; all her things are. She's got nothing with her. Your mother's not here yet. She's had a puncture. The police have just arrived and need to speak to me. They'll want to call you in a minute so keep your phone clear.'

'Where are you? At Susie's, at the house?'

'No, still at the baths. Susie's had to go home to make arrangements so she can be on hand to help. I'm going back to your house soon, with Emma and the police. We've told your mother to come there when she's on the road again – and also not to call you yet, to keep your phone free. I must go, now.'

The sobs come, howling tears; I'm pushing the car, scorching up the motorway. I come to roadworks and have to slow to a crawl. It starts raining, pouring down.

No one's calling. I can't stand it, can't live with the thoughts in my head. She could have gone home. It's five miles; she could have walked. Who might she have met? Anyone could have accosted her. Oh, God.

I need Julian. I've got to speak to him. The police can wait.

CHAPTER 14

'Ursula?'

'Julian, thank God, you're there! I need you desperately. Jessie's missing. I'm sure the police are doing all they can, but,' I'm gulping back sobs, 'there's no sign. Susie was picking them up from swimming this afternoon and Jessie was nowhere, she'd just vanished, completely disappeared. They've been searching since six. I need you to help, tell me what to do, stop me losing control. It's unbearable. I was somewhere quite far away – if only I hadn't been – and still not home. Driving back as fast as I can.'

'What does Emma say happened? She was there, wasn't she? You said them.'

'Yes, but in different classes. Jess hadn't even got changed; her swimming things were still in her bag, Val said, and her mobile. She hadn't wanted to swim, because of some trouble at school, I think, and must have quietly skipped out. I can't imagine her doing that, they know not to. Or really to believe she ran home, it's at least five miles and not even her mobile with her . . .

'I'm sick with fear, Julian. Jessie's got to be somewhere; she has to be. Help me, please, you must, it's so hard to cope.' But what can he do? I think. And if only the rain would stop, I can hardly see the road for the rain and my heaving sobs.

'For God's sake, take care,' he's calling. 'You're not holding that phone and driving, are you – it is hands-free?'

'Yes, yes. Can you come to Brearfield, just jump in your car? It's a lot to ask, but I need you to, Julian. You might think of something, some clue. I'm so frightened. It's too awful to imagine what could have happened.'

'Jessie rang me at lunchtime today . . .'

Hearing that gives me a jolt like jamming on brakes. 'Why – what about? You actually spoke to her?' It's such a surprise, my heart's thudding louder than ever. 'What did she say?' I demand. 'Tell me quick. Was she thanking you for that book?'

Was it to do with the school rumours, I wonder, the fight with Zoë? Had Jess wanted him to know?

'She told me about Elton dying and was starting to say something about a friend being mean – about me, I think, they pick up fag ends – but a bell rang for class and she had to go.'

'Oh, Julian.' I'm crying again, can't keep hold.

'It's been so hot,' he says thoughtfully, as though his mind's running ahead, not wasting time on shocked sympathetic words, 'hardly a day to be making a stand about swimming. She might just have gone outside for some air. Possibly talked to some-one . . .'

He's pondering, sounding vague when I'm desperate for action. 'Can't you get going?' I plead urgently. 'Please, it's Jessie's life that's at stake . . . I must keep the phone clear for the police now. Tell me you'll come, that you'll do it for me?' It strikes me then that the police will probably want to interview him. Erica's falsehoods will surface like flotsam and clog things up, waste police time. There's no point in mentioning it, though.

'You've spoken to William? Is he on his way?' Julian asks.

With a shock it dawns on me that I haven't. I'd needed to call Julian, before anyone, even before Bill, Jessie's own father. 'Not yet,' I mumble, my voice low with shame. 'I just had to talk to you.'

'The police will have got in touch with him. Ursula, listen. Take this in. I'm trying hard to think of all the things Jessie's ever said — to me, to people who came in the shop. There's a tiny niggling thought at the back of my head. It might become clearer, I might think how to act on it. It could come to nothing. I don't want to raise your hopes. Whatever else, just remember that I'll be doing my all. You speak to the police now, and keep strong.'

He clicks off then. I hate the abrupt sound, to be losing contact, but he's going to help, do his best, Julian will find her . . . My mobile's ringing again; I was hardly hearing it.

The hands-free system clicks in, the voice coming through sounds loud and strange. 'This is Detective Chief Inspector Mark Gibson. Am I speaking to Mrs Osborne?'

'Yes, yes, that's me. Is there any news?' Terror rises in my throat. From his tone there seems no hope that she's found.

'Nothing to report yet. Do rest assured, though, we're doing all we can. I know how hard it is, but you must try to stay calm. Ninety per cent of times children are found quite safe and well.' There's a pause before Gibson goes on, 'I've just been speaking to your ex-husband. He actually hadn't heard yet that Jessie was missing.'

There is a hint of reproof in his voice, a critical edge. This Chief Inspector rightly thinks a father deserves to be told. 'I filled him in as best I could, but I'd called on his mobile and he was worried you might be trying to get through. I also had to try to explain . . .' the Chief Inspector pauses again, '. . . that at least for the first few hours, any media coverage would be best avoided. Interest in this case would be intense, given who Mr Osborne is now married to, and it could be counterproductive. It's a different situation if things drag on – but I'm sure she'll be found very quickly and all will be well.'

'Tell me she will be,' I plead desperately, knowing he can't and would never give false hope. There's a moment of painful silence, shared acknowledgement of that fact.

He clears his throat. 'Um, Mr Osborne said he was leaving immediately, driving straight to your house. And we've contacted your son Tom, who'll also soon be on his way. I've checked that your mother's puncture is being seen to, that's all in hand.'

'Tell me what's happening, that people are searching – you have got a good photograph of Jess? Val – Mrs Stockton – would help with things like that, I'm sure.'

'Yes, she has, she's been extremely helpful. We've a very full description, clothes, everything. A special CID incident room has been set up at the force headquarters in Lewes and a large number of uniformed officers are working out of Brearfield, doing door-to-door interviews and searches. You must try not to worry.

'I'm at your house. Your daughter, Emma, and Mrs Stockton are here, too, and Detective Inspector Jamison who is assisting me. And there will be a family liaison officer on hand to give all the help and support she can. Now I do have a few quick questions, if you wouldn't mind?'

'Please – ask anything at all.'

'Would you say Jessie had been acting at all out of character recently? It is often a strong indicator of risk. And I will need to ask when we meet, I'm afraid, about any family or personal problems, even such things as abuse. You mustn't hold back.'

I tell him about Jessie's difficult day at school and her reluctance to swim. I ask in turn a host of questions and discover that as well as the Leisure Centre and all nearby properties, a thorough search has already been made of the house. There was no sign of my beloved Jessie, not in the garden, not at any friend's home, not anywhere. Oh, please God, let her be found.

'There's just one thing more, Mrs Osborne . . .' I stiffen, the Chief Inspector's tone has a slight edge. 'I was trying to reach you earlier. Your phone was busy rather a long time.'

'Yes, I was speaking to a close friend, Julian Bridgewater. He's moved away recently, but had the antiquarian bookshop in Brearfield and knows Jessie well. I was asking him to come back and help.'

'Can I check we have the right mobile number for him? We are having difficulty reaching him and we're anxious to have a word. His name has kept coming up as we've been talking to people – other parents, Jessie's friends, girls in her swimming class . . .'

'You're not, surely, suggesting there's anything suspicious in that?' I demand frostily. 'He's a very good friend of mine, of the whole family. He lives near Cambridge now, I was just speaking to him there. The reason you've been hearing his name is because one of the parents at school, Erica Barkston, took exception to Jessie helping in his bookshop on Saturday mornings. She's been making her views well known,' I say emphatically, with sarcasm. 'It's ridiculous. My ex-husband knew about it; he saw no objection. We were both pleased, in fact. Jessie is bright, a great lover of books, and Mr Bridgewater was wonderful at encouraging and stretching her. She wasn't paid or any-thing and learning so much – all about the antiquarian book trade.'

My voice is cracking up. The Chief Inspector waits patiently for me to regain control.

'We'll be interviewing Mr Bridgewater's ex-assistant, Roy Bishop,' he carries on then, 'although it seems he's had to go to a relation's funeral in Cardiff. We're following that up.'

'There is one thing,' I say cautiously. 'Mr Bridgewater said Jessie called him at lunchtime today. He's been sending her books and . . .'

'Are you sure he said today? We've checked her mobile and she'd made no calls from it in the last twenty-four hours.'

A quiver runs through me, a tightening of the gut. 'She must have deleted the number,' I say, feeling both defensive and disbelieving. 'Isn't there a way to check deleted numbers? Mr Bridgewater said she talked about a school friend being mean and that only just happened today. She must have called, he couldn't have known, otherwise.'

That clinches it for me. I feel better. We end the call with the Chief Inspector taking Julian's mobile number and inquiring after the owners of the house in Cambridgeshire. I tell him they are called Henry and Lauren Pearson.

Soon I'm turning off the motorway and on the familiar roads close to home. There's a blockage in my throat, I'm finding it hard to swallow. Slowing right down as I drive through Brearfield my foot's hovering over the brake. I'm scanning pavements, doorways, peering up paths – willing Jessie to come running out, waving at the car.

There are few people about although it's a hot night and still light. She has got to be somewhere, there has to be a rational explanation. I must stay convinced she's unharmed. Julian will think of something, there'll be a solution over the mobile call. He'll help find my darling sweet bright Jessie, he's got to.

I can't think sensibly. The most sickening horrifying images are looming, pressing and presenting themselves like ghoulish faces in a fairground hall of horrors. Reaching home I turn in the gates, straining to see round shrubs and bushes on the sides of the drive. No Jessie hiding, no sign. There is a tidily parked police car, an unmarked one, and Val's car, too. No family cars yet. Bill can't be very far away.

My legs nearly buckle climbing out, after driving hard with such tension I stumble in my heels and fall against the car. The unsuitable shoes prey on me, I can't wait to get them off and feel sick with self-recrimination and loathing of Perry. If I hadn't gone, hadn't been so blind; it's an unendurable living nightmare.

The front door opens and Emma comes running. Poor darling, what she must have been through. I should have phoned, thought more; I couldn't feel worse. 'Darling Ems, come here quick. If only I hadn't gone, if only – have you kept strong? We've got to get through this together.'

Her face is wet with crying. Wrapping her up, keeping her tightly held, I can feel every shudder of her thin shaking shoulders as she sheds more tears, every rib, every beat of her thudding heart and mine.

We go indoors with my arm still tight round her. 'I only said she was stupid, not wanting to swim, Mum, we didn't have a real fight. She just lost it and shlumped off out of the changing room, all huffy,' Emma tells me, sniffing loudly. 'I had my lesson to go to and didn't think any more about it. No one had taken much notice. And now they all say how they thought Jess hadn't come. She did go to Beth's once; remember? I've been swimming on my own before. I feel so bad, Mum, I can't live with myself – they will find her, won't they? She will be all right?'

'We can only all keep hoping and praying. You can't possibly start blaming yourself in any way.' It's not Emma's fault; it's mine alone. I could have stayed for swimming and gone later. 'You must be exhausted, Ems,' I say, feeling overcome, lifting the hair away from her agonized eyes. 'We must get you to bed. Have you had anything to eat?'

'I couldn't get her to have much,' Val says. She's standing in the kitchen door, looking tiredly, gently compassionate. I stare at her and break down again, with despairing moans, covering my face with both hands. Emma hugs my middle, Val's arms come round too, and with an effort I pull myself together. 'Perhaps I should take Ems home to stay with us,' Val says kindly. 'You're going to be very busy with the police.'

The poor child looks whiter still and so alarmed that Val touches her cheek. 'No,' she smiles, 'better if you stay right here, I think, close to Mum. Come upstairs now, though, and let her meet Chief Inspector Gibson. Then I know she'll be up to say goodnight.'

A middle-height man with combed-forward brown hair comes out of the sitting room, perhaps hearing his name. 'Sleep would be a very good thing, Emma,' he says. 'We'll pray there's good news in the morning.' He's smiling and her face lights up; she's comfortable with him, I think, they've got to be friends.

Val leads her to the stairs and I call after them with a promise to be up as soon as I can. Turning back to Chief Inspector Gibson, his expression is neutral although not unfriendly.

'Good to meet you, Mrs Osborne. We do need to talk, but I think before anything else, you should have a large cup of hot sweet tea.'

We shake hands. His intelligent eyes are a comfort. And there's a quiet unassuming reticence about him that appeals. But is that a good thing? Shouldn't he be more proactive? And in his late thirties he seems young. Promoted fast, I think distractedly, craving reassurance. I can't bear feeling so helpless, just standing here, taking no positive action.

What can I do, though? Much as I'm bursting to rush out combing the streets, calling out Jessie's name, my head is urging me to trust this man. After all, who can I trust if not the police? Who would I turn to?

I meet the family liaison officer, Mary, a tall girl in her late twenties. She has a serene face, short, thick fair hair, broad high cheekbones. Her hands, I notice, are capably large. She's been busy in the kitchen and has tea and coffee ready, biscuits and slices of cheese.

'I'm sure you won't have eaten for hours,' she insists, 'and food helps you stay alert and sharp. Remembering odd incidents and chance remarks could be vital.'

'The tea's a lifesaver,' I say, taking grateful sips, starting to cry again then, thinking it's Jessie's life in need of saving, not mine.

Neither Mary nor the Chief Inspector fusses over me. After a time he says, 'There are one or two things I should ask rather urgently. Ideally before your family arrive.'

In the sitting room a small square table has been erected. It has a laptop, various papers. The man sitting at it gets up the moment we come in and holds out a bony hand. 'Roger Jamison.' He's a tall, lean, wiry sort with hollowed-out cheeks, but his handshake is firm and warm.

'Thanks for all you're doing,' I say awkwardly, my thoughts scattering. The Chief Inspector clearly wants to get on and goes to an upright chair, angling it to face me as I sit down uneasily on the nearby sofa formulating plenty of queries of my own.

Gibson is looking at me thoughtfully. 'First of all, I want you to remember that all the while I'm asking personal questions that may seem unrelated, the incident room is very actively engaged. There's a huge team working on the ground, talking to residents, locating passers-by, doing checks, issuing an all-ports watch — that's airports too, of course. There is some CCTV footage from the Leisure Centre I could show you shortly. Unfortunately it's of little help, although it does establish that Jessie went outside.'

'I do want to see it,' I say. He acknowledges that, still carrying on his flow, watching me with concentrating eyes.

'There was no answer from Mr Bridgewater's mobile, incidentally,' he says. 'I've been calling it at regular intervals. You said he was a good friend of the family, close to Jessie. You've been quite involved with him, haven't you, since your divorce? Is it true you broke off the relationship recently and that was the reason he went away?'

'No, it was rather the reverse. I didn't want him to go. But I was in a mixed-up state and Julian felt, I think, that by going away, shutting himself up and writing a book, it might give me time to work things out.'

The Chief Inspector leaves it at that, although I have a sense he'll be returning to Julian before long. 'And Mr Osborne — how are things there? You get on all right since the divorce, no problems over access, no great tension between you?'

I shake my head mutely then answer, 'No, nothing like that, we've worked it out, we're fine.'

'Was there any awkwardness between him and Mr Bridgewater?'

'None. They met in a neighbourly way from time to time. Julian even mentioned the other day that they'd been at the same dinner party in London.' My mind leaps back to Gibson's starting point.

'Chief Inspector, I can't believe he isn't answering his mobile. Could I just give it a try?'

'By all means.' I get up and go to the phone on a side table. An automated message informs me that the person I'm calling is not available. I leave word that I'm anxious and could Julian hurry and return the call.

'I can't understand it,' I say defensively, returning to my seat, feeling cowed by the impassive gazes of the two senior detectives in the room. 'I expect he's on his way here, concentrating on the driving. He has a fast car. I must go up to Emma now, if you don't mind, and say a quick goodnight.'

'Of course. She's had a very stressful time. We've had to ask a lot of questions. But before you do, Mrs Osborne . . . There is one thing. You see Mr Bridgewater isn't, in fact, in his car. Two officers from our Huntingdon headquarters have called at Mr and Mrs Pearson's house and his car is still there, parked right in front of the garage. It's a Porsche, isn't it? He was nowhere to be found, though. They've searched all over, and the surrounding area. Mr Bridgewater is clearly living there; reference books were scattered, his computer on – and we've done a check on the call you made to him; he was in the vicinity of Cambridge at the time.'

I stare at the mild-faced Chief Inspector, getting no feel for what's going on in his mind. He's implying suspicious circumstances, but not emphatically, and his eyes have no triumphal accusatory glare.

I'm feeling frightened; it's the kind of darting fear like hearing strange unnerving noises in the night. For all my jangling nerves, though, I can't feel any real genuine mistrust. Talking to Julian earlier, there hadn't been a single discordant note. I was frustrated that he hadn't been in a greater rush to leave. Hearing Jessie had called, too, had come as a shock and surprise – although if she'd been feeling got at, it was the sort of thing she might do. But those were pinpricks. Making contact with Julian had been an incredible relief, I'd felt less alone, the pit of my despair less bottomless. I'd known with absolute certainty there was nothing he wouldn't do.

And yet, and yet . . . The fact that he was not in his car has shaken me. It's unnerving, impossible to understand.

Conscious, suddenly, of staring blankly at the Chief Inspector, I scramble to my feet in embarrassment and head for the door.

'Of course Mr Bridgewater wouldn't have used his car if he hadn't wanted to be found,' Gibson says ruminatively, causing me to stop dead and spin facing him again. 'We can track cars quite easily out on the road – and it would be another reason, too, for his mobile being switched off . . .'

My hand is on the door-handle. 'There'll be a perfectly rational explanation for it all,' I say unfazed, staring the man squarely in the eye. 'I'm convinced of that.'

Val comes out of Emma's door with a finger to her lips. 'She's practically asleep, we've been saying a few little prayers. No news, I suppose? You're looking particularly tense – is there some new problem?'

'They seem to be trying to implicate Julian,' I whisper. 'It's got me even more upset, but I suppose they're just doing their job. You must go home now, Val. I won't ever be able to say how grateful I am.'

'They have to think of all the angles. I'd stay, but the liaison officer, Mary, is very sympathetic; she's been up being sweet to Emma. Make use of her, won't you – and call me any time at all, whatever time of night. I'll do anything you want.'

I hug her emotionally, feeling the wrench of parting, and watch her go out of the door.

Emma's eyelids are drooping. 'They'll find Jessie, Mum? I'll never have any fights again.' I kiss her softly, draw her curtains more tightly closed and when I'm sure she's asleep, slip away.

Crossing to my own room to kick off the offending heels and change into jeans I have a mind's-eye flash of the sight of my small holdall. Perry had deposited it on a chair just inside that hotel bedroom door. It's probably still sitting there. I try to expunge all thoughts of him, but even with every fibre, every crevice of my brain focussed on Jess, it's not so easy.

He might call by with the excuse of returning the bag, could even try to pick up where he left off. Surely he would have sensed my revulsion. More likely, with his soaring self-regard, he will have simply put it down to hysteria. I feel sick at the thought of ever having to set eyes on him again. He's so bound up with this nightmare.

There's a car arriving, parking with slow caution. My mother, I think, and run downstairs.

She comes in looking as grey and haggard as though pulled from the rubble of a disaster. I feel overwhelmed with anguish. It brings a sense of the accumulated guilt of years, all the irascible self-centred outbursts, my intolerance and lack of understanding.

'I need you, Mum,' I cry, enveloping her as tightly as I had Emma. 'I love you. I just want Jessie back safe and sound.'

CHAPTER 15

Bill has just arrived and is in with Detective Chief Inspector Gibson. He'll be a difficult interviewee, antagonistic, demanding action and throwing his weight around just as he does at *The Post*. He's that sort of editor. I'm sure, though, Gibson will stay quietly in charge.

I'm in the kitchen with my mother and the solicitous liaison officer, Mary. 'There's always hope, some unexpected lead,' Mary says, trying her best, but I feel at snapping point, like a dry brittle twig, and kind, well-meaning words are somehow making it worse. 'There could be a breakthrough at any time,' she adds.

'And if there isn't?' I mutter bitterly, pacing up and down on the fired-earth tiles, hoping she hasn't heard.

She beams her seraphic smile at me, although, sensing a brick wall, smoothly transfers it to my mother. They're both at the kitchen table with cups of tea.

My mother returns the smile, then looks over to me and lifting her voice says wretchedly, 'If only I'd taken an afternoon off from the surgery. I so much wanted you to have a nice little break, darling. If only I'd come earlier and been there for the girls.'

She's looking revived, for all the pain and misery; her face has a faint pastel-wash of colour and her tired veined hands clasping the mug look less clawed. That's Mary's doing, suggesting a shot of brandy in her tea.

I stop pacing and lean against the sink, crossing and uncrossing my arms. 'Don't go on about "if only", Mum, and for heaven's sake don't start blaming yourself. You can't take it on your own shoulders; the failings are all mine. The buck,' I say, pummelling my chest, releasing pent-up stress, 'stops here. I should never have gone, or at the very least I should have told Jessie's swimming teacher to keep an eye. But how could that woman just *assume* Jess hadn't come, she could so easily have checked with Emma.'

I feel racked with vengeful thoughts, but then turning away screw up my face in private agony. It's not the teacher, not my mother; it's me. I'm the one, the selfish, useless, irresponsible mother who's paying a cruel price.

Standing gripping the sink, head bent, I slowly calm down, and turn back to face the two women. My eyes flick to the kitchen clock yet again. 'It's ten o'clock. Nearly five hours since she went missing.'

'They're doing everything possible,' Mary says, in her reassuring way. 'The DCI and Inspector Jamison are senior investigating officers, they know their job. Come and sit down and conserve your energy. There's plenty of tea still in the pot.'

'No more tea, thanks.' I can't smile, and pulling out a chair, sit down well away from the table. Space, a bit of distance, feels shielding, like a protective husk or shell encasing my private torment. There's a kernel of greater terror deep within, that's telling me with certainty, with Julian-type telepathy, that Jess is in critical danger. Every second is a ticking time bomb. If she isn't found soon . . . There's a whole long menacing night ahead. Please God, let her be found.

'I hope the Chief Inspector isn't feeling too put-upon.' My mother's voice sounds high and reedy. 'William's had such a go at the police, these last few days, in the paper with all those dreadful statistics . . .' She looks down at her mug then, in embarrassed confusion, probably remembering that Mary is a policewoman, herself.

It's the brandy, I know, but my mother does have a knack of making crass, wrong-note remarks in times of stress. 'No one's going to be thinking like that, Mum,' I say curtly, instantly regretting being brusque. 'We just want Jessie back.' I get up and walk about again, feeling blind impatience for Bill's interview to be over, to be seeing the CCTV frames, to have a heart-rending glimpse of Jess. It's driving me mad, being out here, not knowing what's going on.

'The police always show enormous caution with the press,' Mary remarks, her sweet smile aimed at Barbara in a show of solidarity. 'In a situation like this things get separated, the DCI will be seeing Mr Osborne only as the father. He's got children of his own.'

I stare past her. Gibson will be telling Bill the things that don't add up, the strange inconsistencies surrounding Julian – whom Bill has had nothing against. Our relationship has never been an issue; he felt confident, rightly, that Julian and I hadn't had an affair in the past, and accused me only of remoteness over my part in our flaky marriage. He held his job most to blame. And then there was Victoria and all his guilt over that.

The Chief Inspector's suspicions will play on Bill's paternal jealousy, I'm sure. He'll start wondering if all the while Jessie had been the lure. He may look shocked and say, 'Surely not,' even think it for a bit, but the mistrust will be invasive and take hold like a cancer. And no one is swifter than Bill to lay blame. God, it's so cruelly unfair.

A tall thin shadow appears at the door. Detective Inspector Jamison catches my eye. 'Would you like to come back in now, Mrs Osborne? And Mary, could you and Mrs Sinclair, perhaps, wait here a little longer?'

'We'll make some sandwiches,' Mary offers, beaming at my mother. 'They're always very welcome.'

Jamison closes the door and returns to his table. I hesitate a moment, taking things in.

Bill is by the fireplace looking gaunt, grey with the strain. Our eyes meet in shared agony. His have the watchful wariness of a jungle animal; he's ready to pounce, to accuse, to fight to the death for his daughter.

He comes straight over then, giving me a spontaneous hug in the way of two men gripping each other in a brief show of emotion. I understand his need and appreciate it, she's our own beloved Jess, our precious bright solemn youngest child.

'Are you coping, holding up?' Bill touches my face. 'She's got to be all right, got to be found.' Taking hold of my shoulders then, he stares with frightening intensity. 'Ursula, look . . .' He's sounding awkward; it puts me on my guard. 'You've got to try and be completely objective. There's something going on here; you can't shut your mind to it, however unimaginable. Julian is implicated in this, for whatever reason, you must see that? You can't let any . . . *feelings* get in the way.'

I snap free of him, riven with resentment. 'What are you hinting at, Bill? You can't seriously believe, you're not trying to suggest . . .' I'm battling against tears, but struggle on. 'I talked to Julian this very evening, he's coming back to Brearfield, doing all he possibly can.'

Turning then to include and appeal to Gibson, I go on, 'Julian is the most honourable man that could be, so good with Jessie and Emma – and Tom, giving him lifts to London. I'm sure Val Stockton vouched for him, Chief Inspector. She would have said how decent he is, how intelligent and kind.'

'Intelligence is irrelevant.' Bill's anger is gathering, the fight coming out. 'As you very well know. And while we're at it,' he goes on, his lips taut, 'why have you never mentioned all the gossip about Jessie helping at the bookshop?' He's staring with hooded demanding eyes.

I should have done, Bill knows what Erica's like. He would have dismissed it as small-town bitchy silliness – but not now. 'Erica Barkston deserves locking up,' I shoot back, still struggling with tears. 'It was a joke, the way she snooped and spied. Julian knew about it and certainly thought so. It helped him decide on the subject for his biography – the book he's working on.'

Bill looks about to have another go, but Chief Inspector Gibson politely intervenes. 'Perhaps, if you'd both come and sit down? There are things I still need to ask.'

'And remind her about his car,' Bill says to Gibson while glaring at me. He widens his attack. 'You have, of course, been on to every possible car-hire and taxi firm I take it?'

It's possible to detect a flicker of impatience in the Chief Inspector's eyes, just a blink, but he answers evenly. 'I can assure you, Sir, all possible avenues of inquiry are being actively explored.' Standing by his upright chair, he obeys his own instructions and sits down.

'I must see the CCTV footage, Chief Inspector,' I say impatiently, also sitting down. Bill goes to the sofa opposite. He'll have seen it already, I think, he would have insisted.

'Of course, we'll put it on now,' Gibson says. 'Fortunately it's one of the more up-to-date CCTV systems so we've downloaded it on to a DVD.'

He glances at Inspector Jamison, who goes wordlessly to the player, and after a few seconds of jumping lines a picture comes into view. The sight of Jessie coming out of the main Leisure Centre doors, of them swinging shut behind her, causes indescribable pain.

I sit forward tensely. Jessie's head is turned, her attention caught. 'It looks like she's seen someone who was – or was choosing to be – just off camera,' the Chief Inspector comments. 'The playing fields are covered, a wide arc, but not the street to that side. You can see she runs down the steps quite purposefully, as though towards someone. There's a warren of streets and lanes, residential properties and a big housing estate that way, before the open country.

'If we rewind a bit,' he says, which Jamison attends to, 'you'll see her hand was raised. It looks as if she's giving a cautious wave; possibly just a backhanded wipe at her brow, though, on a hot day. Or she was brushing at a wisp of hair – it's hard to be sure.'

'She wouldn't have been waving to anyone she didn't know,' Bill says, with hurtful point-proving emphasis. Turning to him ready to argue, though, I get caught, held like a rabbit in the path of his gleaming persuasive eyes and have to look quickly, furiously, away.

I can't speak. It's the emotional shock of seeing my darling Jessie alive, seeing her in her shorts and trainers, in the T-shirt with its big heart motif saying 'Love'. Silent tears start pouring down my face. Neither Bill nor the Chief Inspector try to give comfort. I'm grateful for that.

It takes a while to regain some composure, discover my bag, dig for a tissue and be capable of replying to Bill.

'But if it was someone she knew very well,' I maintain, imagining how she would have greeted Julian – the clear implication of Bill's accusatory remark, 'she would have been waving much more energetically and had more of a recognizing smile.'

'Not necessarily,' he says, glaring. Bill never gives in, never sees another side. 'You're forgetting her changing-room tiff with Emma, the row with the girl at school. She would have been in quite a sulk, as only Jessie can.'

Jamison holds out a phone to the Chief Inspector, who gets up and takes the call, walking back and forth. Bill and I wait in silence, avoiding further glances.

Returning to his chair Gibson says, 'We're having difficulty in raising Mr or Mrs Pearson. Someone in Mr Pearson's barristers' chambers thinks they were going to a film, which would explain both their mobiles being off.' He looks directly over to me. 'It seems likely they kept a car at their Cambridgeshire house. Do you know, Mrs Osborne, if that's so – did you see one in the garage, possibly, the time you went to stay?'

'But surely you said Julian's car was parked right in front of the garage?'

'Yes, he would have had to repark it, had he taken out the Pearsons' car. That put us off the scent for a bit, but looking again at the registration numbers of the Pearsons' cars I see one of their vehicles is very old. I'm sure it would have been left at the house.'

I mind Gibson's talk of being put off the scent, but his manner is never accusing, he simply makes mild statements of fact. And I had seen a car.

'They do keep one there,' I mutter, remembering Henry proudly showing me his ancient Ford the morning of the overheard conversation. 'But, of course, it needn't always live there. Either of them could have taken it to London; it's obviously roadworthy.'

I can't bear all this finger-pointing. It's making me more trusting of Julian than ever, but it's still insidiously, systematically wearing me down.

'Ursula, you must accept how black this is . . .' Bill begins saying, but Gibson raises a restraining hand. He's not having a dominating editor run the show.

A thought comes to me. 'There was my phone call to Mr Bridgewater, Chief Inspector, his mobile had been on then. Why have it on at all if he was about to go to ground and incriminate himself? And why would he have told me Jessie had called if she hadn't? It simply doesn't make sense.' I feel on stronger ground and meet Bill's eyes. How can he not keep more of an open mind? He knows Julian. Is that what journalism does, black in the shades of grey?

Gibson leans forward, spreading out his hands on his knees. 'I do assure you I'm making no assumptions at all, Mrs Osborne, in what I'm about to say.' He sits up straighter and looks at me levelly. 'Believe me, this is pure surmise on my part – simply a possible answer to your question.' His eyes are sympathetic. 'But Mr Bridgewater could, you see, have been expecting a call other than yours. You hadn't been in contact for quite a while, as I understand it, and your phoning him might have caught him unawares.'

'And the call from Jessie?' I stare back with a trembling lip.

'Well, suppose you had surprised him; it might have just come into his mind to say he'd heard from her. Suppose he was fearful of letting slip something your daughter had just told him. Always assuming, that is, he had just seen her, or picked her up from the baths . . .'

The silence that descends on the room is like a great smothering blanket. I'm imagining everyone's thoughts, they're pressing down on me, and the pain of my need for Jessie is acute.

It can't be true. I long for Julian, to be able to turn to him. Nothing, no one can really dent my trust. I won't let them. He's out looking for her, he promised to do his utmost. He hadn't got her with him, he was so natural when we talked, truthful. But then why is his mobile off, why is he out of contact? The tension is unbearable.

Bill speaks first, trying to be helpful, I think, and inject a more workman-like practical note – even to make amends for such focussed suspicion. 'I wonder, Chief Inspector, about the possibility of someone trying to get at me or my wife – someone bearing a grudge. What do you think?'

Gibson looks faintly dubious. 'We're certainly not ruling anything out at this stage.'

'And just one point on the media front,' Bill goes on. 'I had to get out of doing *The Firing Line* tonight and could only tell the producer a short while before. It's a live show; he wasn't a happy man. I insisted he said nothing on air, just that I couldn't be there for personal reasons. And I refused to explain my crisis even to him.'

Bill stares at the Chief Inspector while clasping and unclasping his hands so tightly, his fingers leave white imprints as they lift away. 'How soon do we put this out? I know you've asked all media for an embargo, I kept it out of *The Post*'s first editions, but half Brearfield has been ringing in to the paper. Something's got to give.' An aggressive tone is creeping in, but he's a desperate father, as raw with pain as I am.

'We don't want any publicity yet,' Gibson replies, 'and I'm confident my request will be respected. We *are* doing all we possibly can.'

Bill looks disbelieving. His mobile goes and from his instantly transformed expression it's Victoria. He talks for a while then clicks off and gives a small pale smile. 'Seems they failed to get a replacement on *The Firing Line* and had to have a general discussion.'

The house phone rings, too. It's Tom, who's almost here and sounding desperate for any news. If only, I think, clutching my arms to me, feeling numb with the agony, buckling under the strain.

Julian is incapable of harming Jessie. I love him. My trust is written in stone, now I've found it, it's in the very marrow of my bones.

Gibson clears his throat. 'The situation as I see it is this. Now that Mr Bridgewater has disappeared we actually have a double missing person's inquiry on our hands. The two may be linked, it's not certain. But it is vital we find both.'

'What about this old car, the Ford, you are looking for that?' Bill demands sharply.

'If it's out on the roads anywhere we should find it. I'm waiting to hear back. And also from the investigating officers at Huntingdon who'll be reporting soon on how things were at the Cambridgeshire house. They found it unlocked, Mr Bridgewater had obviously left in a hurry. They're checking his computer, all the papers on his desk.'

There's the sound of the front door being opened and banged shut. I jump up, needing to see Tom, but fumble too long with the door-handle and he opens it from the other side.

His hug is strength-giving, all the loving support a mother could wish for. He's smiling hello to his father too, and taking in the two plain-clothes detectives in formal suits.

I introduce him to both and Chief Inspector Gibson mentions he will need to have a quick private word.

Jamison slips out and returns with my mother and Mary and for a few moments we all stand about making awkward small talk.

'Shall we go into the kitchen, Tom?' Gibson suggests. 'I've just a few questions, won't take long. Then I believe Mary has some welcome sandwiches and coffee for us all.'

CHAPTER 16

'It's eleven o'clock. She's been missing almost six hours, now.'

'Don't do this, darling.' My mother's voice is cracking, she's ragged with anxiety. 'You're so overwrought, you haven't had a scrap of food. It's dangerous, not eating; it lowers your resistance. You've got to keep going. Can't you manage just one egg sandwich?'

'No, Mum – please don't nag.' I straighten up and come to sit down opposite her. I was standing leaning over the sofa arm, propped on my hands, head bowed in despair.

I try to smile across at her, although it's partly to stop myself crying. She has lost her faint brandy glow, I think; her face is putty-grey again. It's sheer fatigue, the effort of attempting to keep me afloat.

Mary, who is beside her, reads my concern. She gets up and goes to the table behind the sofa where drinks, sandwiches and some fruit are laid out. There's a covered teapot, a flask of coffee, and the brandy bottle is in evidence. Mary waves it at me for confirmation and soon my mother is sipping from a fresh mug of doctored tea.

Gibson's phone keeps going and every time a steel band tightens round my chest. I clench my fists and pray, but the calls are routine, hope-denying. Nothing changes.

I look over to Tom. He's talking to Jamison, but seeing my glance leaves the Inspector and comes to sit down beside me.

'Try to stay calm, Mum,' he urges, putting a warm hand over mine, tight-clenched in my lap. 'There's got to be someone out there who knows something. All the interviews, calling at houses, searching with dogs – I wanted to go knocking on doors and things, but,' he raises his eyes to Jamison, 'they say it's not possible, now. I got here too late.'

Inspector Jamison obviously has eagle ears. 'We'd need you tomorrow, Tom,' he calls, 'when it's daylight, if we're combing an area and it's an organized search.'

I stare at the Inspector. 'Don't say tomorrow, she must be found before that . . .'

He gives me a straight look. 'We're doing all we can, but you must be prepared.'

I drop my eyes. He's right to warn, although it brings plaguing, unbearable images: a trainer of Jessie's upturned in a muddy ditch, a T-shirt with a heart motif found under a hedge, ponds being dragged for a small limp body. I squeeze my eyes tight shut and get up and walk about.

Chief Inspector Gibson takes another call. He's sitting at Jamison's little table, listening, absorbed – looking at me, too. 'Yes, of course you can,' I hear him say. 'She's right here. Yes, fine on this phone.' He lowers the mobile and beckons. 'It's Mrs Pearson. She'd like a quick word.'

I take the phone. 'Hello, Lauren.' My voice is flat and lifeless; I feel incapable of normal interaction.

She pours out her horror and disbelief at Jessie's disappearance and is deeply sympathetic, saying in bemused tones, 'I can't think what's happened, what's with Julian. It's weirder than weird. We'd have been there at the house this evening since it's a Friday, but for a wedding in London tomorrow. A barrister friend of ours – first time married at fifty!'

Lauren is trying to sound normal and natural to combat my wooden responses. I feel mechanical, like a robot, capable only of programmed functions, if any at all.

'Julian knew we weren't coming,' she carries on, 'so he would have felt free to use the car. He does often enough, picking us up from the station when we train it. We can't both fit in his! It's been a boon, having him there; the house lived in. He's working dog hard on that biography, getting on really well, I think, deep into the psyche of his character who acted so normal on the surface, Julian says, but kept a child locked up and turned killer. It'll be a strong book.'

No way has she fully grasped the nightmarish horror-script fact that her very close friend is under suspicion of abducting a child himself. The prime suspect. Considered capable of heinous acts, of being a dangerous paedophile. Gibson hasn't spelled it out.

'Lauren, they think it's possible Julian could have abducted Jessie and have her with him. He's under suspicion. It's very serious.'

The Chief Inspector is hearing my side of the call. He's alert and watchful, anticipating any body language – affecting to look at a notebook, but his need-to-know awareness is palpable.

'That's mad, that's insane!' Lauren exclaims, shocked into full understanding, loudly enough, I hope, for Gibson to hear. 'They don't know Julian, they're reading it all wrong. You know him,

Ursula,' she presses. 'Tell them, say what he's like. Sure, he enjoyed teaching Jessie and having her help in the bookshop, but that was just normal and nice. The guy loves *you*, for Christ's sake, I just hope you know how much.'

'He's disappeared, though, left his car and taken yours.'

'There'll be some simple straightforward explanation,' Lauren says in her usual confident way. 'Could Jessie have run away? Possibly even tried to travel to our house? She was upset about his going, wasn't she, and the shop closing? Jess might have wanted to make a stand and shake people up.'

'She had nothing with her. Her mobile and purse were still in her swimming bag.'

'Guess she'd have taken those. It was just a thought. God, I feel for you,' Lauren says, sounding genuine, telling me how much I'm in her thoughts and prayers.

Giving back the Chief Inspector his phone, I think that if calls to it are monitored, Lauren saying Julian enjoyed teaching Jessie, her comments on the subject matter of his book aren't going to help. Nothing will.

I long to ask Tom about Gibson's questions; he'll probably think it his own private affair, though. I mustn't pry. He's pouring himself coffee and I go over for some, too.

'I feel so spare and helpless, Mum, there *must* be something I can do.' He gives a mournful little grin, turning to offer me his mug. I take it with a look of thanks, thinking of him rushing away from friends on a Friday night, sensing his deep consuming distress. Any normal decent brother would feel that and want to help, but somehow Tom has an extra depth of love and sensitivity. He would withstand harsh tests of his loyalty.

The Chief Inspector wanders over to join us. Gibson has a bland featureless face, it's too regular, lacking defined planes and contours. His light brown hair combed neatly forward looks slightly silly, but that blank canvas can still manage to convey a stash of perceptive humanity. It's all in the eyes.

'There's a police car on its way here, Tom,' he remarks, 'just bringing a couple of things we need. You could help by doing the rounds with two officers. You know the area, places Jessie went, try to think of anyone at all with whom she's had a passing acquaintance. The officers will be able to prompt you. I'd be most grateful.'

'Thanks, I'd love to be doing something useful,' Tom says appreciatively, looking every bit the boy I still think him. 'It's OK, is it, me hearing radio messages and stuff?'

'I can't answer for the odd expletive,' Gibson says deadpan, 'but no, you'll be fine.'

The car's arriving; Tom glances over to his father, but Bill is on his mobile, looking and sounding exasperated. Talking to the paper, probably, sending weary disgruntled reporters out on undisclosed late-night searches for leads.

'I'll tell Dad. Don't hold anyone up. Would the officers like coffee first?' I ask.

'They're on duty,' the Chief Inspector sounds firm. 'They should get on.'

The officers have brought out a small printer. Jamison plugs it into the laptop and gets back to work, going online, bringing up emails. Gibson is standing behind him, reading as he scrolls down.

I pour more coffee and put a sandwich on a plate. I'm not hungry, but must try to eat. And I want my mother to see and approve. She's nodded off and is in quite a deep sleep, I think, with her head lolled to one side like a rag doll. Her mouth is a little open, making her look vulnerable and old.

Am I partly to blame, always moody and making life difficult? It's feeling so unconditionally loved, I think, and having no need of any façade.

Emma's alone in bed upstairs. She could be lying awake or having bad dreams. I can't bear the thought and, telling Mary what I'm doing, I slip out to go to check on her.

There's a strange stillness about the house. A light is on in the hall, but the stairs are plunged in gloom and the darkness seems to be fingering, whispering, beckoning, as though urged by some malevolent force to spread and dispense more fear. I can feel it all around in the atmosphere, ice-cold on my skin, rising, invading like floodwater.

Emma's door is ajar and without switching on any light I can make out her peacefully sleeping face. Her breathing is even; she hasn't stirred, I'm sure. Tiptoeing away, I feel a burning urge to go into Jessie's room. It takes a supreme effort of will to turn away. In my own room it's still impossible to escape the images. I'm seeing the empty bed, the piece of old comfort blanket still under her pillow, the pink-check curtains. They're not drawn tonight, the blackness of night will be coming into the room.

More unstoppable tears. I sit down at the dressing table with elbows resting and bury my head in my hands.

Taking slow deep breaths I stare at my ravaged ghostly face in the mirror. Wouldn't Julian have wanted to keep in touch if he's trying to find her? Could he actually, horrifically, have done something in his past and be capable of perverted crimes?

It's impossible, inconceivable. I love him, he couldn't do Jessie harm. He promised to do his all, I think, violently dragging a brush through my hair. Somehow he'll find her and this nightmare will end. Or will it?

My face is stained with crying; I wipe at the tear-channels with a tissue and find the strength to go back downstairs.

My mother is still sleeping. Bill and the Chief Inspector have drawn up chairs to Jamison's table, Mary, too. They're reading from printed-out sheets of paper.

'I've printed out some information from the SIOs at Huntingdon,' Jamison says.

'Senior Investigating Officers,' Mary decodes, getting up and bringing me a chair.

'Books he had open to work with, the site he had online,' Inspector Jamison goes on, before Bill interrupts, turning on me with a hard penetrating stare.

'Did you know about this book – the kind of research Julian was into?' I'm left no room for reply. Bill goes on furiously, 'It's the biography of a paedophile abductor. That's no coincidence to me.'

'Don't you dare start accusing and making unproven assumptions.' I keep hold of the chair-back for support. 'Of course I knew. I told you only tonight about Erica's comically suspicious attitude, of it reminding him of a long-ago case. Lauren Pearson's a friend of yours; she knows about the book. Talk to her. She'll set you straight.'

Bill chooses to ignore that. 'You look at this list.' He hits at the piece of paper in his hand. 'All these books, old newspaper cuttings: Julian's notes on the original case – which was certainly particularly horrific,' he glares at me coldly, 'and very pertinent to now.'

I pick up one of the copy sheets with pumping adrenaline and start to read a list of the books open on his desk.

Without Conscience: The Disturbing World of the Psychopaths among Us. Robert D. Hare PhD.

The Human Predator: A Historical Chronicle of Serial Murder and Forensic Investigation. Katherine Rausland PhD.

The Psychopath: Emotion and the Brain. James Blair, Derek Mitchell and Katherine Blair.

Snakes in Suits: When Psychopaths Go to Work. Chris Babath PhD and R. D. Hare PhD.

Interpersonal Diagnosis and Treatment of Personality Disorders. L. S. Benjamin.

Could Julian have got so steeped in psychopathy and his subject's character that it corroded his reason . . .? No, I'm going crazy. These are perfectly respectable appropriate reference books – and while I might be guilty of blind faith against all the evidence, Bill is certainly going overboard the other way.

Julian's personal notes have been painstakingly photographed and reproduced. It cuts deep, seeing his actual writing, his untidy scrawl. They're under headings. 'Lack of Remorse', 'Impulsivity' and 'Lessons Learned'.

The headlines from newspaper cuttings are listed: *'Child held captive for weeks, only to die in seconds.' 'Terrible police bungle – unavoidable tragedy?'*

His last emails are listed, too; they're unremarkable, mainly to do with research for the book.

There's one from a girl called Anita, about some good mark her son got at school. It's signed Annie with an x, which I could have done without, but certainly isn't a love note, and there are no emails at all from Lauren. She would have phoned, though.

The police are so meticulous. A half-drunk cup of coffee is noted: a bottle of mineral water. That the house was left unlocked is underlined, emphasizing Julian's hurried departure.

'There's nothing here of any help, is there?' I look at Gibson.

'No, you're right . . .' He seems about to comment further, hesitates then lets it rest.

Bill stands up; his face is shadowed and angry, grief-stricken. He's staring at the Chief Inspector, a thought coming. 'Could Bridgewater have paid someone to take her?'

'Unlikely. Working in pairs is more like professional porn.' Bill looks prepared to lay any form of heinous crime at Julian's door. The Chief Inspector continues, 'If Mr Bridgewater should be found to be involved I feel sure he would have been acting alone.'

'But you said he might have been expecting a call?'

'Yes, well – still making complete assumptions – it is just possible he had left Jessie somewhere, promising to keep in touch, and been about to use the phone himself.'

'He thought up that job in the bookshop just to further his aims, I'm sure. Had it all carefully planned . . .' Bill is desperate for something to latch on to, blindly clutching at any straw and trying to turn it into a strong supporting rope.

I can't bear the injustice and cover my ears, shouting at him, 'Shut up! It was Jessie's idea about helping in the shop, she begged me to let her. You're being monstrously unfair, you've lost all sense of reason – you weren't around, don't know a bloody thing.'

Gibson had talked earlier of checking the sex register for known local offenders, helicopter searches, Special Branch expertise. 'At least the police are spreading a wider net and not closing prejudiced minds,' I throw out, but old-style marital sarcasm is a bitter taste on my tongue. And the paternal agony in Bill's eyes slows me down.

The grouping round the table disperses, we drift to the sofas, other seats, to wait . . .

Bill brings out his mobile. I hear him say, 'Darling,' and know with a pang the strength and support he'll be gaining from the call.

I check a couple of texts on my mobile. They're from Val and Susie, who have obviously compared notes and decided calling might bring false rays of hope. My two friends are there for me, any time, any place, they say. Lifting my head from the messages, it takes great effort to contain another howl of anguish.

Chief Inspector Gibson comes over. I'm sitting on an upright chair by the side table with the telephone and get up since he seems to want a word.

He's looking unexpectedly awkward. 'This isn't really connected,' he mutters, making clear it's between him and me, 'but I thought you might like hearing that the Huntingdon SIOs read a little of Mr Bridgewater's book and were very impressed – in spite of criticisms of the police on that case.' Gibson gives a rare rather humble smile. 'It was on the computer and possibly relevant,' he adds as though to explain that they hadn't been wasting time.

Gibson really is keeping an open mind, I think. 'He does write well,' I say gratefully, finding it hard then not to blurt out emotionally, repetitively, that Julian is also a good caring, decent man.

The Chief Inspector is too, I think. He's not prejudging, not convinced. Somehow I feel he's brought new thinking to bear and revised a previous view. Is it information he's not divulging, some discovery made at the house? Has he worked out a new theory? Whatever else, it's a source of strength and support. I'm not being dismissed as hysterical, blind to facts and circumstantial evidence. Gibson doesn't, after all, think I'm quite out of my mind.

CHAPTER 17

Bill is still talking to Victoria. I'm leaning my head against the wall, keeping it slightly turned his way, and it's hard not to feel a swell of jealousy. He has been looking raw-boned with the strain, but there's a newly relaxed curve to his body, a softening of deeply etched lines. His face has always shown his feelings, always been responsive and animated, but now it has such a look of tender intimacy, even as he's arguing. We never had quite that wonderful closeness, it was never really there for me.

I'm near to going under: seeing Jessie as hunted prey and the hounds closing in, the sense of inevitability, tragedy, disaster, is gaining ground. I shut my mind, but my eyes still slide back to Bill. His long call to Victoria is making me yearn for Julian's tender love. Even if by some miracle, I think, Jessie is found and safe back home, Julian exonerated, could we ever have a chance of happiness after all that has been?

Julian doesn't know I'm feeling unconditional love for him. Or that it took being in a hotel room with Perry, whom he detests, to make me see it. It's hard to imagine him ever forgiving me or believing I got out of that room unscathed. What respect could he possibly have left for me? And I have forfeited any right to his future trust.

I'd been so close to calling and saying I loved him. If only he knew. If he finds Jessie he will always think protestations of love are connected. Will he find her? He said he would do his all. Please God, let her be all right.

I look at my watch. If only there was something, anything, to go on. With midnight fast approaching and no sign of Jessie, any pinpoint of light is dimming and flickering out.

My mother has woken up. I straighten up and meet her eyes. They're pained and sorrowful. 'I wish you'd go up to bed, Mum. There's nothing you can do and you need some proper sleep. I'd be happier about Emma too, if you were upstairs.'

'I'll take up my bag and see she's sleeping, but don't pack me off, I need to be here with you, not lying alone upstairs, worrying.'

I help her up from the sofa and give her bony shoulders an emotional squeeze. 'Of course, Mum, of course.'

She was in the kitchen and doesn't know the things about Julian that don't add up. I'd said he was under suspicion, talking to Lauren, though. My mother must have heard that.

Would Gibson have questioned her earlier, on the phone? He was in touch over the puncture. Would she have told him she'd disapproved about Jessie's job, of her view that Julian would never settle? Surely she couldn't conceivably imagine Julian, whose father she so admired, could have snatched and be in hiding with her granddaughter? Bill's views might colour hers; she thinks he's worldly.

She's taking up her little holdall. The sight of mine on that hotel chair is a constant torture in my mind, the drip, drip, my head banged against a wall. If only I'd seen through Perry in time and not made that fateful journey. But mightn't I as likely have just dropped off the girls myself and gone to the supermarket?

No, Jessie was upset. I'd have lingered, seen she got changed, urged and cajoled her to swim. It was all about Perry.

Where is she? Why is there no clue? Oh, Jessie, please hang on.

Bill is catching my attention, waving his mobile. 'Victoria wants to talk to you.'

He was calling quite loudly and I can sense my mother's keen curiosity – and that of the two detectives and Mary. They, like everyone else in the country, must have read every intrusive humiliating detail of Bill's great affair. The Minister and the Editor, Victoria's accident, it was never off the front pages.

I separate myself from Bill and keep the phone tight-pressed to my ear. Victoria is talking of the strain I must be under; the pain. 'It's beyond imagining,' she says. 'I can't stop thinking of dear sweet Jessie, all her bright curious questions at weekends . . .'

The words seem heartfelt, said with fervour, there's a catch in her voice, too. 'Hang on to hope,' Victoria urges, 'don't lose sight of that. William is desperate, he feels so impotent. I know he's thinking the worst about Julian, being too quick to judge and how hard that must be for you. I've tried telling him . . .'

I grab at the rope she's handing. 'You've met Julian,' I plead. 'You must have seen the sort of man he is, how decent and incapable of anything bad?'

'I liked him,' she replies evenly, 'I can't say more. It's all such purely circumstantial evidence, I'm sure the police are keeping an open mind.'

'Julian's out there looking for Jessie, I know he is. Can't you somehow get it across to Bill?' I'm using every persuasive breath in my body, immune to the audience of listeners in the room.

'I have been trying.' Victoria is beginning to sound embarrassed, caught in the crossfire, tugged at by loyalty to Bill. She continues less emotionally, 'My daughter, Nattie, is right here beside me and wants you to know how very much her thoughts are with you. She's desperately upset.'

'Can you ask about Tom?' I hear the girl butting in. 'He's not answering his phone.'

I explain that Tom is out with the police and end the call. It's left me both warmed and drained, overcome.

Handing Bill back his phone, I can hardly bring myself to look at him civilly. His blinkered, closed-mind attitude over Julian is cruelly unjust.

How can it be that I'm feeling such a bond with Victoria? It's not as though we're two women in the same bind, in shared circumstances. She took Bill; it was despicable behaviour. I've spent a year thinking vile thoughts about her. My jealousy reached a crescendo when, first Tom, then the girls, made it unequivocally clear she was the bloody bees' knees in their view, some kind of wonder-woman. The press gave her a comparatively easy ride . . . And here am I now, seeing good in her, even imagining she can soften Bill.

Chief Inspector Gibson is looking at his watch and conferring with Jamison. They both begin sliding papers into briefcases, Jamison clearing the little table.

They're about to go. I can't bear the strain. Bill and I will be circling like hostile dogs, baring our fangs, snarling over the ever-widening chasm that's opened up between us.

Gripping my mobile tightly enough to make it sweaty, willing it, or any other phone just to ring, I go up to Gibson. 'You've got to go haven't you? You need to get some sleep, Mary, too.'

'Mary's staying, she'll be on hand to help in any way, or a colleague of hers. Someone will be here at all times. The incident room is being manned twenty-four hours.' Gibson gives me his steady gaze. 'We are doing everything we possibly can. Try to get a bit of rest, perhaps take it in turns. And Tom's on his way back; he should get some, too. I pray Jessie will be safe home by morning, but he could be needed.'

The night is stretching ahead like a dead-end tunnel and every tomorrow without Jessie would be a solar eclipse. I stare mutely at the Chief Inspector.

'We're at a hotel just up the road,' he says. 'My mobile will be on; call at any time, the moment you hear anything. I have a strange hunch, somehow, you just might . . .'

Bill snaps out of a private reverie and comes striding up to us with furious eyes. 'I hope you're not relying on fucking hunches now.'

'No, and as I've just said, Sir, my officers are working round the clock. We're not resting in the search for your daughter. You have my mobile number; any developments and we'll be right back.'

The door has closed behind them. Bill is pacing. His mobile rings, but it seems to be someone on the paper who, given the copious lashes of his editor's tongue, must be feeling very sore. Mary pours Bill freshly made coffee and she, too, gets a blast of aggressive questions – about the pool staff, school friends, the parents interviewed. All of which she gamely attempts to answer.

'Funny how Julian's name is in there every time.' Bill's scowls at me are the more menacing for his growth of dark beard; it's giving him a mug-shot look. He was always shattered by Friday night after a week of long newspaper hours. 'Even the school Head,' he says trenchantly, 'had clearly been very concerned about a child of eleven helping in that shop, left alone in Julian's care.'

'I was worried about it too, darling,' my mother pipes up. 'I did say Jessie was too young.' She looks down at her hands then, cringing in the face of my livid frown.

'The Head was only parroting bloody Erica Barkston,' I say furiously, 'and she's no business repeating that woman's petty gossip. She's useless.'

Hearing the front door I feel a slight lifting of the dreadful tension. Tom around will help unwind the tangle of his parents' knots.

'Hi everyone.' His attempt at a bright greeting fades. He has no need of a finger in the air to gauge the atmosphere. ''Fraid there's nothing to report,' he informs us. 'Apart from quite a dramatic pub fight outside the French Horn. No news here, I take it?'

He sits down next to his grandmother and nudges her arm. 'You bearing up, Gran?'

'They didn't tell you anything, Tom, any thoughts they had?' she asks.

He shakes his head. Then at an obvious and understandable loss as to how to communicate further – there are no words, no balm – he rubs at his forehead with three middle fingers, smiles round at us awkwardly and looks immensely relieved when he thinks of reaching behind to the sofa-table and picking up a curling ham sandwich.

I go to the small occasional table by Chief Inspector Gibson's upright chair and lay my mobile carefully down. He'd had a hunch, he said. Was that just to keep up hope? I sit studying my nails, legs tight crossed. Bill is feeling jealous, hurt most likely, hearing so much about Jess's relationship with Julian. He has rushed to completely unreasonable judgement as a desperate father – but just suppose he could be right?

I've had tiny moments of misgiving. There was the time when Jess had kept quiet about the bookshop with my mother – had she been warned that certain people might feel particular concern? I'd felt a kind of mild envy at Jess coming home so bouncy and shining-eyed at lunchtime on Saturdays. And sometimes, too, over Julian's soft fond looks. 'He's my friend,' she had said. But what kind of friend?

His looks have always been gentle. She's a bright child, and precocious. I love him. No one, not Erica, not Bill can make me lose faith and believe Julian a disturbed deranged psychopath. Not possibly, I think, shedding slow silent tears.

I lift my eyes eventually, but stop them from creeping to the mobile on the table. That's one certain way to make it not ring.

CHAPTER 18

My mobile rings. It's vibrating on the polished surface of the table.

It takes a second for me to register, being so deep in chilling thoughts, at that instant, and trying to rid myself of them. My hand is shaking as I grab it, my heart hammering like a road drill.

Julian's name is on the mobile screen. It's hope. I can't believe it. 'Have you found her?' I cry, before he can say a word. 'Tell me she's safe and it's good news . . .' He's not answering, not speaking. 'Are you there, Julian?' I'm trembling, holding in breath, bracing myself.

I can hear him now, thank God, panting and taking in air, as though in shock or physically shattered. 'Just needed a minute,' he says. 'She's here, in the car . . . been very brave . . . Not easy to talk, just now.'

'But she is all right? You are bringing her here? Are *you* all right? Thank God, you've called. Where are you? Can't you say more?'

'It's not great just now . . . don't want, um . . . to upset her. She can't take much more. The police are there? They need to be. And you need to get a . . .' He's gone so faint, I can't hear. 'Soon with you,' he says more clearly, then nothing more.

'Julian?' I'm waiting, hanging on, aching for him to keep talking, burning up with the need. But there's only the noisy throttly sound of the engine, the rattling chassis of an old car.

Bill is by my side now, wanting to take the mobile. I'm still trying to listen, batting him away with a feverish arm, but he will keep hissing questions. 'Has he got her with him? What's he done, the bastard? For Christ's sake, can't you say what's going on? Let me speak to him – give me the phone.'

'Shut up, can't you, I'm trying to hear!' I hang on to the mobile, desperate for Bill to keep quiet. I can just hear Julian talking to someone. He must have put the phone down and it's still on.

He's speaking faintly and softly. 'Soon there, soon home. Back with Mum very soon, keep being brave. It's all over now.'

He's talking to Jessie, my beloved daughter. She's there, in the car, safe – she must be. I'm aching to call, 'Jess, Jess,' down the phone, but my throat has almost closed over. I keep straining to hear, but there's only the noise of the engine.

My mother and Tom are looking on anxiously. 'What's going on?' Tom whispers.

'Somehow or other Julian's found her,' I say, lowering the phone. 'I could hear him talking to her just then.' My cheeks feel fiery and aglow. 'It's unbelievable, she's found, he's bringing her home!'

I tell them every last thing I was able to hear. Mary relays it all into her walkie-talkie. It sounds like she's through to the Chief Inspector.

Bill is staying silent, giving me cold black glares. His face had unwound at the first instance, the pure relief and disbelieving wonder had lifted his brow, sparked pinpoints of light in his tired angry eyes. Now his darkly shadowed face is grimly antagonistic and it's in stark contrast to my own indescribable feelings of joy. Bill is back in the blame game and warming up for a fight.

'He's had Jessie with him all the time, he must have. He hasn't just plucked her out of nowhere. What's he been doing to her? When you think, a whole bloody police force out there looking . . . Christ, it makes you sick. Bringing her back now is all planned, I'll bet, all about covering his tracks.'

The bile is rising, I'm about to fight him, but Mary is attracting our attention. 'I'm on to the DCI,' she says, moving closer. 'They're just leaving the hotel, coming right back. He says Mr Bridgewater's car has been spotted the far side of Brearfield, but, considering what you've heard, Mrs Osborne, he thinks the better course is not to intercept the car, just have it followed on its way here. He said to tell you he's had a forensic doctor on standby all evening, who'll be coming to the house directly. The DCI thinks Jessie may well be traumatized and in need of a sedative. But he'll be here very soon himself now, ahead of Mr Bridgewater, and will be able to tell you more.'

I stare at Mary. Jessie traumatized? I'd been thinking all those hours about her being abused, held at knifepoint and worse, but then hearing Julian's gentle voice had driven out the demons. They're back. Nearly seven hours, Jessie was missing. Where has she been? What has anyone done . . . ? And Julian had sounded in bad shape, too.

Mary's going slightly blurred. Shit, my legs are going, shit; I can't start fainting . . . The chair, is it behind me? Is she guiding me?

'Head right forward,' she says efficiently. 'Don't rush it.'

The feeling passes, life back in my limbs. My mother's holding out a glass of water. 'I told you, you should eat something,' she says predictably. 'You are always so stubborn.'

'I did eat a sandwich. You were asleep at the time!' That gives me

childish satisfaction; my mother looks quite deflated. I smile at her
with such affection, feeling released, light-headed, brought back from
the brink in every sense. Insanely impatient to be seeing Jess, too –
where are they? Anticipation is erupting out of me in a lava of panicky joy. 'I knew Julian would find her, Mum, he said he would do
his all!'

'Hold on a moment,' Bill says, his voice knife-sharp. 'You don't
know what the bastard's done to her. You might not think he's such
a saviour after all, when you do.'

I get to my feet in a fury. 'And *you* might, just once, try not rushing to judgement. Why do you always have to accuse and lay blame?'

'Darling,' my mother's touching my arm, 'don't you think, over
this, you should perhaps, listen to Bill? We don't know anything, yet.
You are always so very trusting.'

I turn on her, furious. 'For God's sake, Mum! And as for you,' I
scream at Bill, 'how about waiting to hear what your own daughter
has to say? She'll know the truth of it all.'

'Mum did just say that Julian asked for the police to be here . . .'
Tom intervenes.

'He'll have some very plausible story lined up, you wait and see.'
Bill is being impossible. It's the firing squad before the trial, the sentence before the crime. He didn't hear the gentleness in Julian's voice.

Misty has been skulking under a table all evening, but animals can
sense unhappiness as keenly as danger, a dog knows when its master
is feeling distress. His sudden growls and barking are unexpected in
all the tension and give everybody a jolt.

'That'll be the DCI and DI back,' Mary says, relief written all over
her face. I think of Emma sleeping upstairs and hurry to quieten
Misty, who's shot into the hall.

'Save that noise for the burglars!' I scold, fondling his ears and smiling up at Gibson. I have faith in the Chief Inspector now, a belief that he will follow a fair course and not be out for any quick target-chasing conviction. He's high calibre, I think, feeling bolstered and more able to do battle with Bill.

'There is a doctor coming?' I query.

'Already here. He's just parking. Mr Bridgewater is not far off now, either.'

I glance over his shoulder. Bill has come to the sitting-room door. The hatred building in him – and for someone he's liked and approved of – is as clear as lights changing from green to red. The way he stiffened merely hearing Julian's name fills me with despair.

There's the sound of footfall, someone at the door. Jamison springs to get it.

Gibson introduces the burly substantial doctor, who sets down a leather bag and offers a firm hand. 'Doctor Jeffries,' he says. 'The DCI has filled me in.'

Bill comes forward and says hello too, and the doctor stands looking appraisingly at us, his head turning from one to the other. He has a pursed, rosebud mouth that gives him the appearance of constantly deliberating. Perhaps he is.

'Come to the sitting room,' I say, 'and meet my son and mother.'

I repeat everything gleaned from Julian to them all, exactly as I'd overheard it. Bill doesn't interrupt, thankfully, and Gibson seems to be concentrating on every detail.

My mother suggests Jessie might need sweet tea and biscuits. I follow after her as she trots off to the kitchen, worried I'd been too quick to jump and put her down.

She seems pleased and delighted to have any little task, telling me, as if it were of some importance and I didn't already know, that Jessie really likes Twiglets.

I leave her filling the kettle and go out into the hall, opening the front door and straining for any sound of a car.

Gibson comes to stand beside me. 'Doctor Jeffries thinks it would be best if Jessie were to come in quietly without having to face an audience. Inspector Jamison and Mary, your mother and Tom are all going to wait in the kitchen, just to give her a chance to get acclimatized. If she's suffering trauma she probably won't speak, you must be prepared for that.'

I turn to stare. He wants me to come away from the door. 'Shouldn't we leave it open?' I say, relieved when he gives one of his thoughtful acceding nods. I feel less reluctant to follow meekly as he leads back into the sitting room.

The room clears with no one saying much. I perch on the nearest sofa-arm, watching the departing backs of Mary and Detective Inspector Jamison.

When it's just Gibson, Bill and me, Dr Jeffries says gravely, 'We don't know her condition, you see. It is possible she's quite badly hurt or abused.'

Bill meets my eyes; he's barely seeing me, I think. There's a nerve pulsing in his temple; he looks both slumped as though wilting from strain and shot through with steel.

Misty's ears prick; he cocks his head. We can hear sounds of the front door being closed. The tension is unbearable. I long to rush out and gather up my child in my arms.

The door is pushing open. 'I think Mum and Dad will be in here.' Julian is talking in the same soothing tones as in the car. We can all hear him, now.

Jessie looks so small holding on to the hand of a man of almost six foot. Her face is badly bruised, swollen and lopsided; one eye is almost closed. It's filthy, too.

A thousand thoughts tear through my head. She must have fallen, Julian found her somewhere – in rough undergrowth perhaps? She's been set on by drugged youths. Her knees aren't grazed, though, no scratches, just that closed-eye tear-stained wretchedly puffed-up little face. Who could have done this?

'Darling Jess!' I'm on my knees, holding her, but she gives nothing; it's a one-way affair. Just my arms round her stiff small body with her never once letting go of Julian's hand.

Gibson has told us not to ask any questions, that we should let her take her time.

Bill drops down beside me and picks up her limp free hand. 'Hello, Jess,' he says, lifting it up to his lips and kissing it gently. She turns to stare at him, then at me, then up at Julian. She's still not letting go of his hand and looks frozen, guardedly afraid.

Julian squats down. 'Time to go to bed, Jess. Do you want to sleep in yours or in Mum's?' Still holding on to his hand she pulls at it to indicate me. It feels like flinging open heavy curtains and letting in bright light. She needs me after all.

My face must have shown it, but I'm crying too, and Jessie stares at my smiling wet face. 'Upstairs to bed, then, Jess,' I say, trying to inject a note of normality, 'and there's a nice doctor here to see you, too.' She turns away instantly at that, hiding her head against Julian's hand.

Julian looks at Bill then me. We're all of us bent-kneed and at the same level. He gets up then, with Jessie still clutching on, and says levelly, taking in the doctor and Gibson, 'It might be best on the whole, if no one has any objection, if I carried Jess up. She was being held captive, you see, when I found her and understandably feels a bit clingy.'

Bill's face is like an angry woodcarving, etched in hard deep lines. 'I'll carry her up myself, if you don't mind,' he mutters, momentarily meeting Julian's eyes.

'She'll be better in the morning, William, it's just the aftermath,' Julian replies mildly, looking round for guidance. He can't have failed to absorb the violence in Bill.

Gibson takes charge. Coming forward he smiles, gently. 'Hello, Jessie. I'm a policeman. Mr Bridgewater is going to stay with you while the doctor gives you a little drink and soon you'll be fast asleep and feeling so much better in the morning.'

He's looking and sounding more like a shy well-meaning parson than a Detective Chief Inspector, I think, not in the least threatening.

'Could you manage the stairs, Jess?' Julian suggests. 'Shall we try that?'

She nods and pulls on his hand as if impatient to get away from us all.

A small crisis averted – pity it hadn't been Julian's first thought. I focus on him for a second. He looks physically and mentally drained, I've never seen him so pale.

'Thank you,' I say, as he's turning to go, 'from the bottom of my heart.'

'Can you come here a minute,' he mutters. 'The Chief Inspector needs to know a few things pretty fast. It'll upset . . .' He nods at Jessie's head. 'But I'll do it soon as poss.'

I can't find any more words, so I nod, meeting his eyes. I'm feeling such overwhelming desperate need for Jessie's arms, such shivering relief and exhaustion, that I'm incapable of functioning much more at all.

Julian looks ready to drop. However bad it's been for us, waiting here, he's been through some terrible hell, too. We've all been in danger of sinking tonight, I think, struggling to keep ourselves from capsizing and somehow staying afloat.

CHAPTER 19

Jessie is sleeping deeply with the sedative. She hasn't said a word. Doctor Jeffries assures us it isn't that unusual in the circumstances, no cause for serious alarm. She is in the grip of shock, he explains, and beyond normal physical exhaustion.

I should go downstairs, but can't leave her side. It's a miracle she's here, in my bed and safe home again. The memories will never fade: the torturing images, the dread fear of loss, of never seeing her again. Those long hours of waiting will stay vivid for ever.

She's lying as still and pale as somebody under anaesthetic; her grimy tear-stained face is bathed clean and the puffy swelling and cut lip are more starkly apparent. What happened? Who struck her so hard? How could anyone do such a thing to a defenceless child?

While Doctor Jeffries was bathing and attending to her, Jessie wouldn't once let go of Julian's hand. He kept whispering it was all over, all better, then, as soon as the sedative began working, slipped away and hurried down to Chief Inspector Gibson.

Tom and my mother creep in soon after Jessie is upstairs. My mother is over in the low Victorian nursing chair and looking anguished. The chintz curtains behind her, their fresh colours echoing the wisteria outside, seem somehow to emphasize her pinched, drawn weariness. She takes on everyone's worries, adopting them and letting them cling on like a plant on a host tree. There hasn't been any shortage tonight.

Tom is terrific with Jess. She's practically asleep, but he sits on the bed chatting about her favourite pop star, Christina Aguilera, and Nattie's week of A levels as if it was a routine uneventful bedtime. I'm sure it helps. How are we going to get back to normal, though? I'll never want to let Jessie out of my sight.

Bill takes Tom's place on the bed, bending to kiss his daughter's swollen face and cover her small limp hand with his. As he gets to his feet I'm sure there is the glint of tears in his eyes.

The burly Doctor Jeffries is about to go, but gives us the benefit of a few thoughts. 'She was hit in the face with a fist, I'd say, and with force – that'll be a corker of a black eye in the morning. Bruises always take time to come out.'

'Any sexual interference?' Bill inquires, flashing me a cold-eyed glance. He can't surely still be thinking Julian has done something to Jess?

'There are no visible signs,' Doctor Jeffries replies. 'Your daughter is going to have to be interviewed, though, as soon as possible, probably first thing. Then, depending on her evidence, a full examination and sample-taking may need to be carried out.'

'Does her trauma indicate it is likely there was sexual abuse?' I ask fearfully.

'Not necessarily. To my mind this crime hadn't quite yet tipped over that particular edge. Her evidence will be vital, but for all sorts of reasons she might be very reluctant to talk. Don't expect an early resolution.' Doctor Jeffries pauses. 'My instinct, for what it's worth, is that she was found just in time. I think you're very lucky to have her home.'

And with that oblique reference to Julian's part in it all, the doctor purses his rosebud lips, snaps his bag shut and says his goodbyes. I go downstairs with him, leaving Bill in my bedroom being polite to my mother.

Chief Inspector Gibson and Julian have been talking in the hall. My heart overturns, going up to them after seeing out the doctor. Julian is looking so emptied out and exhausted, as if tested to the limits of his endurance. God knows what he went through to find Jessie and bring her safe home.

'You must let me get you a shot of brandy,' I smile. 'And some food, you look terrible!'

'I'd settle for a straight scotch . . .' His responding look causes the most aching pull and the look in his eyes, when I come back with the glass, shoots right through me. Will there ever be a chance of being alone together when I can try, however hard it is, to make amends and explain?

Gibson melts back a bit as I talk to Julian. He's waiting to begin the interview, though, and I'm holding them up. They go into the kitchen, Jamison too, and I come upstairs again.

They're been closeted in there quite a time, although is that the door opening now?

'Gibson wants us in the sitting room,' Bill says abruptly, standing in the bedroom door. 'That is if Barbara doesn't mind staying with Jess.' He comes closer in, smiling encouragingly at her.

'Of course not,' she assures him, looking at me.

At least Bill has a more pleasant expression for my mother. His black looks at me have been bad enough, but from his accusing eyes shooting after Julian, Bill might have imagined him about to do a runner and shin down the nearest drainpipe.

My mother comes to my side. 'Will Chief Inspector Gibson say what's going to happen, do you think? Could Julian be arrested on suspicion or anything? He did, after all, go missing and seem to be in hiding from the police.'

'What on earth are you talking about, Mum?' I narrow my eyes. 'Julian almost certainly saved Jessie's life tonight and you talk about arresting him?'

'It might yet come to that,' Bill comments sardonically.

I round on him, completely exasperated. 'Have you lost all reason and sanity? Think of poor little Jess's knocked-about face. Do you really believe she'd have been clinging to Julian like that and not once letting go of his hand if he'd been lashing out?'

'I think he's got her emotionally involved. And it's a fact,' Bill goes on in a lecturing tone before I can argue, 'that women forgive violence. They think it's never really meant; they feel dependent, they believe in the apology, have a sense of responsibility. It all seems to get mixed up. Jess is young and vulnerable, but no less aware of her femininity.'

I stare at Bill in disbelief and confusion. What on earth has got into him, suddenly turning psychologist? 'But she's a little girl!' I cry. 'You're talking about adults in sexual relationships, men with no control; abuse, domestic violence. Not a normal decent human being like Julian. You're off your head.'

'I know about women and violence,' Bill says darkly.

'How – because of a few extreme cases that cross your desk at the paper?'

'No . . .' Bill seems to be weighing up whether to elaborate. He meets my eyes. 'Reasons much closer to home.' I remember suddenly then that there had been newspaper rumours about Victoria's husband, Barney. It had seemed extreme at the time, the suggestion he had hit her — surely it couldn't have been true?

'This is getting us nowhere,' I mumble.

'You don't know a thing,' Bill mutters, seeing he's giving me pause, 'not the half of it. You coming down now?'

He makes for the door, stopping a moment by Jessie's bedside, looking a slumped shattered figure. There's pain in his eyes; he's dishevelled, his pink shirt creased, suit jacket and tie abandoned, his lived-in face more deeply grooved. I stare after him, feeling chastened.

Rumours about Barney would be as a whisper, I think, compared to the siren calls about Julian if Jessie refuses to speak. Suspicion would harden in people's minds like fillings in their teeth. Unproven assumptions become convictions. She must tell the truth about what happened.

My mother gets up and comes beside me, touching my arm. She's looking miserably in need of reassurance, but I can only snap irritably, 'Jess will clear everything up. There'll be tests, forensic evidence.' I give a mean glare. 'And when her abductor is behind bars and Julian exonerated then perhaps you and Bill will have the grace to say sorry.'

I immediately feel sheepish for having a go and force a smile. 'I'll be up soon to release you, Mum — and now shall we, perhaps, just agree to let Chief Inspector Gibson get on with his work?'

She seems relieved at that, the frown lines relaxing, her shoulders more drooped. 'He's a nice sensible-looking man,' she says in her tritely earnest way. 'I'm sure he'll be thorough and fair.'

*

I hurry down. The group in the sitting room is dotted about like actors on places marked with a cross. Smiling round, I go to a sofa-arm, mid-stage.

The atmosphere is tense; no one had been speaking when I came in. Bill is by the small table where I'd had my mobile. He looked up, but is now concentrating on a stone painted to look like a cat that he's holding. It's one that Emma gave me ages ago. Tom is leaning against the wall. Inspector Jamison and Mary are at the worktable, both on laptops, and Gibson and Julian are standing by the mantel-piece looking my way.

'Come and sit down, Mrs Osborne,' Gibson says, his eyes indi-cating I should sit properly on the side of the sofa nearest to them. I duly move. 'Mr Bridgewater has told me all he can,' he contin-ues. 'It had to be under caution and I'm grateful to him for waiving his right to legal representation, as we need to act fast.' Gazing at me distantly, he goes on, 'Mr Bridgewater has suggested he explain everything, just as he told me. I think that's sensible, I'd like to hear it again, too.' Gibson's implying, probably for Bill's benefit, that he can pick up any inconsistencies. 'Although I must, of course, remind you,' he turns to Julian, 'that you are still under caution.'

Julian nods, acknowledging that, and is about to begin when Bill uncrosses his legs and sits forward. 'So let's just establish this,' he says icily. 'We're about to hear an unverified, unproven account from the key suspect.'

Gibson shows a steelier side. 'I'd rather not have interruptions, Sir. Shall we just hear what Mr Bridgewater has to say?'

Bill suppresses a comeback with a supremely irritated face and the Chief Inspector turns to Julian. 'Perhaps you'd like to start by explaining how you knew where she might be?' I swallow, feeling dread and fix my eyes on Julian.

'I didn't, I had no idea at all,' he explains, 'just a vague memory of a man who'd come in the shop once and talked to Jessie. He had been looking in the second-hand box and acting in a way that felt a bit odd. I asked about his interests and what he did. He said he was a security guard. Jess got quite cross later on, when I told her the man had seemed a bit suspicious and to be wary. He was called Martin, she said; he was very nice and they'd talked in the market square. His mother had just died, he had a sweet Jack Russell terrier.'

'I do remember her talking to a man there once,' I remark. Bill looks up from the painted stone, giving me a mistrustful glance. Does he think I'm making it up?

I turn back to Julian, who looks at me with hard-to-read eyes. 'After you'd called,' he says, still looking at me, 'I sat trying to think of places that might employ security guards; shops, businesses, and I tried to contact a few. It was after hours, they were all on answerphone. I hadn't much to go on either, just a name, Martin, that could easily have been assumed.'

'Quite so,' Bill says sarcastically. 'Your mobile was off. Where were you doing all this phoning?'

'On the landline,' Julian says with mild impatience. 'There are two at the house where I'm staying.'

'Shall we get on?' Gibson intervenes firmly.

Julian looks over to Tom. 'Then I suddenly thought of your holiday job at the biochemical laboratory last year, Tom, and that a lab must need security guards. One of the biologists there is a friend of mine and I called him at home. He didn't know any guards personally, but I must have sounded pretty desperate since he agreed to go back to the lab, find someone on duty and see what he could do.'

'And that worked?' I ask.

'Up to a point. A security guard told him there was one called Martin Jackson who was off that night. He knew more or less where he lived, not the exact address. Up an alley off a street called Hill Rise, he thought.'

'Before you go on,' I say, suddenly obsessed with clearing up the whole mobile thing that's so concerning me. 'Why did you have your mobile off? It was on, obviously, when I called you, but not when Chief Inspector Gibson tried to get through soon afterwards. And I believe he'd been trying you earlier, too. It doesn't make sense. You must have known how desperate I'd be to keep in touch all evening.'

'I'm sorry,' he says in a heartfelt way. 'I had to have it off. It's complicated . . .'

'I can believe that,' Bill snorts.

Julian ignores him and stares at me. 'I'll try and explain. I don't have my mobile on the whole time when I'm deep into the writing, I don't even answer the house phone. The Pearsons ring on the other line if they want to get in touch. And that's the number you've got, Ursula. I thought if you ever needed me you'd try that one as well as the mobile. Everyone else has the main number, people like Val Stockton. You'll find the number you have is different from hers – the one she gave the Chief Inspector.'

'But why was your mobile on just at the time I called, not before or after?'

He smiles. 'You might find this hard to believe, but – possibly because of Jessie's call at lunchtime – I was thinking about you then and feeling an instinctive need to be in touch. I switched it on and you called. It seemed uncanny. But with the most awful news, of course, that blew away every other thought in my head. You could still have reached me on the other line, still have been the only one to get through.'

He's looking straight at me, talking of need, and his eyes have lost that unreachable glaze. It's bringing a sort of sharpness of mind that I imagine must happen at times of a struggle to survive. I feel gripped, tingling, aching for him to care. Thoughts of Jessie are still uppermost in my mind, though, and I am able to slot away the feelings of hope and longing, saving them to be revisited.

'But why did you immediately switch your mobile off again?' I query. 'Surely you must have seen the need to keep in touch?'

Julian looks at his hands then up again. 'I had to do this thing entirely on my own – to track down a man who, from memory of that single meeting, seemed not unlike the man I'm researching in detail and so immersed in. It fitted, somehow, that he might be hanging round the baths. I felt sick with worry. If Jess was out of sorts, as she'd sounded, she could easily have been tempted to wander outside and talk to him, even possibly accept a drink on a hot day . . . And then, you see,' Julian says apologetically, turning to Gibson, 'after what happened in the case I'm researching I didn't trust the police not cock things up.'

'And then, and then,' Bill says scathingly, 'this is about as far-fetched as they come.'

I know my ex-husband well enough to suspect he doesn't entirely believe that; he's painted himself into a corner and refusing to budge. And there are a lot of anomalies.

Julian ignores him. 'Going it alone meant having to go to ground. Taking my car was obviously out of the question, which was a pity since it's fast. And I'd lost time calling round about security guards. I pushed that old Ford hard and got to Brearfield about half-past nine.'

He pauses and looks at Gibson. 'Now that I know where the CCTV cameras are it's clear Martin had known, too. He lives the opposite side of the Leisure Centre from the direction Jess turned towards and must have taken her on a circuitous route, doubling round at the back, perhaps. He'd known the angle of the cameras, for sure.

'From my research, people with his sort of antisocial personality disorder can be cunningly deceitful and yet act impulsively as well; he may have taken that elaborate, thought-through route without actually having had a particular plan.'

'You did search in the direction she went out of the baths?' I ask Gibson, hoping it doesn't sound over critical.

'Yes. We had to, logically. We concentrated the search that way, but with dogs trying to pick up the scent. Cars patrolling, police on the ground.'

Julian carries on. 'Without an exact address it was helpful that he lived in a cul-de-sac. There were a couple of houses either side at the beginning, then a bit of wasteland with a scrapyard opposite, then a pair of semi-detached bungalows at the end. One of which was his. The other seemed deserted, with a rusted car, general filth: a broken window. The old Ford was easy to lose in that street . . .'

Bill glares. 'How did you know which was his house in this very convenient cul-de-sac?'

'I didn't. I rang the bell at one or two houses with lights on and asked. Someone seemed almost sure they knew which was his and I inquired after the Jack Russell dog, just to confirm it was the right Martin Jackson.' Julian sips some water and goes on.

'I went into the garden of the other bungalow and sat on an upturned barrel behind the rusted car keeping very still and quiet. The dog might have heard me, but I wanted to stay out of sight from the road, and listen. It was dark by then, about half-past ten.'

His description and my image of the place are making me feel such dread. I swallow back nausea, thinking of Jessie held there and what can have happened.

Bill interrupts again. His face is grey-toned, cloudy with rage, menacing with its growth of beard. 'This is all too damn pat by half. I think, in fact,' he sneers, 'that you'd driven round well in advance of tonight, found a suitable property to fit your fantasy story – which seems to involve pinning the blame on some poor halfwit unsuspecting sod – and then taken advantage of my daughter. It fucking stinks.' He is on his feet now, the venomous rage pouring out.

Mine does too, and I jump up and storm over to him. I'm shaking, in the grip of febrile racing adrenaline.

'Julian has found Jess and brought her home – at God knows what risk to himself.' I'm glaring, my arms stiff at my sides, fists clenching and opening. 'And you're choosing to call him a liar and abuser? Don't you dare! I won't have it.'

'I'll call him what I damn well like.'

That's too much for me. My hand finds a will of its own and swings up making forceful contact with Bill's face. The sound of a stinging slap on his skin rings out alarmingly loudly and soberingly and seems to ricochet round the room. Bill turns his face in the direction it was struck, but does nothing to restrain me. He doesn't need to, I'm shocked out of my skin. I've never hit anyone before in my life.

Tom gets to me first. 'Mum, Mum, what are you doing!' His arm is round me, he's leading me back to the sofa. I've started crying, burying my face in my hands. 'It's not you – you've never even hit one of us!'

He turns to Gibson, whose expression is lost to me. I can't bear to look. 'She hasn't ever, I promise, and I'm sure she must have wanted to often enough. But at least,' Tom goes on, his tone sounding more wry. 'It's quite something, doing it the first time in front of three police officers. It's certainly leaving no doubt.'

'Perhaps I earned it,' Bill says. 'I have been making accusations without proof.'

It's a welcome apology. I take away my covering hands and look up. 'And I'm sorry, too, Bill.' My shoulders relax a bit, I give a few sniffs, but still feel unable to look Julian in the eye.

Finally I brave a glance at Chief Inspector Gibson and there was never a more impassive face. It's cruel of him, not giving me a lead. 'Will you have me up for assault? It is an open and shut case.' I give a weak smile.

'There are a lot of witnesses,' he says sombrely. 'Pity they're never there when we need them. Perhaps we'd better get on now, though, given the hour and what everyone has been through . . .' He looks over to Julian.

I still can't. Julian must be appalled at such lack of control. 'Sorry it's all taking a bit long, this,' he says. 'Would you rather pack up now? Chief Inspector Gibson could tell you everything that happened from then on, tomorrow. I'm actually a bit worried I might have left the Cambridgeshire house unlocked, leaving in such a rush—'

'That's all been seen to, Sir,' Jamison pipes up. 'The house has been made secure.'

'I think you'd better get on, right now,' Bill says. 'I want to hear it all, and from you.'

CHAPTER 20

The mood is less tense. Bill is finally accepting he could be wrong, I think, and seeing a wider landscape. He's been through the same hell as I have tonight, and must have had thoughts as searing as mine. I can't bring myself to forgive him, though, for aiming all his suspicion on Julian like a concentrated beam of torchlight – and it's obvious a corner of distrust is still there.

Bill has come to sit opposite now, on the other white sofa, one of the handsome pair he positioned with a careful eye to the room's symmetry, the width of the large marble fireplace apart. The vibrant paintings he left behind are on the walls, rich slashes of colour, flaunting as peacocks. It must have been extra hard, living through the long hours of crisis in this old familiar walked-out-on home, weighted down with memories and guilty ghosts.

Tom has stayed close by me – keeping in restraining range, I think, after my flash of violent temper. His nearness is making me feel soothed and washed over with love like water flowing over stones, and I reach out a hand. I'm going to find it hard to share him when some lucky girl claims him. It's a worry that he's become completely besotted with Maudie, his green-eyed girlfriend; they're both so young. There'll be others in time, though, I'm sure.

Chief Inspector Gibson is leaning well forward, hands clasped round crossed knees, preparing to concentrate hard. I'm glad he hasn't been eyeing his watch and appearing to hanker after his hotel bedroom. He's looking sharp-eyed and intelligently determined, keen to get on.

Julian's topaz eyes are distant, briefly distracted in thought. I want them focussed on me, but he seems unreachable, retreated into some private shell.

Is he thinking about Lauren or things in his past that I know so little about? Uganda, Aids hospitals, the ways he got involved in local struggles; I can remember Jessie saying, when he came home with gifts from his last trip, that he really cared about all the homeless people out there.

My thoughts are dipping in and out like seabirds. I long to discover those parts of him below the surface, the parts always closed to me where the shades are down.

'So how did you get Jessie away from that bungalow?' Bill demands sharply, snapping me back. 'Assuming she was, in fact, really there, in this god-awful-sounding place . . .'

Julian ignores the combative sarcasm. 'The hard part was trying to stay calm. I knew nothing of Martin Jackson, not his motivation, not his level of aggression. I was up to here in schizoid and personality disorders, but it suddenly all seemed so terrifyingly flimsy and theoretical when Jessie's life was at stake.'

He's lifting me on to a whole new level of stress. It's unbearable, waiting to hear what's to come.

'If Martin did have Jessie in there,' Julian carries on, 'getting her out was going to depend on finding a way to communicate. He was perfectly capable of normal conversations, I'd had a minimal one with him myself, but he must almost certainly have some form of mental illness. I thought it unlikely he was a cold calculating deviant; hard to believe he would have come into the shop and talked to Jessie so openly had he been sexually obsessed. Most probably he was no more than one of life's floundering disordered misfits. That didn't stop him being impulsive and dangerous. Assuming he had Jessie, the situation was grim.'

The room is silent; my spine's gone to jelly.

'People are busy,' Julian says. 'Martin had probably only ever been shown indifference at best. He'd just lost his mother and was lonely. Jessie's sympathetic interest must have made him seek her out. But even had he wanted no more than a friendly companion, he could still have been given to bursts of violent aggression.

'Jessie's intelligence makes her better at communicating than many children of her age. I'm sure she would have responded and probably felt pleased he was appealing to her and in need of company. She has been a bit unsettled by everything, all the recent events, and Elton dying came at a very bad time.'

The implications of Jessie unsettled touch Bill on the raw — although, I think, by 'recent events', Julian was meaning himself and me.

Tautening his lips, Bill reacts with an angry comeback. 'How the hell would you know? Are you such an authority on my daughter's feelings? Has she "responded" and "felt pleased you were appealing to her"?' he demands, throwing Julian's phrases back in his face.

'Think about it, William.' Julian looks him straight in the eye. 'I've been taking Ursula out since you left, coming to this house, having meals, getting to know your children. Jessie especially, of course, because of the books. She's really enjoyed learning about the antiquarian trade – quite the capable little dealer now – but initially, I think, it was an escape route. A distraction, her own private world after all the ups and downs.'

I feel priggishly sanctimonious as Bill studies his nails, showing his sensitivities. Then aware of being as much at fault myself and desperate to move on I ask, 'How did you find out she was definitely there, Julian? Did you talk to Martin – how did you get her away?'

'The dog suddenly barking was a sort of trigger. I'd crept up to the dividing wall trying to see the lie of the land and he started up quite a racket.

'I hopped over the wall and quickly up into the porch. Through the door I could hear a voice inside hissing violently, 'Shut it, lay off – shut it . . .' Then there were yelps of pain, as if something had been chucked at the dog or he'd got a hefty kicking. It was proof of somebody there, almost certainly Martin.'

The dog's treatment, Jessie's bruises: it's hard to contain my shivering. 'Did you start talking through the door? Had you worked out what to say?'

'Only what not to.' Julian smiles. 'Never promise anything, never say no, I've learned are the rules of negotiating. I didn't think that would wash with Martin. He was cornered and dangerous and, since I was way out of order anyway,' he glances at Gibson, 'they were rules I felt uncommitted to, that I could risk breaking if need be.' The Chief Inspector is looking as inscrutable as ever.

'I started talking through the door,' Julian carries on, 'saying I was the man from the bookshop and knew Martin had Jessie in there – that I was quite alone and he needn't worry on that score. "You're in a whole lot of trouble," I said. "You're going to need someone to be a good friend to you. I know you've been through a stressful time from Jessie and I'm prepared to help. You'll have to trust me . . ." I told him people were combing the town, it was only a matter of time, that he'd only get himself into a worse hole. Everyone would understand how distressed he'd been and that he meant no harm . . .

'I went on saying stuff like that interminably. There was nothing, no cough, no heavy breathing – only the sound of the dog sniffing at the door. I felt desperate.'

Julian's eyes are on me alone, he's forgotten the rest of his silent audience. 'I was doing my all, Ursula. I just kept on talking, hoping the man would crack. The strain was awful and I could almost smell Martin's fear and tension too, his adrenaline was creeping round the door like escaping smoke.

'There was no way of knowing for certain that Jessie was still alive. I went on promising no weapons, no knives, telling him not to make things worse for himself, just to open the door a finger and see I was quite alone.

'I was struggling, getting nowhere. Then I said, "Your mother was proud of you, wasn't she, Martin? She wouldn't have wanted this." At that moment Jessie started to cry – just a few jerky tearful little intakes of breath – and I could hear Martin whispering, "Shut it, shut it or it'll be worse. You won't like it." But at last the door opened a needle's width and he peered through the crack. I took a step back and put my hands on my head. He shone a little pencil torch right in my eyes, but I kept on talking. "I need to come in, Martin. Best if I do then we can sort this out. You're in a lot of trouble, serious trouble," I repeated that endlessly.'

'You did get in?' I query faintly. 'Where was Jessie? What had he done to her . . .?' It feels as though there's a stone in my throat, wait-ing on his reply.

'Yes, I got in,' Julian says, with his eyes on me. 'Martin eased open the door a fraction more, but with a carving knife. I had to edge past the blade.' My eyes flash instinctively to his body for marks. One of the sleeves of his blue shirt is torn, there's a largish matt brown stain.

'Martin kicked the door shut and put on a weak passage light; it allowed me to take everything in before starting the unnerving busi-ness of trying to negotiate. I could see into the living room, see a brown armchair, an old-fashioned wooden standard lamp and a dirty orange hearthrug in front of a mock-coals fire.

'Jessie was sitting on an upright chair right in the middle of the room, staring ahead like someone under cross-examination. She wasn't tied, but I could see she'd been hit and, most horrifying, there were kitchen knives laid out on the floor all round her. I couldn't make eye contact, she obviously wasn't daring to look my way.'

It's an arresting, terrifying image; even Bill is silent and unques-tioning.

'It seemed vital to concentrate on Martin – who's shortish, late for-ties I would say, receding fuzzy-brown hair,' Julian describes, looking over to Gibson. 'He was wearing khaki fatigues, black T-shirt, quite fancy trainers and has a flower-design tattoo on one forearm.'

'So? What then?' Bill demands tightly.

'It was an extraordinary thing. He suddenly sent the knife clat-tering and dropped down on his knees – right there where we were in the hall. He kept repeating, "I'm in serious trouble," parroting my phrase, almost savouring the words, their drama and importance. And he was shaking too, a real attack of the shivers. Then he said, "I didn't mean no harm."

'I told him we must let the girl go, trying to make it sound practical, a joint decision. I was straining backwards all the while, trying to unlatch the door and click it to stay unlocked. I called through to Jess to go and sit in the blue Ford car outside in the street. I reeled off the numberplate, said it was unlocked and begged her just to run, get in and wait.

'"She'll talk, she can't go," Martin said. I promised I'd see she didn't. Jess got up, but quite unsteadily and knelt to pat the dog as if taking a minute to find the strength. I was motioning feverishly as she was picking a way over the knives, willing her just to get the hell out. She got past us and to the door, but she was still hesitating; I thought she was frightened of going out in the dark alone, but she actually said, "Bye Martin," almost as though she was talking to a friend, not an unhinged man who had hit her in the face.

'I stayed on a minute repeating he wasn't to worry, people would understand. I pressed a few twenties in his palm hoping that the surprise element of a bit of money would slow him up, and promised again neither Jessie or I would talk. But it was breaking the cardinal rule of never promising anything, which worried me. I told him his mother would have been proud then shifted it as fast as I've ever sprinted and released the latch as I went so the door would slam shut. You know the rest,' he says.

'You did more than your all,' I tell him, trying to get a grip, knowing it must sound so inadequate and useless. He shrugs and smiles faintly, looking worn out from the effort of the telling.

'God, I felt right there,' Tom exclaims, breaking the trance that's descended on the room. 'I was getting so psyched up, waiting for you to describe taking a lunge at that man . . . Just as well Gran wasn't hearing all this, it would have really put her through it.'

'Can you go up to her, Tom? Say I'm just coming and she should get to bed. You must too. I'll be leaning on you for help in the morning. Emma will need careful priming. It's not going to be an easy time.'

I stand up, shaky with nervous exhaustion. Bill gets up too. 'It's very late; hadn't you better stay the night,' I suggest awkwardly, floundering, walking into the hall with him. It sounds more like an offer to a London dinner guest than an ex-husband whom I've just slapped in the face. The raised red mark left by my hand has subsided and calmed, but not my shame.

'No, I'll get straight off,' he says, leaving me jealously imagining him offloading in Victoria's comforting arms. 'I'll want to come back to see Jess, though.' Bill looks straight at me, needing to establish his rights. 'To see how she is. Perhaps tomorrow?'

The thought of him back again so soon is too much for me. I can't take any more of this piercing tension and stress; it's worse than the facing a bull in the ring, lions in the pit.

'What about Sunday? Emma and I will be doing lunch, you'd have time with Jessie.'

He seems content with that – and I think he has honestly begun to accept Julian's account. It would be hard not to with the clarity and honesty of that story, glaring out like the sun cleared of covering cloud.

Gibson is in the hall, waiting while the others pack up, and, saying goodbye on the doorstep, Bill looks past me with a question. 'What about that phantom call? Julian insists he had one from Jessie, but you said none had been made from her mobile all day.'

Julian has come up and joined us, also wanting to go, I think, and chips in, sounding slightly irritated, 'As I told the Chief Inspector, all

I can say is that she called. I was out at a supermarket and had my mobile with me.'

Inspector Jamison has just appeared out of the sitting room. 'We have, um, checked the calls to your mobile, sir,' he says, 'and none of them came from her phone.'

'She did call,' Julian insists. 'It came as a surprise. I don't actually even remember giving her the number. It's as much of a mystery to me.'

'One that I'm sure she herself will soon solve,' Gibson says firmly and Bill has to content himself with that. He hurries out into the night.

Mary leaves next, smiling goodbye and giving my shoulders a warm kindly squeeze.

'I must be off too,' Julian says.

'You're not driving all that way to Cambridgeshire tonight, surely? You could stay here . . .'

'No, not tonight, now that I know the house is OK. I'll go to the shop. It's under offer, but the key's still on my ring.'

Gibson is looking from Julian to me. He has something to say. A bit more than his goodbyes, I think.

'I'm afraid we will need to speak to Jess at the very first opportunity, Mrs Osborne. Early tomorrow; I'm trying to set up an interview for eleven. A highly trained and qualified child protection officer will be asking the questions. Not at a police station, there are specialist suites of rooms for interviewing children. Somewhere designed to put Jess as far as possible at her ease. They're not keen on a parent attending, but I am going to recommend you should be present, Mrs Osborne. I think it will be all right.'

'I would like to be there.'

'The nearest suite is right behind Brearfield Hospital. There's a medical examining room, but, assuming her evidence tallies, it's quite possible Jess won't need a full examination,' Gibson says delicately. 'There is also an observation room, and I shall be listening in from there. I've already arranged for a police car to be here for you at ten-thirty and one to return you home. And lastly, we need to take away Jessie's clothes and trainers for forensic testing. Mary has got them ready, I believe.'

Julian has been waiting to have a word. 'I'm very conscious of keeping you,' he says, 'but there's something on my mind that's exercising me quite a lot.'

'Fire away, sir.' Gibson is all ears and attention, showing no signs of tiredness.

'Well, Jessie obviously formed some sort of avenue of communication with her captor. The way she hesitated and needed to say goodbye to Martin was very genuine. And she'd have certainly heard all my protestations to him that neither of us would talk. I fear she might feel bound by that, possibly quite frightened, too, of the consequences of breaking her word. She has a strong will. I think, if you have no objection, it would be good for me to talk to her before the interview and try to explain how important it is she tells it as it was.'

Gibson ponders that. 'I would need to be present. And I should also remind you, of course, that you would still be under caution. Perhaps if we meet here about ten tomorrow then – if that's all right with Mrs Osborne?'

'Of course.' It brings a powerful sense of relief and reprieve to know Julian will be here again in the morning, and hasn't quite yet walked out of my life. But it's only a stay of execution.

I'm really frightened about Jessie and absolutely understand about

Julian's worries. It's desperate, thinking of her alone with Martin, scared out of her wits and having to communicate, but it would be in her nature to feel honour-bound to stay silent. Surely she'll feel more loyal to Julian and see the need to corroborate his story? I can't tell Jessie that he probably saved her life. It would add to her lingering fear and nightmarish memories and bring extra pressure.

Julian leaves almost immediately, ahead of the two detectives. It seems ironic that despite Jessie being at the bookshop, all the gossip and finger-pointing, far from being irresponsible Julian was watching out for her. He saw the danger signs that I'd missed, he picked up clues to her possible fate – and had the speed of mind and the singular qualities needed to act on them. Independence, unorthodoxy; steadiness in a crisis.

He can't know how my feelings have crystallized and I can imagine how that crisis call will strike him when he gives it thought. It will seem dreadfully anticlimactic after the uncanny timing of his switched-on mobile. I had been calling in a time of need, in anguish, not love.

Julian will see it as a cry for help that couldn't be refused and think of what he did tonight as a duty discharged. He did it with all his heart and guts and ingenuity, but now it's the end. The shop is under offer, all his Brearfield ties cut. He'll have Lauren, probably, for comfort. If I call in the next days and weeks talking of love, he'll assume my feelings are coloured by overwhelming gratitude.

And if he asks or finds out about Perry Maynard, that really will be that.

It's two in the morning. Muggy enough to be the tropics, but I'm feeling a sense of bleakness, cold as an Arctic wind. It's penetrating right to the bone.

Gibson and Jamison are ready to leave. On the doorstep the Chief Inspector shakes my hand. 'Try and get some sleep,' he says, with perceptively understanding eyes. 'Jessie's home and safe from harm; be thankful for that. However bad life looks, it always has unexpected twists along its route.'

CHAPTER 21

The sun is streaming in. I must have forgotten to close the shutters, I think, not really awake, half-absorbing the shafts of bright light slanting in on to the pale honey carpet.

Then everything comes flooding back as fast as a click of the fingers. Turning the other way in panic it's an overwhelming relief to see that Jess is sleeping peacefully beside me.

She's on her back with her head dropped to my side, her mouth slightly open. The bruises have really come out, in all shades from pale mauve to inky prune, the bad eye is puffy, her lips are swollen, the upper one cracked. It makes me feel sickened and very angry.

I ease out of bed and stand in my nightdress, uncertain what to do. It's eight already, Jess needs all the sleep she can get before the ordeal of an interview that as yet she knows nothing about.

It seems best to leave her and get my own show on the road. Emma would be in by now; she can't be awake. I have a quick shower and hair-wash, hurrying back into the bedroom in a towel, but Jess hasn't stirred. Nor does she with the noise of the drier, it's going to be a real job waking her. I have quite a sense of achievement when I'm in navy cotton trousers and pink-striped shirt –

interview-room clothes – with clean blow-dried hair and it's only eight-fifteen.

The thought of the testing, stressful emotional day ahead of us fills me with dread, but I'm also finding it hard to contain a kind of tight-chested elation. We've come through. Jessie's home, alive – it's a feeling like first holding a baby after giving birth.

I'm wiping away a tear or two when Emma comes in. I hold out my arms, but she's too distracted, seeing her sister in the bed, and creeps round to the side Jess is facing. I go beside her and put an arm round her as she stares at Jessie. Then she raises her eyes with a questioning look that's also one of complete horror.

I wrap her up tight. She's keeping her head buried and, sounding muffled and miserable, talks into my chest. 'I can never ever forgive myself, Mum. If only I hadn't been so mean in the changing rooms. I feel so awful. What can I do to make up?'

'She's home, Ems, that's all that matters. It's not you – I'm to blame if anyone, and horrible old life. Just be as normal as possible with her and don't ask any questions, love. That's important. She'll still be in shock and very distressed. You'll hear everything soon enough.'

Will Jessie tell us the whole story from her side? I need to know what happened all those hours she was confined in that house with Martin. How he got her there, how she coped.

I tell Emma that Chief Inspector Gibson is coming back to see Jessie – and Julian, too. Also that Jess has to go and give evidence and be interviewed at a special suite of rooms near Brearfield General Hospital. 'It's going to be a bit fraught,' I say with a smile that I hope conveys the need for us all to keep our cool and be superhumanly understanding.

Emma sits down gingerly on the bed. 'Gran says Julian found her and brought her home.'

'You've seen Gran – she's up?'

'For hours, probably, she always is. She came into my bedroom and we decided we should leave you a bit.'

'You shouldn't have, never think that!'

It was good of my mother, making Emma feel grown-up and needed. She'd have liked that. Emma must be half-traumatized herself. There was all the strain of searching the Leisure Centre, the hours she had to get through before I was home. God, why did I ever get involved with Perry?

My mother looks round the bedroom door. 'I've brought you a cup of tea. Your hair looks nice, darling. It's all over the papers' late editions, according to the radio,' she whispers theatrically, coming to our side of the bed, 'and it was on the radio news. The police have put out a brief statement, that she was missing seven hours before being found and returned. They say they'll be releasing further details later.'

I suppress a sigh at the thought of a whole new batch of press intrusion: journalists calling and asking for quotes, Jessie's school friends seeing it.

As I take the tea from her, my mother says, 'Her poor face is really bad, isn't it? Don't you think perhaps we should start getting her up? It'll be a slow business. Did you know Tom thought of putting the phone on answermachine last night? He said it would never stop ringing today! It'll probably get full up.'

My mother is peering at Jess in the arching-neck way of someone driving past an accident and it jars. I ask tightly how she slept, unable to hide my frayed-nerves irritability. Then I suggest, I hope not too much in the way of pushing her out, that it would be wonderful if she got breakfast ready while I got Jess up.

She seems to accept that and, giving one of her traditional worried smiles, tiptoes out.

Emma stays. 'Will she hate seeing me, Mum?'

'The opposite. She'll feel all the better and know she's really home!'

Sitting on the bed I whisper to Jessie that she has to wake up and lightly brush her bruised cheek with my fingers. I lift her up off the pillow and hold her. She smells of sleeping hot child, a sort of mixture of hay and warm milk, and still faintly of the antiseptic Doctor Jeffries used to bathe her face.

Jess stirs, making complaining grunts, wriggling in a fidgety scratchy way, then suddenly goes completely rigid in my arms. 'No, no don't, I won't.' It's a waking dream, I think, pressing her tighter to me and feeling her slowly calm down.

'Hi Sis. Are you feeling awful? Your face must be so really sore.' Emma touches her hand and Jess focusses, more fully awake. She stares at her sister and then back at me.

'You need to get up and start getting dressed, Jess,' I say. 'Julian is coming to see you, and the nice policeman from last night.' It seems terribly abrupt and premature to bring up the interview, but I've got to warn her and begin getting her used to the idea. It's happening so soon. 'And people will need to ask you questions, a proper serious interview that's recorded on video. It is very important – you do understand?'

'No. I don't want that.' She pulls away from me brusquely. One eye is almost completely closed, but the other is full of fear. 'They can't. I won't say.'

'Julian's going to explain about it,' I plead, trying not to sound too desperate. 'Come in the bathroom now, and then we'll choose some clothes – your denim skirt and blue T-shirt?'

She's not saying another word. Emma tries her best, wonderfully. 'You can wear cool sunglasses with your black eye, Jess! Like those swish ones in *Bliss* that were so good – you were keen on the red-check frame ones, remember?'

Jess stares back grumpily, keeping her lopsided mouth zipped shut. When I hold out her old trainers, though, there's an explosion. 'I'm not wearing those smelly old things!' She grabs them and hurls them across the room like a tantrumming toddler and wails, 'I want my K-Swiss ones.'

Screwing up her face in fury causes visible pain and an outbreak of heaving tears. Trying to explain about the need for forensic testing seems a very bad idea.

Emma hurries out and is back again in no time bearing Jessie's black ballet pumps. I can't believe this wonderful sisterly gentleness will last, but right now it's saving the day.

Julian arrives at quarter to ten. As I answer the bell and let him in, Jessie comes out of the kitchen and stares. 'Hi Jess,' he says easily. 'That's a real boxer's black eye! It must hurt a bit. I hope you didn't have nightmares like me!' She shakes her head then slowly nods it up and down. 'I've brought you a book. It's the *Pied Piper* by Nevil Shute, about children being rescued in the war – you'll understand what they went through!' She takes it without saying thank you and starts reading the first page.

'Coffee, Julian, while we've got a minute?' I hardly dare look at him, feeling shy as a bird, desperate for a few snatched minutes alone. 'Jess, can you go and ping the kettle, please?'

I'm determined to be normal and firm with her for all my agitated anxiety. She had breakfast, half a bowl of cereal, in complete silence, yawning a lot, which hurt and caused her to give in to tears, which was obviously touching her pride. It seems important she stays in the kitchen; it would be awful if Gibson started thinking Julian's had an advance chat with her. Julian must see that, too.

Jess looks up from the book. I can tell her mind is at work. Is it about Julian and me or is she deciding to pit her will and be stubborn? She goes silently back into the kitchen, though, and Julian comes with me into the sitting room. He closes the door behind us. If only I knew the thoughts in his head, too. We sit on opposite sofas, too far apart for him to take my hand.

'How can I begin to thank you?' I say, looking across with a nervous smile that fades as I battle with my thudding heart. 'There are no words. I keep wondering if Jess would even be alive, but for you. It's so momentous, what you did. It feels wrong just to say thank you . . . You do understand?'

'I was as desperate as you. It was vital to find her, I thought we had so little time.'

'You'll probably want to get back,' I say cautiously, 'but can't you stay on a day or two in Brearfield?' I'm feeling the dull leaden ache of instinctive certainty that he won't. He's still looking quite washed out. I want to go beside him, kiss and soothe his eyes and lean his head down on my chest. 'Did you really have nightmares?' I ask lightly, going on in a rush, not needing or waiting for an answer. 'I wish you'd stay over. I . . . do want a chance to say a few things – not least to go on pouring out inadequate thanks!'

He smiles at that. It's a warm smile, wonderful contact. 'You don't need to do that. I could so easily have made things worse. I must get back to Cambridgeshire. I'm leaving straight from here. It's best. There's the book to finish, better all round.'

I look down at my hands then get up with a long slow release of breath that has to take the place of tears. 'I'll just get the coffee,' I say, avoiding his eyes.

Julian gets up, too, and intercepts me, taking hold of my wrists as he had done on the night of the row. I meet his eyes then, with my insides in knots. Will he kiss me? My ribcage feels bound with ropes. He gives me a concentrated look, then frees up a hand to touch my face and brush over my lips. His fingers trail lightly down my neck and span out wide under my jaw, as though holding my head to keep me looking at him.

Taking away his hand and moving back a bit, he says, 'I'll turn up one of these days and see how you are, and Jess.' We can both hear the sound of a car in the drive. 'That'll be my minder.' He grins. 'You'd better go and let him in. Don't know how far I'll get with Jess, I have a feeling she's not going to be very receptive.'

Gibson and Jamison look spruce and neatly combed. I ask after their hotel and whether they got a few hours sleep. 'Julian is in the sitting room. Do go in. I'll just get Jess.'

'May I suggest you leave us alone with her,' Gibson says solemnly.

I want to ask why, feeling cross, but haven't the nerve. It's too delicate an area. 'That's fine,' I reply evenly, 'but you'll tell me afterwards how it went?'

'Of course.'

'I'll bring in the coffee and get Jess.'

Pouring boiling water into the cafetière, I ask Emma to come and say hello to Chief Inspector Gibson. She seemed to have made quite a friend of him last night. 'You as well, Jess – Julian wants to see you, too.'

She's at the table with her head dropped on her hands. I hope she's not going to choose to be difficult and ignore what I've just said. It wouldn't be the first time. I don't want a fight on my hands. She gets up, though, touching her sore lips and my heart.

After pouring the coffee and leaving the sitting room with Emma, I let resentment build up at being excluded. Gibson could at least have given me a reason. It saps my confidence and makes me feel hurt, like a patient kept in the dark, someone not trusted enough to be sensible.

Tom comes into the kitchen in T-shirt and cargoes and makes himself a bowl of muesli and yoghurt, giving a huge yawn. He talks of needing to go and collect some work. 'I'm just so behind, Mum, but I'll be back. And I won't go till after Jess's interview, I'll be here with Emma all morning.'

My mother is staying until Sunday. I must make a serious effort not to bite her head off all day. It would help, I think, if I could talk to her about Julian, but she seems to put up a screen that I find hard to go round behind. She's thought Julian unsuitable from the start.

Am I right to read meaning into his remark about turning up to see me sometime? It's certainly going to ensure I'm jumping at the sound of every car, every mobile beep. On top of that, I'll be terrified of letting Jessie out of my sight for a single moment. I should have asked Doctor Jeffries for some downers, sleeping pills – and some for Jess. Will she need a sedative these first few nights?

It's the right thing that Julian is going back to Cambridgeshire. Jessie needs every ounce of my love and attention now. Emma will need to feel loved and not forgotten, too. Is it going to take weeks, months? What a household we shall be; three frightened females, all jumpy and nervous as maltreated kittens.

Bill's coming back to see Jessie tomorrow and he'll want to know all about her interview. She must back up Julian's account. I couldn't face any more of those black venomous looks. I need Bill to be saying sorry and showing real humility.

'There's a police car just parking, Mum.'

'Thanks, Ems. I suppose it'll wait. Do you want to go and ask if they'd like coffee?' She runs off, looking pleased to have any little task. It's so hard on her, all this.

Chief Inspector Gibson had better speed up the return of Jess's trainers, I think, or we'll be having tantrums every day. Emma's patience and inventiveness won't last for ever. I want to ask Gibson about the press statement, what more they will put out and how soon. I suppose it all depends on Jessie's interview.

The media will certainly keep up the pressure. Once there's a suspect, will they say someone is 'helping the police with their inquiries'? Will that be Martin? Will Jessie confirm he's the one?

What if he's done a bunk? Julian giving him money was probably not a great idea from that point of view. Will he come looking for Jess and seeking revenge if she talks?

Gibson will be at the interview suite. I can ask questions then, although with Jessie there, perhaps not. But he'll soon be gone anyway and we'll be left in this house with no near neighbours, left to cope with our demons alone.

The two police officers settle us in the back. The car is sweaty and stuffy, a male workplace, and, along with the cameramen at the gate, it's making me feel claustrophobic. The whole media shouting match is back again, almost as many as descended on me when Bill's affair was exposed. Whatever Jessie's thoughts about cameras pointed at her, though, she seems now to be quite enjoying the policemen's chat. She's better with men, I think, knowing that the child protection officer about to interview her is a woman.

Julian hadn't got a thing out of her, I gathered from Gibson just as we were leaving.

The suite is a very confusing building with too many doors; single storey, prefab style, but quite streamlined, fresh and modern once we find our way in. Gibson is waiting for us and starts talking to Jess. After the session in the sitting room they've got some kind of a rapport going, I think, hoping that bodes well. My mind inevitably slips to Julian; will he be halfway to Cambridgeshire by now?

'Why do you need all my clothes and stuff,' Jess demands suddenly, 'when you know I was there?' It's such a clear and unexpected question after all her head-shaking and refusal to speak and quite takes me by surprise.

'We don't know anything,' Gibson replies smiling. 'We don't know if you are telling the truth, whether Mr Bridgewater is – even if your mother and father are. Forensics gives us proof. There's a sort of rule of forensics that when two people are in contact, something of each is left behind. Your clothes will have traces of substances that you couldn't possibly see with a naked eye: blood, saliva, anything. We have a whole library of sneaker imprints, too. After trainers have been worn a couple of months every single one has its own unique imprint. All clues to help see justice is done and that no one is wrongly blamed.'

Jess looks about to ask more, but the door is opening. We're in a small airless waiting room with one high-up window and a low table with magazines and comics. The woman coming in has dark glossy hair and perfect skin, the sort that will never line. She's dressed in a neat grey cotton trouser-suit and high heels. She could be any age between thirty and fifty, I think.

'Just thought I'd say hello. I'm Misha Annand, but call me Misha. Everyone does. Someone's bringing you tea. Do you like tea? We've got Coke or orange juice.'

There's nothing patronizing or sickly about her smile, but Jessie doesn't answer. I'm cross and embarrassed, but Gibson has laid on heavily that the reason parents are seldom allowed to be present is because of the great urge to speak for or communicate with their children. I'm impressed that Misha made no reference to the state of Jessie's face. She doesn't wait for Jess to answer and leaves with a friendly look and an incline of the head, but no more smiles.

A busty woman with a bad cold brings us a tray of tea and biscuits. Jess likes tea and has a few sips, but there's a sense among us of a need to get on and be able to put this ordeal behind us.

Gibson soon takes us two doors down the passage and delivers us to Misha. He doesn't mention to Jessie that he'll be watching and listening unobserved, just says he'll see us afterwards. 'Tell what you know, Jessie, answer the questions. You'll be fine.'

I feel despairing. However highly trained and unthreatening this child protection officer is, I think, she's a stranger, and it's not an interview about favourite books, food or film stars. Jess has to relive the hideous trauma of her long hours alone with a man who struck her, and, for reasons of fear, perhaps honouring Julian's promise that she wouldn't talk, unknown sensitivities, whatever it is, something is holding her back. How can this pleasant impersonal interviewer break through the barrier of her stubborn resolve?

CHAPTER 22

The interview gets underway. The room is workmanlike with the video recording equipment clearly in evidence but also a few thought-through touches, as in a dentist's waiting room, to help people feel more relaxed. The chairs are comfortable, upholstered in dark blue, there's a struggling palm in a glazed Chinese-style barrel pot and paintings: a farmyard scene and two tame landscapes with hills and sheep grazing.

Misha pours Jessie a glass of water and explains the reasons for videoing the interview. 'It should save any need for you to go to court. And while things are fresh in your mind now, they mightn't be in a few months time.'

The first questions are routine, name, age, any siblings. I think of Chief Inspector Gibson tucked away in an observation room and wonder whether he feels frustrated at being unable to conduct the interview himself. He has explained about all the strict rules for interviewing children, that there is a five-tiered structure of competence and that Jessie's interviewer will be at level three. The top two tiers are for exceptional cases, highly specialist, dealing with extreme situations such as serial murders where links could be hard to detect.

He also told me, in the few minutes we were alone just now, when Jessie was in the loo, that traumatic events tended to force witnesses and victims to narrow their attention to the core aspects of the frightening experience they had lived through. He thought she may yet give a very fluid account.

It's not easy to imagine she will. Jess is looking petulant, fixing on the farmyard picture with her bruised sulky face.

Misha says. 'I know you won't find it easy to talk about what happened, Jess, but I would just like to paint in some background. For instance, before you went to school yesterday morning had you asked not to go swimming?'

She hadn't, I think quickly, it was only after she got home – after the tiff with a friend.

'No.'

'No, meaning you hadn't asked not to, or no, you didn't want to swim?'

The interview is going to take forever at this rate. 'I didn't talk about swimming before school.' Jess is scowling like a scolded teenager.

'When did you decide you didn't want to swim?'

Jessie shrugs. She's still partly in shock and exhausted, I think, feeling sick with worry.

'Did something happen to upset you at school?' Misha goes on.

There's a considerable pause, but Jess eventually elaborates. 'A girl called Zoe was mean about Julian. She said he was on the sex register.'

'Did that worry you? Did you believe her?'

'No.'

'Did you ring Julian at all during school?'

'Yes.'

'Can you remember about what time it was?'

'In lunch break.'

'But you hadn't made any calls from your mobile all day, yesterday. We've checked.'

'I forgot it at home.'

Misha looks levelly at my daughter. 'What phone did you use, then, Jess?'

She shrugs, but then responds grumpily, 'I borrowed a friend's.'

'Why did you want to ring Julian?'

Another shrug. We wait patiently. 'He didn't know my guinea-pig had died,' Jess says finally. 'I was cross people were being horrible about him and wanted to tell him about Elton.'

'After school you went home, had tea, and left for swimming. Then for a short time you were going to a friend of your mother's, weren't you? Did you mind that?'

Jess lifts her shoulders in an enormous shrug – is she already half-forgetting I'm here?

'Yes. I minded what Mum was doing,' she says unnervingly.

I try to hide my embarrassment and not react, but no one's paying any attention to me anyway. I'm becoming invisible.

'Why did you mind, Jess?' Misha asks, impressing me with her straightforward non-prying way of probing.

After another interminable pause Jess says, 'I didn't want some horrible new man around.'

'Your mobile was in with your swimming things. You remembered to pick it up from home – was there any particular reason for that?'

'No, just to have it. Mum checked we had our phones because of her being away.'

Misha sips from her glass of water then carries straight on. 'And you didn't want to swim because of Zoe?'

'Yes, I've said that.' Jess answers, jutting out her chin with a look of defiance.

'So when your mother had driven off for the evening, you didn't get changed for swimming, you decided to go out, to go off somewhere on your own?'

'Only out on to the steps to get some air. My sister was bugging me, I felt fed up.'

'Who did you see when you went out on the steps?' Jessie looks away. There's a window with a light opaque blind; she stares at it. Then transfers her gaze to the farmyard picture. Misha tries again. 'Was it a man called Martin with his dog?' With her heels dug in my daughter can have a resolve as strong as any spy's. At this moment, not even coercion, which thankfully is hardly likely, would bend that determined will.

'Was it Julian you saw?'

'Why – why should I have seen him?' Jess demands pugnaciously.

'He was nowhere to be found all those hours you were lost and had left home in a great hurry. We don't know anything that went on. You could have been with him. If you don't tell us what happened, the wrong man could be convicted.'

'But you get forensic evidence to stop that.' She's taken on board all Gibson was telling her, I think, proudly.

'Forensic evidence isn't always conclusive. And circumstantial evidence – when everything else seems to fit – can be very persuasive. So you must tell us who it was that you saw when you came out and stood on the steps?'

'No.'

'When did you first see Julian – where did you make contact? You must have at some stage. He brought you home.'

Jess isn't falling for that. She looks up at the picture, pushes at one thumb's cuticle with the other; rubs her bruised eye. I can tell she's very close to tears. It's a quarter to twelve, over half an hour of interviewing gone.

'You care about Martin, don't you?' Misha remarks. 'You think he needs help.'

My daughter goes on pushing at her cuticle, but I feel there's a crack in her armour.

'Would you believe me if I say other people will understand that, too?'

'They'll just say so, but they lock people up in prison and it makes them worse.'

'Sometimes that happens: mostly people who need help do get it. Are you worried Martin might feel you'd let him down or that he might hold it against you?'

Jessie starts to cry. Misha takes no notice and carries straight on. 'When sick people are locked up they do get treatment. You mustn't worry at all about that.'

'They won't think he's sick,' Jess sniffs. 'It doesn't show. He's like a normal person – just someone who's had. . .horrible things happen in his life.'

'Doctors know about people in Martin's situation. Some might have been badly mistreated, not all; either way they need help, they're a danger to themselves and others.'

'Martin's father beat him.'

'Tell us what happened, Jessie.'

The tension contained in her silence is like a drop of rainwater clinging to a windowpane; it can't hold on for much longer, it must lose its grip. She turns my way, looking so abjectly desolate that my heart's ready to break. 'I'm sorry, Mum,' her bruised tear-stained little face is really wretched. 'I knew it was stupid and wrong going with him, but he wasn't a real stranger . . .'

'It's all right Jess, don't think about that. Tell Misha what happened, forget I'm here.'

'When I went out on the steps I saw him just up the road, sitting on a wall with his little Jack Russell dog, Dicky, at his feet. He waved to me so I went over to say hello. Dicky was panting, looking so hot – Martin said he loved ice lollies and it was such a funny sight seeing him lick them. Then he talked about having some in the freezer at home and suggested I come on a little walk and have one with Dicky. It was so hot, I really wanted a lolly and there was nearly a whole hour to go of the swimming . . .'

'It was quite a long way to his home, wasn't it?' Misha queries.

'He kept saying we were nearly there and that Dicky needed his exercise and there was a much shorter way back. I hated the house when we got there, it was so skanky and rank, sort of shut-up and dead looking – it made me think of his dead mother who he'd talked about in the past. I said I'd wait outside.' Jessie leaves it there.

'Then what happened?' Misha coaxes.

'He came back out almost straight away and said Dicky was having the lolly in his bowl and I must come and see. I was quite frightened and not wanting to, I was worried about getting back, not knowing the way. But Martin had been really nice and sympathetic about my guinea pig on the way to his house. I was hacked-off, too: fed-up with Emma and Zoe, cross with Mum, I thought if it had got late and people were a bit worried it was just too bad. I sort of hoped someone would ring Mum: I really wanted her to come home . . .'

Jess couldn't be making me feel much worse. Why had she minded quite so much about my date with a man she didn't know? Was it to do with the bitter row Julian and I had after the dance? We'd got back early, she might have been wakeful and listening out. It had been all about Perry. Could Jessie have assumed I was with him?

'It was horrible of me,' she carries on. 'Not caring much if people were worried. But I hadn't thought like that at the start. It all just sort of happened by accident: getting to that awful place, being so scared. It was more trying to make excuses for being there and really wishing I wasn't.'

It is all suddenly pouring out. I can feel Jess's panicky fear as keenly as if it were my own. I'm imagining stepping in that dark doorway, knowing it was dangerous and wrong.

'I thought it was best going in and trying to be nice,' Jess says. 'I needed his help, getting back.'

'He didn't have any ice lollies, did he?' Misha asks.

Jess looks surprised, 'No, you're right. It was a shock that he'd told a lie like that. Dicky was having water out of a saucepan, though, and I asked for some water, too. I drank it quickly, it was only a little glass, and he filled it up again for me. It was a bit dirty and greasy, wet from the tap, and I dropped it. The glass didn't break, just clattered and rolled on the kitchen lino, but he swore really horribly and gave me such a hard shove. I started to cry. I wanted Mum so badly.

'He said to shut the noise or he'd hit me. It was really hard to stop crying, but I didn't want to be hit. Martin had kicked the door shut coming in, I couldn't easily have run out. Then he said I should sit on the sofa while he thought what to do. He'd told me lies, but it was like he did whatever came into his head, getting me there and everything. I stayed on the sofa while he talked about wanting to kill someone who'd called him a saddo. I said everyone gets called names; someone at school had been horrible to me too, that day.

'It felt so late. I was really scared and needing to pee like mad. Martin said he had some doughnuts and I wasn't to move while he got them. I asked to go to the bathroom, but he wouldn't let me. I ate a doughnut and kept on about needing the loo. It was a bungalow and I think he was worried I'd get out the window or shout for help. He finally let me have a pee, but only with the door open. I was in shorts and it was really embarrassing. I did my pee so quick, trying to stop it making a noise, and he didn't much look, but then when I turned on a tap something awful happened.'

My mind instantly flies to things sexual; Misha's too, I think. She still continues to prompt routinely, with no edge of alarm in her voice. 'What sort of thing, Jess?'

'The tap was so stiff. Suddenly it gave way and shook the basin, which was old and wobbly, not firm to the lino, and had this mug sitting on the bit where the soap goes – a flowery, not very nice one – and it fell in the sink and smashed. Martin went berserk. He grabbed my arm and pulled me out into the hall where he could really take a swipe. I started screaming and he kept on hitting me, saying I had to shut it, shut up. Everything was going black and bright, like with real actual stars and orange flashes. The pain was awful. I couldn't stop crying. It was probably making him worse, kind of like . . . well, a vicious circle.'

Where had she heard that expression, I wonder; it seems so horribly apt.

Misha is studying her appraisingly. 'So what next, Jessie?'

'My head hit the wall. It's really sore here . . .' she touches a point on the side near the back and grimaces, her shoulders going tense. 'Next thing I knew I was on the sofa. He saw me try to stand up and told me not to dare move or else. He was pacing around, swigging out of a beer bottle and muttering to himself. Things like, 'How can I get out of this mess?' Saying them over and over. It was driving me mad. My head was aching, I didn't know what time it was. It made me panic, I so needed Mum, and couldn't help starting to cry again. There was one of those old sideboards on curvy legs like in those old films. Martin went to one of its drawers and got out a big carving knife.'

'What did he do with the knife?'

'Pointed it at me and said I had to shut the noise and whining. He seemed even scareder than me, shaking his head, mumbling. So different from how he'd been on the walk.'

'Did you get him talking, Jessie?'

'Not right away. I couldn't, my mouth was sort of frozen shut. He kept touching the knife. Then I felt brave and said, 'Do you want me to be your friend?' I thought it might help. He didn't answer, went on about not knowing how to get out of it and not trusting me. I felt like I was full of lumps of ice, all cold and heavy and trying not to sink.'

'Were you on the sofa all the time or did you sit on a chair?' Clever question of Misha's, I think, getting Jess to corroborate Julian's evidence. I wonder if Gibson will remember him saying he'd seen from the hall she'd been sitting on a chair.

'I had to go to a chair. Martin made me. He put knives all round and said he'd stick me with one if I got up. He took ages arranging them. I was so wanting to cry again, I was shaking all over.'

'But you still started talking to him?'

'I thought people would be out looking for me, it felt a way of hanging on – and he seemed less nervy with all the knives laid out. I asked if he liked swimming, things like that. He got talking and then he really seemed to want to. He didn't see the sea till he was twenty! His Dad would never go anywhere. They'd lived in Catford, in a house with steep stairs. He pushed his father down them in the end.'

'Did his father die?'

'Well yes. But I mean it wasn't like that. Martin's father beat him – and his mother. His father was always drunk and used a belt and Martin said he could hear his Dad through the thin wall, beating her up the whole time. One night he was so drunk and just at the top of the stairs. Martin gave him a quick little push. He thinks his Dad never knew. And he's sure his mother never had any idea. They moved to the bungalow in Brearfield. It all sounded very true. Only he lied about the lollies, so it's hard to know.'

To think of Jess listening to this, keeping him going, desperate for help to come. I glance at Misha who is looking as inscrutable as ever. She carries on questioning.

'How did Martin react to being talked to through the door?'

'He started sweating and picked up the biggest knife. I thought Julian would have the police with him and if they broke in Martin might hold the knife at me . . . They haven't found him yet, have they?' Jessie queries, 'He won't need to know I've said anything?'

'That's for the police, Jess. It's possible it might come out in court.'

Tears run down her face. 'He thinks I won't talk. Julian told him I wouldn't, too.'

'You've done the right thing. And Martin will get help, which is so vitally important.'

*

The feeling is that on the strength of her evidence Jessie doesn't need a full medical examination. We're not sure if the knock really caused her to pass out or whether, with the other blows and pain, everything just became a bit of a blur. There's an egg of a lump on the back of her head, nothing worse that that.

Out of Jessie's hearing I ask Misha whether it isn't rather unusual that Martin seemed not to have had any sexual intent. She says people with his sort of mental condition can be simply lacking in friendship and someone to confide in, but sometimes that could spill over into more sinister needs. It can be many years before they come to sex offending, often not till late middle age.

As she's speaking, I think in some ways we've actually been very lucky – God knows what could have happened had Julian not done all he did.

Chief Inspector Gibson sees us out. Jessie gets into the car and he has a quick word with me. 'I'll let you know just as soon as there is anything to report. Will you keep her off school a few days?'

'I've been thinking about that. The doctor said everyone reacts differently to trauma, there are no hard and fast rules, and that in a day or two it might be better if she's occupied.'

Gibson nods. 'I'll try and look in on Monday, if I may, and see how she is. Would you like me to call Mr Osborne and tell him all about Jessie's interview? He will want to know.'

The thought of not having to go through it in detail with Bill comes as a relief. Not for the first time I think Detective Chief Inspector Gibson is an unusually intuitive and understanding man.

CHAPTER 23

'Don't you think, darling, you ought to ring your friend Perry Maynard?' My mother smiles encouragingly. 'He'll be worrying and anxious for news after you had to rush away in such terrible panic. Goodness, when you think it was only last night! And if he was on his way to France he might not even know Jessie's been found – perhaps only seen one of the newspapers' early editions.'

We've finished lunch, the ordeal of the interview behind us. I'm washing up and my mother is looking at *The Post*. We must get a late edition; the front page has been changed and carries the story. 'Eleven-year-old daughter of William Osborne, Editor of The Post, missing for seven hours.' There's a photograph from the wedding showing Jessie in a group with Victoria and Bill. All they could find in the time, I suppose, and an excuse to relate the story to Victoria.

No mention of Jessie's own mother. It's trite and irrelevant, beneath me to mind. It must be exhaustion making everything seem depressingly blacker.

'They'd only have had the wedding pictures that late at night,' my mother remarks from the table, as though an expert on newspaper photo-libraries and nightshifts. 'It's sweet of Jess, though, isn't it? *The Post* could just get one off William's desk! His deputy would have taken over last night, wouldn't he? Did you hear what I said about Perry, dear?'

I turn round from the sink and stare at my mother. I can't blame her, it's reasonable suggesting a call. I had said it was dinner with friends of his – spinning the line he had spun to me. And she doesn't know that just hearing his name now makes my skin feel crawled over by maggots.

We're alone. My mother is lingering over a cup of coffee and seems to be enjoying the chance of a chat. Surely she must be as shattered as I am? Jess had done nothing to stifle her yawns and made no fuss at being marched off upstairs for a rest. Even the new book from Julian didn't keep her eyes from closing.

The bruises will heal, but what about the long-term effects, the inner hurt? Trauma can even lead to mental health problems. Doctor Jeffries would only say it takes everyone differently and that Jess seemed to be bearing up, but how can he really know?

Emma is out on a riding lesson. It's thundery, I hope she'll be all right. Val called and offered to take her for me, knowing that I won't go out with the press around. Val is not one for showing emotions, but seeing Jessie's face made her go pale. And she looked angry, muttering about wanting justice done.

I was grateful for the police car taking us to the interview this morning, making it harder for the cameramen to get a good view of Jess in her battered state, although there are sure to be pictures all over tomorrow's Sunday papers. Will we never be free of the press?

Drying my hands on the roller towel, I consider trying to tell my mother all about Perry. It's been hard talking about my feelings with her ever since the break-up with Bill. Perhaps it would be good to let it out, though, and only fair to explain my change of heart.

She looks pleased when I join her and pours a cup of tepid coffee, pushing it firmly my way. No point trying to sweeten the tone, I think, and I plunge in. 'I'm not going to ring Perry, Mum. It took me too long to see it, but he's a shit. A slimy self-obsessed woman-izer who treats people like they were worthless objects, something to be shoved around.'

It wasn't quite what she expected, that's obvious, but she reacts with surprising calm. 'That's a little excessive, darling. Did he say something to upset you? After all you were keen enough to drive all that long way to see him . . .'

'Don't remind me! He'd been very persuasive, saying that it meant something, and I'd probably wanted to believe him. Seeing through the cheap shallow lies, though, even before we'd had a drink, filled me with loathing. I'd been about to walk out on him anyway. I knew what it was all about then, Mum, it lifted a curtain on my own feel-ings. But it's too late now. The man I love has gone away.'

My mother knows I'm not talking about Bill. 'You couldn't see any future in it,' she ventures, probably thinking with very good reason. 'You weren't decided . . .' Her brow looks like a furrowed field, but she carries on. 'Julian's always been a great mystery to me. It didn't seem to fit, living over the bookshop, all those trips to Uganda; I couldn't imagine it lasting. I'm sure, darling, you'll soon see it's really for the best.'

'No, Mum, it's for the worst.'

She's lost for soothing words, looking agonized – and relieved, if startled, when my mobile suddenly rings.

It's Tom. 'Hi Mum! I've just got back. I'm here with Nattie and we were thinking, well, that if she comes down with Dad and me, how much Jessie would love it. Would you mind?'

It's so devious of Tom, uncharacteristically underhand. He knows I can't possibly say no. At least it's not for a whole weekend . . . Emma will be pleased, too . . . 'Mum? You still there?' he calls.

'Sure, sure. Of course Nattie can come. You'll stay for lunch? You won't rush off?'

'I'll check it out with Dad. But don't go to any trouble, she would hate that.'

Clicking off I give a wry grimace. 'Seems we're seven for lunch tomorrow, not four. Better get something out of the freezer.'

Bill's car is drawing up. Jessie has been watching for it and scoots out. Hearing about Nattie coming caused such a shine of delight in her good eye as to do the work of two. She'd had a sad moment at breakfast all the same. 'I wish Elton wouldn't have died, Mum.' Her little chin was trembling. 'Nattie would have loved him, I know.'

I watch from the kitchen window as the car doors are opening. Misty is furiously wagging his tail and Emma's out there too, now. They're both radiating pleased anticipation at the thought of entertaining their stepsister. My hands feel clammy; it's ridiculous, the children think she's wonderful – isn't that good? Julian was right to have got fed up and lectured me about it.

I hurry out, wiping hands on denim thighs. It's cooler after the night's rainstorms with small puffs of frothy cloud like floating islands. The wisteria is showering raindrops; the petunias are a bit drooped in their tubs. Still a beautiful day, though. How will she find us?

'Welcome! The girls have been so excited you were coming.' Not a good start, it must have sounded as if I wasn't.

Nattie gives me a golden smile, genuinely responsive. She has long fair hair and an unusually lovely face with wide hazel eyes, a sort of unselfconscious beauty that's impossible to resent. She is tall, with a slender willowy body. It's all rather unnerving.

'I was worried you'd feel Jess should be kept quiet after her ordeal,' she says anxiously, bending to pat Misty. 'I do seriously hope you'd have said. I can't bear to think of her living through such a brutal experience.'

Jess's face that was eager and welcoming, for all its blackening bruises, darkens. A guarded shadow flits across. She can make people so aware of her moods, every expression a barometer of feelings. 'What is it, Jessie?' Nattie queries. 'Is it something I said?' She gives me a quick sidelong advice-seeking look, but I can't help.

'Martin isn't that sort of brutal,' Jess mutters. 'It isn't like, well, it was planned.'

'You're very understanding,' Nattie says, at which Jessie's brow clears.

Bill looks ill at ease with the Martin talk going on – as well he should. He praises Jessie for her brave interview performance in a muted way, which is hardly surprising since her evidence was undeniable proof that his stance last night had been a travesty of fairness.

We all move indoors and I introduce my mother. Emma's tugging at Nattie's arm. 'Come and see round, there's lots to show you.' With very good grace Nattie allows herself to be dragged off by two young excitable girls.

I become aware of glances between Bill and Tom. 'What's up,

what's this all about?' I raise an eyebrow at Tom, feeling quite out of it.

He grins. 'We've got something in the car for Jess – it's white, furry and female.'

The penny drops. But it's a mistake, I think sadly, hoping I'll be proved wrong. It's too soon, Jessie isn't ready for a new pet. 'She is still very much missing Elton . . .'

'I know,' Bill says. 'I worried about that – and she's probably getting a bit old for guinea pigs. But it's just to do something, seemed worth a try.' He looks uncomfortable, unhappy, and I feel for him. It's clear to him now how fond Jessie is of Julian and he feels more pushed out to the periphery. He walked out on his two young daughters, though, he can't expect the ties not to loosen at all.

'Glass of wine?' I offer.

It had been cause for quite a debate with myself this morning, standing in the larder, eyeing Perry's ten remaining bottles. What the hell, I thought. It'll be some small satisfaction, using them up. Will Perry think of it as one of his less successful investments? I hope he's written it off, though, and that he's chucked away my holdall. I dread seeing his car nosing up the drive ever again.

'That's a nice idea, darling,' my mother says, brightening at the mention of a drink. 'Which of you is driving?' She looks from Bill to Tom, who rolls his eyes in resignation and sets about opening the chilled bottle of Perry's Chablis I've just brought in.

When my mother goes to look at the lunch, Bill takes his glass and wanders to the French windows on to the garden. I join him sensing he has something to offload.

'I've written to Julian to apologize,' he mutters, staring distantly out of the window. 'Difficult letter.' He turns to face me. 'God knows, though, what might have happened if your boyfriend hadn't been quite so alert. And who can blame him for going it alone? You'd think the bloody police might have got their act together and picked up this pathetic Martin character by now. The man's dangerous; it's a disgrace. At least the media are pushing the story and his photograph is out there in every paper. Thank God the lab had one, pity it's so blurred.'

I'm desperate for Martin to be found. I went round the house last night, double-checking doors, windows, seeing shadows move, feeling terror at the scratch of a garden branch on a windowpane. My frustration with the police is as great, but liking and trusting Gibson, I can't help rising to his defence. 'All very well for us to carp,' I say. 'It's not that easy, I'm sure. Some relative might be harbouring him, he could be anywhere in the country . . .'

Bill is looking blackly ahead. He's been feuding with the police in *The Post*, running a campaign against their inefficiency – and now he's in need of their help. A tough editor wants action, results, retribution and Bill is as powerful and forceful as any.

'We'd better round up the girls and get on with this wretched guinea pig business.' He manages a smile and turns on his heel. 'And at some stage I'd like a chat with Jess.'

I call after him. 'Oh, Bill, tell Ems beforehand. Get her involved or she'll feel shut out and jealous.'

He turns and for a camera-flash moment, a glimpse into an album, we come together. Parents, past lovers, a shared impetuous youth; we have new lives and loves, but a hand-touch through time is still possible. The bonds of connection are holding fast through last night's anguish, even strengthened by it. 'Thanks.' He gives me a smile. 'Thanks, I'll go and find her.'

My mother and I watch from the sidelines with fond smiles on our faces. I feel weary at the prospect of another small live creature, more responsibility. This little guinea pig is as different from Elton as can be: pure white, smooth-haired. Chosen for just that reason, I expect. Lucky I'd put off getting rid of the old hutch with its long wired-in run. It's a good solid construction. Jess and her friends used to sit on it, gossiping and cuddling Elton.

'I was wondering what you thought about calling it Madonna,' Bill says sombrely.

Jessie is bending low, stroking the guinea pig's smooth white coat. Her head comes up sharply. 'No, Dad. That's too much like in competition with Elton.'

'What about Blanche?' Nattie suggests diffidently. 'Do you like that? It sort of points up the difference and lets her be more an individual in her own right. And Blanche is French for white!'

Blanche it is. She is delivered, snuffling, looking small, lost and bemused, into her new big-hutch home at the bottom of the garden.

After lunch Bill has his chat with his daughter. They set off down the garden and on the second circuit she's taking his hand. When they come indoors again, he starts calling for Tom and Nattie with a degree of impatience, rounding them up, clearly anxious to get off. Bill has had enough. The strains are showing again. It's another frame – claustrophobic Brearfield, these confining walls, his conscience and all his past dilemmas.

Giving Jessie one last hug before jumping in the car beside Tom at the wheel, he whispers how proud he is, how brave she was. I hear him saying it's all over now, something she has to try to forget. He must know that's never going to happen.

*

The car is off through the big white gate. The girls come in. Emma gets going, rehashing the day with her grandmother – retelling every word of what Nattie had said. 'She's so worried about her A's, Gran. Victoria was at Oxford, you see, and Nattie worries her Mum's expecting too much.' At least Victoria's own daughter dares breathe a word of criticism, however oblique and mild.

Jess stays in the hall looking round aimlessly. Shock and exhaustion will keep her flat and forlorn for days, I think, but it's a particular unhappiness at this moment and I think I understand. Moving close, I put an arm round her. 'Lets go and see if Blanche has eaten that carrot, shall we?'

The tears dribble out. Jess doesn't bother to wipe them.

I have to brush away a few of my own. Elton was irreplaceable. I'm missing him almost as much. He's left such a big empty hole. A proper little charmer with his rough black coat, ginger coxcomb and wicked look in those bright watchful eyes – he could find his way into any girl's heart. Always darting out of his hutch and cheekily rushing up, he knew his family and how much he was loved.

Blanche has abandoned the carrot; it's been barely nibbled. Jessie looks at me with miserable eyes. 'Elton didn't much like cabbage, but we could try her with that.' She gives a sad little smile. 'I know Dad needed to do something, I do understand. But it feels sort of wrong to be filling Elton's place quite so soon.'

'You go and get the cabbage,' I say, with a swelling heart.

We stand watching as Blanche sniffs with her pink twitching nose then cautiously nibbles. My mind is wandering. Martin could be anywhere – somewhere close, hiding behind the garage, crouching below the old garden wall right by where we are . . .

'I want to move the hutch up nearer the kitchen, Jess.'

'Why?'

'This was Elton's special corner – and it'll be good for this bit of grass to have an airing. I'll get Gran to come to help, we'll do it right away.'

CHAPTER 24

It's Monday and Emma has just caught the school bus. I worry about her. The attention has been so one way and now all her friends – Jessie's too, apart from her closest who have been on the phone – will be crowding round, gabbling out questions like a flock of inquisitive goslings. Emma might enjoy the spotlight, but it will remind her of what she herself went through, the searching and building terror and guilt, having to cope without her own mother there for support . . . She's been a brick.

There was so much in Sunday's papers about Jess. My mother took them away last night, thank God, to read in Hove. She hated leaving us, but her short-staffed surgery would have been in a hole and I urged and ordered her to go. I've got to manage alone.

The police have put out a brief statement; Martin's details and a word about Julian's role but no mention of his independent approach. They released the picture Val had given them of Jess and it has been on every front page. A cameraman had managed to snap Jessie through the police-car window too. There's a shocking picture in *The Post* with her puffy closed-up eye and bruises showing up clearly and the blurb alongside is in lurid journalese.

I'd rather Jess wasn't still lingering over breakfast, reading the story. Her elbows are on the table, hands pressed to her head; she's concentrating hard, bent over it, not just glancing at all her pictures together with the indistinct one of Martin. As I watch she turns the page to read the continuation.

'She's in a denim mini and T-shirt saying "Peace". Jessie loves clothes, make-up – she keeps flavoured lip-gloss in her school bag – but for an 11-year-old her level of absorption, her concern, the way she thinks through consequences, even politically inclined solutions at times, seem phenomenal.'

Bill never lets up in that paper of his. It must be unsettling reading, given Jess's sensitivities about Martin. Surely, though, she must want him out of range of harming others?

She looks up. 'I wish I hadn't broken my word. It makes me feel awful. Julian said we wouldn't talk, he promised, Mum. It's horrible of us, so not fair to Martin.'

'But Jess, have you thought? He went on the run right away, before you or Julian had said anything at all. He'd taken all his personal things . . .'

'That just means he didn't trust us – and he was right not to. It's awful.' Her lips start wobbling, tears on the way. She holds them in, though, and bursts out with heartfelt passion, 'Martin needs people to love and hug him; he hasn't even got his mother any more. And now,' she looks down at the paper, 'everyone's going to really hate him. It'll make him worse, more dangerous and I'm the one to blame.'

'But you're only thinking one way. What about you, the victim – and other people who might be at risk?'

'I'm not really a victim. I shouldn't have gone with him. And if I hadn't told on him, he'd have felt that at least somebody cared.'

'Then Julian would have been the one who carried the blame, people thinking he'd held you captive and invented Martin as cover.' I don't add it was exactly what her father had thought.

She sees the dilemma and breaks into tears. We have a hug and I remind her that Chief Inspector Gibson is coming, due in two hours. 'I must get a tray ready for coffee. And shall we take Blanche out a few cabbage leaves now?'

Jessie is rubbing a finger along the table, tracing the grain of the wood; she's not very interested in Blanche at this moment. Her eyes are still glistening as she looks up. 'Mum, what did you say to Julian on Saturday when you didn't want me there? Was it to do with the interview, me telling about Martin, or . . .'

She wants to know where we're at, but I'm desperate for clues myself. 'I wanted to thank him for bringing you home,' I say, feeling a fluttering emptiness inside, 'more than words can say.'

'He went off so quickly and I wasn't being very nice, nor with the policeman. I didn't even thank Julian for the book.'

I sit down with her for a moment feeling the wrench, the strain of uncertainty. 'You should write, he'd like that. He said he might call by sometime and see us – see how you are. I don't know when and it may not be for quite a while, he's very busy writing his book. It's a true story about a real person who was a bit disturbed, like Martin. So Julian must have known a little of the way Martin thought.'

Jess is hesitating, still rubbing at the table. She made clear enough in the interview her feeling that by seeing someone else I'd been deeply disloyal to Julian. 'I'm sure he will be back,' I say, trying to contain the ache, the lurching need that clings like a shadow. 'He does what he says.'

She seems to settle for that. It's over a year since Bill walked out, a month since Julian left Brearfield. Jessie has been pining for stability and Julian was in her life from a very young age. How could I forget the way she used to stare up, listening patiently while he wooed me in a coded way, talking poetry and favourite writers, when we three used to have lunch all those years ago, in the Thai restaurant across from the shop?

He's good with all the children, but has he shown extra fondness for Jess? He knows her best of all – and she knows very well how to be beguiling with her girlish inveigling ways and love of books.

She gets round her father, too. She's always commanded his concentrated attention and brought out proud protective instincts. Bill is decent enough never to show it, Emma has no idea, but I'm quite sure Jess is his secret favourite. It's just possible to understand his extreme jealous reaction and speed of jumping to conclusions over Julian.

I'm reminded of Jessie's mobile call to Julian. He was sure he hadn't given her the number. Feeling a sudden burning need to clear up every ounce of suspicion, I stare at Jess. 'How did you know Julian's number, darling, when you called him from school?'

'I got it off your mobile.'

It's a shock, it seems underhand and unlike her. 'You went snooping in my bag?'

'No, I didn't! You'd left your mobile out on the table where we were doing homework the night you went to that dance. Julian was going away, selling the shop . . . I wrote it on an exercise book, that's all.'

I'm feeling only slightly less dismayed, busying myself getting coffee cups ready. Gibson will be here any minute. Jessie comes to my side and leans her head into me. 'Sorry, Mum. It was why I called him really, on Friday – just seeing his number there, suddenly, on that exercise book. It sort of gave me the idea. I borrowed Blythe's phone.'

Blythe is one of her nicest friends. I kiss Jessie's hair. 'It's all right, love. But it was a bit sneaky!'

She looks up anxiously. 'Will they find Martin soon? What happens when they do?'

'Well, first thing they'll have to charge him and if they want to put him in prison they'll have to go to court. I'm not quite sure of the actual charge: abducting and something called GBH, grievous bodily harm, perhaps. He did actually let you go in the end, although that was really all Julian's doing, and I suppose that might help him later on. He might get a lesser sentence because of that. It's called a mitigating factor in legal talk.'

'I'm frightened, Mum. I don't want to go back to school before he's found. He might come looking for me. Would they just lock him up and not give him any treatment?'

She's being brave, I think, owning up to feeling fear. 'They will need to keep Martin in prison. He's out there feeling hounded, remember, and could easily lose control again.'

'But will he see a doctor?'

'People with mental illnesses do get help,' I say, uncertainly, 'but probably not right away. He'd have to be checked out and I'm not sure that would happen much before the trial. If he pleads guilty, it would still take months for a report on how he is, probably. It's a question of money and everything always taking so long.'

Jess looks appalled. 'But that's awful. Misha said the trial might not be for months, sometimes up to a year. He'd get worse in jail with people being horrible to him and couldn't that end up costing more?'

'You'll have to be a politician, Jessie,' I say, eyeing the kitchen clock in its round red frame, 'then you can sort it all out.' In the big sunny kitchen that looks right down the garden, life suddenly seems less beleaguered and grim. 'You should talk to Victoria,' I add with a smile.

'She's always very busy,' Jess answers taking me seriously, carefully tidying the chocolate digestives and my mother's home-made short-bread I've dumped on a plate.

'But I'm sure she'd love hearing what you think. You could talk to her at mealtimes, perhaps. Now I think we should take Blanche some breakfast. And haven't you got an essay to do? What's the subject?'

'It's a stupid crap one, "The seasons". I'd rather write about the Pied Piper book from Julian or Elton dying.'

'Think of it as a challenge; try to make all the seasons sound beautiful in their different ways.'

I go to the larder for cabbage leaves, thinking how demanding Jess is and imagining, for a rash moment, life with Julian around to help. And Misty needs a decent walk. Where, though? I'd feel very twitchy out in the countryside, just the two of us alone.

'Oh, Mum.' There's a note of command in Jess's tone, a need for my full attention as though to prove a point. 'You did like Nattie, didn't you? I know she's older and things, but kind of always really friendly to us. I like her lots.'

How could I dare to disagree? Victoria's daughter had seemed warm and sensitive to moods, tuned-in; far from a bad example. Jess is looking braced to defend her and it's quite hard keeping a straight face. 'Yes, I did, I really liked her lots – just like you do.'

*

The Chief Inspector arrives promptly at eleven; Jamison too, they seem inseparable. Jessie is with me in the hall. I've got used to her battered bruised face, but they can't help glancing at her the way people do. Gibson gives his grave little smile and asks how she's feeling, then tells her, speaking with the authority of someone who's seen a few in the course of his career, that black eyes can take a surprisingly long time to heal and fade.

'Sleeping all right, Jessie?' he asks.

'I can only lie on one side.' She looks impatient. 'Have you found Martin yet?' Nothing like a direct question. Gibson's smile is no more or less grave, waiting as Jess continues, 'Could he have gone back to Catford, do you think? He knows all round there from when he was young.' She stares challengingly at the senior investigating officer of the Sussex force, demanding to be taken seriously.

'That's exactly where there's been a sighting,' Gibson says. 'You'd make an excellent detective. We're getting close and we'll probably pick him up today.'

'Will you let us know?' I ask, resolving to walk on the downs later and get Jessie out in the air. Perhaps Susie might come too. I'd feel happier with her there and it would be a chance to talk. Pity Val will be working. Somehow I've got to get across to them both the depth of debt I feel. When I think what a hideous responsibility it must have been, there couldn't be any much greater than being in charge of a friend's child who's gone missing.

'I'll call and tell you myself,' the Chief Inspector promises.

He seems in no hurry and there are things I'm keen to ask. Looking at Jess I say hopefully, 'You have got that essay, love – best if you get going with it now.'

'No one could have been braver,' Gibson says as she gets up. 'You did the right things, Jessie, you mustn't feel bad. It's better for Martin to be safe and where people can help him.'

She looks pleased before saying rather incongruously, 'I've got a new guinea pig.'

'Shall I come and see it?' Detective Inspector Jamison offers, rising from his chair.

Had he realized that Jessie mightn't want to be alone? Should I be thinking like that and not be so carelessly insensitive? But perhaps Gibson has things to say too, that Jamison knows about.

'She seems to be coping remarkably well,' Gibson says, when Jessie has led tall dark wiry Jamison out of the room, 'and giving everything a lot of thought. And how are you? Have you managed to catch up on some sleep?'

'I'm the least of anyone's worries! My concern is about Jessie and going back to school. She might start getting things more morbidly out of proportion, like brooding on a row. If her need to defend Martin is hard even for me to understand, her friends wouldn't, I'm sure. Then having broken a promise not to talk, she's frightened about Martin coming looking for her.'

'We'll soon have him behind bars. The doctor thought school might be a good distraction. I'm not sure about that personally, but she's as likely to brood at home.'

While Gibson is speaking my thoughts are on Martin's probable imminent arrest. With Julian conclusively cleared, Erica Barkston can hardly go on stirring it up and telling tales to parents that the children then repeat at school. She'll have a few words to eat, a large helping of humble pie.

I put Erica out of my mind. 'More coffee? Can I ask one or two questions?'

'Try me, I'll do my best.' Gibson moves his cup nearer, his face bland as ever.

'Well, it seemed there was a particular moment when you changed your mind about Julian, the scales lifted from your eyes. Am I right and was it any one thing that swayed you?'

'It was mainly to do with his book, how we found things at the house in Cambridgeshire. There was a feeling of productive normality about it all; the material on his computer was appropriate and practical. And then his scathing view of the police as negotiators made me think of other quite logical reasons why he might have gone to ground. I couldn't, of course, be sure.'

The Chief Inspector produces his grave smile – I've never known anyone able to look perfectly serious and still twitch with amusement. 'That's not to say we condone or approve of what Mr Bridgewater did,' he goes on. 'It was dangerous and irresponsible. Not exactly vigilantism, the opposite really, since he certainly wasn't meting out punishment. It was in fearless-action John Buchan style, but he took a considerable risk that I would most definitely rather he hadn't. I know we don't invariably get it right and absolutely didn't in the case he's been researching, but he should have had more trust.'

Gibson looks defensive; he knows how far they were from finding Jess. 'Things have come on a lot in recent years,' he says sheepishly. 'Sometime I must tell Mr Bridgewater about a few advances, the spy holes that can be silently drilled, even through walls where people are being held, the wide-angle cameras we can insert in them—'

'I have one other question,' I say, interrupting hesitantly and seeing Gibson immediately pick up on the slight pause. 'It's a silly thing, but why didn't you want me there when Julian was trying to persuade Jessie to talk?'

The Chief Inspector gives me a patient spreading-hands look like a teacher preparing to explain. 'Jess had come home not speaking because of exhaustion and trauma, but I could see she was keeping up a wall of silence that morning; responding to Mr Bridgewater in front of you would have been to lose face. I thought, too, that he would be more distracted if you were there and I wanted him to stay focussed on Jess.'

I feel a suffusing flush creep into my face, giving off heat like a blast from a furnace. Gibson's mobile starts ringing, which is a relief – possibly to us both.

Jamison's head comes round the door, we are soon saying good-byes in the hall and then they're disappearing down the drive.

I make my call to Susie, who sounds pleased at the idea of a walk. She has her own troubles, too. I'm not the only mixed-up, mucked-up kid on the block round these parts.

CHAPTER 25

It's good to be up here, striding out along the brow of the downs. It's too hot, though. Yesterday was fresher after the thunderstorms, but the heat is formidable again, now. Strands of hair are sticking to my face and I can feel the sweat trickling.

Susie seemed glad to come out and it's a comfort having her with Jessie and me. There's no one about on a term-time Monday afternoon, not a soul – although it is nearly the holidays. Just to be out of the house is a wonderful release. The view is glorious. Brearfield looks almost like an island in the hazy heat shimmer, the fields seem like rippling lakes.

Bringing myself back I smile down at Jessie. 'All OK?'

'Sure.' She's not relaxed, though, looking to either side of her too often. Her eyes were darting and watchful coming here in the car. As if sensing my thoughts and to prove me wrong, Jessie takes off then, running on ahead of us and calling out to Misty.

While she's out of hearing, I turn to Susie. 'I'm wondering whether to suggest stopping for ice creams on the way home. Martin offered Jess a lolly after all, and every second of Friday night must still be horribly vivid, a real living hell.'

'I'm sure she can handle it – and an ice cream! I could use one, too.'

'Somehow we've got to get back to normal life,' I sigh.

'Wish Phil and I could,' Susie mutters. I squeeze her arm and see a tear in the corner of her eye.

I hate to see Susie so down. It's easy to be depressed in Brearfield, it can feel as confining and inhibiting as a chronic disease at times, but she hasn't the same small-town frustrations as I have. Her problems start and finish with Phil.

Even out walking with an old friend Susie has made an effort: lipliner and gloss, a sexy halter-neck T-shirt and canvasy white short skirt. Her newly bought cutaway trainers look almost like running shoes and she's picking her way with care, negotiating the humpy stony turf. Susie nurtures her looks. She never lets herself go; always trying her best, looking the part on Phil's arm – he should bloody well give her some return. Someone else is sure to otherwise, and I can sense that moment is coming near.

'It's such a wide world, up here, no place for cobwebs and gloom,' I say, which is silly, she's in no mood for forced cheerfulness. I rest a hand on her arm. 'Is it very bad? Would it help to talk?'

She stares ahead to Jessie, who's throwing a stick for Misty, then takes a deep breath. 'He hardly seems to notice I exist, Ursula. You were right and it would have been a good idea, trying to make him jealous, but it's hard when you're feeling right down on the floor. I'm a lousy actress. What's scaring me is I'm beginning not to care. He's slowly destroying everything we've had together, making irreparable holes like a moth; I almost hate him these days. I'm only asking for a little more loyalty and love. If we split up, it would be really terrible for the kids.' Susie and Phil have two teenagers in the midst of exam years.

She's chewing on a forefinger looking embarrassed, probably thinking of my circumstances and that mentioning the children wasn't a good move. She turns apologetically. 'I know you've been there too, but it was a bit different in your case . . .' Two discreet tears slip out. Her shoulders heave up and drop down again.

'Still the flower-shop woman?' I ask, at a loss for comforting words.

'I answered Phil's mobile once, when he was in the shower and someone clicked right off. I took down the number and called it back and it *was* her voice, the cellulite cow. I cut her off too, though – couldn't face a slanging match, yelling at her to get her greedy hands off. He goes on bringing me flowers, can you believe? That's just so he can spend money in her shop, nothing to do with me, of course.' Susie has always been so sweetly eager to please, but her bitterness now is plain to see.

'Phil would be desolate without you,' I say, thinking that at least he isn't devious and ruthless on top of it all like Perry, that he's stupid enough – and cares enough – to bring her flowers. It's small consolation.

Susie is keeping her head bent. Then she looks up and says rather uncannily, given what I was just thinking, 'Perry Maynard's chasing me. He came with our wine the other day, doing his own delivery for some reason, and slipped a note into the back pocket of my jeans. And with Phil right there, just putting away the case!

'It was a very lovey-dovey note, and not the first either, though it seemed much more genuine and serious than usual. It really calls for an answer. Perry flirts, I know; it's just that this latest note does seem so sincere and I am attracted . . . Frightened of getting into an affair, though. I think it would do for me and Phil and be the end of us.'

I swallow away the bad taste in my mouth, hearing her talk about Perry. It's hard, too, being reminded of how dishonestly circumspect I was, not coming clean about my detestable trip to the coast. Still the right instinct, probably. Susie is so vulnerable and to know that Perry was after others, including me, would have pulverized her already crushed pride. Better this way round. She mustn't be taken in, though, and walked all over. It's desperate.

God, how could I ever have sat in that country pub, in that booth with Perry – who had clearly tested the water there with others before – and had even a half-second's thought that he might actually care for me?

Jessie's sitting on a rock waiting for us to catch up, swigging at her water bottle. It's good to stop a moment. The more distant view from up here, I think, would have been of a sprawling new town if the Downsland proposal had been allowed. Thank God, it was turned down in the end.

Everyone fought it so fiercely, feelings rising till they boiled over into a riot . . . If Victoria hadn't been Housing Minister then and hadn't visited the site, would Bill's affair ever have been exposed? My huge humiliation seems so distant now, though, a pinprick, a fly to the elephant of my need for Julian. It was immense enough at the time, blindfolding and spinning me round until I couldn't think or see straight.

Will Julian turn up sometime soon? How soon – days, months? What about Blossom Cottage? Do we move? There are decisions to be taken, life to be kick-started again.

I smile at Jessie. 'Time to go back, you guys!' She gets up from her stone, calls Misty and we start off for home.

I don't know how to advise Susie. Should she just get the hell out?

Their children would survive. If Susie took up with Perry though he'd leave her brutally scarred. 'Have you kept the notes?' I mutter in an undertone when Jess is a little ahead. Susie nods, nervous-eyed. 'Why not leave them lying around somewhere and see what Phil does? Give him one more chance for the children's sake. I don't think he'll challenge you, more likely press you to come out to dinner and change your wine merchant. You've little to lose, you're innocent in it all. Try to stay that way. And take this or leave it as you will, but for what it's worth, Julian knew Perry at school and talked to me about him after your dance. He thinks Perry's a scheming, untrustworthy low-down shit.'

Susie flashes me an extremely suspicious look. 'I'm sure Julian was just jealous, you made a huge hit with Perry that night. It was clear for all to see.'

In the car I say to Jessie, 'I was wondering about stopping for ice creams. What do you think?'

She takes an uncomfortably long time answering. 'It will remind me, Mum – but it's there, it doesn't go away. I don't want never to have lollies again because of Martin.'

We're only just ahead of Emma, getting home. She comes in panting and makes for the fridge to gulp down gallons of the fresh lemon drink I made before the walk. Then she goes clumping off upstairs to change out of her navy pleated skirt. The only summer uniform concession is a short-sleeved shirt. So stupid they can't have cotton dresses, I think, following her up to sit on her bed and hear about the day.

'I wish we could go for a swim,' Emma sighs. 'We can't really because of Jess, can we?'

'The Braggs have said we can use their pool. They're in London in the weekdays, though, Ems; it might be a bit lonely and isolated. Jess is still quite nervy. I'll see what she says.' The Braggs, I think, having loaned their marquee for Susie's charity dance and caused me to meet Perry, have a lot to answer for.

'Um, don't go yet, Mum . . . Some people at school are saying that Julian's the one who took Jess and he's trying to pin the blame on some thicko character. I tried telling them it's not true and that Jess has told us what happened, but they just give me funny looks. It's so mean.'

Emma comes to me for a hug. I feel overflowing with love – and a hard-to-control urge to storm round to Erica Barkston and hurl out a few choice old Anglo-Saxon words at her. The school rumours are Erica's doing, she certainly needs her comeuppance.

'This man, Martin, will soon be arrested and charged, Ems. Try to keep your cool, it'll soon all die down.' Why haven't they found Martin yet? Julian thought he couldn't have got far in the time. It's three days, now.

Going downstairs, my mobile rings and my heart does a flip. I never give out the number because of the press, only my closest friends have it. I hurry to reach it on the hall table. It won't be Julian, I can sense it's not. He'll be thinking of Jessie, leaving things a while. I just wish I knew for how long.

It's Chief Inspector Gibson. 'We arrested Martin Jackson this afternoon,' he says. Did I catch the tiniest smidgen of complacency in his voice? Has he got two private fingers raised, pointing up his back at the journalists on *The Post*? 'We picked him up leaving a corner shop in a backstreet off the South Circular,' Gibson goes on. 'And it was in the Catford area, you can tell Jessie. He was buying a tin of dog food; the shop-owner recognized him and tipped us off.

I sincerely hope Jess will soon be able to start putting it all behind her, now.'

'It does come as a relief,' I say fervently, 'especially after Emma has just been telling me there's still gossip going on at school, rumours flying around.'

'The media coverage will help with that, the press never hold back . . . I'll be in touch again in a couple of weeks, to hear how things are.'

The Chief Inspector ends the call rather formally, as though not alone, and I'm left with a sense of let-down. He was a prop, almost a friend, someone to turn to. After his initial barely veiled disapproval at my desperate call to Julian even before telling Bill, I felt Gibson had come to understand. He'd absorbed so quickly the particular extra stresses and God knows, during those long hours on Friday, they were in plentiful supply.

Staring down at the oak refectory table in the hall, I think quite sorrowfully about Martin. After all he did, though, the physical harm, the terrible trauma he inflicted on Jess, how is it possible to be feeling pity welling up inside?

Perhaps it has something to do with the tin of dog food. His dog, Dicky, was his only real friend, dependable and uncomplaining.

I have a sudden clear memory of Martin sitting on a bird-shitty bench in the market square. I can see him in sharp focus. A flattish nose, small mouth and chin, a backward-sloping forehead; his fuzzy mid-brown hair badly receded on either side of a pronounced widow's peak. He'd been wearing built-up trainers and a black polo that had looked affected and out of place, somehow, on a middle-aged man idling on a town bench.

I look up and see Emma is standing beside me. She must have

come down quietly, hearing me on the phone. 'You look sad, Mum. What is it? Was that Chief Inspector Gibson – have they found Martin? It's probably not an evening to go round to the Braggs for a swim now, is it?'

I put an arm round her. 'No, Ems, I think best not tonight.'

Jess appears at the kitchen door, looking combative and on guard. I'd been half hearing the television and not quite able to believe she was really occupied and watching. She asks truculently, 'Did they find him in Catford? If they put him in prison, Mum, what's going to happen to Dicky?' Her eyes film over.

'I don't know, love. I'm sure Martin will tell them where Dicky is and he'll be looked after.' But Martin might not. It's hard to avoid a distressing image sliding into my mind, of the poor dog left locked up somewhere, possibly not found for weeks. 'The nice liaison officer is coming back to see us tomorrow, we can ask her, perhaps.'

'Could we give him a home, Mum?' Jessie is staring defensively; she knows the answer.

'It wouldn't be right, darling,' I say, heavy-hearted. 'Someone will, though, perhaps a really nice family who'll choose him from a place where stray dogs go.'

It's Thursday and Jessie's just gone off with Emma on the school bus. She still has a black eye, but it is properly open and her lips are no longer swollen like beestings. The bruising to her face, too, has faded and turned less shocking yellows and mauves. I've come in from waving them off, standing watching, waiting till the bus had turned a corner and was right out of sight.

Her friends had been calling and crowding round as she went up the steps. It'll be fine, I tell myself, making purposefully for the study, anticipating a heavy day of tension ahead.

I've been saying to Jess how near the end of term it is, only this week and four days of next, but to little avail. 'That's not the point,' she said, flaring up. She'd accepted the need to go, though, in spite of obvious nerves and looking as pale as any Victorian waif.

My head-hunters' firm is chasing. I'm behind with my research work, a mountain of early-stage phone calls is still outstanding, but a methodical search for the ideal company director for a middle-England pharmaceutical firm isn't guaranteed to lift me to the heights of delirium.

A gremlin gets into the system and I look round to find ways of postponing the task. The middle drawer of my desk is home to a folder of poems, some going way back, a few written in the weeks after Bill had left. That had been a low time.

> Bereft, betrayed, bruised
> In mind and spirit
> Navigating
> Seas of sorrow
>
> Missing silken threads of
> Sharing
> Lacking true and deep
> Affection
> Familiar voices echo in an empty vessel . . .

Bits of poems; useless to me. I want to be writing long joyous passionate ones. It's impossible to write a line in this state of limbo. Do

I call Julian? What I need to say can't easily be done on the phone, not with the complications of Perry. But he must have picked up a little of how I was feeling in those moments we had alone together before Gibson came.

I blew them, though. Why care if it wasn't the moment or there wasn't time to explain? Why hadn't I just said I loved him and what a blind idiotic fool I'd been?

It's no good, this. I have to work, chat in riddles to bored or job-hungry business people playing a hard-to-get game. Why did I have to do the same?

There's a lull. I'm waiting for one or two of them to call me back. I swivel in Bill's old desk chair and gaze out at a laden apple tree. It's a very good year for fruit, they say. No call from school yet. Will Jessie be having a delayed reaction? There are days, weeks, months, ahead when that might happen.

Friday tomorrow, a whole week has gone by. Perry has been on my mind ever since the walk with Susie. I feel a loathing as corrosive and noxious as nitric acid, but it was entirely my own blinkered vain self-ish fault.

He will have put that hysterical dash from the hotel down to the call from Val, a mother's reaction at hearing her child was missing. And he of all people won't have had an inkling of the walkout I'd been about to spring, the satisfaction I was going to derive from it. Perry doesn't know how joyfully my heart was beating at the thought of escaping his clutches and being able to make my call to Julian and tell him I loved him from the bottom of my heart.

Unless he's got rid of it, Perry will soon turn up with that overnight bag, left sitting on a hotel bedroom chair. Enough time will have elapsed, he'll think, since the horror of Jessie's disappearance and he wouldn't want me being the one that got away.

It'll be on a Friday morning again, on his way to France. I'll thank him for returning the bag and ask him most politely to get out of my life. That moment in the hotel bedroom when I felt full of fight and confidence has passed. I simply want never to see him again.

Perhaps he deserves some thanks for ripping away the veils. It's helped me see that what I wanted above all I kept pushing further away, right to the limit, over a cliff face, off the tightrope. And there are always other women waiting with safety nets and open arms.

CHAPTER 26

It's almost time for the girls to come home. There have been no calls from school, no obvious panics.

I've had a day completely on my own. Dolores, my Spanish cleaner, comes on Wednesdays, her husband Carlos drops her off; Cyril, the gardener, comes tomorrow. It's been an ideal time for catching up and yet I've achieved nothing, not even painting my toe-nails or paying a few bills.

As well as my obsessive thoughts about Julian the house has had echoes. I've felt sucked back to the old days of living here with Bill, remembering the force of him, the quiet calm when he was away in his world of scoops and stories.

> Still I hear your voice in an echo
> From a distant moment, sounding
> But losing resonance

They were happy times. We were always separate people, though, never entirely fused.

The school bus has a familiar rumbling engine that's reaching me even in the study. I hurry out, feeling a bubbly impatience to be seeing them, nervous of how it went.

'Hi, Mum, we're back.' Emma comes panting up the drive. 'There's just been such a punch-up on the bus, this girl really socking it to Jess's ex!' I kiss her hot glowing cheek, marvelling at her inexhaustible exuberance. 'Jess did very well,' she announces, as though reporting on a toddler's first day. 'Everyone was so nice and thoughtful.' Jessie is silent, but then she always needs time to unwind.

I put an arm round her, going in. 'Was it all right, no scared funny feelings?' I get nothing back, but know better than to press too hard.

In the hall she deposits her canvas bag on the polished oak chair by the table and takes out a book. She stands holding it. 'Want a drink or anything before tea?' I ask.

Jessie shakes her head then spins round and makes for the stairs. Post-school moods are nothing new, I tell myself, going into the kitchen where Emma's already on the phone to one of her friends.

I fill the kettle, thinking what a wonder it is they find anything left to talk about after nattering for a whole day at school.

It's hard not to half-listen in, scrubbing garden potatoes for supper. 'And she oils her nipples,' Emma says in a goggling way, leaving me wondering what came before. She moves on then to pick holes in the form teacher, who wears too many beads and looks 'bizarre' in her long embroidered skirts.

Worry gets the better of me and I go upstairs to Jess.

She's lying face down on the bed, sobbing. It's exhaustion, I think, it was too soon, a mistake, but so hard to have known. 'Were people being mean to you?' I ask gently.

Jess rolls on to her back, rubbing her eyes. 'It was horrible, Mum.

I hated every minute. My friends kept on about it the whole time. They were asking stupid questions like "did he smell?" and I didn't feel normal with them. It was like . . . well, I didn't fit any more, they just so didn't understand.'

She doesn't have to explain. It's clear she had to build up a relationship with her captor, that it was an instinctive sense of the way to survive, but her friends couldn't be expected to see it and they hear their parents talking. Jessie had become partly in charge and felt almost a kind of responsibility for Martin.

I try to appeal to her pride, suggesting she can't run away from it, that people have silly reactions, but so what? I need to get her to accept – rather as I'm having to – that life has to go on. 'So nearly the holidays, love. See it through, try to last out.'

Jessie climbs off the bed, wiping at her eyes with an arm, muttering about going to feed Blanche. 'I wish Julian would come,' she says then, 'he knows what it was like, he understands about Martin.'

Cyril and I are discussing what needs doing in the garden. He suggests earthing up the celery and leeks, sowing autumn lettuces, pruning the rambler roses that have had their day. He's pushing seventy, lean and weathered as a salty old sailor, crusty and difficult at times, but never whinging and complaining.

'I think that was a car, Mrs Osborne,' he says, listening out. 'Is it a bit far for you to hear the bell down here?'

'Yes, better go. I'll be back soon to finish that bit of weeding.'

The sitting-room doors are open on to the terrace and I go up the two steps and inside, feeling pink and overheated. It's another boiling day. The heavenly scent of jasmine and wall-hugging tobacco plants is a joy, a shaft of spirit-lifting elation. It's very momentary given the sight, through an opposite window, of Perry Maynard's polished-to-gleaming top of the range car drawing up. I had known it wasn't Julian's. Had it been that thrusting sexy-engine sound so often heard on past evenings, arriving early, leaving late, my spirits would have been sky-high.

I make for the door, frustrated to be looking such a mess; not great for cool, confident dismissals of Perry. Tossing my hair back and biting on my lips, I'm picturing him springing on to the doorstep with my holdall in one hand, a bottle of wine in the other. My bile-driven impatience to be shot of him is beyond containing, it's in danger of spilling out in a bitter, frothy diatribe of loathing. I want to preserve what few shreds of dignity I have left.

He's without a bottle of wine or even my overnight bag and his face is composed, calculatedly, in an expression of friendly concern.

'Hello, Ursula, forgive me barging in on you in this rather rude way . . .' Perry's well-toned bulk is filling the doorway and the crinkly eyes are smilingly at it, hard at work. His cleft chin and upper-lip scar look very pronounced in the slanting sun.

He steps in without invitation, supremely confident of disarming me and achieving his ends. 'I've been feeling truly dreadful all week,' he smiles, standing facing me. 'I didn't do too well down on the coast, a bit overkeen, I know – but, well . . .' He's allowing self-effacing sheepishness to temper his creased-eyed smile.

'And then the real agony, the real pain I've been feeling, is impossible to describe. I can hardly live with myself, remembering how casual I was over that disastrous call. I'd just felt it couldn't be all that serious, I really had no idea . . . Perhaps you can imagine my distress when it all became clear, seeing pictures of your beautiful young daughter all over the papers . . .'

He touches my cheek, quite unaware, I think, of my skin's instant shrinkage. 'How is she? Better now they've picked up that monster, I'm sure – know what I'd do with him, given half a chance . . .'

The eyes are crinkling overtime; it's an anguished smile, such deep manufactured concern that I'm surprised he can't sense how much he's overdoing it.

Standing in my hall, his eyes become more expectant; he's ready to accept the offer of coffee he assumes, not unreasonably, is on its way, and preparing to make himself most charmingly at home.

It's quite impressive that he's worked out a *mea culpa* approach is the best way, that whispered sweet nothings about blonde pubes hadn't hit the spot, and, however seething his resentment at my bitterly hysterical, very public departure, a large dose of pride had to be swallowed in the interests of recovery of ground and pitching in again.

'My daughter's safe, that's all that matters,' I say unsmiling, with no mention of coffee or cold drink, no apologetic explanation that I'm too busy, that he's caught me at a bad time. 'You're passing through – on another trip to France?' I ask, trying to edge his bulk backwards and out of the door. 'And other calls to make in Brearfield, too?'

'Now, you're teasing and rapping my knuckles,' he grins, keeping any irritated pique under wraps. He takes hold of my hand. 'You know flirting with Susie is just my way,' he says, playing with my fingers. 'You know that very well, you're no fool, far from it. But yes, I do have to call in there with a case of wine, and yes, I am on my way to France. I'd love to have a quick cup of coffee with you, though – and don't tell me to take one off Susie instead!'

He brings my hand to his lips, oozing charm over the top of it like squeezed-out synthetic cream. God, he's so stomach-churningly cocksure. I may not be falling into his palm at this very minute, but he's certainly determined to keep trying, to hang on and keep hold. Perry Maynard could never be knocked off his perch.

And at worst, if it came to it, he'd relish a spiteful revenge, telling all his friends he knows a thing or two about why William Osborne fled the nest. I can imagine the carefully crafted phrases and clever lies.

There's another car turning in. No mistaking the sound. I can't believe this is happening to me. It's as though my whole future has been barely breathing, surviving on a life support machine, and the switch is about to be flicked, the plug removed, the patient's slim hopes denied.

Pulling away my hand as if Perry has held a match to it, just managing to avoid hurling out a stream of abuse, I'm trying desperately to think of some flimsy line, a way to move Perry on, to get him to go while retaining any vestige of dignity. It's a lost cause, Julian will have seen him, but I need Julian alone, I'm so desperate for a chance to talk.

'Really sorry, Perry,' I say, secreting out a smile quite as false as his own, 'but you really are going to have to beg a cup of coffee off Susie instead! That's Julian's car arriving and well, there are things that need finalizing . . . He won't have much time and it is rather important to clear up a few ends. I'm sure you'll understand.' I'm hoping that my smile – given great good luck, which is hardly in evidence so far – might just manage to suggest it could be to Perry's advantage to give me space, that I'm about to draw an old relationship to its close . . .

Phoney smile, concentrated eye contact, I try everything. Perry's a match for me. Blocking my way, not budging an inch, the bastard, he's keeping me contained in my own hall, determined to get ahead of me and be in first with Julian. He knows underneath I'm feeling loathing and the look on his face is cat-like, he's savouring every second of this very convenient and unexpected golden opportunity to get his own back, to pounce and move in for the kill.

As soon as Julian switches off the engine, Perry is out of the house approaching, ambling confidently across the small circle of grass looking for all the world like the master of the house who's about to make an unexpected guest warmly welcome.

'Well, well, well,' he calls, 'the wanderer's return!' He glances at me as I catch up alongside and says in Julian's hearing, 'It's really time I was off now, I'm afraid, Ursula, my dear, but I must just pay my respects to an old school friend – oh, and I must get that overnight bag of yours out of the car. I did remember to bring it back and there I was, stupidly almost going off with it again!'

'I don't need it, you shouldn't have bothered.'

'Don't be silly!' His hand stays my arm. 'It's right there. I'm sure it'll come in very handy on some other occasion . . .'

He's milking this for all it's worth. I can't bear that grin on his insufferably smug face, my hand's itching again . . . but that really wouldn't do. I look away, giving up the fight. There's no way round it. I'm going to have to receive that dreadful little holdall in full view. Nothing could be worse. I'm beyond crying, dry-eyed and despairing.

Julian gets out of the car and leans against it, looking at Perry, not at me.

'Hi!' I start saying, 'I'm so glad—'

'So how are you, Julian,' Perry interrupts. 'You were just off to Uganda last time – good trip?'

'Fine. Jane well?'

'Excellent, thanks.' Perry's beam is as broad as his back. He's stand-ing his ground. Turning and directing his beam fully on me then, he's about to say something else annihilating, but I find a bit of fight.

Cutting Perry, refusing to look his way, I speak warmly to Julian. 'Thanks for coming, I'm so glad – I've been hoping you would . . . Perry has just called in unexpectedly on his way to France. He's doing the rounds and on to Phil and Susie's, now. Just leaving, and on a tight schedule, I think.'

Julian's giving no hint as he turns to stare at me. He's unsmiling. There's nothing showing in his eyes, they're blank, a champion poker player would give more away. He ignores my flustered explanations and asks after Jessie.

'How is she? I've brought her a couple of books, but it seems,' he says tonelessly, glancing at Perry, 'she's back at school. I should have thought of that.'

'Yes, back yesterday.' I try to hold his eyes and fail.

Perry's are hardening, I can tell without looking, smell the fixative, the setting agent. I keep up a hopeless smile at Julian, dreading what's coming, what Perry's next cruel thrust will be.

He squeezes my arm warmly. 'Guess I'd better hit the road. You two obviously have things to discuss. I'll just get that bag of yours, Ursula – the one you forgot the other day . . .'

Perry, in his open-neck shirt and casually creased linen jacket, strides back across the circle of grass to his silvery sunlit car, parked right by the front door. I can imagine the mean-minded private smile on his face while his back is turned. There's no way out, he's going to eke out the very last drop of his revenge.

Julian reaches over into the open car for a carrier that must contain the books for Jess. Our hands touch as he passes it over, but there's no eye contact.

'I know she'd love to see you . . .' Can't he look at me and read the agony in my eyes? He always used to say that *he* knew I loved him, even if I didn't know it. Can't he see how I'm suffering, can't he sense my craving need?

'Give Jess lots of love,' Julian says, making clear he's not staying. 'I hope you're beginning to put the horrors behind you, now. You look very well and recovered.' How can he say that without so much as a glance? Can't he react; show some anger?

He could, at least, about Perry, who's almost upon us with the wretched navy canvas bag – it has a single white stripe that somehow seems to draw extra attention.

Perry holds it out with a triumphal gleam. Transferring the carrier of books to my other hand, I have no option but to take it.

'I think you'll find it's all intact,' he says, with no need for any arch looks or verbal emphasis.

Julian's face is no longer closed. His eyes have become fastened on mine and they're full of pain. Hurt surprise and obvious feelings of betrayal have supplanted that neutral mask. He does care. It's there, showing in his reaction, showing behind his topaz eyes. I've always loved him; I know his feelings.

He's reacting to Perry's deliberately damning, last throwaway line, but not looking coldly satisfied at having his worst suspicions confirmed. It's shaken him, his look is disbelieving. Perhaps there's a sort of threadbare hope, it's a sign of some real emotion at last, a more eggshell-like quality to his protective exterior wall. Julian may be in a new relationship or close as ever to Lauren, but he feels something, he still cares.

Opening his car door he turns. 'I'll give Jess a call. I chose a bad time to come, sorry.'

I drop down the carrier and bag on the gravel drive, but he's already in the car. He can't go, I need him. I'm craving touch, contact – he can't do this to me. I'm oblivious of Perry still beside me as I say passionately, 'You're not going back to Cambridgeshire? You can't, I need to talk, I have to – you must let me . . .'

Julian squints up at me from the driving seat of his open car. He's tanned, a good gold colour, not nut-brown; his face is drawn, still pained.

His answer sounds so formal. 'I'm going to the shop first. Then I'll need to get back. Good to see you looking so well again, Ursula, after that ordeal.' He turns on the ignition and looks past me. 'Bye Perry – give my regards to Jane.'

The engine kicks into life with a pulsing powerhouse roar. It's punching out a message of finality, finish, which perhaps will be giving the driver some small sense of release. The car surges forward, leaving Perry and me standing staring after it, two motionless statues.

Mine is dissolving; I feel everything draining away. Perry's is a large lump of granite, but soon developing all too human form.

'Sorry you didn't get to have your chat, Ursula. Frustrating for you. And it's probably a bit late for that cup of coffee, now. Better be off, I guess. I'll call again sometime, and see how you're doing.'

'Don't, Perry. I'd hate you to be wasting your valuable time. And you might have made yourself late at Susie's, too, now. Phil usually comes home for lunch.'

He ignores that, slings into his car and glides noiselessly off down the drive.

I rush into the house and pick up the phone. Julian's mobile is switched off. He must surely listen to any message I leave? He has to: he's got to.

Speaking urgently into the phone I plead, 'I love you. I've got a lot of explaining to do about Perry, but it's not at all as you think. I've been so very stupid for months on end, but I've always loved you, I know that so well now. Don't go away and leave me, you must come back, now, today, the moment you pick up this message. I can come to the shop, but call me, tell me you want me to – tell me you understand.'

CHAPTER 27

I'm standing clutching the phone, staring out of the kitchen window at the barren expanse of gravel and grass. Surely he'll check his mobile for messages soon. Won't he turn right round and come back when he hears how desperate I am? Come pounding back up the drive and allow me my say? No, he'll more likely press delete in a bitter rage and come nowhere near.

And if I chase after him and go straight to Brearfield now? We might cross on the way. He might be with the shop's buyers; Roy might be there, people, callers, passers-by. What do I care about any of that? I just have to see him, and reach him with my eyes. It would be so much easier if he's heard my message first, a cry of pain from the heart. If only there was a chance I'd find him there with open arms.

Oh God, why did Perry have to come? Couldn't he have given in gracefully like normal people and left me alone? And then Julian choosing the exact same time – was that no coincidence? He knows Perry's business, had he worked out the most probable time that shit might be turning up and pushing into my hall? Did he come out of a need to have his suspicions about Perry confirmed? How can life be so cruel?

My legs are trembling. I can't break down in tears, they won't come, not with this highly charged current coursing through – my heart's thumping inside me like a desperate fist on a door.

Did Julian stop just down the road and turn off his mobile? He'd left Brearfield saying it would always be on. And now it's switched off. It couldn't be more symbolic. He's obviously convinced I've slept with Perry. But was he uncertain of that before? Was it hearing about my bag being 'intact' that caused such a hurt look of shocked betrayal finally to show?

I can't stand here feeling wretched, trembling and hoping, being limp as a wet rag for a minute longer . . . Grabbing my bag, I race through past the larder and into the garage and aim the remote at the door.

Light floods in as the heavy door rolls up and over. I roar off, leaving Misty rushing out after me. He stops midway down the drive. Looking in the mirror, I see him standing forlornly, watching me pull away.

I haven't locked up, but Cyril's there for another half-hour. He'll hang on for a bit too, I'm sure. I drive too fast, seeing nothing, grimly determined, seized with the need to get to Brearfield before Julian leaves. Reaching the market square I park on a yellow line right outside the bookshop and leap out of the car.

The door is locked and he's not answering either my knocking or rings of the bell. I hurry round to the narrow lane at the back, heart hammering, and have a joyous surge of adrenaline at the sight of Julian's car. It's firmly parked in its allocated resident's bay with the top up as though he is staying a while, not just calling in. He hasn't gone to Cambridgeshire yet, he'll surely be back before long, won't he?

A woman pushing a buggy passes by and I run after her. 'Have you seen Julian Bridgewater anywhere, the bookshop man?'

'Nope,' she says boredly, but giving me a funny look before moving on. Am I such a sight in my dirty old shorts, banging on someone's back door?

I walk slowly round to the front again. He's probably just out having lunch. I hurry across the square to the Thai restaurant opposite. It's one o'clock on a Friday, not very busy. No sign of Julian. I feel covered in embarrassment, peering round, looking like God knows what in my shorts and sticking T-shirt. There's even the smell of some pungent garden weed still clinging to my hands. Wasn't it obvious I hadn't been expecting Perry? I'd have been wearing something clean, at least, and had no earth under my nails. Men don't think like that, though; Julian certainly wouldn't.

There's a warden approaching the car. I rush back and make it in the nick of time. Maybe my luck's changing. Where is he, why can't he just appear?

After reparking the car and searching in a few shops and the teashop I try his mobile again. It's still switched off. In desperation I leave another message. 'I've got to talk to you – I'm in Brearfield, but can't find you. You're nowhere. Have to go home to lock up, but I'll be right back. Just listen to my first message, that's all I ask.'

Cyril is waiting by his van, looking anxious. I jump out and hurry over with effusive apologies and his face lightens. 'Thought you wouldn't be long. I wasn't sure you had a key or I'd have locked up. All's well, I hope?'

'Sure, sure – I was just trying to catch Mr Bridgewater . . .'

Cyril was asking after Jessie earlier, with real concern, and I had explained a little of Julian's part. From the look on his face now, mine, which is raging hot, flushed as a sprinter's, must be showing every frustrated desperate secret emotion that I own.

'You'll be all right,' he says cryptically, then flashes me one of his salty smiles and opens the door of his van.

The house phone is ringing. 'Bye,' I shout and hurry indoors and into the kitchen, nearly falling over Misty, who's sticking close by me after being left behind.

My hands are so moist and fumbling that I drop the receiver and send it crashing down on a worktop. Rubbing sweaty palms on my shorts, I get a better grip.

It's my mother. 'What was that awful noise, darling, did you just drop the phone?'

'Yes, it slipped.' I'm curt, in no mood for coping with her. 'Not a great time, Mum,' which is something I say almost every time she rings. 'How are you?' I add, guiltily. 'I do need to dash into Brearfield, really must go now . . .'

'Just tell me how Jessie was about school this morning.' She had called last night and I'd told her about Jess's first day back.

'She was very strong-minded. I was proud.'

'It's good the holidays are so soon – you have sent the cheque for the Algarve, dear?'

My mother knows there's a deadline, a waiting list of others wanting to step in. It's so irritating of her. 'Don't always nag so. It'll get done, I promise.'

I return the phone feeling selfish. I keep putting off making out the cheque. My mother is coming again – as she did last year. She had taken Bill's place at the last minute that time, when he had used the holiday to make the break and end our marriage. I was hardly great company and my mother had borne the brunt. It was more from bitter envy of Bill's newfound freedom and happiness than jealousy of Victoria, but just as blighting of a sunny summer holiday as an oil slick over the beach.

This year's looks set to be as bad. Why doesn't Julian call? I try his mobile again. Still switched off. I go round closing windows and locking doors, thinking that it's after two; he'll probably be gone by now, speeding round the M25 to Cambridgeshire and consoling friends and out of my life.

Back in the car I can't bear Misty's mournful eyes looking up at me through the window and have to get out again and let him in. If Julian's car has gone from its bay at the back of the shop, walking Misty will help stop me from trailing home and weakly going under.

The traffic has built up. I'm drumming my fingers on the approach roads, feeling a sense of defeat, staring out at dry brown front lawns, violent, brassy dahlias that I hate.

There's still no free space in the square. I park on a yellow line again, open the car windows for Misty, and hurry to try the book-shop door. Still no answer. The blinds look different, some up, some down. My pulse starts racing. He's been here since I was – but does that mean I've missed him now and he's gone?

I rush round to the rear and have to gulp back the tears. Julian's Porsche is nowhere to be seen.

Coming round into the square for a second time, walking more slowly, wording a letter, planning calls to Cambridgeshire, I meet the last person on earth I could wish to see. But it seems only fitting somehow, the final nail.

'Are you looking for Julian?' Erica inquires, with her infuriatingly knowing air. 'You've missed him by minutes, actually. He went revving off in that fast car of his; so bad for carbon emissions. You'd probably have crossed over, but for the one-way system – which has helped the flow, though, don't you think? I was surprised to see him around the place again actually,' she says, giving the once-over to my dishevelled state in a very superior way.

'People still feel a little uncomfortable about it all, you know. I mean, can you really lay your hand on your heart and be quite certain of what went on, Ursula? Don't you wonder a bit how Julian just happened to able to find and return your poor child? It is very coincidental.'

There's something distinctly bilious about her smile. Mine is equally sickly in return.

'I don't wonder at all. Jessie's word is fine by me. Now if you'll just . . .'

Erica is observing me from under lowered lids, noting the earth on my shorts, I think. Raising her eyes, she gives a calculated shared-confidence stare. 'Perhaps it's best I tell you,' she pauses, 'but Julian was with a girl. I saw them in the new café bar in College Street when I came by that way – it opened only last week, you may not have tried it yet – and they were together at the shop for quite a while, too. I happened to see them at an upstairs window . . .'

I'm tempted to say a pity she hadn't brought her binoculars, but restrain myself. She patrols the town like a Gestapo guard – does she never stay home?

Erica looks across to the bookshop. 'He opened up the blinds. A bit slack, not closing up again properly, there's so much crime about. One can't be too careful.'

'No, quite so. You're very observant, Erica.'

She beams. 'I like to think so. And do slightly pride myself on being a good judge of character actually. There is something fishy about Julian's past; people question his morals. You're well out of him, Ursula, as I've told you before . . .'

'Very true,' I say, holding on with difficulty. 'Although I wouldn't call raising the blinds a particularly immoral activity and I shall be eternally in Julian's debt for all he did for Jessie. Now I really must go, my poor dog . . .'

Nothing can touch Erica. Her face is wreathed in self-congratulation. Then glancing beyond me, she brings her eyes back with a look of solicitude. 'Oh dear, sorry to say the warden has beaten you to it. He's ticketing your windscreen as we speak.'

Clear of the town centre, the tears – held at bay, with hope, adrenaline, pride while with Erica – break free.

My desolation is complete. Julian brought Jessie books, he was being caring. Maybe he'd wanted to see me too, or to check up on me, but he had a date with a girl the whole while. It's bringing out in me the most poignant sense of betrayal and let-down – the very emotions I had thought had been showing in him.

I've no right to feel betrayed. If he suspected me of sleeping with Perry, or even if he didn't, Julian wasn't tied or beholden. Maybe he's always had girls; so much of his life has been closed to me. Surely, though, Lauren hadn't been meaning other women when she spoke of a part of him where the shades were down.

I can't stop to walk Misty, I just want to get home, to be alone, hugging my misery in the empty house, sobbing it out for the short time before the girls are back from school.

Turning in the gate, Misty is suddenly alert, on his feet, fidgeting round in his space behind the dog screen. He's seen something. I immediately tense up too, my nerves shot to pieces since the terror of what happened only a week ago.

It's Julian. He is out of his car – he was sitting on the front steps when I first saw him – but now he's beside my car, opening the car door before I've turned off the engine, leaving me for a second to swing up the back, Misty's going quite mad. I'm in Julian's arms then, sweaty and dirty with tears streaming down my face.

'I hated your mobile being off, it felt so final . . .' I say when I'm able.

'I found your second message – then the first . . .' His kisses are real; he can't let go.

'I've missed you all over, been twice to Brearfield – but then Erica said you had a date so perhaps it was just as well.'

Julian lets go of my mouth and hugs me. He's breaking up laughing. 'Sure I had a date, an appointment with the girl who's buying the shop. I took her for a coffee and a sandwich. She loves the place, especially the flat, she even wants to buy the little four-poster, although I'm not sure about that and certainly didn't demonstrate how it's best used . . .' He's scooping me off my feet and carrying me towards the front door. 'Which is what I'm going to do now, with yours.'

'You're going the wrong way, you won't get in, the keys are in my bag in the car.'

We're still in bed and it's nearly four; the girls will be back in minutes. The lovemaking on a humid airless afternoon has been a voyage taken together, moments we could hold and make last, lengthening the sweet joy and intoxicating climaxes. Earthier passions too, we've been everywhere, sticking to each other, wet with exertion.

Julian has traced over my body, every curve and crevice. Making a checklist he said, telling me my profile was delicate, my neck Grecian, that I had violet eyes and silky thighs. I said he wasn't seeing straight, that it was the sweat in his eyes.

'This is terrible,' I say, flinging away from him, 'I've got under five minutes to get dressed and downstairs.'

Cleaner and pulling on a sundress, I say, 'A step up from filthy gardening shorts, I was weeding when my two unexpected callers turned up this morning . . .'

'Really unexpected?'

'I'll give you the full Perry story when you'll let me . . .' I've tried to tell Julian, but he put a hand over my mouth saying the talking comes later.

'And I've got something to tell you too, but later, when we're in bed.'

'We are now! Well, you are . . . Can't you get going?' I say, feeling shivers of anxiety at what he might have to say. 'Are you going to greet the girls like that?'

'I might consider a towel, possibly a toga . . .'

'Will you stay at the shop tonight – you're not going all the way to Cambridge . . .?

'Are you joking? I've just planted my flag, pitched my tent – although you might not want me around when you hear everything I have to say.'

CHAPTER 28

'Why's your car in this funny place, blocking the way?' Emma calls, coming past it up the drive. 'And isn't that Julian's? How did he get past yours?'

'I'd gone into Brearfield and he came while I was out. School all OK? And you, Jess, darling,' I ask as she catches up, 'you got through it all right?'

Jessie is clearly in no mood to answer or give me the slightest clue. She says, looking to the house, 'Is Julian inside? Where is he? I want to say hello.'

'Hold on, don't go rushing off. I want a kiss and to hear if it was at all a better day.'

She shrugs her shoulders, then looking impatiently sulky, rather grudgingly offers a hot cheek. Kissing it, holding her tense little body close for an instant, I'm thinking Julian must have got some clothes on by now.

As she hurries on in, my mind is filled with what he can possibly be going to tell me. How bad can it be? A spell in jail? For what? Nothing to do with Aids, I'm sure. He only suggested I *might* not want him around, not that I wouldn't. Is it going to be all right . . .?

'Julian's here this evening, Ems,' I say, feeling overwhelmingly shy all of a sudden. 'Any ideas for supper?'

'Your chicken thing with the avocado, he likes that.' She's not really paying attention, anxious to go indoors and see what's happening.

They'll go and change, I think, and he won't have made the bed. It's too late to worry about any of that. He's moving in, here to stay. No fuss, my life turned on its head, easy as flipping a coin.

Shouldn't the girls be consulted and given a little warning? Am I leaping in with two besotted feet, getting carried away – not seeing straight? And all before I know what he's going to say. We'll manage. I love him and the decision was taken a week ago in that hotel bedroom. I knew what I wanted then. Nothing can sway me. My star is set.

I go indoors to find Julian and Jessie sitting on the polished oak refectory table with dangling legs. He jumps down and puts an arm round me. 'I've been hearing all about Jess's day at school,' he says, looking back fondly at Jess. 'How hard it is with her friends, the problems. There are a few . . .'

She nods, sliding down from the table, then goes running upstairs without troubling to give her mother a second glance.

It makes me feel inadequate, almost jealous; I got an irritated shrug when I asked about school outside, but she's been pouring it out to Julian. It's the surprise of him being here, I think, trying to bury the feeling, wishing he'd buttoned up his shirt.

'When should we tell them?' I ask, feeling insubstantial, leaning into him and gaining strength from his welded body like a supportive sturdy splint. 'Over supper? Or perhaps I should do it in advance . . .'

His arm tightens. 'You mustn't be sensitive about Jess, she's still very shocked and shaken. It'll take time. I could tell them myself if you'd like – warn them that life's going to be a lot tougher now, with a man around the place.'

I look up at him, feeling grateful, a sense of relief seeping in. It would be so much help, I'd be bound to feel painfully self-conscious . . . But it's my job to tell them. Where's my backbone? Am I so much of a reed? There can be no sliding backwards and letting him take over like Bill.

Julian is watching me with a grin. He's only bloody reading my mind, I think, infuriated. 'Well, shall I do it – what do you reckon,' he says, still grinning.

'We'll tell them together over supper,' I say, compressing my lips before breaking away and adding pointedly, 'I'd better get going in the kitchen now, and get it ready.'

'Did I ever tell you I can cook – well, after a fashion? Oh, and it's tidy upstairs, in case you were wondering. The cover's pulled up, at least.'

Julian takes the lead in the telling, saying we love each other and he's moving in. His foot is on mine under the table, delivering pressure – as well as a statement that leaves no room for dissent. The girls hear him out, both with their heads cocked. Playing to the drama of the occasion, I think, loving the sight of them, so summery and golden like an advertisement for some healthy buttery spread. Jess is in a pink sundress, Emma in check shorts.

I feel an ice-cold hand massaging my heart; Jessie might not have been here.

'Why did you put the shop up for sale and go away?' Emma asks. 'Mum was so mopey.'

I'm saved the need to speak as Jessie turns to her sister. 'They weren't getting on,' she says with great authority, really lording it.

'That's not exactly true, Jess,' I interject. 'Julian wanted to start work on his book and he thought I needed space.'

His pressure on my foot increases. 'Was I right?'

I feel myself going berry red. He's enjoying this, but it's not something I want to get into, certainly not now, at this supper table, in front of two inquisitive girls.

'When will you move in properly, Julian?' Emma asks, coming to the rescue.

'I just did, a couple of hours ago!' Could she see I was struggling? She's been so intuitive, the most wonderful support. I do hope he knows she must never be overlooked.

'I will go back to the Cambridgeshire house tomorrow, though, Emma,' he carries on, 'just to collect a few things – that's if I can borrow Mum's car. Mine has to go, I think. It's never going to be big enough now.'

We three turn to stare at each other in amazement then say in unison, 'But you love that car!'

'Not as much as this new family of mine . . . Now – and it's not just to get out of the washing up – I should go and check on how I left the shop. You'll like the new owner,' he says, mainly to the girls. 'She had a job in the City, but wanted to try her hand at something new. And her parents live in Hemple Benton where she can keep a horse, so that clinched it!'

He's out of the door before I remember my car's in the way – and with the key still in it. I think of something else too, and open the kitchen drawer.

Julian is already driving my car up to the garage, locating the remote on the ring. While the heavy door is swinging up and over, I come to the driver's window.

'You're going to need this now,' I say, handing him the spare key to the house.

Transferring to his own car he gets in and squints up. 'Won't need it for long. We'll be moving, and very far from here – and with luck in time for the start of the new term.'

With that he puts his foot down, shooting off, burning enough carbon to give Erica a fit, leaving me with another of life's coins flipped over.

I'm glad of the hour or so alone with the idea of moving to add to my febrile thoughts. I feel too much for Julian to worry about whatever it is he wants to tell me later, but tossing out the notion of moving has got me in a complete tizz. What about my mother, the girls' friends; mine too? I don't want to lose Val and Susie. It needs serious thought and has to be a joint decision, I think crossly, going into the kitchen. He needn't think he's laying down the law.

Emma is busily putting food in the fridge while Jessie is looking out to the garden from the open backdoor. Her hair is tousled and clammy with the heat; she's seems taller suddenly, growing as leggy as her sister. Turning round she gives me a concentrated stare. 'Why is Julian still selling the shop, Mum, if he's moving in?' She's anticipating a possible move, I think, and other than to Blossom Cottage. Jessie's got there ahead of me.

'He's very hard at work on his book . . .'

'I expect he'll carry on selling on the Net,' she suggests. 'I hate thinking the shop will be all new books now, just like any other boring old bookshop, but the lady does sound OK. Perhaps I can do Saturdays with her.'

I say nothing. Jessie must know that's out of the question after Martin. The very thought of it brings me out in skin-pricking shivers. Is it her way of probing about moving? Well, she can ask all the oblique questions she likes, but the answers will have to wait.

The next hurdle is going to be telling my mother. God knows how she's going to take it – and whatever else is to come.

I decide to do some advance cooking for Sunday lunch with her and set about making cheat's mayonnaise. Emma stands beside me, talking loudly over the blender. 'Julian didn't say anything about getting married, Mum. Are you? I didn't quite like to ask.'

'You're never usually one to hold back.' I dribble in more olive oil, well aware of ducking the question, thinking whimsically how much Emma would love another wedding. Whether or not she feels she's been given the brush-off, she leaves it there.

I add a last splash of oil. Do I really want to be married again? It didn't work last time. Nothing could be worse than to have Julian feeling trapped and tied, going off on his travels and only coming back out of a sense of duty. Perhaps I encouraged it, but I've been a Good Wife once, an English Rose stuck out in the sticks – saddled with that sexless image while Bill lived it up in London, I never to want to feel as written-off and dependent again.

Isn't it a question of commitment? I don't need Julian to marry me to show that. It's not as though there'll be babies . . . Marriage becomes meaningless if the love dries up, and he loves my children already, he would feel a natural commitment – particularly after what he did for Jessie, probably saving her life.

Julian will be trustworthy and responsible, I'm sure. And if things go wrong between us, far better he feels untrammelled and able to move on. Bill will always support the girls. I can work.

The whirring is done. Emma has obviously been waiting her moment. 'But are you, Mum – going to get married?' she says, not letting me off the hook.

'Your guess is as good as mine,' I smile, feeling more satisfyingly in control.

From her knowing look she's deciding that's a tease and I'm just not letting on. Maybe it's no bad thing for her to read it that way, for the moment at least.

'Where will Julian keep all his books?' Jess asks, ever practical. 'And is he going to share your study?'

'That would be very fraught! Isn't it time you fed Blanche? And Ems, I'm going to the study to make some calls, but I'll use the work line, so you can still get going, and phone round all your friends.'

I'm about to ring my mother, but click off. Surely it's better to wait till morning when I'll have the full picture; I don't want to have to make two difficult calls.

Julian will be back soon too, and I must phone Val. She, more than anyone, has lived through my deepest seabed lows and I do need to let out some of this fizzing euphoria – and my bottled up scary nerves.

She listens, making a few amused appreciative asides – until I bring up my mother and the effort it will be, explaining that we're not getting married. 'Julian obviously doesn't want to, Val, and it'll surprise you, this, but I don't either!'

'You serious, Ursula? What a breakthrough! You're finally shaking off the mothballs and getting a life.'

'He's talking about moving right away from Brearfield, but I'd miss you and Susie so much and it would be hard on my mother. With my brother Harry out in Colombia, I'm all she's got.'

'She's the least of your worries. She drives, still has a job – you concentrate on Emma and Jess. They're the ones who've been through the mill, it'll be their lives that are going to be most affected.'

I end the call feeling chastened. Thinking of the children makes me all the keener not to be browbeaten about moving; Julian must surely understand. Everything is so up in the air, I feel wound up as a yoyo and terrified of hitting the ground.

Hearing his car I wander outside in the warm evening air, standing by as he parks. He gets out and pulls me close for a kiss. We turn to go in and see we have an audience. Emma and Jess have come out on to the steps. They were watching that intimate kiss, but with solemnly amenable looks on their young faces. To know they accept and welcome Julian, that they don't feel sidelined or threatened, seems more than I deserve.

Behind them the house is making my heart swell, too. I've always loved its mellow symmetry. The wisteria is bright lime green in the evening light with shy hidden splashes of lavender, a token second flowering. It's the only home the children have known.

'Plenty of space in the cupboards,' I call from the bathroom. Julian has brought a few last remaining clothes that were at the flat.

As I come back in he closes the one drawer in Bill's Regency chest he's using. 'I don't need space, I'm not bringing much stuff before we move. It's so spread around: in store, Cambridgeshire, some still in Africa.' He's stepping me out of my sundress, undoing my bra, lowering his head to my breasts. 'And moving has to be soon,' Julian says, looking up and kissing me before I can argue, his hands on my breasts, his eyes holding mine.

He pulls me over to sit down on the bed and turns my shoulders. 'I want you to come and live in the West Country. I'll be writing books, dealing in old ones, dabbling in farming, taking you travelling. There's a big Californian book fair in February, I'm not leaving you behind.' He's watching me, gauging any reaction. 'I want you to give up that job of yours, help me and do things of your own.'

Now I'm being laid back on the bed with Julian beside me, hitched up on an elbow and still watching, his hand lightly pressing on my stomach, easing further down.

'Where do the children fit into this sybaritic, bucolic idyll?' I say distractedly, feeling aroused.

'Neatly. Top billing after you – but I want to talk about them in conjunction with something else.'

'Which is?' I move Julian's hand away, keeping hold of it – I'm not that malleable.

'The thing I've been keeping from you. Possibly stupidly, but I have. Set that aside for a moment, though, would you love or hate life on a farm and having me home for lunch?'

He's lived hard and farmed in testing places, I think fondly, imagining him in the role. 'Of course I'd love it, but . . .'

'I know there's your mother. When she sees you happy she'll be fine, I think, and she might even begin to accept me,' he says, his hand working free of my hold and beginning to roam. 'We can have her close by. I've got my eye on a farm with a couple of cottages near Lyme Regis. Barbara would make friends soon enough. We'd help her settle down.'

He rolls me over, kissing me then keeping me held. 'I could have shown you the particulars,' he says with a wry edge, 'only I binned them this morning. Tore them to shreds like a love letter before going on to keep my appointment with the girl buying the shop.'

'When I'm sure you were charm itself. Is she pretty?' I ask flippantly, shuddering at the memory of Erica's revelations.

'Quite. A bit . . . county. Brearfield will love her.'

'Do you want to hear about Perry?' I ask in a small voice, needing to clear the decks, failing to stay Julian's distracting, caressing hand.

'If I must. It was obvious where you were last Friday, when Jessie went missing.' I can sense a new tension in him and I'm feeling defensive and tense myself. 'But for what happened,' Julian goes on, 'you'd have been shacked up with the adulterous Maynard all night. I'd had to accept that and decide if I could live with it. You had called me before William, that's when I knew you needed me. But arriving this morning and seeing Maynard's car . . . Still, the body language was hopeful – until he produced that wretched little holdall. It was very clear then that he'd had you last week after all, probably even as you were hearing Jessie was lost.'

I struggle to be sitting upright, turning to stare at him. 'Perry didn't have me then or any other time. You're wrong, darling, about everything except about my being with him that evening. He'd booked a room in a fancy little east Kent hotel – in case of need. He'd reached into my car as I arrived and picked up the bag I'd brought – just in case. Then he'd insisted I use the room he'd booked to freshen up, instead of the Ladies downstairs. That made me suddenly see him for what he is, a ghastly shit who's all too accustomed to having his pick, like eating cherries, and who couldn't give a toss what happens to the spit-out stones.'

'So what did you do?' Julian still sounds edgy.

'I stalled. I had a drink with him and waited for the perfect time to tell him to have a cosy dinner for one, walk out and ring you and ask forgiveness for being such a stupid blind fool.'

'And then Val phoned?'

'It was the worst moment of my life. But you were there – and you did your all.'

Julian pulls me backwards into his arms. 'I like you calling me darling,' he says, as he begins taking off clothes of his own.

We're lying under a sheet together, sticky and entwined. It feels like another bed, another country with Julian in it and I'm floating on feathers, on a lingering high.

'You slipped Perry's net,' Julian says, 'I was so sure you'd succumbed, and the thought of it would have always been there.'

'You should have had more faith.'

'You'd never even told me you loved me.'

'No good. You always said you knew my thoughts better than me. And you still haven't told me your hidden secret. There's Lauren, too. Have you ever been more than friends . . .?'

'You can't possibly have been thinking that! Of course not; I'm not Perry. She's a wonderful friend, though, and she always believed I should tell you. It seemed too complicating, never the right time. I've got a son out in Uganda, you see. He's called James and he's nearly sixteen. I want him to come to England and live with us now – if you'll agree.'

It was the last thing I was expecting. The room is in near darkness, the light still on in the bathroom, but the daylight has gone. Julian is towards me, on his side. I can't see his face clearly, his features seem to be making their own shade. And in those shadowy contours his expression seems held, suspended, like a suitor fearing rejection, a captive awaiting his fate.

He's watchful, eyeing me, as I take my time, as the implications slowly seep in and a sinking feeling takes over, as a trapdoor begins to open under my feet. I've had self-deluding fears about Lauren, but this is a deeper dread.

'And James's mother? Have you got a wife out there, too?'

'No, not a wife, not even an ex-one. I've only been married once, to Marion. James's mother is a doctor, a Ugandan. Anita Ssali, she's called, Annie to her friends. I did nearly marry her sixteen years ago, but she knew it would have been partly out of a sense of duty and she wouldn't have it. My father thought I should have insisted and brought her to live in England. It was his only grandchild, whom he never saw. Anita wouldn't come, though. It was for unselfish reasons. She knew I wasn't completely in love, and she's also totally committed to her work. She runs a little hospital for children with Aids, almost single-handed. I've been supporting her and helping where I can. It was hard for her when I fell in love with you. She knew immediately.'

I can't properly sort out my feelings or find the appropriate words. I'm remembering an email on the police list from the Cambridgeshire house. The one signed, 'Annie x'. It's all falling into place. 'She's always looked after your son,' I say. 'Surely she won't want to lose him?'

'She knows it's the right time. You see she's marrying a minister in the Ugandan government now. Her life will be extra busy and she wants James to have the best possible sixth form education, just as I do. Will you take on my half-Ugandan son, darling? He's very strictly brought up, but still a tall hungry teenager. I worry slightly about your mother needing to adjust; he's more Anita's colour than mine.'

I'm recovering from a series of punches, but taking on Julian's son isn't one of them. 'Of course I will, that's not an issue, you shouldn't even need to ask. And,' I say, quite angry that he should have even entertained the thought, 'my mother might be a hopeless case, painfully conventional, but whatever else she's not prejudiced. How could you possibly think such a thing?' I look down then, fighting ridiculous tears.

Julian picks up my chin. 'If that's not a problem, what is? Tell me how you really feel about this, I need to know.'

'It's nothing.' I can't tell him the trapdoor is still there, the ground shifting, bleakness setting in. Anita is still part of his life, I think; she means something, the mother of his only child. He admires her and feels involved.

'It's not nothing.'

I look at him with agonized eyes. 'Well, all those trips out to Uganda. You stayed with her, didn't you, seeing your son? Did you sleep with her as well?'

There's a silence. He obviously did. Everything's slowly imploding.

'Only in the very early years,' he says finally, looking boyishly rueful, 'only when you were still married to William. Once I'd had carnal knowledge of you . . . That was it, I couldn't – not even when I went off feeling so angry with you after that dreadful dance.'

I turn away. Had I known then that he was going to the home of a woman he'd wanted to marry, who had borne him a child, a woman whom he still cares about – what would I have done? Run to Perry? I hope not. It's easy to see why Julian didn't want to tell me.

He knew it would have crushed me to a powder, reduced me to scattered remains.

'It's wonderful she's getting married,' Julian says, sounding anxious and entwining our fingers. 'I'm delighted for her. Annie would never consider such a step unless she was truly in love. And she's very happy for me too – has been since the start . . . But you must tell me how you're feeling, I need to know.' His eyes are on mine.

I'm suddenly on a high again, lifted up, dreaming once more of a picture-book future. God knows what sort of a farmer I'd make, but I'm bursting to give it a try.

'I'm feeling in love,' I say smiling, touching his damp brow, curling my fingers in the hairs on his chest. 'But this won't do. Your son feels part of the family already, but you've fitted a very rosy filter to the viewfinder, it's not really how life works. What about schools? Have you thought how hard it would be for Emma and Jess, leaving all their friends? They're both doing well and so settled here.'

'Jessie isn't and it'll go on being hard for her, too. I had thought about boarding school . . .'

'No, out of the question!' I sit bolt upright. 'I couldn't do that to them and there's an end to it. If we do move to the West Country – and it's a very big if – they're going to a local school.'

I've often told Julian how much I hated being stuck in a boarding school with my parents abroad – the solitude of my girlhood. Effortful terms with only the grandparents to take me out: then the exhilarated delight of long-haul flights with my brother Harry, seeing our parents again. We would breeze into their formal, tightly correct lives, strutting briefly on to the stage like cocky young actors with cameo roles; having fun and being feted – only to have to leave again for another long term.

'And Bill has an equal say in their schooling,' I add pugnaciously.

'At least give it some thought,' Julian says, mildly persistent. 'Perhaps you should ask the girls . . .'

They don't know about James yet, or this business of moving. Nor does my mother, nor does Bill. 'I'm not up to any more tonight,' I say smiling. 'I want to go to sleep now. Don't vanish in the night, into this fantasy world you're living in; I want to wake up and find you beside me and carry on arguing this out in the hard cold light of day.'

CHAPTER 29

I'm putting out breakfast things and heating up some croissants out of the freezer. It's the weekend after all, so this is not just in honour of the new member of the family.

'What about our holiday?' Emma says, pouring out orange juice. 'Will Julian be coming with us to the Algarve?'

'That was just what I wanted to talk about!' She turns with a start. He's at the door and comes into the kitchen and gives her a squeeze. 'I've got a plan to take you all on safari, instead.'

It stops us in our tracks. Jessie's reading *The Post* at the table and her head shoots up. Of the three pairs of eyes on him Emma's are really lighting up. Her two best friends have been on safari holidays and talked of nothing else. She's been nagging about going for ages.

'Barbara must come too, of course,' Julian adds with no hint of facetiousness, glancing at me. 'She'd love a taste of the tropics again, I'd have thought, after places like Jakarta, Accra and Mexico.'

He knows about my father's diplomatic postings and has been to most of the places, too. And he's right, my mother did love the tropics. Perhaps they'll find some common ground.

I'm glad the cheque for the Algarve holiday never made it into the post yesterday, but why didn't he talk to me about it first? So irresponsible, getting the girls all excited.

'It's a wonderful idea, but you can't possibly take us,' I say firmly, frowning at him, 'it would cost a fortune. And it's fanciful to think we'll get in anywhere, it's the height of the season, there'll be no chance.'

'I know people, I can fix it. Kenya, I thought, a week in a game park and a week on the coast. We could drive up from Mombasa to Kilifi Creek; it's halfway to Malindi and the most stunning setting. You'll love seeing the dhows and it's steeped in history. The Mnarani Hotel is the place to stay . . .'

'Oh, Mum, please don't say we can't go!' Emma starts bombarding Julian with questions. It's hard to stay angry with him, seeing their faces, but what if it comes to nothing?

My thoughts stray back to my mother. The postings hadn't been easy for her. I had never known in childhood, in those days of being spoiled on school holidays, what life was really like for her. Some of the places had been rough and it was all about keeping up appearances. She had even found herself laundering the shirts and smalls of visiting politicians, on occasion, when there were local problems, shortages of staff.

My mother would love to go back to Africa, I think. It would remind her of the high spots, not the hard times. But she's not going to love the fact of Julian moving in. It'll open up still more avenues of worry and she's never short of those. School breaks up in days; it's hard to imagine us all gaily setting off together on an exotic holiday, happy and well adjusted as clams.

*

Julian has just left for Cambridgeshire, dropping off Emma at a friend's house on the way. She's being brought back at lunchtime and that's when I must tell her and Jessie about James. And about moving. God, how difficult it all could be.

I pick up the phone to my mother. A large part of me is dying to tell her everything, to take her through the highs, share the troughs and lows, to say how electrifyingly in love I feel. What holds me back are all her doubts and reservations hinted at over the years. I've had to defend Julian all the way.

It's not a time I would usually call and she sounds surprised. 'Nothing wrong, darling?'

'The opposite really, life has been turning several revolutions, but I do need to talk. Can you come today and stay over? Julian has moved in, you see.' It seems better to get it out straight away. 'He's gone to Cambridgeshire for some things and won't be around till later, I'd have you to myself for a while.'

'Goodness, what big news. You do sound awfully happy about it.' She does too, really quite cheerful, I think with astonishment. I might have been Emma chatting about a sleepover, not her only daughter taking up with an 'unsuitable' man. 'I can come about two,' my mother says. 'Sure you both want me to stay the night, though?'

I assure her we do, that Julian suggested it, and end the call.

It's eleven. I can't settle to a thing and take a bottle of mineral water out to the terrace. My mother still has the ability to surprise me, I think, feeling a rush of fondness and a longing to be hugging her and smiling into those faded anxious blue eyes. She has a special face-powdery smell, and a thin frailness that makes me feel so protective – there's too little of her to hug these days.

I'm in cool cotton shorts and a bathing top and still expiring.

Sitting at the round wrought-iron table with my water bottle I think it's far too hot for gardening or doing anything useful. The sky is oppressive and heavy with low-slung clouds that look like bunched-up reverse parachutes, billowing and dark-edged. Misty has slunk under the table; he's anticipating the thunder and lying hard against my calf.

Jessie has Blanche out on the lawn. They're not very involved, the guinea pig is sniffling about and Jess is reading, leaning on wide-apart knees, her book on the grass between them. She's in an old pair of shiny exercise pants and her kicked-off trainers are at right angles, upside-down on the grass. It would make a painting – or a poem. But I must phone Bill.

I'm feeling stupid trepidation about it. I'm not a teenager with a boyfriend under the bed, he can't reasonably make a fuss, he hasn't got a leg to stand on. He might not thank me for having to drive all the way to the West Country and I don't know what his views will be about schools, but there is the sale of the house, compensating factors.

Julian and I briefly carried on arguing about schools and moving before he left this morning. He suggested sending Emma to Nattie's old school – near Newbury, well placed for Bill – he's already talked to the head about James going there, and probably, knowing him, mentioned the possibility of Emma going, too. He thinks Jessie would benefit from a highly academic girls' school. I do agree it might suit her to be separated from Emma . . .

Resisting the idea of boarding is instinctive, but for the most con-trary and sensitive of reasons as well. I'm fighting a deep-seated terror about the girls travelling to and from a country day school after what happened with Martin. Forcing the responsibility upon myself, of taking them in each day, is a sort of hair-shirt mechanism, a way of standing up to the constant fear and facing up to my demons. But then Jessie will have hers, too . . .

Julian understands, I think. He's talked obliquely round it, about Jessie being unsettled, the continuing aftermath of the publicity.

He'll leave schools to me, but his pressure about moving is unrelenting. He thinks, passionately, that I need to get the hell out of Brearfield – which I agree with, although in a way it's giving in to Erica – that Emma is wonderfully adaptable and that Jessie will never be happy where she is any more. 'They'll miss their friends, the phone bills will be high,' he said. 'But they'll rise to the excitement of change.'

My thoughts have been crystallizing as I sit here. We'll share buying a farm, I'll have my half of the house sale to contribute. I'm going to grow soft fruit and start a specialist jam business. Julian planted the seed of an idea when he talked of doing things of my own. It's the sort of thing I'd love to do; the business might even take off. And I'll write poems.

And schools? There's Bill to consider . . . That's just postponing the decision.

But I can't postpone phoning him a moment longer. Bill has to know about my flipped-over life and all its repercussions. I must go inside and get it over with.

'It doesn't sound to me,' he says coldly, after listening without interruption, 'as though you've given any great thought to this son of Julian's. He pops up from nowhere: we know nothing about him. And sixteen is a very experimental age. If you take him in as one of the family he'll be living hugger-mugger with Emma and Jess and they're growing up fast – doesn't that worry you just a bit?'

'No, it does not! You've had Tom living in the same house as Nattie and Victoria didn't think that way. And you can bet James's upbringing was a whole lot stricter than Tom's.' I almost have a go about absent fathers, but then remember Julian has been one, too. 'Don't you trust your own daughters?' I demand. 'James will be at boarding school, going home in the holidays to see his mother . . .' I leave it there, hoping Bill will too, and even pick up on the mention of school. Be good to know where we stand.

He doesn't, just says, sounding querulous, 'So you're putting the house on the market?' I'm used to his aggressive tone. Bill always gets cross first and then calms down. He always needs time to digest things.

It doesn't stop me snapping back. 'Any objections?'

I can feel myself scowling into the phone. This is going badly. I don't want to get into a sparring contest. 'Why not come down tomorrow for lunch,' I say, trying to be accommodating. 'We can talk everything through. Bring Tom and Nattie if you can – and Victoria, of course, if she's free.' Unlikely, but she'd be a peacekeeper and I could handle it now – all the more so with Julian around.

'I'll check it out,' Bill says abruptly and clicks off.

It's beginning to thunder; I must get Jessie indoors.

She locks Blanche back in her hutch and we stand watching, each wrapped in our own thoughts, as the little thing settles in. It's funny how Elton had so much more personality. It makes me pine.

Bill had revealed conflicting emotions, I think. His relief at my news was obvious. I've been a drain, a resentful millstone; a constant reminder, a trailer attached to his fast car. But in some ways, I think, having the responsibility has made him feel cleaner and partly absolved. And Bill likes being in charge, yelling at people, charming them, pulling strings.

Now that I'm unhooked and freewheeling he'll mind losing control. And he'll feel his daughters slipping away. They get on so well with Julian. I'm sure Bill will be picturing scenes of the proper cosy family life that I pray we're going to be having. And he'll feel for ever in debt to Julian over Jessie and find that hard.

The sky is suddenly as black as the Phantom's cape and Jessie and I scuttle inside as the rain tips down. She's at a slight loose end. I tell her to look up the places in Kenya Julian talked about on the Internet and the idea appeals and keeps her occupied. I feel quietly excited about it after my mother's encouraging reaction. It might really be going to happen after all.

Bill calls back sounding more relaxed. Victoria must have got at him. They will come tomorrow morning, but in two cars. Tom and Nattie staying on for lunch, he and Victoria only for a short time. 'Must have some time in the office on Sunday,' Bill says, 'there's so much going on. We're after the Defence Secretary's head. Victoria's not speaking to me, actually,' he adds with great pride. 'She will go on defending that berk of a colleague of hers.'

I call Jess to have a word with her father. She's muted, talking to him. It's nothing to do with Bill, I think, watching her. Just that her eyes are distant, as though her thoughts are pulling her another way.

As she puts down the phone keeping her head low, I ask gently, 'Is it bad memories?'

She looks round. 'Sort of. It's . . . well, just sort of always there.' Jess is running to me then and bursting into tears in my arms.

*

Emma is back, wet-haired from the torrential rain and very talkative. She's telling Jess all about her friend Sal's older brother. 'He's a real fat minger, so crude and so really *personal* and he walks in that funny lumpy way so who's he to talk?'

I send her off to dry her hair. Then over lunch while Emma is eating hungrily and Jess is pushing cold ham and quiche around her plate, I face up to explaining about leaving Brearfield. It seems best to get it out of the way before tackling the more monumental news about a brand new brotherly addition to the family. I have no idea how it's going to take them.

'We'll have a little farm. It would give me the chance of starting a business, there are all sorts of reasons,' I say rather desperately, without producing a single other one. 'You do both understand?'

'It's because of Jessie really, isn't it?' Emma says, slightly melodramatically, with a glaze to her eyes. 'She needs to get right away from here with all the bad vibes, doesn't she, Mum? Would I be able to have friends to stay? And it's my birthday at the end of the hols – would we still be here for the party?'

I promise her parties, a continuous trail of friends – thinking nervously of gaggles of just-thirteen-year-olds, who will need watching over with eagle eyes. Emma's still blaming herself and feeling guilty, but that glazed look of hers makes me sad. It's lucky in one sense, her guilt, as it's making her wonderfully accommodating, but I think she's very aware of everything being tailored to Jessie's needs, and naturally beginning to expect a little consideration given to hers.

If I was thinking entirely of the children's wants and needs, not Julian's and my own, would I decide the West Country was the place to go? Am I being typically selfish? It is lovely country and it will keep them from becoming too sophisticated and adult too soon.

Julian wants us to have a London base, too. 'I wouldn't use it like William does,' he said grinning, 'and the girls will need it in a few years.' It is such a plunge in the dark, all this. Perhaps a happy home is the key to it all.

Jess is still fiddling with her food. She's given no indication so far, no clue as to whether distance from Brearfield will help and her feelings about it. She looks up. 'Do you mean a real farm, Mum, with animals and people working on it and stuff?'

'Yes, but not a very big one. Sheep possibly and a few chickens; it'll be mainly down to crops, and perhaps some soft fruit like gooseberries and raspberries.'

I wait till they're scooping ice cream out of plastic tubs before talking about James.

It matters so much to me how they respond. I want Julian's son, who will be in a strange country, his father the only person he knows, to be made truly to feel he belongs. I'll be no substitute for his mother, but I long to form a real bond. It's not from indebtedness to Julian, simply a gut need to do right by his son. I *think* the girls will be cautiously excited and curious and want to make him welcome. They've so loved having Nattie in their lives.

They hear me out with fast draining faces. Their reaction is the greater shock for its unexpectedness, like a dropped tray of glasses or a burst tyre. My quiet confidence was very misplaced.

From Emma's expression you'd think it was her friend Sal's 'fat minger' brother moving in. 'Oh, Mum, it will be *awful*, you're not really serious? He's going to be *living* with us? I mean, I'm sure he's very nice and all that, but he won't know anyone and he'll be so hanging around and bringing home horrible friends who'll sneer and stare. And we won't be able to talk girls' things and not be overheard. *And* sharing a bathroom! It'll be really *gruesome*.'

'He's four years older, Ems, he's not going to hassle you. And you've shared a bathroom with Tom all these years. James will be just like another brother.'

'Tom's eight years older and he didn't stare and things. And he's, well, you know, family . . .'

Jess pushes back her chair and rushes out and upstairs. I feel momentarily cross; she's got to get out of that babyish habit. The thought pulls me up sharp. At some stage we'll have to start treating her with normal toughness, but it is hardly more than a week since she came home traumatized. She'd been hit in the face, bruised, had to live through a unique hell and survive on her wits alone. She needs a lot of love and understanding. Jessie has always bottled it up, it's so hard to know what's going on inside, she says so little.

Emma needs gentle handling too, she's really upset about James. 'Suppose you actually like him?' I try, with an anxious smile. 'You were thrilled to meet Nattie – good friends from the start.'

'She's a girl and was never going to be living here full time. It's different – you know it is, Mum.'

'Think how hard life is out in Uganda, darling, all the luxuries James has missed out on that you two take for granted. Try to make him feel at home. Suppose it was the other way round and you'd been the one going abroad for the first time, say to live with Dad's new wife – think how you'd feel.' She gives me a funny look. 'All right, so I'm not quite exactly Julian's wife . . . Don't be so difficult!' Emma gives a small half-hearted smile.

*

By the time my mother arrives the girls have worn me out. Jessie's problem with James, it seems, stemmed more from worry about Julian's divided loyalties than shared bathrooms. I told her she must make him feel part of the family, that having a son has never affected Julian's love for her in the past and certainly won't do in the future. 'You're like a daughter to him, he'd expect it of you.'

I reminded her of how the people have suffered in James's country, the past terrible hardships. 'And you've been so brave, you know all about feeling fear and terror, I want you to try to imagine how hard it would be for an older boy having to keep his feelings secret. There will be times when he's bound to feel lonely and insecure.'

There was a risk it would make her feel James would be garnering all the sympathy and she'd get forgotten. I think, though, Jess quite liked the idea of being a sort of mother figure. She appears to be taking it all in, but it is so hard to tell.

A lot depends on the boy, I think, trying to imagine Julian's son.

It's still raining heavily and my mother suggests taking the girls on a shopping spree for holiday clothes. I had wanted to keep the safari holiday secret till suppertime and let Julian tell her himself, but Emma was spilling it out before my mother was in the door. She seems as unfazed about the idea as with my earlier news this morning and really quite full of anticipation. There's a new lightness about her. I don't understand what's going on.

We have an exhausting time at a nearby huge retail-shopping outlet. I buy my mother a safari-style cotton trouser suit, thinking it would look fine if we end up going to Portugal after all. And she gets the girls cute cotton cut-offs in neutral colours, saying they would be suitable camouflage out on drives in game parks.

She stocks up on insect repellent, too. It's too much for me. When the girls are absorbed, rifling through cut-price CDs, while we're shattered, collapsed on two small chairs waiting patiently, and all other shoppers around seem in a self-absorbed disinterested daze, I tackle my mother on her apparent Julian U-turn.

'You've never seen his point, never been the slightest bit positive. So what's changed?'

'You, your decision. It was obvious you loved him; not so obvious it was going to work out. I thought either he had someone abroad or that he would eventually give up hanging around for you to make up your mind. It seemed best to keep warning you. I dreaded you getting genuinely hurt and badly burned – unlike with William.'

I flash her a look. 'You never understood how utterly humiliating and hateful it all was, Bill's great love for another woman on every front page. I just thought I deserved a little more sympathy . . .'

'You did labour it all a bit, though, darling . . .' My mother looks down at her lap. 'You know it won't be easy, taking on Julian's son? First time out of the country, people staring, having to settle into a new school.'

'Of course, and there's the problem of how the girls will take to him, too.'

I tell her a little of that, but feeling prickly, she's got me riled. And I'm not quite yet ready to let her off the hook about Julian. 'What I want to know, Mum, is why, since you thought the very worst of him only a week ago when Jess was missing – *and* had all those doubts before – should you now suddenly be all so relaxed and rosy about Julian?'

'It did look awfully bad, darling. And William's a newspaperman, he sees it all, I suppose that influenced me slightly. Jessie's at that stage, you see, of being quite a flirt, but with no idea of the effect it can have on a man. It seemed impossible to believe, obviously, but life can be so horrifying at times. There's something unbelievably shocking every day.'

'Couldn't you have trusted your own daughter, when I was so certain and unshakable?'

'You were in love, not seeing straight. But your instincts were right, I'm very glad to say!'

My blood's up, I'm not letting her off. 'And it's a bit rich, calling it "warning me", the way you kept on about Julian having been a disappointment to his father. That was an opinion, your own view.'

'No, it was just a fact. He was a disappointment to his father — only a very slight one. I did know Julian's father a little, you see.' My mother's going a bit pink; this is a revelation. 'Peter wanted Julian to go into the Foreign Office, he thought it was right for him and couldn't accept that he chose a different path. Having mapped out his son's future, he found it hard to accept that children aren't clones.' I'm staring, needing to know more. 'Our paths crossed during Dad's last posting,' my mother explains, pinker than ever. 'He actually got in touch a year after his wife's terrible car accident. I'd seen him once or twice before his cancer was diagnosed . . .'

I start thinking back. She had come to the funeral and mentioned then that they had met, but I'd thought nothing of it at the time. Why play things so close to her chest? My mother's smiling. 'I have had one or two dates over the years,' she says, a remark overheard by Emma, coming up to show off her new CD – who looks amazed.

When Julian and I finally get to bed I can't wait to tell him about my mother and his father. He is surprised. 'Is it true you fought against going into the Foreign Office?' I ask.

'My father wanted it, but it wasn't for me. He was very disappointed.'

I smile to myself, tucked in the crook of Julian's arm. 'I've missed you,' I say, looking up. 'It hasn't been an easy day. I think we're all in need of this mythical holiday!'

'That's all fixed, all booked . . .' I lean up and kiss him, prepared to believe anything now. 'Was it Emma and Jess?' Julian asks. 'They're unhappy about James?'

'Jessie thinks you'll be off her with a son of your own and Emma thinks it will be *gruesome* sharing a bathroom.'

'She's got a point. We'll have a fleet of bathrooms, at least three, in the new house. Look, I know it's your call,' he says, fingering my hand, 'but are you going to talk schools with William tomorrow?'

I go quiet. Does he just want the freedom of no children around? He's not, after all, going to have my mother living conveniently close by now.

She continued to shock and surprise us this evening, saying she was very flattered and honoured that Julian wanted her with us – and a cottage on a farm sounded lovely – but Hove was home. She would come and stay and help out on occasion; it wasn't all that far . . . The clear implication had been that she wasn't about to be an on-tap babysitter and had her own life to lead. 'I love coming to Sunday lunch,' she'd said, smiling serenely, 'I shall miss that. And I know you think I'm a bit lonely, darling, but I do have a circle of friends. I like my little bit of bridge . . .'

I haven't answered Julian's question about Bill and schools. My silence is hanging rather heavy. Julian hitches me higher up, to be on the pillow beside him. 'Don't think bad of me. It's not really selfishness. I do want to take you to places, theatres, have a few nights in London, but you'd never relax, leaving Emma and Jess with a sitter after Martin. It's a grim fact of life and something you're going to have to live with and face up to. But as I said, why not let the girls decide for themselves?'

'If they chose the wrong way you'd feel hard-done-by and we'd have rows.'

'We'll have plenty of those. You've got form, I know what I'm taking on. Quite something, though, defending my honour and taking a swipe at William, I enjoyed that. It was a good sign.'

CHAPTER 30

Over lunch on Sunday Nattie tells the girls about her old school, which makes Emma immensely keen and Jessie want to go there, too. She agrees, though, to look at her father's choice for her. We talked briefly before lunch, before he and Victoria left to be slaves to their busy careers. It also happens to be the school Julian has suggested. I'm reserving judgement, but agreeing to see it, just like Jess.

The house is on the market; the estate agent confidently predicts a buyer by the time we're back from holiday. We all feel sorry for Tom, staying behind, doing his holiday job at the biochemical laboratory for another year and looking after Misty — until it becomes clear, again via Nattie and relayed by Emma, that Tom has bamboozled his girlfriend Maudie's parents into letting her come to stay. I hope they realize there won't be a parent in sight. Tom swears they really do know . . .

Maudie paints, too, and she's longing to potter and paint all day, Tom says. It sounds a pretty idyllic couple of weeks to me. But then I'm biased, a besotted mother. As long as they don't leave the place in chaos, of course, when the estate agent is showing prospective asking-price purchasers around.

I hate the constant reminders of Martin, such as the biochemical lab. To think that last year he was a security guard at the lab while Tom was working there. They might even have chatted in passing. It makes me feel quite quivery, but I'm forcing myself not to ask Tom.

We've been having lunch on the terrace and he follows me into the kitchen while the others are still outside. 'The girls had told me all about James, Mum. Even before you could. I've got the flavour of their feelings, but I'm sure it's little wrinkles that'll iron out. I did the stern brother bit and came on quite strong – I told them what a relief it will be, to have a bit of male backup after all these years.' I smile at Tom, remembering how he used to struggle to stay awake, needing to see his father coming back late on his commuting trains. How much Tom, as a boy, had minded when Bill was home less and less.

'And don't forget,' he says with a twinkle, lifting an eyebrow, 'that you'll have Julian for support, right there, taking an active hand. You're not used having to a man on tap,' he grins. 'Dad was never around, after all . . .' Was he reading my thoughts? 'Your life's going to be so changed – I mean Julian won't be taking off for Uganda any more.'

Before we leave for Kenya I have a tearful lunch with Val and Susie, in Val's architect-sleek, space-worshipping house. A summery artistic spread. It won't be the last lunch, I'll have them back, see them again after the holiday, before we leave Brearfield, offer to have them to stay. Press plants on them out of the garden, I'm sure a few won't be missed.

Val and Susie will be, though, dreadfully. Is it the right thing, moving right away and losing friends? I've been such a mess of uncertainties for so long, like a weathervane, swinging on any whim, any drift of my thoughts.

Do I really know what I'm doing, what I'm feeling? How deep is my love and trust? I'm driving back from Val's, alone in the car and a great Cheshire-cat smile spreads wide, all over my face. I can't stop it, can't stop the hammering in my chest, the hot flow in my veins. I love him, I can't stop smiling, I want blasting music in the car, want to wind down the windows and shout it out loud. 'It's a given,' he said once, talking of his love for me. I know what he meant by that now.

We have an evening in London with Lauren and Henry before going. Myrtle comes to babysit. Julian tells her she must come to Dorset and have a busman's holiday.

We'll be using the Pearsons' basement when we need to be in London and I'm grateful to see it and feel more at home. 'I wanted to knock your two heads together,' Lauren says, beaming at us. 'What a hopeless pair you were. Everyone could see how in love you both were . . .'

'Including me,' Julian says sounding quite injured. 'I knew my own mind, Ursula was the one . . .'

'No kidding . . . And who kept holding back, not coming clean with her . . .?' Lauren gives me a large American wink and Henry pours us all some more wine.

I've never felt more relaxed than over dinner with them. Lauren is fast becoming a genuine friend. I have confessed to Julian that even at my worst, blackest moments I found her very hard to hate.

With the holiday only two days away I do some last-minute shopping in Brearfield. It's market day, which takes me back, seeing Bert on the plant stall, his ruddy, pitted old face. I buy up half his stall in the interests of selling the house.

Erica is there, poking suspiciously at some polythene-packed bacon on a cheap groceries stall. She's in a green shirt and white skirt with cabbage roses on it. I can't help wondering if it might get a few caterpillars confused.

I seek her out, which is an unusual enough event to put her on guard – some animal instinct warning her to beware. 'How are you, Erica? Any holidays planned?' I ask pleasantly.

'We always go bicycling in France. It's so important, I think, don't you, for the young to familiarize themselves and improve their accents.' She's more cheered, delivering a mini homily.

'Julian is taking us all on safari in Kenya in a couple of days,' I say, 'my mother, too. It'll make a nice change. Then we're moving from Brearfield, actually, buying a farm in Dorset. And Julian's son is going to be living with us, which is a joy.'

My face breaks out in an almost genuine smile. 'I'll miss our little chats, though, Erica. Oh, and in case you didn't know, there's a charming young woman buying the bookshop – I think you saw her at lunch with Julian the other day. Brave of her really, giving a new venture a try.'

Erica is speechless, which is definitely a first. She's clocking up all the riveting gossip, though; it's an interesting reversal of roles.

The packing, all the excitement, we're behaving like swarming bees, whooshing around the house and homing in on our suitcases. When we finally collapse into bed, I'm feeling wakeful, my head buzzing with all the last-minute details. Julian is still awake, too.

The return journey is complicated. He's staying behind, seeing us on to our plane then going to Uganda to travel back with James. 'Are you sure you don't mind? It will be less stressful for him than making the journey alone.'

'We'll be waiting at the airport to meet you. I'll have had time to stock up and get his room ready. It's a good plan.'

We turn over, trying to get some sleep that won't come. Julian reaches out for my hand in the dark. 'Are you in a receptive mood?'

'What's coming, now? What have you forgotten to do . . .?' I ask suspiciously, dreading anything cropping up to mar the holiday.

'I only wanted to ask you to marry me,' he says wryly. 'You may not like the idea, of course, but you could sleep on it perhaps . . .'

It comes as a singular surprise. I've so convinced myself it's unnecessary and not going to happen anyway, that I feel completely lost for words. My love for Julian is different from anything in the past with Bill, with anyone. It's not wide-eyed young love, it's the grown-up real McCoy. With Julian anything is possible. 'I, well, I thought it might change things and they're not, actually, so bad as they are . . .'

'True. But perhaps we could revisit the subject occasionally?' I feel that's slightly rhetorical and doesn't need an answer. 'Suppose,' he carries on, 'we were to have a baby, would you feel differently then?'

I spin round and turn on a light. 'You're not serious? We're not revisiting that one in a hurry! Do you know how old I am? I've got a couple of years at most before it's quite out of the question – and I thought you wanted us to have a bit of life of our own? That would be one certain way of getting me really tied. If you ever do that to me . . . I'll go out to work and you can farm and stay home and change nappies, and wipe up the sick and . . .'

'Perhaps it's a bit late for this discussion. You need to be in a calmer frame of mind.'

'And you need to be in your right one. We have got a long journey to make tomorrow; how about getting some sleep instead of having any more of these cock-eyed ideas.'

I reach up to turn out the light and catch his amused smile.

It's strange being back at the airport in the arrivals hall, meeting another flight from Uganda. We were only two months ago, in very different circumstances, innocent of the fateful events to come.

We're nervous, all three of us; back from our thrilling safari, suntanned, fidgeting, wearing carefully chosen clothes.

Emma's panicking about moving; she wants time to see all her friends and tell them about the leopards she saw mating in a tree, every last word on the holiday. Changing schools is suddenly causing terror.

Not so with Jess, she's intensely relieved to be going. Chief Inspector Gibson thought it was an excellent thing. He called just before we left. Only to see how we were, not with any update or news on Martin's trial. That's still to be faced, there will be more reminders to come.

There is a diverse mix of people waiting at arrivals, holding up boards; straining and looking out. Other planeloads are coming through; the Kampala flight has only just touched down.

I watch people reuniting. The quick grip of an arm around shoulders: girls jumping up and down squealing as a friend appears. The brief embarrassed pat-on-the-back hug of two men, probably father and son. Then the lovers; the embrace you almost feel part of in all its urgency, one couple have tears streaming down as they walk away still clinging fast. Each of these people has to cope with dramas, loss and disappointments, I think, the burning need of another.

Here's Julian now, and James. They look much the same height though James is probably still growing. He has an elegance about him that's surprising. He's less his mother's colour than expected: not his father's son either – although it is there, showing through in those brown eyes, something of Julian's special blend of strength and reticence.

We three on our home ground move forward cautiously, smiling.